Busman's Honeymoon

MYSTERIES BY DOROTHY L. SAYERS:

Busman's Honeymoon
Clouds of Witness
The Documents in the Case
The Five Red Herrings
Gaudy Night
Hangman's Holiday
Have His Carcase
In the Teeth of the Fvidence
Lord Peter: A *Collection of All the Lord Peter Wimsey Stories*
Lord Peter Views the Body
Murder Must Advertise
Strong Poison
Unnatural Death
The Unpleasantness at the Bellona Club
Whose Body?

DOROTHY L. SAYERS

Busman's Honeymoon

♦

Harper & Row, Publishers, New York
Grand Rapids, Philadelphia, St. Louis, San Francisco
London, Singapore, Sydney, Tokyo, Toronto

A hardcover edition of this book is published by Harper & Row, Publishers, Inc. It is here reprinted by arrangement with the estate of Anthony Fleming.

First PERENNIAL LIBRARY edition published 1986.

Library of Congress Cataloging-in-Publication Data

Sayers, Dorothy L. (Dorothy Leigh), 1893–1957.
Busman's honeymoon.

Reprint. Originally published: New York: Harper & Row, 1937.
I. Title.
PR6037.A95B8 1986 823'.912 86-45139
ISBN 0-06-055021-X
ISBN 0-06-080823-3 (pbk.) 92 93 94 95 96 OPM 15 14 13 12 11

TO MURIEL ST. CLARE BYRNE, HELEN SIMPSON AND MARJORIE BARBER

◆

Dear Muriel, Helen and Bar,

With what extreme of womanly patience you listened to the tale of *Busman's Honeymoon* while it was being written, the Lord He knoweth. I do not like to think how many times I tired the sun with talking—and if at any time they had told me you were dead, I should easily have believed that I had talked you into your graves. But you have strangely survived to receive these thanks.

You, Muriel, were in some sort a predestined victim, since you wrote with me the play to which this novel is but the limbs and outward flourishes; my debt and your long-suffering are all the greater. You, Helen and Bar, were wantonly sacrificed on the altar of that friendship of which the female sex is said to be incapable; let the lie stick i' the wall!

To all three I humbly bring, I dedicate with tears, this sentimental comedy.

It has been said, by myself and others, that a love-interest is only an intrusion upon a detective story. But to the characters involved, the detective-interest might well seem an irritating intrusion upon their love-story. This book deals with such a situation. It also provides some sort of answer to many kindly inquiries as to how Lord Peter and his Harriet solved their matrimonial problem. If there is but a ha'porth of detection to an intolerable deal of saccharine, let the occasion be the excuse.

Yours in all gratitude,

Dorothy L. Sayers

That will ask some tears in the true performing of it: if I do it, let the audience look to their eyes; I will move storms, I will condole in some measure. . . . I could play Ercles rarely, or a part to tear a cat in, to make all split . . . a lover is more condoling.

—Shakespeare, A *Midsummer Night's Dream*

CONTENTS

◆

PROTHALAMION

♦

MARRIAGES

WIMSEY-VANE. On the 8th October, at St. Cross Church, Oxford, Peter Death Bredon Wimsey, second son of the late Gerald Mortimer Bredon Wimsey, 15th Duke of Denver, to Harriet Deborah Vane, only daughter of the late Henry Vane, M.D. of Great Pagford, Herts.

MIRABELLE, COUNTESS OF SEVERN AND THAMES, TO HONORIA LUCASTA, DOWAGER DUCHESS OF DENVER

My dear Honoria,

So Peter is really married: I have ordered willow-wreaths for half my acquaintance. I understand that it is a deciduous tree; if nothing is available but the bare rods, I shall distribute them all the same, for the better beating of breasts.

Honestly, as one frank old woman to the other, how do you feel about it? A cynic should have cause to be grateful, since to see your amorous sweet devil of a son wedded to an Oxford-Bloomsbury bluestocking should add considerably to the gaiety of the season. I am not too blind to see through Peter, with all his affectations, and if I had been half a century younger I would have married him myself, for the fun of it. But is this girl flesh and blood? You say she is passionately devoted to him, and I know, of course, that she once had a half-baked affair with a poet—but, Heaven deliver us, what's a poet? Something that can't go to bed without making a song about it. Peter wants more than a devoted admirer to hold his hand and recite verses to him; and he has a foolish, pleasant trick of keeping to one woman at a time, which he may find inconvenient in a permanent relationship. Not that many marriages can be called permanent these days, but I can't see Peter exhibiting himself in the Divorce Courts for his own amusement, though, no doubt, if asked to oblige, he would carry it through with an air. (Which reminds me that my idiot great-nephew, Hughie, has bungled matters as usual. Having undertaken to do the thing like a gentleman, he sneaked off to Brighton with a hired nobody, and the Judge wouldn't believe either the hotel bills or the chambermaid—knowing them all too well by sight. So it means starting all over again from the beginning.)

Well, my dear, we shall see what we shall see, and you may be sure I shall do my best for Peter's wife, if only to spite Helen, who will doubtless make everything as unpleasant as possible for her new sister-in-law. Naturally, I pay no attention to her snobbish nonsense about misalliances, which is ridiculous and out-of-date. Compared with the riff-raff we are getting in now from the films and the night-clubs, a country doctor's daughter, even with a poet in her past, is a miracle of respectability. If the young woman has brains and bowels, she will suit well enough. Do you suppose they intend to have any children? Helen will be furious if they do, as she has always counted on Peter's money going to Saint-George. Denver, if I know anything about him, will be more concerned to secure the succession in case Saint-George breaks his neck in that car of his. Whatever they do, somebody will be indignant, so I imagine they will please themselves.

I was sorry I could not come to the reception—you seem to have diddled the Press very neatly—but my asthma has been very bad lately. Still, I must be thankful to have retained my faculties and my sense of humour so long. Tell Peter to bring his Harriet to see me as soon as they return from this mysterious honeymoon of theirs, and believe me, dear Honoria, always (in spite of my venomous old tongue) most affectionately yours,

Mirabelle Severn and Thames

MRS. CHIPPERLY JAMES TO HON. MRS. TRUMPE-HARTE

. . . Well, dear, prepare for a shock! Peter Wimsey is married—yes, actually *married*—to that extraordinary young woman who lived with a Bolshevist or a musician or something, and murdered him, or something—I forget exactly, it was all ages ago, and such odd things happen every day, don't they? It seems a sad waste, with all that money—but it does rather go to show, doesn't it, that there is something not quite right about the Wimseys—the third cousin, you know, the one that lives shut up in a little villa at Monte, is *more* than eccentric—and in any case Peter must be forty-five if he's a day. You know, dear, I always thought you were a little unwise to try to get him for Monica, though of course I didn't like to say so when you were working so hard to bring it off. . . .

MRS. DALILAH SNYPE TO MISS AMARANTH SYLVESTER-QUICKE

. . . Of course, *the* sensation is the Wimsey-Vane marriage. It must be a sort of sociological experiment, I should think, because, as *you* know, darling, he is the *world's* chilliest prig and I'm *definitely* sorry for the girl, in spite of the money and the title and everything, because *nothing* would make up for being tied to a chattering icicle in an eyeglass, my dear, *too* weary-making. Not that it's likely to last. . . .

HELEN, DUCHESS OF DENVER, TO LADY GRUMMIDGE

My dear Marjorie,

Thank you for your kind inquiries. Tuesday was indeed

a most exhausting day, though I am feeling rather more rested this evening. But it has been a very trying time for all of us. Peter, of course, was just as tiresome as he could be, and that is saying a good deal. First of all, he insisted on being married in church, though, considering everything, I should have thought the Registrar's Office would have been more appropriate. However, we resigned ourselves to St. George's, Hanover Square, and I was prepared to do everything in my power to see that the thing was done properly, if it had to be done at all. But my mother-in-law took it all out of my hands, though I am sure we were distinctly given to understand that the wedding would take place on the day *I* had suggested, that is, next Wednesday. But this, as you will see, was just one of Peter's monkey tricks. I feel the slight *very much*, particularly as we had gone out of our way to be civil to the girl, and had asked her to dinner.

Well! Last Monday evening, when we were down at Denver, we got a wire from Peter, which coolly said, "If you really want to see me married, try St. Cross Church, Oxford, tomorrow at two." I was furious—all that distance and my frock not ready, and to make things worse, Gerald, who had asked sixteen people down for the shooting, laughed like an idiot, and said, "Good for Peter!" He insisted on our both going, just like that, leaving all our guests to look after themselves. I strongly suspect Gerald of having known all about it beforehand, though he swears he didn't. Anyway, Jerry knew all right, and that's why he stayed in London. I am always telling Jerry that his uncle means more to him than his own parents; and I needn't tell *you* that I consider Peter's influence most pernicious for a boy of his age. Gerald, manlike, said Peter had a right to get married when and where he liked; he never considers the embarrassment and discomfort these eccentricities cause to other people.

We went to Oxford and found the place—an obscure little church in a side-street, very gloomy and damp-looking.

It turned out that the bride (who, *mercifully*, has no living relations) was being married from a Women's College, of all places. I was relieved to see Peter in proper morning dress; I really had begun to think he meant to get married in a cap and gown. Jerry was there as best man, and my mother-in-law arrived in great state, beaming away as though they had all done something clever. And they had raked out old Uncle Paul Delagardie, creaking with arthritis, poor old creature, with a gardenia in his buttonhole and trying to look sprightly, which at his age is disgusting. There were all kinds of queer people in the church—practically none of our own friends, but that ridiculous old Climpson woman, and some hangers-on that Peter had picked up in the course of his "cases," and several policemen. Charles and Mary appeared at the last moment, and Charles pointed out to me a man in a Salvation Army uniform, who he *said* was a retired burglar; but I can scarcely believe this, even of Peter.

The bride came attended by the most incredible assortment of bridesmaids—all female dons!—and an odd, dark woman to give her away, who was supposed to be the Head of the College. I am thankful to say, considering her past history, that Harriet (as I suppose I must now call her) had enough sense of propriety not to get herself up in white satin and orange-blossom; but I could not help thinking that a plain costume would have been more suitable than cloth of gold. I can see that I shall have to speak to her presently about her clothes, but I am afraid she will be difficult. I have never seen anybody look so indecently triumphant—I suppose, in a way, she had a right to; one must admit that she has played her cards very cleverly. Peter was as white as a sheet; I thought he was going to be sick. Probably he was realising what he had let himself in for. Nobody can say that I did not do my best to open his eyes. They were married in the old, coarse Prayer-book form, and the bride said "Obey"—I take this to be their idea of humour, for she looks as obstinate as a mule.

There was a great deal of promiscuous kissing in the

vestry, and then all the oddities were bundled into cars (at Peter's expense, no doubt) and we started back to Town, closely pursued by the local newspaper men. We went to my mother-in-law's little house—*all* of us, including the policemen and the ex-burglar—and after a wedding-breakfast (which I must admit was very good) Uncle Delagardie made a speech, garnished with flowers of French eloquence. There were a lot of presents, some of them very absurd; the ex-burglar's was a thick book of ranting and vulgar hymns! Presently the bride and bridegroom vanished, and we waited a long time for them, till my mother-in-law came down, all smiles, to announce that they had been gone half an hour, leaving no address. At this moment, I have no idea *where* they are, nor has anybody.

The whole business has left us in a most painful and ridiculous position. I consider it a disgraceful ending to a most disastrous affair, and it is no consolation to think that I shall have to produce this appalling young woman as my sister-in-law. Mary's policeman was bad enough, but he is, at any rate, quiet and well behaved; whereas, with Peter's wife, we may look for notoriety, if not for open scandal, from one day to another. However, we must put as good a face on it as we can; I wouldn't say as much as I *have* said to anybody but you.

With all gratitude for your sympathy,

Yours affectionately,

Helen Denver

MR. MERVYN BUNTER TO MRS. BUNTER, SENR.

Dear Mother,

I write from an "unknown destination" in the country, hoping this finds you as it leaves me. Owing to a trifling domestic catastrophe, I have only a candle to see by, so trust you will excuse my bad writing.

Well, Mother, we were happily married this morning and a very pretty wedding it was. I only wish you could have been present at his lordship's kind invitation, but as I said to him, at eighty-seven some physical infirmities are only to be expected. I hope your leg is better.

As I told you in my last, we were all set to escape Her Grace's interfering ways, and so we did, everything going off like clockwork. Her new ladyship, Miss Vane that was, went down to Oxford the day before, and his lordship with Lord Saint-George and myself followed in the evening, staying at the Mitre. His lordship spoke very kindly to me indeed, alluding to my twenty years' service, and trusting that I should find myself comfortable in the new household. I told him I hoped I knew when I was well suited, and should endeavour to give satisfaction. I am afraid I said more than was my place, for his lordship was sincerely affected and told me not to be a bloody fool. I took the liberty to prescribe a dose of bromide and got him to sleep at last, when I could persuade his young lordship to leave him alone. Considerate is not the term I would employ of Lord Saint-George, but some of his teasing must be put down to the champagne.

His lordship appeared calm and resolute in the morning, which was a great relief to my mind, there being a good deal to do. A number of humble friends arriving by special transport, it was my task to see that they were made comfortable and not permitted to lose themselves.

Well, dear Mother, we partook of a light and early lunch, and then I had to get their lordships dressed and down to the church. My own gentleman was as quiet as a lamb and gave no trouble, not even his usual joking, but Lord Saint-George was in tearing high spirits and I had my hands full with him. He pretended five times that he had lost the ring, and just as we were setting out he mislaid it in earnest; but his lordship, with his customary detective ability, discovered it for him and took charge of it personally. In spite of this misadventure, I had them at the chancel steps dead on time, and I will say they both did me credit. I do not know where you would beat his young lordship for handsome looks, though to my mind there is no comparison which is the finer gentleman.

The lady did not keep us waiting, I am thankful to say,

and very well she looked, all in gold, with a beautiful bouquet of chrysanthemums. She is not pretty, but what you would call striking-looking, and I am sure she had no eyes for anyone but his lordship. She was attended by four ladies from the College, not dressed as bridesmaids, but all neat and ladylike in appearance. His lordship was very serious all through the ceremony.

Then we all went back to a reception at Her Grace the Dowager's Town house. I was very much pleased with her new ladyship's behaviour towards the guests, which was frank and friendly to all stations, but, of course, his lordship would not choose any but a lady in all respects. I do not anticipate any trouble with her.

After the reception, we got the bride and bridegroom quietly away by the back door, having incarcerated all the newspaper reporters in the little drawing-room. And now, dear Mother, I must tell you...

MISS LETITIA MARTIN, DEAN OF SHREWSBURY COLLEGE, OXFORD, TO MISS JOAN EDWARDS, LECTURER AND TUTOR IN SCIENCE IN THE SAME FOUNDATION

Dear Teddy,

Well! we have had our wedding—quite a red-letter day in College history! Miss Lydgate, Miss de Vine, little Chilperic and yours truly were bridesmaids, with the Warden to give the bride away. No, my dear, we did *not* array ourselves in fancy costumes. Personally, I thought we should have looked more symmetrical in academic dress, but the bride said she thought "poor Peter" would be *quite* sufficiently harrowed by headlines as it was. So we just turned up in our Sunday best, and I wore my new furs. It took all our united efforts to *put* Miss de Vine's hair up and *keep* it put.

The Denver family were all there; the Dowager is a darling, like a small eighteenth-century marquise, but the

Duchess looked a tartar, *very* cross, and as stiff as a poker. It was great fun seeing her try to patronise the Warden—needless to say, she got no change out of *her!* However, the Warden had her turn to be disconcerted in the vestry. She was advancing upon the bridegroom with outstretched hand and a speech of congratulation, when he firmly took and kissed her, and *what* the speech was to have been we shall now never know! He then proceeded to kiss us all round (brave man!) and Miss Lydgate was so overcome by her feelings that she returned the salute good and hearty. After that, the best man—(the good-looking Saint-George boy)—started in, so there was quite an orgy of embraces, and we had to put Miss de Vine's hair up again. The bridegroom gave each bridesmaid a lovely crystal decanter and set of cut glasses (for sherry-parties, bless his frivolous heart!) and the Warden got a cheque for £250 for the Latymer Scholarship, which I call handsome.

However, in my excitement I am forgetting all about the bride. I had never imagined that Harriet Vane could look so impressive. I'm always apt to think of her, still, as a gawky and dishevelled First-Year, all bones, with a discontented expression. Yesterday she looked like a Renaissance portrait stepped out of its frame. I put it down first of all to the effect of gold lamé, but on consideration, I think it was probably due to "lerve." There was something rather splendid about the way those two claimed one another, as though nothing and nobody else mattered or even existed; he was the only bridegroom I have ever seen who looked as though he knew exactly what he was doing and meant to do it.

On the way up to Town—oh! by the way, Lord Peter put his foot *resolutely* down on Mendelssohn and *Lohengrin*, and we were played out with Bach—the Duke was mercifully taken away from his cross Duchess and handed over to me to entertain. He is handsome and stupid in a county-family kind of way, and looks rather like Henry VIII, de-bloated and de-bearded and brought up to date. He asked me, a little anxiously, whether I thought "the girl" was really keen on his brother, and when I said I was sure of it, confided to me that he had never been able to make Peter out, and had never expected him to settle down, and hoped it would turn out all right, what? Somewhere in the dim recesses of his mind, I think he has a lurking suspicion that Brother Peter may have that little extra something he hasn't got himself, and that it might even be a good thing to have, if one didn't have to consider the County.

The reception at the Dowager's was great fun—and for once, at a wedding, one got enough to eat!—and drink! The people who came off badly were the unhappy reporters, who by this time had got wind of something, and turned up in battalions. They were firmly collared at the doors by two gigantic footmen, and penned up in a room, with the promise that "his lordship would see them in a few moments." Eventually "his lordship" did go to them—not Lord Peter, but Lord Wellwater, the F.O. man, who delivered to them at great length a highly important statement about Abyssinia, to which they didn't dare not listen. By the time he had finished, *our* lord and lady had sneaked out by the back door, and all that was left them was a roomful of wedding-presents and the remains of the cake. However, the Dowager saw them and was quite nice to them, so they tooled off, fairly happy, but without any photographs or any information about the honeymoon. As a matter of fact, I don't believe anybody, except the Dowager, knows where the bride and bridegroom really have gone to.

Well—that was that; and I do hope they'll be most frightfully happy. Miss de Vine thinks there is too much intelligence on both sides—but I tell her not to be such a confirmed pessimist. I know heaps of couples who are both as stupid as owls and not happy at all—so it doesn't really follow, one way or the other, does it?

Yours ever,
Letitia Martin

EXTRACTS FROM THE DIARY OF HONORIA LUCASTA, DOWAGER DUCHESS OF DENVER

20 May.—Peter rang up this morning, terribly excited, poor darling, to say that he and Harriet were really and truly engaged, and that the ridiculous Foreign Office had ordered him straight off to Rome again after breakfast—so like them—you'd think they did it on purpose. What with exasperation and happiness, he sounded perfectly distracted. Desperately anxious I should get hold of H. and make her understand she was welcome—poor child, it is hard for her, left here to face us all, when she can scarcely feel sure of herself or anything yet. Have written to her at Oxford, telling her as well as I could how very, very glad I was she was making Peter so happy, and asking when she would be in Town, so that I could go and see her. Dear Peter! Hope and pray she really loves him in the way he needs; shall know in a minute when I see her.

21 May.—Was reading *The Stars Look Down* (Mem. very depressing, and not what I expected from the title—think I must have had a Christmas carol in mind, but remember now it has something to do with the Holy Sepulchre—must ask Peter and make sure) after tea, when Franklin announced "Miss Vane." Was so surprised and delighted, I jumped up quite forgetting poor Ahasuerus, who was asleep on my knee, and was dreadfully affronted. I said, "My dear, how sweet of you to come"—she looked so different I shouldn't have known her—but of course it was 5½ years ago, and nobody can look her best in the dock at that dreary Old Bailey. She walked straight up to me, rather as if she was facing a firing-squad, and said abruptly, in that queer deep voice of hers, "Your letter was so kind—I didn't quite know how to answer it, so I thought I'd better come. Do you honestly not mind too much, about Peter and me? Because I love him quite dreadfully, and there's just nothing to be done about it." So I said, "Oh, do please go on loving him, because he wants it so much, and he really is the dearest of all my children, only it doesn't do for parents to say so—but *now* I *can* say it to *you*, and I'm so glad about it." So I kissed her, and Ahasuerus was so furious that he ran *all* his claws *hard* into her legs and I apologised and smacked him and we sat down on the sofa, and she said, "Do you know, I've been saying to myself all the way up from Oxford, 'If only I can face her and it really is all right, I shall have somebody I can talk to about Peter.' That's the one thing that kept me from turning back half-way." Poor child, that really was all she wanted—she was quite in a daze, because apparently it all happened quite late on Sunday evening, and they sat up half the night, kissing one another madly in a punt, poor things, and then he had to go, making no arrangements for anything, and if it hadn't been for his signet-ring that he put on her hand all in a hurry at the last moment it might have been all a dream. And after holding out against him all these years, she'd given way all of a piece, like falling down a well, and didn't seem to know what to do with herself. Said she couldn't remember ever having been absolutely and shatteringly happy since she was a small child, and it made her feel quite hollow inside. On inquiry, I found she must be *literally* hollow inside, because as far as I could make out she hadn't eaten or slept to speak of since Sunday. Sent Franklin for sherry and biscuits, and made her—H., I mean—stay to dinner. Talked Peter till I could almost *hear* him saying, "Mother dear, you are having an orgy" (or is it orgie?). . . . H. caught sight of that David Bellezzi photograph of Peter which he dislikes so much, and I asked what she thought of it. She said, "Well, it's a nice English gentleman, but it isn't either the lunatic, the lover or the poet, is it?" Agree with her. (Can't think why I keep the thing about, except to please David.) Brought out family album. *Thankful* to say she didn't go all broody and possessive over Peter kicking baby legs on a rug—can't stand maternal young women, though P. really a very comic infant with his hair in a tuft, but he controls it very well now, so why rake up the past? She instantly seized on the ones Peter calls "Little Mischief" and "The Lost Chord" and said, "Somebody who understood him took those—was it Bunter?"—which looked like second sight. Then she confessed she felt horribly guilty about Bunter and hoped his feelings weren't going to be hurt, because if he gave notice it would break Peter's heart. Told her quite frankly it would depend entirely on her, and I felt sure Bunter would never go unless he was pushed out. H. said, "But you don't think I'd do that. That's just it. I don't want Peter to lose *anything.*" She looked quite distressed, and we both wept a little, till it suddenly struck us as funny that we should both be crying over Bunter, who would have been shocked out of his wits if he'd known it. So we cheered up and I gave her the photographs and asked what plans they had, if they had got so far. She said P. didn't know when he'd be back, but she thought she'd better finish her present book quickly, so as to be ready when the time came and have enough money for clothes. Asked if I could tell her the right tailor—shows sense, and would pay for really *inspired* dressing, but must be careful what I advise, as find I have *no* idea what people make by writing books. Ignorant and stupid of me—so important not to hurt her pride. . . . Altogether most reassuring evening. Telephoned long enthusiastic wire to Peter before bed. Hope Rome is not too stuffy and hot, as heat does not suit him.

24 May.—Harriet to tea. Helen came in—very rude and tiresome when I introduced Harriet. Said, "Oh, really! and where *is* Peter? Run off abroad again? How absurd and unaccountable he is!" Went on to talk Town and Country solidly, saying every so often, "Do you know the so-and-so's, Miss Vane? No? They're *very* old friends of Peter's." "Do you hunt, Miss Vane? No? What a pity! I do hope Peter doesn't mean to give it up. It does him good to get out." Harriet very sensibly said "No" and "Certainly" to everything, without any explanations or apologies, which are always so dangerous (dear Disraeli!). I asked Harriet how the book was getting on and if Peter's suggestions had helped. Helen said, "Oh, yes, you write, don't you?" as if she'd never heard of her, and asked what the title was, so that she could get it from the library. Harriet said, quite gravely, "That is very kind of you, but do let me send you one—I am allowed six free copies, you know." First sign of temper, but I don't blame her. Apologised for Helen after she'd gone, and said I was glad my *second* son was marrying for love. Fear my vocabulary remains hopelessly old-fashioned in spite of carefully chosen reading. (Must remember to ask Franklin what I have done with *The Stars Look Down.)*

1 June.—Letter from Peter, about taking the Belchesters' house in Audley Square from Michaelmas and furnishing it. H., thank Heaven, ready to prefer eighteenth-century elegance to chromium tubes. H. alarmed by size of house, but relieved she is not called upon to "make a home" for Peter. I explained it was his business to make the home and take his bride to it—privilege now apparently confined to aristocracy and clergymen, who can't choose their vicarages, poor dears, usually much too big for them. H. pointed out that Royal brides always seemed to be expected to run about choosing cretonnes, but I said this was duty they owed to penny papers which like domestic women—Peter's wife fortunately without duties. Must see about housekeeper for them—someone capable—Peter insistent wife's work must not be interrupted by uproars in servants' hall.

5 June.—Sudden outburst of family feeling in most tiresome form. Gerald first—worried of course by Helen—to ask if girl is presentable and has she got modern ideas, meaning children of course, that is to say not wanting children. Told Gerald to mind his own business, which is Saint-George. Next Mary, to say Small Peter sickening for chicken-pox and will this girl really look after Peter? Told her, Peter perfectly capable of looking after himself, and probably not wanting wife with head stuffed with chicken-pox and best way to boil fish. Found beautiful Chippendale mirror and set tapestry chairs at Harrison's.

25 June.—Love's dream troubled by solemn interview with Murbles about Settlements—appalling long document providing for every conceivable and inconceivable situation and opening up ramifications into everybody's death and remarriage, "covered," as Murbles observes, "by THE WILL" (in capitals).

Had not realised Peter was doing so well out of the London property. H. more and more uncomfortable at every clause. Rescued her in depressed state and took her to tea at Rumpelmeyer's. She finally told me, "Ever since I left College, I've never spent a penny I hadn't earned." Said to her, "Well, my dear, tell Peter what you feel, but do remember he's just as vain and foolish as most men and not a chameleon to smell any sweeter for being trodden on." On consideration, think I meant "camomile" (Shakespeare? Must ask Peter.) Considered writing to P. about this, but better not—young people must fight their own battles.

10 August.—Returned from country yesterday to find question of Settlements settled. H. showed me three pages of intelligent sympathy from P., beginning, "Of course I had foreseen the difficulty," and ending, "Either your pride or mine will have to be sacrificed—I can only appeal to your generosity to let it be yours." H. said, "Peter can always see the difficulty—that's what's so disarming." Agree heartily—can't stand people who "can't see what the fuss is about." H. now meekly prepared to accept suitable income, but has solaced pride by ordering two dozen silk shirts in Burlington Arcade, and paying cash for them. Evinces dogged determination to do thing properly while she is about it—has grasped that if Helen can pick holes, Peter will suffer for it—has grasped that if Helen can pick holes, Peter will suffer for it, and resolutely applies intelligence to task. Something apparently to be said for education—teaches grasp of facts. H. grappling with fact of P.'s position—interesting to watch. Long letter from Peter, very dubious about League of Nations, and sending detailed instructions about library shelving and a William-and-Mary bedstead, also irritable about being left in Rome, "like a plumber, to stop diplomatic leaks." English very unpopular in Italy, but P. had soothing discussion with the Pope about a historical manuscript—must have made a pleasant change for both of them.

16 August.—Harriet, who has been down to the country to look at a water-mill (something to do with her new book), said she had motored back through Herts, and paid a visit to her old home at Great Pagford. Talked about her people—quiet country doctor and wife. Father made quite good income, but never thought of saving anything (thought he'd live for ever, I suppose)—very anxious, however, H. should have good education—just as well, as things turned out. H. said her own childish ambition had been to make enough money to buy quaint old farmhouse called Talboys in next village. Had seen it again on her trip—Elizabethan, very pretty. Said how differently things turned out from what one expected. I said it sounded just the sort of place she and P. would want for week-end cottage. H. rather taken aback—said, Yes, she supposed so. Left it at that.

19 August.—Found the exact right hangings for the bedstead. Helen says all that kind of thing highly insanitary. Says Gerald has had bad reports of the partridges and thinks country going to the dogs.

20 August.—H. has written to Peter about buying Talboys. Explained she thought Peter "liked giving people things." So he does, poor boy! Facts now apparently faced once for all—looks as though he was going to get five-and-a-half years' arrears of patience repaid in a lump. Said mildly I thought nothing would give P. greater pleasure. When she had gone, danced quiet jig in drawing-room, to surprise of Franklin (silly woman—she ought to know me by this time).

21 August.—Harriet's book finished and sent to publisher. This unfortunately leaves her mind free to worry about Abyssinia, so tiresome. Convinced civilisation will perish and Peter never be seen again. Like cat on hot bricks saying she wasted five years of P.'s life and can't forgive herself and it's no good saying he's over age because he has M.I. written all over his conscience and if he was seventy he might still be gassed or bombed in an air-raid. Earnestly hope we shall *not* have another war with meat-coupons and no sugar and people being killed—ridiculous and unnecessary. Wonder whether Mussolini's mother spanked him too much or too little—you never know, these psychological days. Can distinctly remember spanking Peter, but it doesn't seem to have warped him much, so psychologists very likely all wrong.

24 *August.*—Peter has instructed agent to negotiate for Talboys with present owner—man called Noakes. His letter to me very discreet—but he *is* delighted. Situation in Rome apparently clearing, so far as his own job is concerned. H. still uneasy about prospects of war.

30 *August.*—Harriet completely exalted by letter from Peter saying, "Even if it is the twilight of the world, before night falls I will sleep in your arms." . . . (How well I recognise the old, magniloquent Peter of twenty years back) . . . and adding that his plumbing is done and he has asked for his papers, which is more to the point.

4 *September.*—They have made a good job of the chandeliers for the hall and great saloon. Gerald says they can have the tapestries from the Blue Room—they will look well on the upper landing, I think—have sent them to be overhauled and cleaned, which they badly need. (Peter would say, so do my pronouns, but I know quite well what I mean.) Ahasuerus sick in Franklin's bedroom—funny how fond he is of her, seeing she doesn't really like cats.

7 *September.*—Peter wires he will be back next week. Harriet insisted on taking me out to dinner and standing me champagne. Said, hilariously, her last opportunity, as Peter doesn't care for champagne. Condoled with her on loss of freedom in brief and witty speech (brief for me, anyway). Should like to see Helen taking me out to dinner and listening to a speech.

14 *September.*—Peter came back. He dined somewhere with Harriet and then came round to see me—alone, so nice of them, because of course I had said, bring her too. He looks

thin and tired, but I think that must be Mussolini or the weather or something, because he obviously has no doubts about anything (except the League, naturally)—and it struck me so much that he sat absolutely quiet for nearly two hours without fidgeting or saying very much, so unusual, because as a rule peas on a hot shovel are nothing to it. Very sweet about what I had done as regards the house. Will leave it to me to engage staff, as Harriet not experienced. They will need about eight servants, besides Bunter and the housekeeper—so I shall have a nice busy time.

15 September.—Harriet came round this morning to show me her ring—big solitaire ruby—old Abrahams had it cut and set specially to instructions. Poor H. laughed at herself, because when Peter gave it to her yesterday she was looking at *him* and ten minutes afterwards, when challenged, couldn't even tell him the colour of the stone. Said she was afraid she never would learn to behave like other people, but Peter had only said it was the first time his features had ever been prized above rubies. Peter joined us at lunch—also Helen, who demanded to see the ruby and said, sharply, "Good Heavens! I hope it's insured." To do her justice, I can't see that she could have found anything nastier to say if she'd thought it out with both hands for a fortnight. She then went on to say she supposed they intended to get married quietly before the Registrar, but Peter said, No, he would as soon be married in a railway-station waiting-room, and that if Helen had developed religious scruples she need not lend her countenance to the proceedings. So Helen said, "Oh, I see—St. George's Hanover Square, I suppose"—and went on to arrange everything for them, including the date, the parson, the guests and the music. When she got to "The voice that Breathed o'er Eden," Peter said, "Oh, for God's sake, cut out the League of Nations!" and he and Harriet began to invent rude rhymes, which left Helen rather out of it, as she never was good at drawing-room games.

16 September.—Helen obligingly presented us with a copy of the new form of marriage service, with all the vulgar bits left out—which was asking for trouble. Peter very funny about it—said he knew all about the "procreation of children," in theory though not in practice, but that the "increase of mankind" by any other method sounded too advanced for him, and that, if he ever did indulge in such dangerous amusements, he would, with his wife's permission, stick to the old-fashioned procedure. He also said that, as for the "gift of continence," he wouldn't have it as a gift, and had no objection to admitting as much. At this point, Helen got up and left the house, leaving P. and Harriet to wrangle over the word "obey." P. said he would consider it a breach of manners to give orders to his wife, but H. said, Oh, no—he'd give orders fast enough if the place was on fire or a tree falling down and he wanted her to stand clear. P. said, in that case they ought both to say "obey," but it would be too much jam for the reporters. Left them to fight it out. When I came back, found Peter had consented to be obeyed on condition he might "endow" and not "share" his worldly goods. Shocking victory of sentiment over principle.

18 September.—Must really say "*Damn!*" Disgusting newspapers have raked up all that old story about Harriet and Philip Boyes. Peter *furious*. Harriet says, "Only to be expected." Was horribly afraid she might offer to release P. from engagement, but she controlled herself nobly—expect she realises it would nearly kill him to go through that again. Think it is probably fault of that Sylvester-Quicke woman who tried so hard to get hold of Peter—have always suspected her of writing gossip-column for Sunday papers. Helen (coming down strong, but heavy-footed, on family side) determined that best plan is to have colossal Society wedding and face it out. Has decided, for reasons best known to herself, 16th October most suitable date. Kindly undertaken choice of bridesmaids—our own friends, as H.'s friends "obviously impossible"—and offered loan of house for reception—also ten villas belonging to impoverished nobility for honeymoon. Peter, losing patience, said, "Who's getting married, Helen? You or we?" Gerald tried to take Head of Family line—well snubbed all round. Helen again gave her views, and ended by saying, "Then I take it the

16th is settled." Peter said, "Take what you like." Helen said she would take her departure till he chose to realise she was only doing her *best* for them—and Gerald looked so imploring that Peter apologised for incivility.

20 *September.*—Agent reports price for Talboys settled. Many alterations and repairs needed, but fabric sound. Agreement to purchase with immediate possession—present owner to be left there till after honeymoon, when Peter will go down and see what they want done and send the workmen in.

25 *September.*—Situation, what with Helen and newspapers, becoming impossible. Peter upset at idea of St. George's and general hullaballoo. Harriet suffering from return of inferiority complex which she tries hard not to show. Have held up all invitations.

27 *September.*—Peter came to me and said that if this went on they would both be driven mad. He and H. have decided to do the whole thing quietly, without telling anybody except their own personal friends. Small wedding at Oxford, reception *here*, honeymoon in some peaceful spot in the country. I have readily agreed to help them.

30 *September.*—They have fixed up with Noakes to have honeymoon at Talboys, nobody to know anything about it. Apparently N. can clear out at short notice and lend all furniture, &c. I asked, "What about DRAINS?" Peter said, Damn drains—no drains (to speak of) at the Hall when he was a boy (well I remember it!). Wedding (Archbp's licence) on the 8th October and let Helen think what she likes till last moment—also newspapers. Harriet very much relieved. Peter adds, anyway, honeymoon in hotels disgusting—own roof (especially if Elizabethan) much more suited to English gentleman. Fierce bustle about wedding-dress—Worth's—period gown in stiff gold brocade, long sleeves, square neck, off-the-face head-dress, no jewels except my long ear-rings that belonged to great-aunt Delagardie. (*N.B.*—Publisher must have come well up to scratch

on new book.) H. to be married from her College (rather nice, I think)—tremendous wirings and swearings to secrecy. Bunter to go ahead and see that all is in order at Talboys.

2 *October*.—We have had to cancel Bunter. He is being dogged by pressmen. Found one forcing his way into Peter's flat via service lift. B. narrowly escaped summons for assault. P. said, better take Talboys (including drains) on trust. Payment completed, and Noakes says he will have everything ready—quite accustomed to letting house for summer holidays, so it should be all right—Helen agitated because no invitations yet sent out for 16th. Told her I believed 16th not yet officially settled (!) Helen asked, Why the delay? Had Peter got cold feet, or was that girl playing him up again? . . . I suggested, wedding their own affair, both being well over age. . . . They are taking no servants but Bunter, who is a host in himself, and can do all they want, with local help. I fancy Harriet rather shrinks from starting off at once with a strange staff, and Peter wants to spare her. And Town maids are always a perfect nuisance in the country. If Harriet can once establish herself with Bunter, she will have no further trouble with domestics!

4 *October*.—Went round to Peter's flat to advise about settings for some stones he picked up in Italy. While there, registered post brought large, flat envelope—Harriet's writing. Wondered what it was she wanted to send and not bring! (Inquisitive me!) Watched Peter open it, while pretending to examine zircon (such a lovely colour!). He flushed up in that absurd way he has when anybody says anything rather personal to him, and stood staring at the thing till I got quite wound up, and said, "What is it?" He said, in an odd sort of voice, "The bride's gift to the bridegroom." It had been worrying me for some time how she'd grapple with that, because there isn't an awful lot, *really*, one can give a very well-off man, unless one is frightfully well off oneself, and the wrong thing is worse than nothing, but all the same, nobody really wants to be kindly told that they can't bring a better gift than their sweet selves—very pretty but so patronising and Lord of Burleigh—and after

all, we all have human instincts, and giving people things is one of them. So I dashed up to look, and it was a letter written on a single sheet in a very beautiful seventeenth-century hand. Peter said, "The funny thing is that the catalogue was sent to me in Rome, and I wired for this, and was ridiculously angry to learn it had been sold." I said, "But you don't collect manuscripts." And he said, "No, but I wanted this for Harriet." And he turned it over, and I could read the signature, "John Donne," and that explained a lot, because of course Peter has always been queer about Donne. It seems it's a very beautiful letter from D. to a parishioner—Lady Somebody—about Divine and human love. I was trying to read it, only I never can make out that old-fashioned kind of writing (wonder what Helen will make of it—no doubt she'll think a gold cigarette-lighter would have been much more suitable)—when I found Peter had got on the phone, and was saying, "Listen, dear heart," in a voice I'd never heard him use in his life. So I shot out of the room, and ran slap into Bunter, just coming in from the hall-door. Afraid Peter is getting out of hand, because when he came out after telephoning, Bunter reported that he had "booked the best room at the Lord Warden, my lord, for the night of the 16th, and reserved cabin and train accommodation for Mentone as instructed." P. asked, were the hell-hounds on the trail? B. said, Yes—leading hell-hound had approached him as expected with pump working full blast. Had asked, Why Lord Warden and not night boat or aeroplane? B. had replied, Lady a martyr to sea-and-air-sickness. Hound appeared satisfied and tipped B. 10*s*., which B. says he will take liberty of forwarding to Prisoners' Aid Society. I said, "Really, Peter!" but he said, Why shouldn't he arrange continental trip for deserving couple? and posted off reservations to Miss Climpson, for benefit of tubercular accountant and wife in reduced circumstances. (Query: How does one reduce a circumstance?)

5 *October*.—Worth has made magnificent effort and delivered dress. Few select friends invited to see trousseau—including Miss Climpson, miraculously reduced to *speechlessness* by Peter's gift of mink cloak—950 guineas admittedly

perhaps a trifle extravagant, but his *sole* contribution, and he looked as scared and guilty when he presented it as he did when he was a small boy and his father caught him with his pocket full of rabbits after a night out with that rascally old poacher Merryweather he took such a fancy to—and *how* that man's cottage did *smell!* But it *is* a lovely cloak, and H. hadn't the heart to say more than, "Oh, Mr. Rochester!"—in fun, and meaning Jane Eyre, who I always think behaved so ungraciously to that poor man—so gloomy to have your bride, however bigamous, insisting on grey alpaca or merino or whatever it was, and damping to a lover's feelings. . . . Hell-hound's paragraph in *Morning Star*—discreetly anonymous but quite unmistakable. Helen rang up to know if it was true. I replied, with exactness, that it must be all invention! In evening, took Peter and Harriet to Cheyne Walk to dine with Paul—who insists on coming to wedding, arthritis or no arthritis. Noticed unusual constraint between P. and H., who had been all right when I saw them off to dinner and theatre last night. Paul gave one look at them, and started off to chatter about his eternal *cloisonné* and the superiority of naturally matured French wines over port. Uncomfortable evening, with everybody unlike themselves. At last, Paul sent P. and H. off by themselves in a taxi, saying he wanted to talk business with me—obvious excuse. I asked, did he think anything was wrong? Paul said, "*Au contraire, ma sœur, c'est nous qui sommes de trop. Il arrive toujours le moment où l'on apprend à distinguer entre embrasser et baiser*"—adding with one of his grins, "I was wondering how long Peter would last before he let the bars down—he's his father all over again, with a touch of myself, Honoria, with a touch of myself!" Couldn't waste time and breath being annoyed with Paul—who has always been the complete polygamist—and so was Peter's father, of course, dearly as I loved him—so I said, "Yes, but, Paul, do you think Harriet—?" Paul said, "Bah! the wine she drinks is made of grapes. *Il y a des femmes qui ont le génie—*" I really could *not* stand Paul on *le génie de l'amour*, because he goes on and *on*, getting more and more conscientiously French every moment, with illustrative anecdotes from his own career, and anyway, he's only as much

French as I am—exactly one-eighth—so I told him hastily I was sure his diagonal was the right one (wonder whether I meant "angle" or "diagnosis"), and I expect it is—have never known Paul mistaken about the progress of a love-affair. Realise that this explains why he and Harriet have always got on so well together, though one would never have expected it, considering her reserve and his usual taste in women. Suggested to Paul it was time he went to bed; so he said rather dismally, "Yes, Honoria—I'm getting very old and my bones ache. My sins are deserting me, and if I could only have my time over again I'd take care to commit more of them. Confound Peter! *Il ne sait pas vivre. Mais je voudrais bien être dans ses draps.*" "You'll be in your own winding-sheet soon," I said, very crossly; "no wonder Peter calls you Uncle Pandarus, you evil old wretch." Paul said, "Well, you can't deny I had him taught his job, and he's no disgrace to either of us." There was no answer to that, so I came away. . . . Tried *The Stars Look Down* again, and found it full of most unpleasant people. . . . The fact is, one never really *visualises* one's own son. . . . But I needn't have been so cross with Paul.

7 *October.*—Harriet came to see me before starting for Oxford—very nice to me. I think she will give Peter *all* he wants—yes, I really do. If anybody can. . . . Felt depressed, all the same, for nearly half an hour. . . . Later on, while coping with preparations for wedding-breakfast—all made more difficult by need for secrecy—interrupted by Peter on phone, gone suddenly all fractious because it had rained in the night and roads would be slippery, and convinced Harriet would have a skid and be killed on way to Oxford. Begged him not to behave like a half-wit and said, if he wanted healthy occupation he could come and help Franklin wash all the ornaments out of drawing-room cabinets. He didn't come—but Jerry did, in high spirits at idea of being best man, and broke a Dresden shepherdess.

Later.—Peter and Jerry got (thank goodness!) safely out of the way to Oxford. Preparations completed and all wished-for guests summoned and transport arranged for the impecunious. . . . In evening, furious trunk-call from Helen at Denver, having had wire from Peter and demanding what we meant by inconsiderate behaviour. Took great pleasure in telling her (at considerable length and her expense) nothing to thank but her own tactlessness.

8 October.—Peter's wedding-day. Too exhausted to do more than put down that it all went off very well. H. looked genuinely lovely, like a ship coming into harbour with everything shining and flags flying at wherever modern ships do fly flags—Peter terribly white, poor darling, like the day he had his first watch, and could hardly bear himself for fear it would come to pieces in his hands or turn out not to be real, or something—but he pulled himself together to be specially nice to all the guests (believe if he were in Inquisition he would exert social talents to entertain executioners). . . . Got back to Town at 5:30 (Peter's face a study when he realised he had to go 60 miles over crowded roads in a closed car with somebody else driving!—but one really couldn't let him drive H. back in the open Daimler, all in wedding-garments and a top-hat!) . . . Got them smuggled out of the house at a quarter to 7—Bunter was waiting for them with the car on the far side of the Park. . . .

11 p.m. Hope all is really well with them—must stop now and try to get some sleep or shall be a rag in the morning. Find *The Stars Look Down* not quite soothing enough for a bed-book—will fall back on *Through the Looking-Glass.*

CHAPTER I

♦

New-Wedded Lord

I agree with Dryden, that "Marriage is a noble daring."
—Samuel Johnson, *Table Talk*

Mr. Mervyn Bunter, patiently seated in the Daimler on the far side of Regent's Park, reflected that time was getting on. Packed in eiderdowns in the back of the car was a case containing two and a half dozen of vintage port, and he was anxious about it. Great speed would render the wine undrinkable for a fortnight; excessive speed would render it undrinkable for six months. He was anxious about the arrangements—or the lack of them—at Talboys. He hoped everything would be found in good order when they arrived—otherwise, his lady and gentleman might get nothing to eat till goodness knew when. True, he had brought ample supplies from Fortnum's, but suppose there were no knives or forks or plates available. He wished he could have gone ahead, as originally instructed, to see to things. Not but what his lordship was always ready to put up with what couldn't be helped; but it was unsuitable that his lordship should be called on to put up with anything—besides, the lady was still, to some extent, an unknown factor. What his lordship had had to put up with from *her* during the past five or six years, only his lordship knew, but Mr. Bunter could guess. True, the lady seemed now to be in a very satisfactory way of amendment; but it was yet to be ascertained what her conduct would be under the strain of trivial inconvenience. Mr. Bunter was professionally accustomed to judge human beings by their behaviour, not in great crises, but in the minor adjustments of daily life. He had seen one lady threatened with dismissal from his lordship's service (including all emoluments and the enjoyment of an *appartement meublé*, Ave. Kléber) for having, in his presence, unreasonably lost her temper with a lady's maid: but wives were not subject to peremptory dismissal. Mr. Bunter was anxious, also, about how things were going at the Dowager's; he did not really believe that anything could be suitably organised or carried out without his assistance.

He was unspeakably relieved to see the taxi arrive and to assure himself that there was no newspaper man perched on the spare wheel, or lurking in a following vehicle.

"Here we are, Bunter. All serene? Good man. I'll drive. Sure you won't be cold, Harriet?"

Mr. Bunter tucked a rug about the bride's knees.

"Your lordship will bear in mind that we are conveying the port?"

"I will go as gingerly as if it were a baby in arms. What's the matter with the rug?"

"A few grains of cereal, my lord. I have taken the liberty of removing approximately a pound and three-quarters from among the hand-luggage, together with a quantity of assorted footgear."

"That must have been Lord Saint-George," said Harriet.

"Presumably so, my lady."

"*My lady*"—she had never really thought it possible that Bunter would accept the situation. Everybody else, perhaps, but not Bunter. Yet apparently he did. And that being so, the incredible must have happened. She must be actually married to Peter Wimsey. She sat looking at Peter, as the car twisted smoothly in and out of the traffic. The high, beaked profile, and the long hands laid on the wheel had been familiar to her for a long time now; but they were suddenly the face and hands of a stranger. (Peter's hands, holding the keys of hell and heaven . . . that was the novelist's habit, of thinking of everything in terms of literary allusions.)

"Peter!"

"My dear?"

"I was just wondering whether I should recognise your voice—your face seems to have got rather remote, somehow."

She saw the corner of his long mouth twitch.

"Not quite the same person?"

"No."

"Don't worry," he said, imperturbably, "it'll be all right on the night."

Too much experience to be surprised, and too much honesty to pretend not to understand. She remembered what had happened four days earlier. He had brought her home after the theatre, and they were standing before the fire, when she had said something—quite casually, laughing at him. He had turned and said, suddenly and huskily:

"Tu m'enivres!"

Language and voice together had been like a lightning-flash, showing up past and future in a single crack of fire that hurt your eyes and was followed by a darkness like thick, black velvet. . . . When his lips had reluctantly freed themselves, he had said:

"I'm sorry. I didn't mean to wake the whole zoo. But I'm glad, my God! to know it's there—and no shabby tigers either."

"Did you think mine would be a shabby tiger?"

"I thought it might, perhaps, be a little daunted."

"Well, it isn't. It seems to be an entirely new tiger. I never had one before—only kindness to animals."

> *"My lady gave me a tiger,*
> A *sleek and splendid tiger,*
> A *striped and* shining *tiger,*
> *All under the leaves of life."*

Nobody else, thought Harriet, had apparently suspected the tiger—except of course, old Paul Delagardie, whose ironic eyes saw everything.

Peter's final comment had been:

"I have now completely given myself away. No English

vocabulary. No other Englishwoman. And that is the most I can say for myself."

Gradually, they were shaking off the clustering lights of London. The car gathered speed. Peter looked back over his shoulder.

"Not waking the baby, are we, Bunter?"

"The vibration is at present negligible, my lord."

That led memory farther back.

"This question of children, Harriet. Do you feel strongly about it?"

"Well, I'm not quite sure. I'm not marrying you for the sake of having them, if that's what you mean."

"Thank Heaven! He does not wish to regard himself, nor yet to be regarded, in that agricultural light. . . . You don't particularly care about children?"

"Not children, in the lump. But I think it's just possible that I might some day come to want—"

"Your own?"

"No—yours."

"Oh!" he had said, unexpectedly disconcerted. "I see. That's rather—Have you ever considered what kind of a father I should make?"

"I know quite well. Casual, apologetic, reluctant and adorable."

"If I was reluctant, Harriet, it would only be because I have a profound distrust of myself. Our family's been going a pretty long time. There's Saint-George, who has no character, and his sister, with no vitality—to say nothing of the next heir after Saint-George and myself, who is a third cousin and completely gaga. And if you think about my own compound of what Uncle Paul calls nerves and nose—"

"I am reminded of what Clare Clairemont said to Byron: 'I shall always remember the gentleness of your manners and the wild originality of your countenance.'"

"No, Harriet—I mean that."

"Your brother married his own cousin. Your sister married a commoner and *her* children are all right. You wouldn't be doing it all yourself, you know—*I'm* common enough. What's wrong with *me*?"

"Nothing, Harriet. That's true. By God, that's true. The fact is, I'm a coward about responsibility and always have been. My dear—if you want it and are ready to take the risk—"

"I don't believe it's such a risk as all that."

"Very well. I leave it to you. If you will and when you will. When I asked you, I rather expected you to say, No."

"But you had a horrible fear I might say, 'Yes, of course'!"

"Well, perhaps. I didn't expect what you did say. It's embarrassing to be taken seriously—as a person."

"But, Peter, putting aside my own feelings and your morbid visions of twin gorgons or nine-headed hydras or whatever it is you look forward to—would *you* like children?"

She had been amused by the conflict in his self-conscious face.

"Egotistical idiot that I am," he had said finally, "yes. Yes. I should. Heaven knows why. Why does one? To prove one can do it? For the fun of boasting about 'my boy at Eton'? or because—?"

"Peter! When Mr. Murbles drew up that monstrous great long will for you, after we were engaged—"

"Oh, Harriet!"

"How did you leave your property? I mean, the real estate?"

"All right," he said with a groan, "the murder's out. Entailed.—I admit it. But Murbles expects that every man—damn it, don't laugh like that, I couldn't argue the point with Murbles—and *every* contingency was provided for."

A town, with a wide stone bridge, and lights reflected in the river—taking memory no further back than that morning. The Dowager's closed car, with the Dowager discreetly seated beside the chauffeur; herself in cloth of gold and a soft fur cloak, and Peter, absurdly upright in morning dress, with a gardenia in his lapel, balancing a silk hat on his knee.

"Well, Harriet, we've passed the Rubicon. Any qualms?"

"No more than when we went up the Cherwell that night and moored on the far bank, and you asked the same question."

"Thank God! Stick to it, sweetheart. Only one more river."

"And that's the river of Jordan."

"If I kiss you now I shall lose my head and something irreparable will happen to this accursed hat. Let us be very strange and well bred—as if we were not married at all."

One more river.

"Are we getting anywhere near?"

"Yes—this is Great Pagford, where we used to live. Look! that's our old house with the three steps up to the door—there's a doctor there still, you can see the surgery lamp. . . . After two miles you take the right hand turn for Pagford Parva, and then it's another three miles to Paggleham, and sharp left by a big barn and straight on up the lane."

When she was quite small, Dr. Vane had had a dog-cart—just like doctors in old-fashioned books. She had gone along this road, ever so many times, sitting beside him, sometimes allowed to pretend to hold the reins. Later on, it had been a car—a small and noisy one, very unlike this smooth, long-bonneted monster. The doctor had had to start on his rounds in good time, so as to leave a margin for break-downs. The second car had been more reliable—a pre-war Ford. She had learnt to drive that one. If her father had lived, he would be getting on for seventy—his strange new son-in-law would have been calling him "sir." An odd way, this, to be coming home, and not home. This was Paggleham, where the old woman lived who had such terrible rheumatism in her hands—old Mrs., Mrs., Mrs. Warner, that was it—*she* must have gone long ago.

"That's the barn, Peter."

"Right you are. Is that the house?"

The house where the Batesons had lived—a dear old couple, a pleasantly tottering, Darby and Joan pair, always ready to welcome little Miss Vane and give her strawberries and seedy-cake. Yes—the house—a huddle of black gables, with two piled chimney-stacks, blotting out the stars. One would open the door and step straight in, through the sanded entry into the big kitchen with its wooden settles and its great oak rafters, hung with home-cured hams. Only, Darby and Joan were dead by now, and Noakes (she vaguely remembered him—a hard-faced, grasping man who hired out bicycles) would be waiting to receive them. But—there was no light in any of the windows at Talboys.

"We're a bit late," said Harriet, nervously; "he may have given us up."

"Then we shall firmly hand ourselves back to him," said Peter, cheerfully. "People like you and me are not so easily got rid of. I told him, any time after eight o'clock. This looks like the gate."

Bunter climbed out and approached the gate in eloquent silence. He had known it; he had felt it in his bones; the arrangements had fallen through. At whatever cost, even if he had had to strangle pressmen with his bare hands, he ought to have come ahead to see to things. In the glare of the headlights a patch of white paper showed clearly on the top bar of the gate; he looked suspiciously at it, removed, with careful fingers, the tintack that secured it to the wood and brought it, still without a word, to his master.

"NO BREAD AND MILK" (it said) "TILL FURTHER NOTISE."

"H'm!" said Peter. "The occupier, I gather, has already taken his departure. This has been up for several days, by the look of it."

"He's got to be there to let us in," said Harriet.

"He's probably deputed somebody else. He didn't write this himself—he can spell 'notice' in his letter to us. The 'somebody' is a little lacking in thought not to realise that *we* might want bread and milk. However, we can remedy the matter."

He reversed the paper, wrote in pencil on the back "BREAD AND MILK, PLEASE," and restored it to Bunter, who tin-tacked it back and gloomily opened the gate. The car moved slowly past him, up a short and muddy approach, on either side of which were flower-beds, carefully tended and filled with chrysanthemums and dahlias, while behind them rose the dark outlines of some sheltering bushes.

"A load of gravel would have done them no harm," observed Bunter to himself, as he picked a disdainful way through the mud. When he reached the door—massive and uncompromising, within an oaken porch having seats on either side—his lordship was already performing a brisk fantasia upon the horn. There was no reply; nothing stirred in the house; no candle darted its beams; no casement was thrown open; no shrill voice demanded to know their business; only, in the near distance, a dog barked irritably.

Mr. Bunter, gloomily self-restrained, grasped the heavy knocker and let its summons thunder through the night. The dog barked again. He tried the handle, but the door was fast.

"Oh, dear!" said Harriet.

This, she felt, was her fault. Her idea in the first place. Her house. Her honeymoon. Her—and this was the incalculable factor in the thing—her husband. (A repressive word, that, when you came to think of it, compounded of a grumble and a thump.) The man in possession. The man with rights—including the right not to be made a fool of by his belongings. The dashboard light was switched off, and she could not see his face; but she felt his body turn and his left arm move along the back of the seat as he leaned to call across her:

"Try the back!"—and something in his assured tone reminded her that he had been brought up in the country and knew well enough that farm houses were more readily assailable in the rear. "If you can't find anybody there, make for the place where the dog is."

He tootled on the horn again, the dog responded with a volley of yelps, and the shadowy bulk that was Bunter moved round the side of the building.

"That," continued Peter, with satisfaction, and throwing his hat into the back of the car, "will keep him busy for quite a bit. We shall now give one another that attention which, for the last thirty-six hours, has been squandered on trivialities. . . . *Da mihi basia mille, deinde centum.* . . . Do you realise, woman, that I've done it? . . . that I've got you? . . . that you can't get rid of me now, short of death or divorce? . . . *Et tot millia millies quot sunt sidera cœlo*. . . . Forget Bunter. I don't care a rap whether he goes for the dog or the dog goes for him."

"Poor Bunter!"

"Yes, poor devil! No wedding bells for Bunter. . . . Not fair, is it? All the kicks for him and all the kisses for me. . . . Stick to it, old son! Wake Duncan with thy knocking. But there's no hurry for the next few minutes."

The fusillade of knocks had begun again, and the dog was growing hysterical.

"Somebody must come sometime," said Harriet, still with a sense of guilt that no embraces could stifle, "because, if not—"

"If not . . . Last night you slept in a goosefeather bed, and all that. But the goosefeather bed and the new-wedded lord are inseparable only in ballads. Would you rather wed with the feathers or bed with the goose—I mean the gander? Or would you make shift with the lord in the cold open field?"

"He wouldn't be stranded in a cold open field if I hadn't been so idiotic about St. George's, Hanover Square."

"No—and if I hadn't refused Helen's ten villas on the Riviera! . . . Hurray! somebody's throttled the hound—that's a step in the right direction. . . . Cheer up! the night is yet young, and we may even find a goosefeather bed in the village pub—or in the last resort sleep under a haystack. I believe, if I'd had nothing but a haystack to offer you, you'd have married me years ago."

"I shouldn't be surprised."

"Damnation! think what I've missed."

"Me too. At this moment I could have been tramping at your heels with five babies and a black eye, and saying to a sympathetic bobby, 'You leave 'im be—'e's my man, ain't 'e?—'E've a right to knock me abaht.'"

"You seem," said her husband, reprovingly, "to regret the black eye more than the five babies."

"Naturally. You'll never give me the black eye."

"Nothing so easily healed, I'm afraid. Harriet—I wonder

what sort of shot I'm going to make at being decent to you."

"My dear Peter—"

"Yes, I know. But I've never—now I come to think of it—inflicted myself on anyone for very long together. Except Bunter, of course. Have you consulted Bunter? Do you think he would give me a good character?"

"It sounds to me," said Harriet, "as though Bunter had picked up a girl friend."

The footsteps of two people were, in fact, approaching from behind the house. Somebody was expostulating with Bunter in high-pitched tones:

"I'll believe it w'en I sees it, and not before. Mr. Noakes is at Broxford, I tell you, and has been ever since last Wednesday night as ever is, and he ain't never said nothing to me nor nobody, not about sellin' no 'ouse nor about no lords nor ladies neither."

The speaker, now emerging into the blaze of the headlights, was a hard-faced angular lady of uncertain age, dressed in a mackintosh, a knitted shawl, and a man's cap secured rakishly to her head with knobbed and shiny hatpins. Neither the size of the car, the polish of its chromium plating nor the brilliance of its lamps appeared to impress her, for advancing with a snort to Harriet's side she said, belligerently:

"Now then, 'oo are you and wot d'you want, kicking up all this noise? Let's 'ave a look at yer!"

"By all means," said Peter. He switched on the dashboard light. His yellow hair and his eye-glass seemed to produce an unfortunate impression.

"H'mph!" said the lady, "film actors, by the look of yer. And—" (with a withering glance at Harriet's furs) "no better than you should be, I'll be bound."

"We are very sorry to have disturbed you," began Peter, "Mrs.—er—"

"Ruddle is my name," said the lady of the cap. "Mrs. Ruddle, and a respectable married woman with a grown son of her own. He's a-coming over from the cottage now with his gun, as soon as he's put his trousis on, which he had just took 'em off to go to bed in good time, 'aving to be up early to 'is work. Now then! Mr. Noakes is over at Broxford, same as I was sayin' to this other chap of yours, and you can't get nothing out of me, for it ain't no business of mine, except that I obliges 'im in the cleaning way."

"Ruddle?" said Harriet. "Didn't he work at one time for Mr. Vickey at Five Elms?"

"Yes, 'e did," said Mrs. Ruddle quickly, "but that's fifteen years agone. I lost Ruddle last Michaelmas five year, and a good 'usband 'e was, when he was himself, that is. 'Ow do you come to know Ruddle?"

"I'm Dr. Vane's daughter, that used to live at Great Pagford. Don't you remember him? I know your name, and I think I remember your face. But you didn't live here then. The Batesons had the farm, and there was a woman called Sweeting at the cottage who kept pigs and had a niece who wasn't quite right in the head."

"Lor' now!" cried Mrs. Ruddle. "To think o' that! Dr. Vane's daughter, is you, miss? Now I come to look at you, you *'ave* got a look of 'er. But it's gettin' on for seventeen years since you and the doctor left Pagford. I did 'ere as 'e'd passed away, and sorry I was—'e was a wonderful clever doctor, was your dad, miss—I 'ad 'im for my Bert, and I'm sure it's a mercy I did, 'im comin' into the world wrong end up as you might say, which is a sad trial for a woman. And how *are* you, miss, after all this time? We *did* 'ear as you'd been in trouble with the perlice, but as I said to Bert, you can't believe the stuff they puts into them papers."

"It was quite true, Mrs. Ruddle—but they'd got hold of the wrong person."

"Just like 'em!" said Mrs. Ruddle. "There's that Joe Sellon. Tried to make out as my Bert 'ad been stealin' Aggie Twitterton's 'ens. ''Ens,' I said. 'You'll be making out next as 'e took that there pocket-book of Mr. Noakes's, wot 'e made all the fuss about. You look for your 'ens in George Withers's back kitchen,' I says, and sure enough, there they was. 'Call yourself a perliceman,' I says, 'I'd make a better perliceman than you any day, Joe Sellon.' That's what I ses to 'im. I'd never believe nothing none of them perlicemen said, not if I was to be paid for it, so don't you think it, miss. I'm sure I'm very pleased to see you, miss, looking so well, but if you and the gentleman was wanting Mr. Noakes—"

"We did want him, but I expect you can help us. This is my husband and we've bought Talboys and we arranged with Mr. Noakes to come here for our honeymoon."

"You don't say!" ejaculated Mrs. Ruddle. "I'm sure I congratulate you, miss—mum, and sir." She wiped a bony hand on the mackintosh and extended it to bride and groom in turn. "'Oneymoon—well, there!—it won't take me a minnit to put on the clean sheets, which is all laying aired and ready at the cottage, so if you'll let me 'ave the keys—"

"But," said Peter, "that's just the trouble. We haven't got the keys. Mr. Noakes said he'd make all the preparations and be here to let us in."

"Ho!" said Mrs. Ruddle. "Well, 'e never told me nothing about it. Off to Broxford 'e was, by the ten o'clock bus Wednesday night, and never said nothing to nobody, not to mention leave me my week's money."

"But," said Harriet, "if you do his cleaning, haven't you got a key to the house?"

"No, I have *not*," replied Mrs. Ruddle. "You don't ketch *'im* givin' me no keys. Afraid I'll pinch sommink, I suppose. Not that *'e* leaves much as 'ud be worth pinchin'. But there you are, that's 'im all over. *And* burglar-proof bolts on all the winders. Many's the time I've said to Bert, supposin' the 'ouse was to go on fire with 'im away an' no keys nearer than Pagford."

"Pagford?" said Peter. "I thought you said he was at Broxford."

"So 'e is—sleeps over the wireless business. But you'd 'ave a job ter get him, I reckon, 'im bein' a bit deaf and the bell ringin' inter the shop. Your best way'll be ter run over ter Pagford an' git Aggie Twitterton."

"The lady who keeps hens?"

"That's 'er. You mind the little cottage down by the river, miss—mum, I should say—where old Blunt useter live? Well, that's it, an' she's got a key to the 'ouse—comes over ter see ter things w'en 'e's away, though, come ter think of it, I ain't seen 'er this last week. Maybe she's poorly, because, come to think of it, if 'e knowed you was coming it's Aggie Twitterton, 'e'd a-told about it."

"I expect that's it," said Harriet. "Perhaps she meant to let you know, and got ill and couldn't see to it. We'll go over. Thank you very much. Do you think she could let us have a loaf of bread and some butter?"

"Bless you, miss—mum—I can do that. I got a nice loafer bread, 'ardly touched, and 'arf a pound er butter at 'ome this minnit. And," said Mrs. Ruddle, not for an instant losing her grasp upon essentials, "the clean sheets, like I was sayin'. I'll run and fetch them up directly, and it won't take no time to get straight w'en you and your good gentleman comes back with the keys. Excuse me, mum, wot might your married name be?"

"Lady Peter Wimsey," said Harriet, feeling not at all sure that it was her name.

"I never!" said Mrs. Ruddle. "That's wot 'e said"—she jerked her head at Bunter—"but I didn't pay no 'eed to 'im. Begging your pardon, mum, but there's some of these commercial fellers 'ud say anythink, wouldn't they, sir?"

"Oh, we all have to pay heed to Bunter," said Wimsey. "He's the only really reliable person in the party. Now, Mrs. Ruddle, we'll run over and get the keys from Miss Twitterton and be back in twenty minutes. Bunter, you'd better stay here and give Mrs. Ruddle a hand with the things. Is there room to turn?"

"Very good, my lord. No, my lord. I fancy there is *not* room to turn. I will open the gate for your lordship. Allow me, my lord. Your lordship's hat."

"Give it to me," said Harriet, Peter's hands being occupied with the ignition switch and the self-starter.

"Yes, my lady. Thank you, my lady."

"After which," said Peter, when they had reversed through the gate and were once again headed for Great Pagford, "Bunter will proceed to make it quite plain to Mrs. Ruddle—in case she hasn't grasped the idea—that Lord and Lady Peter Wimsey are my lord and lady. Poor old Bunter! Never have his feelings been so harrowed. Film-actors, by the look of you! No better than you should be! These commercial fellers will say anythink!"

"Oh, Peter! I wish I could have married Bunter. I do love him so."

"Bride's Wedding-Night Confession; Titled Clubman Slays Valet and Self. I'm glad you take to Bunter—I owe him a lot. . . . Do you know anything about this Twitterton woman we're going to see?"

"No—but I've an idea there was an elderly labourer of that name in Pagford Parva who used to beat his wife or something. They weren't Dad's patients. It's funny, even if she's ill, that she shouldn't have sent Mrs. Ruddle a message."

"Dashed funny. I've got my own ideas about Mr. Noakes. Simcox—"

"Simcox? Oh, the agent, yes?"

"He was surprised to find the place going so cheap. It's true it was only the house and a couple of fields—Noakes seems to have sold part of the property. I paid Noakes last Monday, and the cheque was cleared in London on Thursday, I shouldn't wonder if another bit of clearing was done at the same time."

"What?"

"Friend Noakes. It doesn't affect our purchase of the house—the title is all right and there's no mortgage, I made sure of that. The fact that there was no mortgage cuts both ways. If he was in difficulties, you'd expect a mortgage; but if he was in great difficulties, he might have kept the property free for a quick sale. He kept a bicycle shop in your day. Was he ever in difficulties with that?"

"I don't know. I think he sold it and the man who bought it said he'd been cheated. Noakes was supposed to be pretty sharp over a bargain."

"Yes. He got Talboys dirt cheap, I fancy from what Simcox

said. Got some kind of squeeze on the old people and put the brokers in. I've an idea he was fond of buying and selling things as a speculation."

"He used to be spoken of as a warm man. Always up to something."

"All sorts of little enterprises, h'm? Picking things up cheap on the chance of patching 'em up for resale at a profit—that sort?"

"Rather that sort."

"Um. Sometimes it works, sometimes not. There's a London tenant of mine who started twenty years ago with a few second-hand oddments in a cellar. I've just built him a very handsome block of flats with sunshine balconies and vitaglass and things. He'll do very well with them. But then he's a Jew, and knows exactly what he's doing. I shall get my money back and so will he. He's got the knack of making money turn over. We'll have him to dinner one day and he'll tell you how he did it. He started in the War, with the double handicap of a slight deformity and a German name, but before he dies he'll be a damn sight richer than I am."

Harriet asked a question or two, which her husband answered, but in so abstract a tone that she realised he was giving only about a quarter of his mind to the virtuous Jew of London and none of it to herself. He was probably mulling over the mysterious behaviour of Mr. Noakes. She was quite accustomed to his sudden withdrawals into the recesses of his own mind, and did not resent them. She had known him stop short in the middle of a proposal of marriage to her because some chance sight or sound had offered him a new piece to fit into a criminal jig-saw. His meditations did not last long, for within five minutes they were running into Great Pagford, and he was obliged to rouse himself to ask his companion the way to Miss Twitterton's cottage.

CHAPTER II

♦

Goosefeather Bed

But for the Bride-bed, what were fit,
That hath not been talk'd of yet.
—Drayton, *Eighth Nimphall*

The cottage, which had three yellow brick sides and a red-brick front, like the uglier kind of doll's house, stood rather isolated from the town, so that it was perhaps not unreasonable in Miss Twitterton to interrogate her visitors, in sharp and agitated tones from an upper window, as to their intentions and *bona fides*, before cautiously opening the door to them. She revealed herself as a small, fair and flustered spinster in her forties, wrapped in a pink flannel dressing-gown, and having in one hand a candle and in the other a large dinner-bell. She could not understand *what* it was all about. Uncle William had said *nothing* to her. She did not even know he was away. He *never* went away without letting her know. He would *never* have sold the house without telling her. She kept the door on the chain while repeating these asseverations, holding the dinner-bell ready to ring in case the odd-looking person in the eye-glass should become violent and oblige her to summon assistance. Eventually, Peter produced Mr. Noakes's last letter from his pocketbook (where he had thoughtfully placed it before starting, in case of any difference of opinion about the arrangements) and passed it in through the partly-opened door. Miss Twitterton took it gingerly, as though it were a bomb, shut the door promptly in Peter's face, and retired with the candle into the front room to examine the document at her leisure. Apparently the perusal was satisfactory, and at the end of it she returned, opened the door wide and begged her visitors to enter.

"I beg your pardon," said Miss Twitterton, leading the way into a sitting-room furnished with a suite in green velvet and walnut veneer, and a surprising variety of knick-knacks, "for receiving you like this—do please sit down, Lady Peter—I do hope you will both forgive my attire—dear me!—but my house is a little lonely and it's only a *short* time ago since my *henroost* was robbed—and really, the whole thing is so *inexplicable*, I scarcely know what to think—it really is *most* upsetting—so *peculiar* of uncle—and what you must be thinking of both of us I cannot *imagine*."

"Only that it's a great shame to knock you up at this time of night," said Peter.

"It's only a quarter to ten," replied Miss Twitterton, with a deprecating glance at a little china clock in the shape of a pansy, "nothing, of *course*, to you—but you know we keep *early* hours in the country. I have to be up at *five* to feed my birds, so I'm rather an *early bird* myself—except on choir-practice nights, you know—Wednesday, such an awkward day for me with Thursday market-day, but then it's more convenient for the dear Vicar. But, of *course*, if I'd had the *smallest* idea that Uncle William would *do* such an *extraordinary* thing, I'd have come over and been there to let you in. If you could wait five—or perhaps *ten*—minutes while I made a more suitable toilet, I could come now—as I see you have your beautiful *car*, perhaps—"

"Please don't bother, Miss Twitterton," said Harriet, a little alarmed at the prospect. "We have plenty of supplies with us and Mrs. Ruddle and our man can look after us quite well for tonight. If you could just let us have the keys—"

"The keys—yes, of course. So *dreadful* for you not being able to get in and really such a cold night for the time of year—what Uncle William can have been *thinking* of—and did he say—dear me! his letter upset me so I hardly knew what I was reading—your honeymoon, didn't you say?—how terrible for you—and I do hope at any rate you've had supper? No *supper?*—I simply can't *understand* how Uncle could—but you *will* take a little bit of cake and a glass of my homemade wine?"

"Oh, really, we mustn't trouble you—" began Harriet, but Miss Twitterton was already hunting in a cupboard. Behind her back, Peter put his hands to his face in a mute gesture of horrified resignation.

"There!" said Miss Twitterton, triumphantly, "I'm sure you will feel better for a little refreshment. My parsnip wine is really *extra* good this year. Dr. Jellyfield always takes a glass when he comes—which isn't very often, I'm pleased to say, because my health is always *remarkably* good."

"That will not prevent me from drinking to it," said Peter, disposing of the parsnip wine with a celerity which might have been due to eagerness but, to Harriet, rather suggested a reluctance to let the draught linger on the palate. "May I pour out a glass for yourself?"

"How kind of you!" cried Miss Twitterton. "Well—it's *rather* late at night—but I really *ought* to drink to your wedded happiness, oughtn't I?—*Not* too much, Lord Peter, please. The dear Vicar always says my parsnip wine is not *nearly* so innocent as it looks—dear me!—But *you* will take just a little more, won't you? A gentleman always has a stronger head than a lady."

"Thanks so much," said Peter, meekly, "but you must remember I've got to drive my wife back to Paggleham."

"*One* more I'm *sure* won't do any harm—Well, just *half* a glass, then—there! Now of course, you want the keys. I'll run upstairs for them at once—I know I mustn't keep you—I won't be a *minute*, Lady Peter, so *please* have another slice of cake—it's home-made—I do all my own baking, and Uncle's too—whatever can have come over him I can't *think*!"

Miss Twitterton ran out, leaving the pair to gaze at one another in the light of the candle.

"Peter, my poor, long-suffering, heroic lamb—pour it into the aspidistra."

Wimsey lifted his eyebrows at the plant.

"It looks rather unwell already, Harriet. I think my constitution is the better of the two. Here goes. But you might kiss me to take the taste away. . . . Our hostess has a certain refinement (I think that's the word) about her which I had not expected. She got your title right first shot, which is unusual. Her life has had some smatch of honour in it. Who was her father?"

"I think he was a cowman."

"Then he married above his station. His wife, presumably, was a Miss Noakes."

"It comes back to me that she was a village school-mistress over at some place near Broxford."

"That explains it. . . . Miss Twitterton is coming down. At this point we rise up, buckle the belt of the old leather coat, grab the gent's soft hat and make the motions of imminent departure."

"The keys," said Miss Twitterton, arriving breathless with a second candle. "The big one is the *back* door, but you'll find that *bolted*. The *little* one is the *front* door—it's a *patent*, *burglar-proof* lock—you may find it a little *difficult* if you don't know the way it works. Perhaps, after all, I ought to come over and show you—"

"Not a bit of it, Miss Twitterton. I know these locks quite well. Really. Thank you ever so much. Good night. And many apologies."

"*I* must apologise for Uncle. I really *cannot* understand his treating you in this *cavalier* way. I *do* hope you'll find everything all right. Mrs. Ruddle is *not* very intelligent."

Harriet assured Miss Twitterton that Bunter would see to everything, and they succeeded at length in extricating themselves. Their return to Talboys was remarkable only for Peter's observing that unforgettable was the epithet for Miss Twitterton's parsnip wine and that if one was going to be sick on one's wedding night one might just as well have done it between Southampton and Le Havre.

Bunter and Mrs. Ruddle had by now been joined by the dilatory Bert (with his "trousis" but without his gun); yet even thus supported, Mrs. Ruddle had a chastened appearance. The door being opened, and Bunter having produced an electric torch, the party stepped into a wide stone passage strongly permeated by an odour of dry-rot and beer. On the right, a door led into a vast, low-ceilinged, stone-paved kitchen, its rafters black with time, its enormous, old-fashioned range clean and garnished under the engulfing chimney-breast. On the whitewashed hearth stood a small oil cooking-stove and before it an arm-chair whose seat sagged with age and use. The deal table held the remains of two boiled eggs, the heel of a stale loaf and a piece of cheese, together with a cup which had contained cocoa, and a half-burnt candle in a bedroom candlestick.

"There!" exclaimed Mrs. Ruddle. "If Mr. Noakes 'ad a-let me know, I'd a-cleaned all them things away. That'll be 'is supper wot 'e 'ad afore 'e caught the ten o'clock. But me not knowing and 'avin' no key, you see, I couldn't. But it won't take me a minnit, m'lady, now we *are* here. Mr. Noakes took all 'is meals in 'ere, but you'll find it comfortabler in the settin'-room, m'lady, if you'll come this way—it's a much brighter room, like, and furnished beautiful, as you'll see, m'lord." Here Mrs. Ruddle dropped something like a curtsy.

The sitting-room was, indeed, "brighter" than the kitchen. Two ancient oak-settles, flanking the chimney-piece at right angles, and an old-fashioned American eight-day clock on the inner wall, were all that remained of the old farm-house furniture that Harriet remembered. The flame of the kitchen candle, which Mrs. Ruddle had lit, danced flickeringly over a suite of Edwardian chairs with crimson upholstery, a top-heavy sideboard, a round mahogany table with wax fruit on it, a bamboo what-not with mirrors and little shelves sprouting from it in all directions, a row of aspidistras in pots in the window-ledge, with strange hanging plants above them in wire baskets, a large radio cabinet, over which hung an unnaturally distorted cactus in a brass Benares bowl, mirrors with roses painted on the glass, a chesterfield sofa upholstered in electric blue plush, two carpets of violently coloured and mutually intolerant patterns juxtaposed to hide the black oak floor-boards—a collection of objects, in fact, suggesting that Mr. Noakes had furnished his house out of auction-sale bargains that he had not been able to re-sell, together with a few remnants of genuine old stuff and a little borrowing from the stock-in-trade of the wireless business. They were allowed every opportunity to inspect this collection of bric-à-brac, for Mrs. Ruddle made the round of the room, candle in hand, to point out all its beauties.

"Fine!" said Peter, cutting short Mrs. Ruddle's panegyric on the radio cabinet ("which you can hear it lovely right over at the cottage if the wind sets that way"). "Now, what we want at the moment, Mrs. Ruddle, is fire and food. If you'll get us some more candles and let your Bert help Bunter to bring in the provisions out of the back of the car, then we can get the fires lit—"

"Fires?" said Mrs. Ruddle in doubtful accents. "Well, there, sir—m'lord I should say—I ain't sure as there's a mite of coal in the place. Mr. Noakes, 'e ain't 'ad no fires this long time. Said these 'ere great chimbleys ate up too much of the 'eat. Oil-stoves, that's wot Mr. Noakes 'ad, for cookin' an' for settin' over of an evenin'. I don't rackollect w'en there was fires 'ere last—except that young couple we 'ad 'ere August four year, w'en we had sich a cold summer—and they couldn't get the chimbley to go. Thought there must be a bird's nest in it or somethink, but Mr. Noakes said 'e wasn't goin' to spend good money 'aving they chimbleys cleared. Coal, now. There ain't none in the oil-shed, that I do know—without there might be a bit in the wash'us—but it'll have been there a long time," she concluded dubiously, as though its qualities might have been lost by keeping.

"I might fetch up a bucket or so of coal from the cottage, mum," suggested Bert.

"So you might, Bert," agreed his mother. "My Bert's got a wonderful 'ead. So you might. And a bit o' kindlin' with it. You can cut across the back way—and, 'ere, Bert—jest shet that cellar door as you goes by—sech a perishin' draught as it do send up. And, Bert, I declare if I ain't forgot the sugar—you'll find a packet in the cupboard you could put in your pocket. There'll be tea in the kitchen, but Mr. Noakes never took no sugar, only the gran, and that ain't right for 'er ladyship."

By this time, the resourceful Bunter had ransacked the kitchen for candles, which he was putting in a couple of tall brass candlesticks (part of Mr. Noakes's more acceptable possessions) which stood on the sideboard; carefully scraping the guttered wax from the sockets with a penknife with the air of one to whom neatness and order came first, even in a crisis.

"And if your ladyship will come this way," said Mrs. Ruddle, darting to a door in the panelling, "I'll show you the bedrooms. Beautiful rooms they is, but only the one of 'em in use, of course, except for summer visitors. Mind the stair, m'lady, but there—I'm forgettin' you knows the 'ouse. I'll jest pop the bed again the fire, w'en we gets it lit, though damp it cannot be, 'avin' been in use till last Wednesday, and the sheets is aired beautiful, though linen, which, if folks don't suffer from the rheumatics, most ladies and gentlemen is partial to. I 'opes as you don't mind them old four-posters, miss—mum—m'lady. Mr. Noakes did want to sell them, but the gentleman as come down to look at them said as 'ow they wasn't wot 'e called original owing to being mended on account of the worm and wouldn't give Mr. Noakes the price 'e put on 'em. Nasty old things I calls 'em—w'en Ruddle and me was to be wedded I says to 'im, 'Brass knobs,' I ses, 'or nothink'—and, bein' wishful to please, brass knobs it was, beautiful."

"How lovely," said Harriet, as they passed through a deserted bedroom, with the four-poster stripped naked and the rugs rolled together and emitting a powerful odour of mothballs.

"That it is, m'lady," said Mrs. Ruddle. "Not but what some o' the visitors likes these old-fashioned things—quaint, they calls 'em—and the curtains you will find in good order if wanted, Miss Twitterton and me doin' of 'em up careful at the end of the summer, and I do assure you, m'lady, if you and your good gentleman—your good lord, m'lady—was a-wantin' a bit of 'elp in the 'ouse you will find Bert an' me allus ready to oblige, as I was a-sayin' only jest now to Mr. Bunter. Yes, m'lady, thank you. Now, this"—Mrs. Ruddle opened the farther door—"is Mr. Noakes's own room, as you may see, and all ready to okkerpy, barrin' 'is odds-and-ends, which it won't take me a minnit to put aside."

"He seems to have left all his things behind him," said

Harriet, looking at an old-fashioned nightshirt laid ready for use on the bed and at the shaving tackle and sponge on the washstand.

"Oh, yes, m'lady. Kept a spare set of everythink over at Broxford, 'e did, so 'e 'adn't to do nothing but step into the 'bus. More often at Broxford than not 'e was, lookin' after the business. But I'll 'ave everythink straight in no time—only jest to change the sheets and run a duster over. Maybe you'd like me to bile yer a kittle of water on the Beetrice, m'lady—*and,*" Mrs. Ruddle's tone suggested that this consideration had often influenced the wavering decision of prospective summer visitors—"*down* this 'ere little stair—mind yer 'ead, mum—everythink is modern, put in by Mr. Noakes w'en 'e took to lettin' for the summer."

"A bathroom?" asked Harriet hopefully.

"Well, no, m'lady, not a *bath*room," replied Mrs. Ruddle, as though that were too much to expect, "but everythink else is quite modern as you'll find—only requirin' to be pumped up night and morning in the scullery."

"Oh, I see," said Harriet, "how nice." She peered from the lattice. "I wonder if they've brought in the suit-cases."

"I'll run and see this minnit," said Mrs. Ruddle, gathering all Mr. Noakes's toilet apparatus dexterously into her apron as she passed the dressing-table and whisking his nightgear in after it; "and I'll 'ave it all up before you can look round."

It was Bunter, however, who brought the luggage. He looked, Harriet thought, a little worn, and she smiled deprecatingly at him.

"Thank you, Bunter. I'm afraid this is making a lot of work for you. Is his lordship—?"

"His lordship is with the young man they call Bert, clearing out the woodshed to put the car away, my lady." He looked at her and his heart was melted. "He is singing songs in the French language, which I have observed to be a token of high spirits with his lordship. It has occurred to me, my lady, that if you and his lordship would kindly overlook any temporary deficiencies in the arrangements, the room adjacent to this might be suitably utilised as a dressing-room for his lordship's use, so as to leave more accommodation here for your ladyship. Allow me."

He opened the wardrobe door, inspected Mr. Noakes's garments hanging within, shook his head over them, removed them from the hooks and carried them away over his arm. In five minutes, he had cleared the chest of drawers of all its contents and, in five minutes more, had re-lined all the drawers with sheets of the *Morning Post*, which he produced from his coat-pocket. From the other pocket he drew out two new candles, which he set in the two empty sticks that flanked the mirror. He took away Mr. Noakes's chunk of yellow soap, his towels and the ewer, and presently returned with fresh towels and water, a virgin tablet of soap wrapped in cellophane, a small kettle and a spirit-lamp, observing, as he applied a match to the spirit, that Mrs. Ruddle had placed a ten-pint kettle on the oil-stove, which, in his opinion, would take half an hour to boil, and would there be anything further at the moment, as he rather thought they were having a little difficulty with the sitting-room fire, and he would like to get his lordship's suit-case unpacked before going down to give an eye to it.

Under the circumstances, Harriet made no attempt to change her dress. The room, though spacious and beautiful in its half-timbered style, was cold. She wondered whether, all things considered, Peter would not have been happier in the Hotel Gigantic somewhere-or-other on the Continent. She hoped that, after his struggles with the woodshed, he would find a good, roaring fire to greet him and be able to eat his belated meal in comfort.

Peter Wimsey rather hoped so, too. It took a long time to clear the woodshed, which contained not very much wood, but an infinite quantity of things like dilapidated mangles and wheelbarrows, together with the remains of an old pony-trap, several disused grates and a galvanised iron boiler with a hole in it. But he had his doubts about the weather, and was indisposed to allow Mrs. Merdle (the ninth Daimler of that name) to stand out all night. When he thought of his lady's expressed preference for haystacks, he sang songs in the French language;

but from time to time he stopped singing and wondered whether, after all, she might not have been happier at the Hotel Gigantic, somewhere-or-other on the Continent.

The church clock down in the village was chiming the three-quarters before eleven when he finally coaxed Mrs. Merdle into her new quarters and re-entered the house, brushing the cobwebs from his hands. As he passed the threshold a thick cloud of smoke caught him by the throat and choked him. Pressing on, nevertheless, he arrived at the door of the kitchen, where a first hasty glance convinced him that the house was on fire. Recoiling into the sitting-room, he found himself enveloped in a kind of London fog, through which he dimly decried dark forms struggling about the hearth like genies of the mist. He said "Hallo!" and was instantly seized by a fit of coughing. Out of the thick rolls of smoke came a figure that he vaguely remembered promising to love and cherish at some earlier period in the day. Her eyes were streaming and her progress blind. He extended an arm, and they coughed convulsively together.

"Oh, Peter!" said Harriet, "I think all the chimneys are bewitched."

The windows in the sitting-room had been opened and the draught brought fresh smoke billowing out into the passage. With it came Bunter, staggering but still in possession of his faculties, and flung wide both the front door and the back. Harriet reeled out into the sweet cold air of the porch and sat down on a seat to recover herself. When she could see and breathe again, she made her way back to the sitting-room, only to meet Peter coming out of the kitchen in his shirt-sleeves.

"It's no go," said his lordship. "No can do. Those chimneys are blocked. I've been inside both of them and you can't see a single star and there's about fifteen bushels of soot in the kitchen chimney-ledges, because I felt it." (As indeed his right arm bore witness.) "I shouldn't think they'd been swept for twenty years."

"They ain't been swep' in *my* memory," said Mrs. Ruddle, "and I've lived in that cottage eleven year come next Christmas quarter-day."

"Then it's time they were," said Peter, briskly. "Send for the sweep tomorrow, Bunter. Heat up some of the turtle soup on the oil-stove and give us the foie gras, the quails in aspic and a bottle of hock in the kitchen."

"Certainly, my lord."

"And I want a wash. Did I see a kettle in the kitchen?"

"Yes, m'lord," quavered Mrs. Ruddle, "oh, yes—a beautiful kittle as 'ot at 'ot. And if I was jest to put the bed down before the Beetrice in the settin'-room and git the clean sheets on—"

Peter fled with the kettle into the scullery, whither his bride pursued him.

"Peter, I'm past apologising for my ideal home."

"Apologise if you dare—and embrace me at your peril. I am as black as Belloc's scorpion. He is a most unpleasant brute to find in bed at night."

"Among the clean sheets. And, Peter—oh, Peter! the ballad was right. It *is* a goosefeather bed!"

CHAPTER III

♦

Jordan River

The feast with gluttonous delays
Is eaten . . .
. . .night is come; and yet we see
Formalities retarding thee. . . .
A bride, before a "Good-night!" could be said,
Should vanish from her clothes into her bed,
As souls from bodies steal, and are not spied.
But now she's laid; what though she be?
Yet there are more delays, for where is he?
He comes and passeth through sphere after sphere;

First her sheets, then her arms, then anywhere.
Let not this day, then, but this night be thine;
Thy day was but the eve to this, O Valentine.
—John Donne, *An Ephithalamion*
on the Lady Elizabeth and Count Palatine

Peter, dispensing soup and pâté and quails from a curious harlequin assortment of Mr. Noakes's crockery, had said to Bunter:

"We'll do our own waiting. For God's sake get yourself some grub and make Mrs. Ruddle fix you up something to sleep on. My egotism has reached an acute stage tonight, but there's no need for you to pander to it."

Bunter smiled gently and vanished, with the assurance that he should "do very well, my lord, thank you."

He returned, however, about the quail stage, to announce that the chimney in her ladyship's room was clear, owing (he suggested) to the circumstance that nothing had been burned in it since the days of Queen Elizabeth. He had consequently succeeded in kindling upon the hearthstone a small fire of wood which, though restricted in size and scope by the absence of dogs, would, he trusted, somewhat mitigate the inclemency of the atmosphere.

"Bunter," said Harriet, "you are marvellous."

"Bunter," said Wimsey, "you are becoming thoroughly demoralised. I told you to look after *yourself*. This is the first time you have ever refused to take my orders. I hope you will not make it a precedent."

"No, my lord. I have dismissed Mrs. Ruddle, after enlisting her services for tomorrow, subject to her ladyship's approval. Her manner is unpolished, but I have observed that her brass is not and that she has hitherto maintained the house in a state of commendable cleanliness. Unless your ladyship desires to make other arrangements—"

"Let's keep her on if we can," said Harriet, a little confused at being deferred to (since Bunter, after all, was likely to suffer most from Mrs. Ruddle's peculiarities). "She's always worked here and she knows where everything is, and she seems to be doing her best."

She glanced doubtfully at Peter, who said:

"The worst I know of her is that she doesn't like my face, but that will hurt her more than it will me. I mean, you know, she's the one that's got to look at it. Let her carry on. . . . In the meantime, there is this matter of Bunter's insubordination, from which I refuse to be diverted by Mrs. Ruddle or any other red herring."

"My lord?"

"If, Bunter, you do not immediately sit down here and have your supper, I will have you drummed out of the Regiment. My God!" said Peter, putting a formidable wedge of foie gras on a cracked plate and handing it to his man, "do you realise what will happen to us if you die of neglect and starvation? There appear to be only two tumblers, so your punishment shall be to take your wine in a teacup and make a speech afterwards. There was a little supper below-stairs at my mother's on Sunday night, I fancy. The speech you made then will serve the purpose, Bunter, with suitable modifications to fit it for our chaste ears."

"May I respectfully inquire," asked Bunter, drawing up an obedient chair, "how your lordship comes to know about that?"

"You know my methods, Bunter. As a matter of fact, James blew—if I may call it so—the gaff."

"Ah, James!" said Bunter, in a tone that boded James no good. He brooded a little over his supper, but, when called upon, rose without overmuch hesitation, teacup in hand.

"My orders are," said Mr. Bunter, "to propose the health of the happy couple shortly to—the happy couple now before us. To obey orders in this family has been my privilege for the last twenty years—a privilege which has been an unqualified pleasure, except perhaps when connected with the photography of deceased persons in an imperfect state of preservation."

He paused, and seemed to expect something.

"Did the kitchen-maid shriek at that point?" asked Harriet.

"No, my lady—the housemaid; the kitchen-maid having

been sent out for giggling when Miss Franklin was speaking."

"It's a pity we let Mrs. Ruddle go," said Peter. "In her absence we will deem the shriek to have been duly uttered. Proceed!"

"Thank you, my lord. . . . I should, perhaps," resumed Mr. Bunter, "apologise for alarming the ladies with so unpleasant an allusion, but that her ladyship's pen has so adorned the subject as to render the body of a murdered millionaire as agreeable to the contemplative mind as is that of a ripe burgundy to the discriminating palate. (*Hear, hear!*) His lordship is well known as a connoisseur, both of a fine body (*Keep it clean, Bunter!*)—in every sense of the word (*Laughter*)—and of a fine spirit (*Cheers*)—also in every sense of the word (*Renewed laughter and applause*). May I express the hope that the present union may happily exemplify that which we find in a first-class port—strength of body fortified by a first-class spirit and mellowing through many years to a noble maturity. My lord and my lady—your very good health!" (*Prolonged applause, during which the orator drained his cup and sat down.*)

"Upon my word," said Peter, "I have seldom heard an after-dinner speech more remarkable for brevity and—all things considered—propriety."

"You'll have to reply to it, Peter."

"I am no orator as Bunter is, but I'll try. . . . Am I mistaken, by the way, in imagining that that oil-stove is stinking to heaven?"

"It's smoking, at any rate," said Harriet, "like nothing on earth."

Bunter, whose back was towards it, got up in alarm.

"I fear, my lord," he observed, after some minutes of silent struggle, "that some catastrophe has occurred to the burner."

"Let's have a look," said Peter.

The ensuing struggle was neither silent nor successful.

"Turn the blasted thing out and take it away," said Peter at length. He came back to the table, his appearance in no way improved by several long smears from the oily smuts which were now falling in every part of the room. "Under the present conditions, I can only say, Bunter, in reply to your good wishes for our welfare, that my wife and I thank you sincerely and shall hope that they may be fulfilled in every particular. For myself, I should like to add that any man is rich in friends who has a good wife and a good servant, and I hope I may be dead, as I shall certainly be damned, before I give either of you cause to leave me (as they say) for another. Bunter, your health—and may heaven send her ladyship and you fortitude to endure me, so long as we all shall live. I may as well warn you that I for one am firmly resolved to live as long as I possibly can."

"To which," said Mr. Bunter, "always excepting the fortitude as being unnecessary, I should wish—if the expression may be permitted—to observe, Amen."

Here everybody shook hands, and there was a pause, broken by Mr. Bunter's saying with slightly self-conscious haste, that he thought he had better attend to the bedroom fire.

"And in the meantime," said Peter, "we can have a final cigarette over the Beatrice in the sitting-room. I suppose, by the way, Beatrice is capable of heating us a little washing water."

"No doubt of it, my lord," said Mr. Bunter, "always supposing that one could find a new wick for it. The present wick appears, I regret to say, inadequate."

"Oh!" said Peter, a little blankly.

And indeed, when they reached the sitting-room, Beatrice was seen to be at her last expiring blue glimmer.

"You must see what you can do with the bedroom fire," was Harriet's suggestion.

"Very good, my lady."

"At any rate," said Peter, lighting the cigarettes, "the matches still seem to strike on the box; all the laws of Nature have not been suspended for our confusion. We will muffle ourselves in overcoats and proceed to keep each other warm in the accepted manner of benighted travellers in a snowbound country. 'If I were on Greenland's coast,' and all that. Not that I see any prospect of a six-months' night; I wish I did; it is already past midnight."

Bunter vanished upstairs, kettle in hand.

"If," said her ladyship a few minutes later, "you would

remove that contraption from your eye, I could clean the bridge of your nose. Are you sorry we didn't go to Paris or Mentone after all?"

"No, definitely not. There is a solid reality about this. It's convincing, somehow."

"It's beginning to convince me, Peter. Such a series of domestic accidents could only happen to married people. There's none of that artificial honeymoon glitter that prevents people from discovering each other's real characters. You stand the test of tribulation remarkably well. It's very encouraging."

"Thank you—but I really don't know that there's a great deal to complain of. I've got you, that's the chief thing, and food and fire of sorts, and a roof over my head. What more could any man want?—Besides, I should hate to have missed Bunter's speech and Mrs. Ruddle's conversation—and even Miss Twitterton's parsnip wine adds a distinct flavour to life. I might, perhaps, have preferred rather more hot water and less oil about my person. Not that there is anything essentially effeminate about paraffin—but I disapprove on principle of perfumes for men."

"It's a nice, clean smell," said his wife, soothingly, "much more original than all the powders of the merchant. And I expect Bunter will manage to get it off you."

"I hope so," said Peter. He remembered that it had once been said of "*ce blond cadet de famille ducale anglaise*"—said, too, by a lady who had every opportunity of judging—that "*il tenait son lit en Grand Monarque et s'y démenait en Grand Turc.*" The Fates, it seemed, had determined to strip him of every vanity save one. Let them. He could fight this battle naked. He laughed suddenly.

"*Enfin, du courage! Embrasse-moi, chérie. Je trouverai quand même le moyen de te faire plaisir. Hein? tu veux? dis donc!*"

"*Je veux bien.*"

"Dearest!"

"Oh, Peter!"

"I'm sorry—did I hurt you?"

"No. Yes. Kiss me again."

It was at some point during the next five minutes that Peter was heard to murmur, 'Not faint Canaries but ambrosial"; and it is symptomatic of Harriet's state of mind that at the time she vaguely connected the faint canaries with the shabby tigers—only tracing the quotation to its source some ten days later.

Bunter came downstairs. In one hand he held a small and steaming jug, and in the other a case of razors and a spongebag. A bath-towel and a pair of pyjamas hung from his arm, together with a silk dressing-gown.

"The fire in the bedroom is drawing satisfactorily. I have contrived to heat a small quantity of water for your ladyship's use."

His master looked apprehensive.

"But what to me, my love, but what to me?"

Bunter made no verbal reply, but his glance in the direction of the kitchen was eloquent. Peter looked thoughtfully at his own finger-nails and shuddered.

"Lady," said he, "get you to bed and leave me to my destiny."

The wood upon the hearth was flaring cheerfully, and the water, what there was of it, was boiling. The two brass candlesticks bore their flaming ministers bravely, one on either side of the mirror. The big four-poster, with its patchwork quilt of faded blues and scarlets and its chintz hangings dimmed by age and laundering, had, against the pale, plastered walls, a dignified air as though of exiled royalty. Harriet, warm and powdered and free at last from the smell of soot, paused with the hair-brush in her hand to wonder what was happening to Peter. She slipped across the chill dark of the dressing-room, opened the farther door, and listened. From somewhere far below came an ominous clank of iron, followed by a loud yelp and a burst of half-suffocated laughter.

"Poor darling!" said Harriet. . . .

She put out the bedroom candles. The sheets, worn thin by age, were of fine linen, and somewhere in the room there was a scent of lavender. . . . Jordan river. . . . A branch broke and fell upon the hearth in a shower of sparks, and the tall shadows danced across the ceiling.

The door-latch clicked, and her husband sidled apologetically through. His air of chastened triumph made her chuckle, though her blood was thumping erratically and something seemed to have happened to her breath. He dropped to his knees beside her.

"Sweetheart," he said, his voice shaken between passion and laughter, "take your bridegroom. Quite clean and not the least paraffiny, but dreadfully damp and cold. Scrubbed like a puppy under the scullery pump!"

"Dear Peter!"

("*. . . en Grand Monarque. . . .*")

"I think," he went on, rapidly and almost indistinguishably, "I *think* Bunter was enjoying himself. I have set him to clean the blackbeetles out of the copper. What does it matter? What does anything matter? We are here. Laugh, lover, laugh. This is the end of the journey and the beginning of all delight."

Mr. Mervyn Bunter, having chased away the beetles, filled the copper and laid the fire ready for lighting, wrapped himself up in two great-coats and a rug and disposed himself comfortably in a couple of arm-chairs. But he did not sleep at once. Though not precisely anxious, he was filled with a kindly concern. He had (with what exertions!) brought his favourite up to the tape and must leave him now to make the running, but no respect for the proprieties could prevent his sympathetic imagination from following the cherished creature every step of the way. With a slight sigh he drew the candle towards him, took out a fountain-pen and a writing-pad, and began a letter to his mother. The performance of this filial duty might, he thought, serve to calm his mind.

"Dear Mother,—I write from an 'unknown destination—'"

"What was that you called me?"

"Oh, Peter—how absurd! I wasn't thinking."

"*What* did you call me?"

"My lord!"

"The last two words in the language I ever expected to get a kick out of. One never values a thing till one's earned it, does one? Listen, heart's lady—before I've done I mean to be king and emperor."

It is no part of the historian's duty to indulge in what a critic has called "interesting revelations of the marriage-bed." It is enough that the dutiful Mervyn Bunter at length set aside his writing materials, blew out the candle and composed his limbs to rest; and that, of the sleepers beneath that ancient roof, he that had the hardest and coldest couch enjoyed the quietest slumbers.

CHAPTER IV

♦

Household Gods

> *Sir, he made a chimney in my father's house,*
> *and the bricks are alive to this day to testify it.*
> —William Shakespeare, *II Henry VI: IV.2*

Lady Peter Wimsey propped herself cautiously on one elbow and contemplated her sleeping lord. With the mocking eyes hidden and the confident mouth relaxed, his big, bony nose and tumbled hair gave him a gawky, fledging look, like a schoolboy. And the hair itself was almost as light as tow—it was ridiculous that anything male should be as fair as that. No doubt when it was damped and sleeked down for the day his head would go back to its normal barley-corn colour. Last night, after Bunter's ruthless pumping, it had affected her much as the murdered Lorenzo's glove affected Isabella, and she had

had to rub it dry with a towel before cradling it where, in the country phrase, it "belonged to be."

Bunter? She spared him a stray thought from a mind drugged with sleep and the pleasure that comes with sleep. Bunter was up and about; she could faintly hear doors opening and shutting and furniture being moved down below. What an amazing muddle it had all been! But he would miraculously put everything right—wonderful Bunter—and leave one free to live and not bother one's head. One vaguely hoped Bunter had not spent the whole night chasing blackbeetles, but for the moment what was left of one's mind was concentrated on Peter—being anxious not to wake him, rather hoping he would soon wake up of his own accord and wondering what he would say when he did. If his first words were French one would at least feel certain that he retained an agreeable impression of the night's proceedings; on the whole, however, English would be preferable, as showing that he remembered quite distinctly who one was.

As though this disturbing thought had broken his sleep, he stirred at that moment, and, without opening his eyes felt for her with his hand and pulled her down against him. And his first word was neither French nor English, but a long interrogative, "M'mmm?"

"M'm!" said Harriet, abandoning herself. *"Mais quel tact, mon dieu! Sais-tu enfin qui je suis?"*

"Yes, my Shulamite, I do, so you needn't lay traps for my tongue. In the course of a mis-spent life I have learnt that it is a gentleman's first duty to remember in the morning who it was he took to bed with him. You are Harriet, and you are black but comely. Incidentally, you are my wife, and if you have forgotten it you will have to learn it all over again."

"Ah!" said the baker. "I *thought* there was visitors here. You don't catch old Noakes or Martha Ruddle putting 'please' into an order for bread. How many loaves would you be wanting? I calls every day. Rightyho! a cottage and a sandwich. And a small brown? Okay, chief. Here they are."

"If," said Bunter, retreating into the passage, "you would kindly step in and set them on the kitchen table, I should be obliged, my hands being covered with paraffin."

"Okay," said the baker, obliging him. "Trouble with the stove?"

"A trifle," admitted Bunter. "I have been compelled to dismantle and reassemble the burners, but I am in hopes that it will now function adequately. We should, however, be more comfortable if we could induce the fires to draw. We have sent a message by the milkman to a person called Puffett who, as I understand, is willing to oblige in the chimney-sweeping way."

"That's okay," agreed the baker. "He's a builder by rights, is Tom Puffett, but he ain't above obliging with a chimbley. You stopping here long? A month? Then maybe you'd like me to book the bread. Where's old Noakes?"

"Over at Broxford as I understand," said Mr. Bunter, "and we should like to know what he means by it. No preparations made for us and the chimneys out of order, after distinct instructions in writing and promises of compliance which have *not* been adhered to."

"Ah!" said the baker. "It's easy to promise, ain't it?" He winked. "Promises cost nothing, but chimbleys is eighteen-pence apiece and the soot thrown in. Well, I must scram. Anything I can do for you in a neighbourly way in the village?"

"Since you are so good," replied Mr. Bunter, "the dispatch of the grocer's assistant with streaky rashers and eggs would enable us to augment the deficiencies of the breakfast menu."

"Say, boy," said the baker, "that's okay by me. I'll tell Willis to send his Jimmy along."

"Which," observed Mrs. Ruddle, suddenly appearing from the sitting-room in a blue-checked apron and with her sleeves rolled up, "there's no call to let George Willis think 'e's to 'ave all me lord's custom, seein' the 'Ome and Colonial is a 'apenny cheaper per pound not to say better and leaner and I can ketch 'im w'en he goes by as easy as easy."

"You'll 'ave to do with Willis today," retorted the baker, "unless you wants your breakfast at dinner-time, seein' the

'Ome and Colonial don't get here till past eleven or nearer twelve more like. Nothing more today? Okay. 'Mornin', Martha. So long, chief."

The baker hastened down the path, calling to his horse, and leaving Bunter to deduce that somewhere at no great distance the neighbourhood boasted a picture-palace.

"Peter!"

"Heart's desire?"

"Somebody's frying bacon."

"Nonsense. People don't fry bacon at dawn."

"That was eight by the church clock and the sun's simply blazing in."

"Busy old fool, unruly sun—but you're right about the bacon. The smell's coming up quite distinctly. Through the window, I think. This calls for investigation. . . . I say, it's a gorgeous morning. . . . Are you hungry?"

"Ravenous."

"Unromantic but reassuring. As a matter of fact, I could do with a large breakfast myself. After all, I work hard for my living. I'll give Bunter a hail."

"For God's sake put some clothes on—if Mrs. Ruddle sees you hanging out of the window like that she'll have a thousand fits."

"It'd be a treat for her. Nothing so desirable as novelty. I expect old man Ruddle went to bed in his boots. Bunter! Bunter! . . . Damn it, here *is* the Ruddle woman. Stop laughing and chuck me my dressing-gown. . . . Er—good-morning, Mrs. Ruddle. Tell Bunter we're ready for breakfast, would you?"

"Right you are, me lord," replied Mrs. Ruddle (for after all, he *was* a lord). But she expressed herself later in the day to her friend, Mrs. Hodges.

"Mother-naked, Mrs. 'Odges, if you'll believe *me*. I declare I was that ashamed I didden know w'ere to look. And no more 'air on 'is chest than wot I 'as meself."

"That's gentry," said Mrs. Hodges, referring to the first part of the indictment. "You've only to look at the pictures of them there sun-bathers as they call them on the Ly-doh. Now, my

Susan's first were a wunnerful 'airy man, jest like a kerridge-rug if you take my meaning. But," she added cryptically, "it don't foller, for they never 'ad no family, not till 'e died and she married young Tyler over at Pigott's."

When Mr. Bunter tapped discreetly at the door and entered with a wooden bucket full of kindling, her ladyship had vanished and his lordship was sitting on the window-ledge smoking a cigarette.

"Good morning, Bunter. Fine morning."

"Beautiful autumn weather, my lord, very seasonable. I trust your lordship found everything satisfactory."

"H'm. Bunter, do you know the meaning of the expression *arrière-pensée?*"

"No, my lord."

"I'm glad to hear it. Have you remembered to pump up the cistern?"

"Yes, my lord. I have put the oil-stove in order and summoned the sweep. Breakfast will be ready in a few minutes, my lord, if you will kindly excuse tea for this morning, the local grocer not being acquainted with coffee except in bottles. While you are breakfasting, I will endeavour to kindle a fire in the dressing-room, which I would not attempt last night, on account of the time being short and there being a board in the chimney—no doubt to exclude draughts and pigeons. I fancy, however, it is readily removable."

"All right. Is there any hot water?"

"Yes, my lord—though I would point out there is a slight leak in the copper which creates difficulty as tending to extinguish the fire. I would suggest bringing up the baths in about forty minutes' time, my lord."

"Baths? Thank God! Yes—that'll do splendidly. No word from Mr. Noakes, I suppose?"

"No, my lord."

"We'll see to him presently. I see you've found the fire-dogs."

"In the coal-house, my lord. Will you wear the Lovats or the grey suit?"

"Neither—find me an open shirt and a pair of flannel bags and—did you put in my old blazer?"

"Certainly, my lord."

"Then buzz off and get breakfast before I get like the Duke of Wellington, nearly reduced to a skellington. . . . I say, Bunter."

"My lord?"

"I'm damned sorry you're having all this trouble."

"Don't mention it, my lord. So long as your lordship is satisfied—"

"Yes. All right, Bunter. Thanks."

He dropped his hand lightly on the servant's shoulder in what might have been a gesture of affection or dismissal as you chose to take it, and stood looking thoughtfully into the fireplace till his wife rejoined him.

"I've been exploring—I'd never been in that part of the house. After you go down five steps to the modern bit you turn a corner and go up six steps and bump your head and there's another passage and a little ramification and two more bedrooms and a triangular cubby-hole and a ladder that goes up to the attics. And the cistern lives in a cupboard to itself—you open the door and fall down two steps *and* bump your head, and bring up with your chin on the ball-cock."

"My God! You haven't put the ball-cock out of order? Do you realise, woman, that country life is entirely conditioned by the ball-cock in the cistern and the kitchen boiler?"

"I do—but I didn't think you would."

"Don't I? If you'd spent your childhood in a house with a hundred and fifty bedrooms and perpetual houseparties, where every drop had to be pumped up by hand and the hot water carried because there were only two bathrooms and all the rest hip-baths, and had the boiler burst when you were entertaining the Prince of Wales, what you didn't know about insanitary plumbing wouldn't be worth knowing."

"Peter, I believe you're a fraud. You may play at being a great detective and a scholar and a cosmopolitan man-about-town, but at bottom you're nothing but an English country gentleman, with his soul in the stables and his mind on the parish pump."

"God help all married men! You would pluck out the heart of my mystery. No—but my father was one of the old school and thought that all these new-fangled luxuries made you soft and merely spoilt the servants. . . . Come in! . . . Ah! I have never regretted Paradise Lost since I discovered that it contained no eggs-and-bacon."

"The trouble with these here chimneys," observed Mr. Puffett oracularly, "is that they wants sweeping."

He was an exceedingly stout man, rendered still stouter by his costume. This had reached what, in recent medical jargon, is known as "a high degree of onionisation," consisting as it did of a greenish-black coat and trousers and a series of variegated pullovers one on top of the other, which peeped out at the throat in a graduated scale of *décolleté*.

"There ain't no sweeter chimneys in the county," pursued Mr. Puffett, removing his coat and displaying the outermost sweater in a glory of red and yellow horizontal stripes, "if they was given half a chance, as who should know better than me what's been up them time and again as a young lad me ole Dad bein' in the chimney-sweeping line."

"Indeed?" said Mr. Bunter.

"The law wouldn't let me do it now," said Mr. Puffett, shaking his head, which was crowned with a bowler hat. "Not as me figure would allow of it at my time of life. But I knows these here chimneys from 'earth to pot as I may say, and a sweeter-drawing pair of chimneys you couldn't wish for. Not when properly swep'. But no chimney can be sweet if not swep', no more than a room can, as I'm sure you'll agree with me, Mr. Bunter."

"Quite so," said Mr. Bunter. "Would you be good enough to proceed to sweep them?"

"To oblige *you*, Mr. Bunter, and to oblige the lady and gentleman, I shall be 'appy to sweep them. I'm a builder by trade, but always 'appy to oblige with a chimney when called upon. I 'ave, as you might say, a soft spot for chimneys, 'avin' been brought up in 'em, like, and though I says it, Mr. Bunter, there ain't no one 'andles a chimney kinder nor wot I does. It's knowing 'em, you see, wot does it—knowing w'ere they wants easin' and 'umourin' and w'ere they wants the power be'ind the rods."

So saying, Mr. Puffett turned up his various sleeves, flexed his biceps once or twice, picked up his rods and brushes, which he had laid down in the passage, and asked where he should begin.

"The sitting-room will be required first," said Mr. Bunter. "In the kitchen I can, for the immediate moment, manage with the oil-stove. This way, Mr. Puffett, if you please."

Mrs. Ruddle, who, as far as the Wimseys were concerned, was a new broom, had made a clean and determined sweep of the sitting-room, draping all the uglier pieces of furniture with particular care in dust-sheets, covering the noisy rugs with newspaper, decorating with handsome dunce's caps two exceptionally rampageous bronze cavaliers which flanked the fireplace on pedestals and were too heavy to move, and tying up in a duster the withered pampas-grass in the painted drain-pipe near the door, for, as she observed, "them things do 'old the dust so."

"Ah!" said Mr. Puffett. He removed his top sweater to display a blue one, spread out his apparatus on the space between the shrouded settles and plunged beneath the sacking that enveloped the chimney-breast. He emerged again, beaming with satisfaction. "What did I tell you? Full o' sut this chimney is. Ain't bin swep' for a mort o' years I reckon."

"We reckon so too," said Mr. Bunter. "We should like to have a word with Mr. Noakes on the subject of these chimneys."

"Ah!" said Mr. Puffett. He thrust his brush up the chimney and screwed a rod to its hinder end. "If I was to give you a pound note, Mr. Bunter"—the rod jerked upwards and he added another joint—"a pound note for every penny"—he added another joint—"every penny Mr. Noakes has paid me"—he added another joint—"or any other practical sweep for that matter"—he added another joint—"in the last ten years or maybe more"—he added another joint—"for sweeping of these here chimneys"—he added another joint—"I give you my word, Mr. Bunter"—he added another joint and swivelled round on his haunches to deliver his peroration with more emphasis—"you wouldn't be one 'apenny better off than you are now."

"I believe you," said Mr. Bunter. "And the sooner that chimney is clear, the better we shall be pleased."

He retired into the scullery, where Mrs. Ruddle, armed with a hand-bowl, was scooping boiling water from the copper into a large bath-can.

"You had better leave it to me, Mrs. Ruddle, to negotiate the baths round the turn of the stairs. You may follow me with the cans, *if* you please."

Returning thus processionally through the sitting-room he was relieved to see only Mr. Puffett's ample base emerging from under the chimney-breast and to hear him utter loud groans and cries of self-encouragement which boomed hollow in the funnel of the brickwork. It is always pleasant to see a fellow-creature toiling still harder than one's self.

In nothing has the whirligig of time so redressed the balance between the sexes as in this business of getting up in the morning. Woman, when not an adept of the Higher Beauty Culture, has now little to do beyond washing, stepping into a garment or so, and walking downstairs. Man, still slave to the button and the razor, clings to the ancient ceremonial of potter and gets himself up by instalments. Harriet was knotting her tie before the sound of splashing was heard in the next room. She accordingly classed her new possession as a confirmed potterer and made her way down by what Peter, with more exactness than delicacy, had already named the Privy Stair. This led into a narrow passage, containing the modern convenience before-mentioned, a boot-hole and a cupboard with brooms in it, and debouched at length into the scullery and so to the back door.

The garden, at any rate, had been well looked after. There were cabbages at the back, and celery trenches, also an asparagus bed well strawed up and a number of scientifically pruned apple trees. There was also a small cold-house sheltering a hardy vine with half a dozen bunches of black grapes on it and a number of half-hardy plants in pots. In front of the house, a good show of dahlias and chrysanthemums and a bed of scarlet salvias lent colour to the sunshine. Mr. Noakes apparently had some little taste for gardening, or at any rate a good gardener; and this was the pleasantest thing yet known of Mr. Noakes, thought Harriet. She explored the potting-shed, where the tools were in good order, and found a pair of scissors, armed with which she made an assault upon the long trail of vine-leaves and the rigid bronze sheaves of the chrysanthemums. She grinned a little to find herself thus supplying the statutory "feminine touch" to the household and, looking up, was rewarded with the sight of her husband. He was curled on the sill of the open window, in a dressing-gown, with *The Times* on his knee and a cigarette between his lips, and was trimming his nails in a thoughtful leisurely way, as though he had world and time enough at his disposal. At the other side of the casement, come from goodness knew where, was a large ginger cat, engaged in thoroughly licking one forepaw, before applying it to the back of its ear. The two sleek animals, delicately self-absorbed, sat on in a mandarin-like calm till the human one, with the restlessness of inferiority, lifted his eyes from his task, caught sight of Harriet and said "Hey!"—whereupon the cat rose up, affronted, and leapt out of sight.

"That," said Peter, who had sometimes an uncanny way of echoing one's own thoughts, "is a very dainty, ladylike occupation."

"Isn't it?" said Harriet. She stood on one leg to inspect the pound or two of garden mould adhering to her stout brogue shoe. "A garden is a lovesome thing. God wot."

"Her feet beneath her petticoat like little mice stole in and out," agreed his lordship gravely. "Can you tell me, rosy-fingered Aurora, whether the unfortunate person in the room below me is being slowly murdered or only having a fit?"

"I was beginning to wonder myself," said Harriet; for strange, strangled cries were proceeding from the sitting-room. "Perhaps I had better go and find out."

"Must you go? You improve the scenery so much. I like a landscape with figures. . . . Dear me! what a shocking sound—like Nell Cook under the paving-stone! It seemed to come right up into the room beside me. I am becoming a nervous wreck."

"You don't look it. You look abominably placid and pleased with life."

"Well, so I am. But one should not be selfish in one's happiness. I feel convinced that somewhere about the house there is a fellow-creature in trouble."

At this point Bunter emerged from the front door, walked backwards across the strip of turf, with eyes cast upwards as though seeking a heavenly revelation, and solemnly shook his head, like Lord Burleigh in *The Critic*.

"Ain't we there yet?" cried the voice of Mrs. Ruddle from the window.

"No," said Bunter, returning, "we appear to be making no progress at all."

"It seems," said Peter, "that we are expecting a happy event. *Parturiunt montes*. At any rate, the creation seems to be groaning and travailing together a good deal."

Harriet got off the flower-bed and scraped the earth from her shoes with a garden label.

"I shall cease to decorate the landscape and go and form part of a domestic interior."

Peter uncoiled himself from the window-sill, took off his dressing-gown and pulled away his blazer from under the ginger cat.

"All that's the matter with this chimney, Mr. Bunter," pronounced Mr. Puffett, "is, sut." Having thus, as it were, come out by the same road as he had gone in, he began to withdraw his brush from the chimney, unscrewing it with extreme deliberation, rod by rod.

"So," said Mr. Bunter, with an inflection of sarcasm quite lost on Mr. Puffett, "so we had inferred."

"That's it," pursued Mr. Puffett, "corroded sut. No chimney can't draw when the pot's full of corroded sut like this 'ere chimney-pot is. You can't ask it. It ain't reasonable."

"I don't ask it," retorted Mr. Bunter. "I asked you to get it clear, that's all."

"Well now, Mr. Bunter," said Mr. Puffett with an air of injury, "I put it to you to just take a look at this 'ere sut." He extended a grimy hand filled with what looked like clinkers. "'Ard as a crock, that sut is, corroded 'ard. That's wot your chimney-pot's full of, and you can't get a brush through it, not with all the power you puts be'ind it. Near forty feet of rod I've got up that chimney, Mr. Bunter, trying to get through the pot, and it ain't fair on a man nor his rods." He pulled down another section of his apparatus and straightened it out with loving care.

"Some means will have to be devised to penetrate the obstruction," said Mr. Bunter, his eyes on the window, "and without delay. Her ladyship is coming in from the garden. You can take out the breakfast tray, Mrs. Ruddle."

"Ah!" said Mrs. Ruddle, peeping under the dish-covers before lifting the tray from the radio cabinet where Bunter had set it down, "they're taking their vittles well—that's a good sign in a young couple. I remember when me and Ruddle was wed—"

"And the lamps all need new wicks," added Bunter austerely, "and the burners cleaned before you fill them."

"Mr. Noakes ain't used no lamps this long time," said Mrs. Ruddle with a sniff. "Says 'e can see well enough by candlelight. Comes cheaper, I suppose." She flounced out with the tray and, encountering Harriet in the doorway, dropped a curtsy that sent the dish-covers sliding.

"Oh, you've got the sweep, Bunter—that's splendid! We thought we heard something going on."

"Yes, my lady. Mr. Puffett has been good enough to oblige. But I understand that he has encountered some impenetrable obstacle in the upper portion of the chimney."

"How kind of you to come, Mr. Puffett. We had a dreadful time last night."

Judging from the sweep's eye that propitiation was advisable, Harriet extended her hand. Mr. Puffett looked at it, looked at his own, pulled up his sweaters to get at his trousers pocket, extracted a newly laundered red-cotton handkerchief, shook it slowly from its fold, draped it across his palm and so grasped Harriet's fingers, rather in the manner of a royal proxy bedding his master's bride with the sheet between them.

"Well, me lady," said Mr. Puffett, "I'm allus willin' to oblige. Not but what you'll allow as a chimney wot's choked like this chimney is ain't fair to a man nor yet to 'is rods. But I will make bold to say that if any man can get the corroded sut out of this 'ere chimney-pot, I'm the man to do it. It's experience, you see, that's wot it is, and the power I puts be'ind it."

"I'm sure it is," said Harriet.

"As I understand the matter, my lady," put in Bunter, "it is the actual pot that's choked—no structural defect in the stack."

"That's right," said Mr. Puffett, mollified by finding himself appreciated, "the pot's where your trouble is." He stripped off another sweater to reveal himself in emerald green. "I'm a-goin' to try it with the rods alone, without the brush. Maybe, with my power be'ind it, we'll be able to get the rod through the sut. If not, then we'll 'ave to get the ladders."

"Ladders?"

"Access by the roof, my lady," explained Bunter.

"What fun!" said Harriet. "I'm sure Mr. Puffett will manage it somehow. Can you find me a vase or something for these flowers, Bunter?"

"Very good, my lady."

(Nothing, thought Mr. Bunter, not even an Oxford education, would prevent a woman's mind from straying away after inessentials; but he was pleased to note that the temper was, so far, admirably controlled. A vase of water was a small price to pay for harmony.)

"Peter!" cried Harriet up the staircase. (Bunter, had he remained to witness it, might after all have conceded her an instinct for essentials.) "Peter darling! the sweep's here!"

"Oh, frabjous day! I am coming, my own, my sweep." He pattered down briskly. "What a genius you have for saying the right thing! All my life I have waited to hear those exquisite words, *Peter darling, the sweep's come*. We are married, by God! we are married. I thought so once, but now I know it."

"Some people take a lot of convincing."

"One is afraid to believe in good fortune. The sweep! I crushed down my rising hopes. I said, No—it is a thunderstorm, a small earthquake, or at most a destitute cow dying by inches in the chimney. I dared not court disappointment. It is so long since I was taken into anybody's confidence about a sweep. As a rule, Bunter smuggles him in when I am out of the house, for fear my lordship should be inconvenienced. Only a wife would treat me with the disrespect I deserve and summon me to look upon the—good Lord!"

He turned as he spoke to look upon Mr. Puffett, only the soles of whose boots were visible. At this moment a bellow so loud and prolonged issued from the fireplace that Peter turned quite pale.

"He hasn't got stuck, has he?"

"No—it's the power he's putting behind it. There's corroded soot in the pot or something, which makes it very hard work. . . . Peter, I do wish you could have seen the place before Noakes filled it up with bronze horsemen and bamboo whatnots and aspidistras."

"Hush! never blaspheme the aspidistra. It's very unlucky. Something frightful will come down that chimney and *get* you—boo! . . . Oh, my God! look at that bristling horror over the wireless set!"

"Some people would pay pounds for a fine cactus like that."

"They must have very little imagination. It's not a plant—it's a morbid growth—something lingering happening to your kidneys. Besides, it makes me wonder whether I've shaved. Have I?"

"M'm—yes—like satin—no, that'll do! I suppose, if we shot the beastly thing out, it'd die to spite us. They're delicate, though you mightn't think it, and Mr. Noakes would demand its weight in gold. How long did we hire this grisly furniture for?"

"A month, but we might get rid of it sooner. It's a damn

shame spoiling this noble old place with that muck."

"Do you like the house, Peter?"

"It's beautiful. It's like a lovely body inhabited by an evil spirit. And I don't mean only the furniture. I've taken a dislike to our landlord, or tenant, or whatever he is. I've a fancy he's up to no good and that the house will be glad to be rid of him."

"I believe it hates him. I'm sure he's starved and insulted and ill-treated it. Why, even the chimneys—"

"Yes, of course, the chimneys. Do you think I could bring myself to the notice of our household god, our little Lar? . . . Er—excuse me one moment, Mr.—er—"

"Puffett is the name."

"Mr. Puffett—hey, Puffett! Just a second, would you?"

"Now then!" expostulated Mr. Puffett, swivelling round on his knees. "Who're you a-poking of in the back with a man's own rods? It ain't fair to a man *nor* his rods."

"I beg your pardon," said Peter. "I did shout but failed to attract your attention."

"No offence," said Mr. Puffett, evidently conceding something to the honeymoon spirit. "You'll be his lordship, I take it. Hope I sees you well."

"Thank you, we are in the pink. But this chimney seems to be a little unwell. Shortness of wind or something."

"There ain't no call to abuse the chimney," said Mr. Puffett. "The fault's in the pot, like I was saying to your lady. The pot, you see, ain't reconcilable to the size of the chimney, and it's corroded that 'ard with sut as you couldn't 'ardly get a bristle through, let alone a brush. It don't matter 'ow wide you builds the chimney, all the smoke's got to go through the pot in the end, and that—if you foller my meaning—is where the fault is, see?"

"I follow you. Even a Tudor chimney winds somewhere safe to pot."

"Ah!" said Mr. Puffett, "that's just it. If we 'ad the Tooder pot, now, we'd be all right. A Tooder pot is a pot as any practical chimney-sweep might 'andle with pleasure and do justice to 'isself *and* 'is rods. But Mr. Noakes, now 'e tuk down some of the Tooder pots and sold 'em to make sundials."

"Sold them for sundials?"

"That's right, me lady. Catch penny, I calls it. That's 'im all over. And these 'ere fiddlin' modern pots wot 'e's put on ain't no good for a chimney the 'ighth and width of this chimney wot you've got 'ere. It stands to reason they'll corrode up with sut in a month. Once that there pot's clear, the rest is easy. There's loose sut in the bends, of course—but that don't 'urt—not without it was to ketch fire, which is why it didn't oughter be there and I'll 'ave it out in no time once we're done with the pot—but while the sut's corroded 'ard in the pot, you won't get no fire to go in this chimney, me lord, and that's the long and the short of it."

"You make it admirably clear," said Peter. "I see you are an expert. Please go on demonstrating. Don't mind me—I'm admiring the tools of your trade. What is this affair like a Brobdingnagian corkscrew? There's a thing to give a man a thirst—what?"

"Thank-you, me lord," replied Mr. Puffett, evidently taking this for an invitation. "Work first and pleasure afterwards. W'en the job's done, I won't say no."

He beamed kindly at them, peeled off his green uppermost layer and, arrayed now in a Fair-Isle jumper of complicated pattern, addressed himself once more to the chimney.

CHAPTER V

Fury of Guns

So Henny-penny, Cocky-locky, Ducky-daddles,
Goosey-poosey, Turkey-lurkey, and Foxy-woxy
all went to tell the king the sky was a-falling.

—Joseph Jacobs, *English Fairy Tales*

"I do *hope* I'm not disturbing you," exclaimed Miss Twitterton anxiously. "I felt I *must* run over and see how you were getting on. I really couldn't sleep for thinking of you—so strange of Uncle to behave like that—so dreadfully inconsiderate!"

"Oh, please!" said Harriet." It was so nice of you to come, won't you sit down? . . . Oh, *Bunter!* Is that the best you can find?"

"Why!" cried Miss Twitterton, "you've got the Bonzo vase! Uncle won it in a raffle. So *amusing*, isn't it, holding the flowers in his mouth like that, and his little pink waistcoat?—Aren't the chrysanthemums lovely? Frank Crutchley looks after them, he's *such* a good gardener. . . . Oh, thank you, thank you so much—I really mustn't inflict myself on you for more than a moment. But I couldn't help being anxious. I do *hope* you passed a comfortable night."

"Thank you," said Peter, gravely. "Parts of it were excellent."

"I always think the *bed* is the important thing—" began Miss Twitterton. Mr. Puffett, scandalised and seeing Peter beginning to lose control of his mouth, diverted her attention by digging her gently in the ribs with his elbow.

"Oh!" ejaculated Miss Twitterton. The state of the room and Mr. Puffett's presence forced themselves together upon her mind. "Oh, dear, what *is* the matter? *Don't* say the chimney has been smoking again? It always *was* a tiresome chimney."

"Now, see here," said Mr. Puffett, who seemed to feel to the chimney much as a tigress might feel to her offspring, "that's a good chimney, that is. I couldn't build a better chimney meself, allowin' for them upstairs flues and the 'ighth and pitch of the gable. But when a chimney ain't never been swep' through, on account of persons' cheeseparin' 'abits, then it ain't fair on the chimney, nor yet it ain't fair on the sweep. And you knows it."

"Oh, dear, oh, dear!" cried Miss Twitterton, collapsing upon a chair and immediately bouncing up again. "What you must be thinking of us all. Where *can* Uncle be? I'm sure if I'd known—Oh! there's Frank Crutchley! I'm so glad. Uncle may have said something to him. He comes every Wednesday to do the garden, you know. A most *superior* young man. Shall I call him in? I'm sure he could help us. I always send for Frank when anything goes wrong. He's so clever at finding a way out of a difficulty."

Miss Twitterton had run to the window without waiting for Harriet's, "Yes, do have him in," and now cried in agitated tones:

"Frank! Frank! Whatever can have happened? We can't find Uncle!"

"Can't find him?"

"No—he isn't here, and he's sold the house to this lady and gentleman, and we don't know *where* he is and the chimney's smoking and everything upside down; what *can* have become of him?"

Frank Crutchley, peering in at the window and scratching his head, looked bewildered, as well he might.

"Never said nothing to me, Miss Twitterton. He'll be over at the shop, most like."

"Was he here when you came last Wednesday?"

"Yes," said the gardener, "he was here then all right." He paused, and a thought seemed to strike him. "He did ought to be here today. Can't find him, did you say? What's gone of him?"

"That's just what we don't know. Going off like that without telling anyone! What did he say to you?"

"I thought I'd find him here—leastways—"

"You'd better come in, Crutchley," said Peter.

"Right, sir!" said Crutchley, with some appearance of relief at having a man to deal with. He withdrew in the direction of the back door, where, to judge by the sounds, he was received by Mrs. Ruddle with a volume of explanatory narrative.

"Frank would run over to Broxford, I'm sure," said Miss Twitterton, "and find out what's happened to Uncle. He might be ill—though you'd think he'd have sent for me, wouldn't you? Frank could get a car from the garage—he drives for Mr. Hancock at Pagford you know, and I tried to get him this morning before I came, but he was out with a taxi. He's very clever with cars, and such a good gardener. I'm sure you won't mind my mentioning it, but if you've bought the house and want someone to do the garden—"

"He's kept it awfully well," said Harriet. "I thought it looked lovely."

"I'm so glad you think so. He works so hard, and he's so anxious to get on—"

"Come in, Crutchley," said Peter.

The gardener, hesitating now at the door of the room with his face to the light, showed himself as an alert, well-set-up young man of about thirty, neatly dressed in a suit of working clothes and carrying his cap respectfully in his hand. His crisp dark hair, blue eyes and strong white teeth produced a favourable impression, though at the moment he looked slightly put out. From his glance at Miss Twitterton, Harriet gathered that he had overheard her panegyric of him and disapproved of it.

"This," went on Peter, "comes a little unexpected, what?"

"Well, yes, sir." The gardener smiled, and sent his quick glance roving over Mr. Puffett. "I see it's the chimney."

"It ain't the *chimney,*" began the sweep indignantly; when Miss Twitterton broke in:

"But, Frank, don't you understand? Uncle's sold the house and gone away without telling anybody. I can't make it out, it's not *like* him. Nothing done and nothing ready and nobody here last night to let anybody in, and Mrs. Ruddle knew *nothing* except that he'd gone to Broxford—"

"Well, have you sent over there to look for him?" inquired the young man in a vain endeavour to stem the tide.

"No, not yet—unless Lord Peter—did you?—or no, there wouldn't be time, would there?—no keys, even, and I really was ashamed you should have had to come last night like that, but of course I never *dreamt*—and you could so easily have run over this morning, Frank—or I could go myself on my bicycle—but Mr. Hancock told me you were out with a taxi, so I thought I'd better just call and see."

Frank Crutchley's eyes wandered over the room as though seeking counsel from the dust-sheets, the aspidistras, the chimney, the bronze horsemen, Mr. Puffett's bowler, the cactus and the radio cabinet, before at length coming to rest on Peter's in mute appeal.

"Let's start from the right end," suggested Wimsey. "Mr. Noakes was here last Wednesday and went off the same night to catch the ten o'clock bus to Broxford. That was nothing unusual, I gather. But he expected to be back to deal with the matter of our arrival, and you, in fact, expected to find him here today."

"That's right, sir."

Miss Twitterton gave a little jump and her mouth shaped itself into an anxious O.

"Is he usually here when you come on Wednesdays?"

"Well, that depends, sir. Not always."

"Frank!" cried Miss Twitterton, outraged, "it's Lord Peter Wimsey. You ought to say 'my lord.'"

"Never mind that now," said Peter, kindly, but irritated by this interference with his witness. Crutchley looked at Miss Twitterton with the expression of a small boy who has been publicly exhorted to wash behind the ears, and said:

"Some days he's here, some not. If he ain't" (Miss Twitterton frowned), "I gets the key from her" (he jerked his head at Miss Twitterton) "to come in and wind the clock and see to the pot-plants. But I did reckon to see him this morning, because I had particular business with him. That's why I come up to the house first—came, if you like" (he added, crossly, in response to Miss Twitterton's anxious prompting), "it's all one, I dessay, to my lord."

"To his lordship," said Miss Twitterton, faintly.

"Did he actually tell you he'd be here?"

"Yes—my lord. Leastways he said as he'd let me have back some money I'd put into that business of his. Promised it back today."

"Oh, Frank! You've been worrying Uncle *again*. I've *told* you you're just being *silly* about your money. I *know* it's quite safe with Uncle."

Peter's glance crossed Harriet's over Miss Twitterton's head.

"He said he'd let you have it this morning. May I ask

whether it was any considerable sum?"

"Matter o' forty pounds," said the gardener, "as he got me to put into his wireless business. Mayn't seem a lot to you," he went on a little uncertainly, as though trying to assess the financial relationship between Peter's title, his ancient and shabby blazer, his manservant and his wife's non-committal tweeds, "but I've got a better use for it, and so I told him. I asked for it last week and he palavered as usual, sayin' he didn't keep sums like that in the house—puttin' me off—"

"But, Frank, of course he didn't. He might have been robbed. He did lose ten pounds once, in a pocketbook—"

"But I stuck to it," pursued Crutchley, unheeding, "sayin' I must have it, and at last he said he'd let me have it today, as he'd got some money coming in—"

"He said that?"

"Yes, sir—my lord—and I says to him, I hope you do, I says, and if you don't, I'll have the law on you."

"Oh, Frank, you shouldn't have said that!"

"Well, I did say it. Can't you let me tell his lordship what he wants to know?"

Harriet's glance had caught Peter's again, and he had nodded. The money for the house. But if he had told Crutchley as much as that—"

"Did he say where this money of his was coming from?"

"Not him. He's not the sort to tell more than he has to. Matter of fact, I never thought he was expecting no money in particular. Making excuses, he was. Never pays out money till the last moment, and not then if he can 'elp it. Might lose 'arf a day's interest, don't you see," added Crutchley with a sudden half-reluctant grin.

"Sound principle, so far as it goes," said Wimsey.

"That's right; that's the way he's made his bit. He's a warm man, is Mr. Noakes. Still, all the same for that, I told him I wanted the forty pound for my new garridge—"

"Yes, the garahge," put in Miss Twitterton, with a corrective little frown and shake of the head. "Frank's been saving up a long time to start his own garahge."

"So," repeated Crutchley with emphasis, "'wantin' the

money for the garridge,' I said, 'I'll see my money Wednesday,' I said, 'or I'll 'ave the law on you.' That's what I said. And I went out sharp and I ain't seen him since."

"I see. Well—" Peter glanced from Crutchley to Miss Twitterton and back again. "We'll run over to Broxford presently and hunt the gentleman up, and then we can get it straight. In the meantime, we shall want the garden kept in order, so perhaps you'd better carry on as usual."

"Very good, my lord. Shall I come Wednesdays same as before? Five shillings, Mr. Noakes give me by the day."

"I'll give you the same. Do you know anything about running an electric light plant, by the way?"

"Yes, my lord; there's one at the garridge where I work."

"Because," said Peter, with a smile at his wife, "though candles and oil-stoves have their romantic moments and all that, I think we shall really have to electrify Talboys."

"You'll electrify Paggleham if you do, my lord," said Crutchley, with sudden geniality. "I'm sure I'd be very willing—"

"Frank," said Miss Twitterton brightly, "knows *everything* about machinery!"

The unfortunate Crutchley, on the verge of an explosion, caught Peter's eye and smiled in some embarrassment.

"All right," said his lordship. "We'll talk it over presently. Meanwhile, carry on with whatever it is you do on Wednesdays." Whereupon the gardener thankfully made his escape, leaving Harriet to reflect that school-marming seemed to have got into Miss Twitterton's blood and that nothing was so exasperating to the male sex in general as an attitude of mingled reproof and showmanship.

The click of the distant gate and a footfall on the path broke in on the slightly blank pause which followed Crutchley's exit.

"Perhaps," cried Miss Twitterton, "that's Uncle coming now."

"I hope to God," said Peter, "it's not one of those infernal reporters."

"It's not," said Harriet, running to the window. "It's the vicar—he's coming to call."

"Oh, the dear vicar! perhaps he may know something."

"Ah!" said Mr. Puffett.

"This is magnificent," said Peter. "I collect vicars." He joined Harriet at her observation-post. "This is a very well-grown specimen, six foot four or thereabouts, short-sighted, a great gardener, musical, smokes a pipe—"

"Good gracious!" cried Miss Twitterton, "do you know Mr. Goodacre?"

"—untidy, with a wife who does her best on a small stipend; a product of one of our older seats of learning—1890 vintage—Oxford, at a guess, but not, I fancy, Keble, though as high in his views as the parish allows him to be."

"He'll hear you," said Harriet, as the reverend gentleman withdrew his nose from the middle of a clump of dahlias and cast a vague glance through his eyeglasses towards the sitting-room window. "To the best of my knowledge and belief, you're right. But why the strictly limited High Church views?"

"The Roman vest and the emblem upon the watch-chain point the upward way. You know my methods, Watson. But a bundle of settings for the Te Deum under the arm suggest sung Matins in the Established way; besides, though we heard the church clock strike eight, there was no bell for a daily Celebration."

"However you think of these things, Peter!"

"I'm sorry," said her husband, flushing faintly. "I can't help taking notice, whatever I'm doing."

"Worse and worse," replied his lady. "Mrs. Shandy herself would be shocked." While Miss Twitterton, completely bewildered, made haste to explain:

"It's choir practice tonight, of *course*. Wednesdays, you know. Always Wednesdays. He'll be taking them up to the church."

"Of course, as you say," agreed Peter with relish. "Wednesday always *is* choir practice. *Quod semper, quod ubique, quod ab omnibus*. Nothing ever changes in the English countryside.

Harriet, your honeymoon house is a great success. I am feeling twenty years younger."

He retired hastily from the window as the vicar approached, and declaimed with considerable emotion:

> "Give me just a country cottage, where the soot of ages falls,
> And, to crown a perfect morning, look! an English vicar calls!

I, too, Miss Twitterton, though you might not think it, have bawled Maunder and Garrett down the neck of the blacksmith's daughter singing in the village choir, and have proclaimed the company of the spearmen to be scattered abroad among the beasts of the people, with a little fancy pointing of my own."

"Ah!" said Mr. Puffett, "that's an orkerd one, is the beasts of the people."

As though the word "soot" had struck a chord in his mind, he moved tentatively in the direction of the fireplace. The vicar vanished within the porch.

"My dear," said Harriet, "Miss Twitterton will think we are both quite mad; and Mr. Puffett knows it already."

"Oh, no, me lady," said Mr. Puffett. "Not mad. Only 'appy. I knows the feeling."

"As man to man, Puffett," said the bridegroom, "I thank you for those kind and sympathetic words. Where, by the way, did *you* go for your honeymoon?"

"'Erne Bay, me lord," replied Mr. Puffett.

"Good God, yes! Where George Joseph Smith murdered his first Bride-in-the-Bath. We never thought of that! Harriet—"

"Monster," said Harriet, "do your worst! There are only hip-baths here."

"There!" cried Miss Twitterton, catching at the only word in this conversation that appeared to make sense, "I was *always* saying to Uncle that he really *ought* to put in a bathroom."

Before Peter could give further proofs of insanity, Bunter mercifully announced:

"The Reverend Simon Goodacre."

The vicar, thin, elderly, clean-shaven, his tobacco-pouch bulging from the distended pocket of his suit of "clerical grey" and the left knee of his trousers displaying a large three-cornered tear carefully darned, advanced upon them with that air of mild self-assurance which a consciousness of spiritual dignity bestows upon a naturally modest disposition. His peering glance singled out Miss Twitterton from the group presented to his notice, and he greeted her with a cordial shake of the hand, at the same time acknowledging Mr. Puffett's presence with a nod and a cheerful, "'Morning, Tom!"

"Good morning, Mr. Goodacre," replied Miss Twitterton in a mournful chirp. "Dear, dear! Did they tell you—?"

"Yes, indeed," said the vicar. "Well, this *is* a surprise!" He adjusted his glasses, beamed vaguely about him, and addressed himself to Peter. "I fear I am intruding. I understand that Mr. Noakes—er—"

"Good morning, sir," said Peter, feeling it better to introduce himself than to wait for Miss Twitterton. "Delighted to see you. My name's Wimsey. My wife."

"I'm afraid we're all at sixes and sevens," said Harriet. Mr. Goodacre, she thought, had not changed much in the last seventeen years. He was a little greyer, a little thinner, a little baggier about the knees and shoulders, but in essentials the same Mr. Goodacre she and her father had occasionally encountered in the old days, visiting the sick of Paggleham. It was clear that he had not the faintest recollection of her; but, taking soundings as it were in these uncharted seas, his glances encountered something familiar—an ancient dark-blue blazer with "O. U. C. C." embroidered on the breast pocket.

"An Oxford man, I see," said the vicar, happily, as though this did away with any necessity for further identification.

"Balliol, sir," said Peter.

"Magdalen," returned Mr. Goodacre, unaware that, by merely saying "Keble," he could have shattered a reputation. He grasped Peter's hand and shook it again. "Bless me! Wimsey of Balliol. Now, what is it I—?"

"Cricket, perhaps," suggested Peter, helpfully.

"Yes," said the vicar, "ye—yes. Cricket and—Ah, Frank! Am I in your way?"

Crutchley, coming briskly in with a step-ladder and a watering-pot, said, "No, sir, not at all," in the tone of voice which means, "Yes, sir, very much." The vicar dodged hastily.

"Won't you sit down, sir?" said Peter, uncovering a corner of the settee.

"Thank you, thank you," said Mr. Goodacre, as the step-ladder was set down on the exact spot where he had been standing. "I really ought not to take up your time. Cricket, of course, and—"

"Getting into the veteran class now, I'm afraid," said Peter, shaking his head. But the vicar was not to be diverted.

"Some other connection, I feel sure. Forgive me—I did not precisely catch what your manservant said. Not Lord *Peter* Wimsey?"

"An ill-favoured title, but my own."

"Really!" cried Mr. Goodacre. "Of course, of course. Lord Peter Wimsey—cricket and crime! Dear me, this is an honour. My wife and I were reading a paragraph in the paper only the other day—most interesting—about your detective experiences—"

"Detective!" exclaimed Miss Twitterton in an agitated squeak.

"He's quite harmless, really," said Harriet.

"I hope," continued Mr. Goodacre, gently jocose, "you haven't come to detect anything in Paggleham."

"I sincerely hope not," said Peter. "As a matter of fact, we came here with the idea of passing a peaceful honeymoon."

"Indeed!" cried the vicar. "That is delightful. I hope I may say, God bless you and make you very happy."

Miss Twitterton, overcome by the thought of the chimneys and the bed-linen, sighed deeply, and then turned to frown at Frank Crutchley, who, from his point of vantage upon the step-ladder, was indulging in what seemed to her to be an unbecoming kind of grimace over the heads of his employers. The young man instantly became unnaturally grave and gave his attention to mopping up the water which, in his momentary distraction, had overflowed the rim of the cactus-pot. Harriet earnestly assured the vicar that they were very happy, and Peter concurred, observing:

"We have been married nearly twenty-four hours, and are still married; which in these days may be considered a record. But then, you see, padre, we are old-fashioned, country-bred people. In fact, my wife used to be a neighbour of yours, so to speak."

The vicar, who had seemed doubtful whether to be amused or distressed by the first part of this remark, at once looked all eager interest, and Harriet hastened to explain who she was and what had brought them to Talboys. If Mr. Goodacre had ever heard or read anything of the murder trial, he showed no sign of such knowledge; he merely expressed the greatest delight at meeting Dr. Vane's daughter once more and at welcoming two new parishioners to his fold.

"And so you have bought the house! Dear me! I hope, Miss Twitterton, your uncle is not deserting us."

Miss Twitterton, who had scarcely known how to contain herself during this prolonged exchange of introductions and courtesies, broke out as though the words had released a spring:

"But you don't *understand*, Mr. Goodacre. It's *too* dreadful. Uncle never let me know a word about it. Not a *word*. He's gone off to Broxford or somewhere, and left the house like this!"

"But he's coming back, no doubt," said Mr. Goodacre.

"He told Frank he would be here today—didn't he, Frank?"

Crutchley, who had descended from the steps and appeared to be occupied in centralising the radio cabinet with great precision beneath the hanging pot, replied:

"So he *said*, Miss Twitterton."

He folded his lips firmly, as though, in the vicar's presence, he preferred not to make the comments he might have made, and retired into the window with his watering-pot.

"But he isn't *here*," said Miss Twitterton. "It's all a terrible muddle. And poor Lord and Lady Peter—"

She embarked on an agitated description of the previous night's events, in which the keys, the chimneys, Crutchley's new garage, the bed-linen, the ten o'clock bus, and Peter's intention of putting in an electric plant were jumbled into hopeless confusion. The vicar ejaculated from time to time and looked increasingly bewildered.

"Most trying, most trying," he said at length, when Miss Twitterton had talked herself breathless. "I am so sorry. If there is anything my wife and I can do, Lady Peter, I hope you will not hesitate to make use of us."

"It's awfully good of you," said Harriet. "But really, *we* are quite all right. It's rather fun, picnicking like this. Only, of course, Miss Twitterton is anxious about her uncle."

"No doubt he has been detained somewhere," said the vicar. "Or"—a bright thought occurred to him—"a letter may have gone wrong. Depend upon it, that is what has happened. The post-office is a wonderful institution, but even Homer nods. I am sure you will find Mr. Noakes at Broxford safe and sound. Pray tell him I am sorry to have missed him. I had called to ask him for a subscription to the concert we are getting up in aid of the Church Music Fund—that explains my intrusion upon you. I fear we parsons are sad mendicants."

"Is the Choir still going strong?" inquired Harriet. "Do you remember once bringing it over to Great Pagford for a great combined Armistice Thanksgiving? I sat beside you at the Rectory tea, and we discussed Church music very seriously. Do you still do dear old Bunnett in F?"

She hummed the opening bars. Mr. Puffett, who all this time had remained discreetly withdrawn and was, at the moment, assisting Crutchley to sponge the aspidistra leaves, looked up, and joined in the melody with a powerful roar.

"Ah!" said Mr. Goodacre, gratified; "we have made a great deal of progress. We have advanced to Stanford in C. And last Harvest Festival we tackled the Hallelujah Chorus with great success."

"Hallelujah!" warbled Mr. Puffett, in stentorian tones. "Hallelujah! Hal-le-lu-jah!"

"Tom," said the vicar, apologetically, "is one of my most enthusiastic choirmen. And so is Frank."

Miss Twitterton glanced at Crutchley, as though to check

him if he showed signs of bursting into riotous song. She was relieved to see that he had dissociated himself from Mr. Puffett, and was mounting the steps to wind the clock.

"And Miss Twitterton, of course," said Mr. Goodacre, "presides at the organ."

Miss Twitterton smiled faintly and looked at her fingers.

"But," pursued the vicar, "we sadly need new bellows. The old ones are patched past mending, and since we put in that new set of reeds they have become quite inadequate. The Hallelujah Chorus exposed our weaknesses sadly. In fact, the wind gave out altogether."

"So embarrassing," said Miss Twitterton. "I didn't know *what* to do."

"Miss Twitterton must be saved embarrassment at all costs," said Peter, producing his note-case.

"Oh, dear!" said the vicar. "I didn't mean. . . . Really, this is most generous. Too bad, your very first day in the parish. I—really—I am almost ashamed to—So very kind—so large a sum—Perhaps you would like to look at the programme of the concert. Dear me!" His face lit up with a childlike pleasure. "Do you know, it is quite a long time since I handled a *proper* Bank of England note."

For the space of a moment, Harriet saw every person in that room struck into a kind of immobility by the magic of a piece of paper as it crackled between the vicar's fingers. Miss Twitterton awestruck and open-mouthed; Mr. Puffett suddenly pausing in mid-action, sponge in hand; Crutchley, on his way out of the room with the step-ladder over his shoulder, jerking his head round to view the miracle; Mr. Goodacre himself smiling with excitement and delight; Peter amused and a little self-conscious, like a kind uncle presenting a teddy-bear to the nursery; they might have posed as they stood for the jacket-picture of a thriller: *Bank-Notes in the Parish*.

Then Peter said meaninglessly, "Oh, not at all." He picked up the concert-programme which the vicar had let fall in clutching at the note; and all the arrested motion flowed on again like a film. Miss Twitterton gave a small ladylike cough, Crutchley went out, Mr. Puffett dropped the sponge into the watering-can, and the vicar, putting the ten pound note carefully away in his pocket, inscribed the amount of the subscription in a little black note-book.

"It's going to be a grand concert," said Harriet, peering over her husband's shoulder. "When is it? Shall we be here?"

"October 27th," said Peter. "Of course we shall come to it. Rather."

"Of course," agreed Harriet; and smiled at the vicar.

Whatever fantastic pictures she had from time to time conjured up of married life with Peter, none of them had ever included attendance at village concerts. But of course they would go. She understood now why it was that with all his masking attitudes, all his cosmopolitan self-adaptations, all his odd spiritual reticences and escapes, he yet carried about with him that permanent atmosphere of security. He belonged to an ordered society, and this was it. More than any of the friends in her own world, he spoke the familiar language of her childhood. In London, anybody, at any moment, might do or become anything. But in a village—no matter what village—they were all immutably themselves; parson, organist, sweep, duke's son and doctor's daughter, moving like chessmen upon their alloted squares. She was curiously excited. She thought, "I have married England." Her fingers tightened on his arm.

England, serenely unaware of his symbolic importance, acknowledged the squeeze with a pressure of the elbow. "Splendid!" he said, heartily. "Piano solo, Miss Twitterton—we mustn't miss that, on any account. Song by the Reverend Simon Goodacre, 'Hybrias the Cretan'—strong, he-man stuff, padre. Folksongs and Sea-shanties by the Choir . . ."

(He took his wife's caress to indicate that she shared his appreciation of the programme. And, indeed, their minds were not far apart, for he was thinking: How these old boys run true to form! "Hybrias the Cretan"! When I was a kid, the curate used to sing it—"With my good sword I plough, I reap, I sow"—a gentle creature who wouldn't have harmed a fly . . . Merton, I think or was it Corpus? . . . with a baritone bigger than his whole body . . . he fell in love with our governess. . . .)

"Shenandoah," "Rio Grande," "Down in Demerara." He

glanced round the dust-sheeted room. "That's exactly how we feel. That's the song for us, Harriet." He lifted his voice:

> *"Here we sit like birds in the wilderness—"*

All mad together, thought Harriet, joining in:

> *"Birds in the wilderness—"*

Mr. Puffett could not bear it and exploded with a roar:

> *"BIRDS in the wilderness—"*

The vicar opened his mouth:

> *"Here we sit like birds in the wilderness,*
> *Down in Demerara!"*

Even Miss Twitterton added her chirp to the last line.

> *"Now this old man, he took and died-a-lum,*
> *Took and died-a-lum,*
> *Took and died-a-lum,*
> *This old man, he took and died-a-lum,*
> *Down in Demerara!"*

(It was just like that poem by someone or other: "Everyone suddenly burst out singing.")

> *"So here we sit like birds in the wilderness,*
> *Birds in the wilderness,*
> *Birds in the wilderness!*
> *Here we sit like birds in the wilderness,*
> *Down in Demerara!"*

"Bravo!" said Peter.

"Yes," said Mr. Goodacre, "we rendered that with great spirit."

"Ah!" said Mr. Puffett. "Nothing like a good song to take your mind off your troubles. Is there, me lord?"

"Nothing!" said Peter. "Begone, dull care! *Eructavit cor meum.*"

"Come, come," protested the vicar, "it's early days to talk about troubles, my dear young people."

"When a man's married," said Mr. Puffett, sententiously, "his troubles begin. Which they may take the form of a family. Or they may take the form of sut."

"Soot?" exclaimed the vicar, as though for the first time he was asking himself what Mr. Puffett was doing in the domestic chorus. "Why, yes, Tom—you do seem to be having a little trouble with Mr. Noakes's—I should say, Lord Peter's—chimney. What's the matter with it?"

"Something catastrophic, I gather," said the master of the house.

"Nothing like that," dissented Mr. Puffett, reprovingly. "Just sut. Corroded sut. Doo to neglect."

"I'm sure—" bleated Miss Twitterton.

"No call to blame present company," said Mr. Puffett. "I'm sorry for Miss Twitterton, and I'm sorry for his lordship. It's corroded that 'ard you can't get the rods through."

"That's bad, that's bad," ejaculated the vicar. He braced himself as a vicar should, to deal with this emergency occurring in his parish. "A friend of mine had sad trouble with corroded soot. But I was able to assist him with an old-fashioned remedy. I wonder now—I wonder—is Mrs. Ruddle here? the invaluable Mrs. Ruddle?"

Harriet, receiving no guidance from Peter's politely impassive expression, went to summon Mrs. Ruddle, of whom the vicar instantly took charge.

"Ah, good morning, Martha. Now, I wonder if you could borrow your son's old shotgun for us. The one he uses for scaring the birds."

"I could pop over and see, sir," said Mrs. Ruddle, dubiously.

"Let Crutchley go for you," suggested Peter. He turned abruptly as he spoke and began to fill his pipe. Harriet, studying his face, saw with apprehension that he was brimming over with an awful anticipatory glee. Whatever cataclysm impended, he would not put out a finger to stop it, he would let the heavens fall and tread the antic hay on the ruins.

"Well," conceded Mrs. Ruddle, "Frank's quicker on his feet nor what I am."

"Loaded, of course," cried the vicar after her, as she vanished through the door. "There's nothing," he explained to the world at large, "like one of those old duck-guns, discharged up the chimney, for clearing corroded soot. This friend of mine—"

"I don't 'old with that, sir," said Mr. Puffett, every bulge in his body expressing righteous resentment and a sturdy independence of judgment. "It's the power be'ind the rods as does it."

"I assure you, Tom," said Mr. Goodacre, "the shotgun cleared my friend's chimney instantly. A most obstinate case."

"That may be, sir," replied Mr. Puffett, "but it ain't a remedy as I should care to apply." He stalked gloomily to the spot where he had piled his cast-off sweaters and picked up the top one. "If the rods don't do it, then it's ladders you want, not 'igh explosive."

"But, Mr. Goodacre," exclaimed Miss Twitterton anxiously, "are you *sure* it's quite safe? I'm always very nervous about guns in the house. All these accidents—"

The vicar reassured her. Harriet, perceiving that the owners of the house, at any rate, were to be relieved of all responsibility for their own chimneys, nevertheless thought it well to placate the sweep.

"Don't desert us, Mr. Puffett," she pleaded. "One can't hurt Mr. Goodacre's feelings. But if anything happens—"

"Have a heart, Puffett," said Peter.

Mr. Puffett's little twinkling eyes looked into Peter's, which were like twin grey lakes of limpid clarity and wholly deceptive depth.

"Well," said Mr. Puffett, slowly, "anything to oblige. But don't say I didn't warn you, m'lord. It's a thing I don't 'old with."

"It won't bring the chimney down, will it?" inquired Harriet.

"Oh, it won't bring the *chimney* down," replied Mr. Puffett. "If you likes to 'umour the old gentleman, on your 'ead be it. In a manner of speaking, m'lady."

Peter had succeeded in getting his pipe to draw, and, with both hands in his trousers-pockets, was observing the actors in the drama with an air of pleased detachment. At the entrance of Crutchley and Mrs. Ruddle with the gun, however, he began to retreat, noiselessly and backwards, like a cat who has accidentally stepped in a pool of spilt perfume.

"My God!" he breathed delicately. "Waterloo year!"

"Splendid!" cried the vicar. "Thank you, thank you, Martha. Now we are equipped."

"You *have* been quick, Frank!" said Miss Twitterton. She eyed the weapon nervously. "You're *sure* it won't go off of its own accord?"

"Will an army mule go off of its own accord?" queried Peter, softly.

"I never like the idea of fire-arms," said Miss Twitterton.

"No, no," said the vicar. "Trust me, there will be no ill effects." He possessed himself of the gun and examined the lock and trigger mechanism with the air of one to whom the theory of ballistics was an open book.

"It's all loaded and ready, sir," said Mrs. Ruddle, proudly conscious of her Bert's efficiency.

Miss Twitterton gave a faint squeak, and the vicar, thoughtfully turning the muzzle of the gun away from her, found himself covering Bunter, who entered at that moment from the passage.

"Excuse me, my lord," said Bunter, with superb nonchalance but a wary eye; "there is a person at the door—"

"Just a moment, Bunter," broke in his master. "The fireworks are about to begin. The chimney is to be cleared by the natural expansion of gases."

"Very good, my lord," Bunter appeared to measure the respective forces of the weapon and the vicar. "Excuse me, sir. Had you not better permit me—?"

"No, no," cried Mr. Goodacre. "Thank you. I can manage it perfectly." Gun in hand, he plunged head and shoulders beneath the chimney-drape.

"Humph!" said Peter. "You're a better man than I am, Gunga Din."

He removed his pipe from his mouth and with his free hand gathered his wife to him. Miss Twitterton, having no husband to cling to, flung herself upon Crutchley for protection, uttering a plaintive cry:

"Oh, Frank! I know I shall scream at the noise."

"There's no occasion for alarm," said the vicar, popping out his head like a showman from behind the curtain. "Now—are we all ready?"

Mr. Puffett put on his bowler hat.

"*Ruat cœlum!*" said Peter; and the gun went off.

It exploded like the crack of doom, and it kicked (as Peter had well foreseen) like a carthorse. Gun and gunman rolled together upon the hearth, entangled inextricably in the folds of the drape. As Bunter leaped to the rescue, the loosened soot of centuries came plunging in a mad cascade down the chimney; it met the floor with a soft and deadly violence and mushroomed up in a Stygian cloud, while with it rushed, in a clattering shower, masonry and mortar, jackdaws' nests and the bones of bats and owls, sticks, bricks and metal-work, with fragments of tiles and potsherds. The shrill outcry of Mrs. Ruddle and Miss Twitterton was drowned by the eruptive rumble and boom that echoed from bend to bend of the forty-foot flue.

"Oh, rapture!" cried Peter, with his lady in his arms. "Oh, bountiful Jehovah! Oh, joy for all its former woes a thousand-fold repaid!"

"There!" exclaimed Mr. Puffett, triumphantly. "You can't say as I didn't warn yer."

Peter opened his mouth to reply, when the sight of Bunter, snorting and blind, and black as any Nubian Venus, struck him speechless with ecstasy.

"Oh, dear!" cried Miss Twitterton. She fluttered round,

making helpless little darts at the swaddled shape that was the vicar. "Oh, dear, dear, dear! Oh, Frank! Oh, goodness!"

"Peter!" panted Harriet.

"I knew it!" said Peter. "Whoop! I knew it! You blasphemed the aspidistra and something awful *has* come down that chimney."

"Peter! it's Mr. Goodacre in the sheet."

"Whoop!" said Peter again. He pulled himself together and joined Mr. Puffett in unwinding the clerical cocoon; while Mrs. Ruddle and Crutchley led away the unfortunate Bunter.

Mr. Goodacre emerged in some disorder.

"Not hurt, sir, I hope?" inquired Peter with grave concern.

"Not at all, not at all," replied the vicar, rubbing his shoulder. "A little arnica will soon put that to rights!" He smoothed his scanty hair with his hands and fumbled for his glasses. "I trust the ladies were not unduly alarmed by the explosion. It appears to have been effective."

"Remarkably so," said Peter. He pulled a pampas grass from the drain-pipe and poked delicately among the débris, while Harriet, flicking soot from the vicar, was reminded of Alice dusting the White King. "It's surprising, the things you find in old chimneys."

"No dead bodies, I trust," said the vicar.

"Only ornithological specimens. And two skeleton bats. And eight feet or so of ancient chain, as formerly worn by the mayors of Paggleham."

"Ah!" said Mr. Goodacre, filled with antiquarian zeal, "an old pot-chain, very likely."

"That's what it'll be," concurred Mr. Puffett. "'Ung up on one of them ledges, as like as not. See 'ere! 'Ere's a bit of one o' they roasting-jacks wot they used in the old days. Look, see! That's the cross-bar and the wheel wot the chain went over, like. My grannie had one, the dead spit of this."

"Well," said Peter, "we seem to have loosened things up a bit, anyhow. Think you can get your rods through the pot now?"

"If," said Mr. Puffett, darkly, "the pot's still there." He

dived beneath the chimney breast, whither Peter followed him. "Mind your 'ead, me lord—there might be some more loose bricks. I will say as you can see the sky if you looks for it, which is more than you'd see this morning."

"Excuse me, my lord!"

"Hey?" said Peter. He crawled out and straightened his back, only to find himself nose to nose with Bunter, who appeared to have undergone a rough but effective cleansing. He looked his servitor up and down. "By God, Bunter, my Bunter, I'm revenged for the scullery pump."

The shadow of some powerful emotion passed over Bunter's face; but his training held good.

"The individual at the door, my lord, is inquiring for Mr. Noakes. I have informed him that he is not here, but he refuses to take my word for it."

"Did you ask if he would see Miss Twitterton? What does he want?"

"He says, my lord, that his business is urgent and personal."

Mr. Puffett, feeling his presence a little intrusive, whistled thoughtfully, and began to collect his rods together and secure them with string.

"What sort of an 'individual,' Bunter?"

Mr. Bunter lightly shrugged his shoulders and spread forth his palms.

"A financial individual, my lord, to judge by appearances."

"Ho!" said Mr. Puffett, *sotto voce*.

"Name of Moses?"

"Name of MacBride, my lord."

"A distinction without a difference. Well, Miss Twitterton, will you see this financial Scotsman?"

"Oh, Lord Peter, I really don't know *what* to say. I know *nothing* about Uncle William's business. I don't know if he'd *like* me to interfere. If only Uncle—"

"Would you rather I tackled the bloke?"

"It's too kind of you, Lord Peter. I'm sure I oughtn't to bother you. But with Uncle away and everything so awkward—

and gentlemen always understand so much better about business, *don't* they, Lady Peter? Dear me!"

"My husband will be delighted," said Harriet. She was wickedly tempted to add, "He knows *everything* about business," but was fortunately forestalled by the gentleman himself.

"Nothing delights me more," pronounced his lordship, "than minding other people's business. Show him in. And, Bunter! Allow me to invest you with the Most Heroic Order of the Chimney, for attempting a rescue against overwhelming odds."

"Thank you, my lord," said Mr. Bunter, woodenly, stooping his neck to the chain and meekly receiving the roasting jack in his right hand. "I am much obliged. Will there be anything further?"

"Yes. Before you go—take up the bodies. But the soldiers may be excused from shooting. We have had enough of that for one morning."

Mr. Bunter bowed, collected the skeletons in the dust-pan and departed. But as he passed behind the settle, Harriet saw him unwind the chain and drop it unobtrusively into the drainpipe, setting the roasting-jack upright against the wall. A gentleman might have his joke; but a gentleman's gentleman has his position to keep up. One could not face inquisitive Hebrews in the character of Mayor of Paggleham and Provincial Grand Master of the Most Heroic Order of the Chimney.

CHAPTER VI

◆

Back to the Army Again

The days have slain the days
And the seasons have gone by,
And brought me the Summer again;

And here on the grass I lie
As erst I lay and was glad
Ere I meddled with right and with wrong.
—William Morris, *The Half of Life Gone*

Mr. MacBride turned out to be a brisk young man, bowler-hatted, with sharp black eyes that seemed to inventory everything they encountered, and a highly regrettable tie. He rapidly summed up the vicar and Mr. Puffett, dismissed them from his calculations, and made a bee-line for the monocle.

"'Morning," said Mr. MacBride. "Lord Peter Wimsey, I believe. Very sorry to trouble your lordship. Understand you're stopping here. Fact is, I have to see Mr. Noakes on a little matter of business."

"Just so," said Peter, easily. "Any fog in Town this morning?"

"Ow naow," replied Mr. MacBride. "Nice clear day."

"I thought so. I mean, I thought you must have come from Town. Bred an' bawn in a briar-patch, Brer Fox. But you might, of course, have been elsewhere since then, so I asked the question. You didn't send in your card, I fancy."

"Well, you see," explained Mr. MacBride, whose native accents were, indeed—apart from a trifling difficulty with his sibilants—pure Whitechapel, "my business is with Mr. Noakes. Personal and confidential."

At this point, Mr. Puffett, finding a long piece of twine on the floor, began to roll it up slowly and methodically, fixing his gaze upon the stranger's face in no very friendly manner.

"Well," resumed Peter, "I'm afraid you have had your journey for nothing. Mr. Noakes isn't here. I only wish he was. But you'll probably find him over at Broxford."

"Oh, no," said Mr. MacBride again. "That won't work. Not a bit of it." A step at the door made him swing round sharply, but it was only Crutchley, armed with a pail and a broom and shovel. Mr. MacBride laughed. "I've been over to Broxford, and *they* said I should find him here."

"Did they indeed?" said Peter. "That's right, Crutchley. Sweep up this mess and get these papers cleared. Said he was here, did they? Then they were mistaken. He's not here and we don't know where he is."

"But," cried Miss Twitterton, "it isn't possible! Not over at Broxford? Then where *can* he be? It's most worrying. Oh, dear, Mr. Goodacre, can't *you* suggest something?"

"Sorry to make such a dust," said Peter. "We have had a slight domestic accident with some soot. Excellent thing for the flower-beds. Garden pests are said to dislike it. Yes. Well now, this is Mr. Noakes's niece, Miss Twitterton. Perhaps you can state your business to her."

"Sorry," said Mr. MacBride, "nothing doing. I've got to see the old gentleman personally. And it's no good trying to put me off, because I know all the dodges." He skipped nimbly over the broom that Crutchley was plying about his feet, and sat down, uninvited, on the settle.

"Young man," said Mr. Goodacre, rebukingly, "you had better keep a civil tongue in your head. Lord Peter Wimsey has given you his personal assurance that we do not know where to find Mr. Noakes. You do not suppose that his lordship would tell you an untruth."

His lordship, who had wandered over to a distant whatnot, and was hunting through a pile of his personal belongings placed there by Bunter, glanced at his wife and cocked a modest eyebrow.

"Oh, wouldn't he, though?" said Mr. MacBride. "There's nobody like the British aristocracy to tell you a good stiff lie without batting an eyelid. His lordship's face would be a fortune to him in the witness-box."

"Where," added Peter, extricating a box of cigars from the pile and addressing it in confidence, "it is not unknown."

"So you see," said Mr. MacBride, "that cock won't fight."

He stretched his legs out negligently, to show that he intended to stay where he was. Mr. Puffett, groping about his feet, discovered a stray stub of pencil and put it in his pocket with a grunt.

"Mr. MacBride." Peter had returned, box in hand. "Have a cigar. Now then, who do you represent?"

He stared down at his visitor with an eye so shrewd and

a mouth so humorous that Mr. MacBride, accepting the cigar and recognising its quality, pulled himself together, sat up and acknowledged his intellectual equal with a conspiratorial wink.

"Macdonald & Abrahams," said Mr. MacBride. "Bedford Row."

"Ah, yes. That clannish old North British firm. Solicitors? I thought so. Something to Mr. Noakes's advantage? No doubt. Well, you want him and so do we. So does this lady here. . . ."

"Yes, indeed," said Miss Twitterton, "I'm very worried about Uncle. We haven't seen him since last Wednesday, and I'm sure—"

"But," pursued Peter, "you won't find him in my house."

"Your house?"

"My house. I have just purchased this house from Mr. Noakes."

"Whew!" exclaimed Mr. MacBride excitedly, blowing out a long jet of smoke, "so *that's* the nigger in the woodpile. Bought the house, eh? Paid for it?"

"Really, really!" cried the vicar, scandalised. Mr. Puffett, struggling into a sweater, remained with arms suspended.

"Naturally," said Peter, "I have paid for it."

"Skipped, by thunder!" exclaimed Mr. MacBride. His sudden gesture dislodged his bowler from his knee and sent it spinning and skipping to Mr. Puffett's feet. Crutchley dropped the heap of papers he had collected and stood staring.

"Skipped?" shrieked Miss Twitterton. "What do you mean by that? Oh, what *does* he mean, Lord Peter?"

"Oh, hush!" said Harriet. "He doesn't really know, any more than we do."

"Gone away," explained Mr. MacBride. "Vamoosed. Done a bunk. Skipped with the cash. Is that clear enough? If I've said it to Mr. Abrahams once, I've said it a thousand times. If you don't come down sharp on that fellow Noakes, he'll skip, I said. And he has skipped, ain't it?"

"It looks like it, certainly," said Peter.

"Skipped?" Crutchley was indignant. "It's easy for you to say skipped. What about my forty pound?"

"Oh, Frank!" cried Miss Twitterton.

"Ah, you're another of 'em, are you?" said Mr. MacBride, with condescending sympathy. "Forty pounds, eh? Well, what about us? What about our client's money?"

"But what money?" gasped Miss Twitterton in an agony of apprehension. "*Whose* money? I don't understand. What's it all got to do with Uncle William?"

"Peter," said Harriet, "don't you think—?"

"It's no good," said Wimsey. "It's got to come out."

"See this?" said Mr. MacBride. "That's a writ, that is. Little matter of nine hundred pound."

"Nine 'undred?" Crutchley made a snatch for the paper as though it were negotiable security for that amount.

"Nine hundred *pounds!*" Miss Twitterton's was the top note in the chorus. Peter shook his head.

"Capital and interest," said Mr. MacBride, calmly. "Levy, Levy & Levy. Running five years. Can't wait for ever, you know."

"My uncle's business—" began Miss Twitterton. "Oh, there must be some *mistake*."

"Your uncle's business, miss," said Mr. MacBride, bluntly but not altogether unsympathetically, "hasn't got a leg to stand on. Mortgage on the shop and not a hundred pounds' worth of stock in the place—and I don't suppose *that's* paid for. Your uncle's broke, that's what it is. Broke."

"Broke?" exclaimed Crutchley, with passion. "And how about my forty quid what he made me put into his business?"

"Well, you won't see that again, Mr. Whoever-you-are," returned the clerk, coolly. "Not without we catch the old gentleman and make him cough up the cash. Even then—might I ask, my lord, what you paid for the house? No offense, but it does make a difference."

"Six-fifty," said Peter.

"Cheap," said Mr. MacBride, shortly.

"So we thought," replied his lordship. "It was valued at eight hundred for mortgage; but he took our offer for cash."

"Looking for a mortgage, was he?"

"I don't know. I took pains to make sure that there were, in fact, no encumbrances. Further, I did not inquire."

"Ha!" said Mr. MacBride. "Well, you got a bargain."

"It will need a good bit of money spent on it," said Peter. "As a matter of fact, we'd have paid what he wanted if he'd insisted, my wife had a fancy for the place. But he accepted our first offer; ours not to question why. Business is business."

"Hum!" said Mr. MacBride, with respect. "And some people think the aristocracy's a soft proposition. Then I gather you're not altogether surprised."

"Not in the least," said Peter.

Miss Twitterton looked bewildered.

"Well, it's all the worse for our client," said Mr. MacBride, frankly. "Six-fifty won't cover us, even if we get it; and now he's gone and beat it with the money."

"Given me the slip, the swindlin' old devil!" ejaculated Crutchley, in angry tones.

"Steady, steady, Crutchley," implored the vicar. "Remember where you are. Think of Miss Twitterton."

"There's the furniture," said Harriet. "That belongs to him."

"If it's paid for," said Mr. MacBride, summing up the contents of the room with a contemptuous eye.

"But it's dreadful!" cried Miss Twitterton. "I can't *believe* it! We always thought Uncle was so well off."

"So he is," said Mr. MacBride. "Well off out of this. About a thousand miles by this time. Not heard of since last Wednesday? Well, there you are. A nice job, I don't think. Fact is, with all these transport facilities, it's too easy nowadays for absconding debtors to clear out."

"See here!" cried Crutchley, losing all control of himself. "You mean to say, even if you find him, I shan't get my forty pounds? It's a damn disgrace, that's what it is—"

"Hold hard," said Mr. MacBride. "He didn't take you into partnership or anything, I suppose? No? Well, that's a bit of luck for you, anyway. We can't come on you for what's missing. You thank your stars you're out of it for your forty pounds. It's all experience, ain't it?"

"Curse you!" said Crutchley. "I'll 'ave my forty pounds out o' somebody. Here, you, Aggie Twitterton—you know he promised to pay me. I'll 'ave the law on you!—Crooked, swindlin'—"

"Come, come," interposed Mr. Goodacre again. "It's not Miss Twitterton's fault. You must not fly into a passion. We must all try to think calmly—"

"Quite," said Peter. "Definitely. Let us beget a temperance that may give it smoothness. And talking of temperance, how about a mild spot? Bunter!—Oh, there you are. *Have* we any drink in the house?"

"Certainly, my lord. Hock, sherry, whisky—"

Here Mr. Puffett thought well to intervene. Wines and spirits were scarcely in his line.

"Mr. Noakes," he observed, in a detached manner, "alwaykep' a good barrel of beer in the 'ouse. I will say that for him."

"Excellent. Strictly speaking, I suppose, Mr. MacBride, it's your client's beer. But if you have no objection—"

"Well," conceded Mr. MacBride, "a drop of beer's neither here nor there, is it now?"

"A jug of beer, then, Bunter, and the whisky. Oh, and sherry for the ladies."

Bunter departed on this mollifying errand, and the atmosphere seemed to grow calmer. Mr. Goodacre seized on the last words to introduce a less controversial topic:

"Sherry," he said, pleasantly, "has always appeared to me a most agreeable wine. I was so glad to read in the newspaper that it was coming into its own again. Madeira, too. They tell me that both sherry and madeira are returning to favour in London. And in the Universities. That is a very reassuring sign. I cannot think that these modern cocktails can be either healthful or palatable. Surely not. But I can see no objection to a glass of sound wine now and again—for the stomach's sake, as the Apostle says. It is undoubtedly restorative in moments of agitation, like the present. I am afraid, Miss Twitterton, this has been a sad shock to you."

"I couldn't have thought it of Uncle," said Miss Twitterton sadly. "He has always been so much looked-up to. I simply can't believe it."

"I can—easily," said Crutchley, in the sweep's ear.

"You never know," said Mr. Puffett, struggling into his topcoat. "I always thought Mr. Noakes was a warm man. Seems like he was 'ot stuff."

"Gone off with my forty quid!" Automatically, Crutchley picked up the papers from the floor. "And never paid me only 2 per cent, neither, the old thief! I never did like that wireless business."

"Ah!" said Mr. Puffett. He caught at a loose end of string dangling from among the papers and reeled it out on his fingers, so that they looked absurdly like a stout maiden lady and her companion engaged in winding knitting wool. "Safe bind, safe find, Frank Crutchley. You can't be too careful where you puts your money. Pick it up where you finds it and put it away careful, same as I does this bit of twine, and there it is, 'andy when you wants it." He stowed the string away in a remote pocket.

To this piece of sententiousness, Crutchley returned no answer. He went out, giving place to Bunter, who, with an inscrutable face, was balancing upon a tin tray a black bottle, a bottle of whisky, an earthenware jug, the two tumblers of the night before, three cut-glass goblets (one with a chipped foot), a china mug with a handle and two pewter pots of different sizes.

"Good Lord!" said Peter. (Bunter's eyes lifted for a moment like those of a scolded spaniel.) "These must be the Baker Street Irregulars; the chief thing is that they all have a hole in the top. I am told that Mr. Woolworth sells a very good selection of glassware. In the meantime, Miss Twitterton, will you take sherry as a present from Margate or toss off your Haig in a tankard?"

"Oh!" said Miss Twitterton. "I'm sure there are some in the chiffonier—Oh, thank you so much, but at this time in the morning—and then they would need dusting, because Uncle didn't use them—Well, I really don't know—"

"It'll do you good."

"I think you need a little something," said Harriet.

"Oh, *do* you, Lady Peter? Well—if you insist—Only sherry, then, and only a *little* of that—Of course, it isn't really so early any longer, is it?—Oh, please, really, I'm sure you're giving me *far* too much!"

"I assure you," said Peter, "you will find it as mild as your own parsnip wine." He handed her the mug gravely, and poured a small quantity of sherry into a tumbler for his wife, who accepted it with the remark:

"You are a master of meiosis."

"Thank you, Harriet. What's your poison, padre?"

"Sherry, thank you, sherry. Your health, my dear young people." He clinked the tumbler solemnly against Miss Twitterton's mug, taking her by surprise. "Take courage, Miss Twitterton. Things mayn't be as bad as they seem."

"Thank you," said Mr. MacBride, waving away the whisky. "I'll wait for the beer if it's all the same to you. No spirits in office hours is my motto. I'm sure it's no pleasure to me, bringing all this unfortunate disturbance into a family. But business is business, ain't it, your lordship? And we've got our clients to consider."

"You're not to blame," said Peter. "Miss Twitterton realises that you are only doing your rather unpleasant duty. They also serve who only serve writs, you know."

"I'm sure," cried Miss Twitterton, "if we could only find Uncle, he would explain *everything*."

"*If* we could find him," agreed Mr. MacBride, meaningly.

"Yes," said Peter, "much virtue in if. If we could find Mr. Noakes—" The door opened, and he dismissed the question with an air of relief. "Ah! Beer, glorious beer!"

"Excuse me, my lord." Bunter stood on the threshold empty-handed. "I'm afraid we have found Mr. Noakes."

"*Afraid* you've found him?" Master and man stared at one another, and Harriet, reading the unspoken message in their eyes, came up to Peter and laid a hand on his arm.

"For God's sake, Bunter," said Wimsey, with a strained note in his voice, "don't say you've found—Where? Down the cellar?"

The voice of Mrs. Ruddle broke the tension like the wail of a banshee:

"Frank! Frank Crutchley! It's Mr. Noakes!"

"Yes, my lord," said Bunter.

Miss Twitterton, unexpectedly quick-witted, sprang to her feet. "He's dead! Uncle's dead!" The mug rolled from her hands to crash on the hearth-stone.

"No, no," said Harriet, "they can't mean that."

"Oh, no, impossible," said Mr. Goodacre. He looked appealingly at Bunter, who bent his head.

"I am very much afraid so, sir."

Crutchley, thrusting him aside, burst in. "What's happened? What's Ma Ruddle shouting about? Where's—?"

"I knew it, I knew it!" shrieked Miss Twitterton, recklessly. "I knew something terrible had happened! Uncle's dead and all the money's gone!"

She burst into a fit of hiccupping laughter, made a dart towards Crutchley, who recoiled with a gasp, broke from the vicar's supporting hand and flung herself hysterically into Harriet's arms.

"Here!" said Mr. Puffett, "let's 'ave a look."

He made for the door, cannoning into Crutchley. Bunter profited by the confusion to fling the door to and set his back against it.

"Wait a minute," said Bunter. "Better not touch anything."

As if the words were a signal for which he had been waiting, Peter took up his cold pipe from the table, knocked it out on his palm and flung the crushed ashes upon the tray.

"Perhaps," said Mr. Goodacre, as one who hopes against hope, "he has only fainted." He rose eagerly. "We might be able to assist him—"

His voice trailed away.

"Dead some days," said Bunter, "from the looks of him, sir." His eye was still on Peter.

"Has he got the money on him?" inquired MacBride. The vicar, unheeding, flung another question, like a wave, against the stone wall of Bunter's impassivity:

"But how did it happen, my man? Did he fall down the stairs in a fit?"

"Cut his throat, more likely," said Mr. MacBride.

Bunter, still looking at Peter, said with emphasis: "It isn't *suicide.*" Feeling the door thrust against his shoulder, he moved aside to admit Mrs. Ruddle.

"Oh, dear! oh, dear!" cried Mrs. Ruddle. Her eyes gleamed with a dismal triumph. "'Is pore 'ead's bashed in something shocking!"

"Bunter!" said Wimsey, and spoke the word at last: "Are you trying to tell us that this is murder?"

Miss Twitterton slid from Harriet's arms to the floor.

"I couldn't say, my lord; but it looks most unpleasantly like it."

"Get me a glass of water, please," said Harriet.

"Yes, my lady. Mrs. Ruddle! Glass of water—sharp!"

"Very well," said Peter, mechanically pouring water into a goblet and giving it to the charwoman. "Leave everything as it is. Crutchley, you'd better go for the police."

"If," said Mrs. Ruddle, "if it's the perlice you're wanting, there's young Joe Sellon—that's the constable, a-standing at my gate this very minnit a-yarning with my Albert. I seen 'im not five minutes agone, and if I knows anything o' them boys when they gits talking—"

"The water," said Harriet. Peter stalked over to Crutchley, carrying with him a stiff peg of neat spirits.

"Take this and pull yourself together. Then run over to the cottage and get this chap Sellon or whatever his name is. Quick."

"Thank you, my lord." The young man jerked himself from his daze and swallowed the whisky at a gulp. "It's a bit of a shock."

He went out. Mr. Puffett followed him.

"I suppose," said Mr. Puffett, nudging Bunter gently in the ribs, "you didn't manage to get that beer up afore—eh? Oh, well—there's worse happens in war."

"She's better now, pore thing," said Mrs. Ruddle. "Come on, don't give way now, there's a dear. What you want is a nice lay-down and a cupper tea. Shall I take 'er upstairs, me lady?"

"Do," said Harriet. "I'll come in a moment."

She let them go and turned to Peter, who stood motionless,

staring down at the table. Oh, my God! she thought, startled by his face, he's a middle-aged man—the half of life gone—he mustn't—

"Peter, my poor dear! And we came here for a quiet honeymoon!"

He turned at her touch and laughed ruefully.

"Damn!" he said. "And damn! Back to the old grind. *Rigor mortis* and who-saw-him-last, blood-prints, finger-prints, foot-prints, information received and it-is-my-dooty-to-warn-you. *Quelle scie, mon dieu, quelle scie!*"

A young man in a blue uniform put his head in at the door.

"Now then," said Police-constable Sellon, "wot's all this?"

CHAPTER VII

◆

Lotos and Cactus

I know what is and what has been;
Not anything to me comes strange,
Who in so many years have seen
And lived through every kind of change.
I know when men are good or bad,
When well or ill, he slowly said;
When sad or glad, when sane or mad,
And when they sleep alive or dead. . . .

And while the black night nothing saw,
And till the cold morn came at last,
That old bed held the room in awe
With tales of its experience vast.

It thrilled the gloom; it told such tales
Of human sorrows and delights,
Of fever moans and infant wails,
Of births and deaths and bridal nights.
—James Thomson, *In the Room*

Harriet left Miss Twitterton tucked up on the nuptial couch with a hot-water bottle and an aspirin and, passing softly into the next room, discovered her lord in the act of pulling his shirt over his head. She waited for his face to reappear and then said, "Hullo!"

"Hullo! all serene?"

"Yes. Better now. What's happening downstairs?"

"Sellon's telephoned from the post-office and the Super's coming over from Broxford with the police-surgeon. So I came up to put on a collar and tie."

Of course, thought Harriet, secretly entertained. Someone has died in our hour, so we put on a collar and tie. Nothing could be more obvious. How absurd men are! And how clever in devising protective armour for themselves! What kind of tie will it be? Black would surely be excessive. Dull purple or an unobtrusive spot? No. A regimental tie. Nothing could be more proper. Purely official and committing one to nothing. Completely silly and charming.

She smoothed the smile from her lips and watched the solemn transference of personal property from blazer pockets to appropriate situations about a coat and waistcoat.

"All this," observed Peter, "is a damned nuisance." He sat on the edge of the naked bedstead to exchange his slippers for a pair of brown shoes. "It's not worrying you too much, is it?" His voice was a little smothered with stooping to fasten the laces.

"No."

"One thing, it's nothing to do with us. That is, he wasn't killed for the money we paid him. He had it all in his pocket. In notes."

"Good heavens!"

"There's not much doubt he meant to make a bolt of it when somebody intervened. I can't say I feel any strong personal regret. Do you?"

"Far from it. Only—"

"M'm? . . . It *is* worrying you. Blast!"

"Not really. Only when I think of him, lying down there in the cellar all the time. I know it's perfectly idiotic of me—but I can't help wishing we hadn't slept in his bed."

"I was afraid you might feel like that." He got up and stood for a moment looking from the window over the sloping field and woodland that stretched away beyond the lane. "And yet, you know, that bed must be pretty nearly as old as the house—the original bits of it, anyhow. It could tell a good many tales of births and deaths and bridal-nights. One can't escape from these things—except by living in a brand-new villa and buying one's furniture in the Tottenham Court Road. . . . All the same, I wish to God it hadn't happened. I mean, if it's going to make you uncomfortable every time you think about—"

"Oh, Peter, no. I didn't mean that. It's not as though—It would be different if we had come here in another sort of way—"

"That's the point. Supposing I'd come here to disport myself with somebody who didn't matter twopence, I should be feeling a complete wart. Quite unreasonably, I dare say, but I can be just as unreasonable as anyone else, if I put my mind to it. But as things are, no! Nothing that you or I have done is any insult to death—unless you think so, Harriet. I should say, if anything could sweeten the atmosphere that wretched old man left behind him, it would be the feeling we—the feeling I have for you, at any rate, and yours for me if you feel like that. I do assure you, so far as I am concerned, there's nothing trivial about it."

"I know that. You're absolutely right. I won't think about it that way any more. Peter—there weren't—there weren't *rats* in the cellar, were there?"

"No, dearest, no rats. And all quite dry. Just a perfectly good cellar."

"I'm glad. I was sort of imagining rats. Not that I suppose it matters very much after one's dead, but I don't seem to mind all the rest nearly so much if I don't have to think of rats. In fact, I don't mind at all, not now."

"We shall have to stick round till after the inquest, I'm afraid, but we could easily get put up somewhere else. That's one thing I was going to ask you about. There's probably a decent inn at Pagford or Broxford."

Harriet considered this.

"No. I don't care about that. I think I'd rather stay here."

"Are you sure?"

"Yes. It's our house. It never was his—not really. And I'm not going to let you think there's any difference between your feelings and mine. That would be worse than rats, even."

"My dear, I'm not proposing to make staying here a test of your affections. Not love, quoth he, but vanity, sets love a task like that. It's easy enough for me. I was begotten and born in the bed where twelve generations of my forefathers were born and wedded and died—and some of them made pretty poor ends from the parson's point of view—so I don't suffer much from hauntings of that kind. But there's no reason at all why you shouldn't feel rather differently."

"Don't say another word about it. We're going to stay here and exorcise the ghosts. I'd rather."

"Well, if you change your mind, tell me," he said, still uneasy.

"I shan't change my mind. We'd better go down now, if you're ready, because Miss Twitterton ought to get some sleep if she can. Now I come to think of it, *she* didn't ask for another bedroom, and it's her own uncle."

"Country people are very matter-of-fact about life and death. They live so close to reality."

"So do your sort of people. It's my sort that go all sanitary and civilised, and get married in hotels and do their births and deaths in nursing-homes where they give offence to nobody. I say, Peter, do we have to feed all these doctors and superintendents and people? And does Bunter carry on all by himself, or ought I to give him some orders?"

"Experience has taught me," said Peter, as they moved down the stair, "that no situation finds Bunter unprepared. That he should have procured *The Times* this morning by the simple expedient of asking the milkman to request the post-mistress to telephone to Broxford and have it handed to the 'bus-conductor to be dropped at the post-office and brought up by the little girl who delivers the telegrams is a trifling example of his resourceful energy. But he would probably take it as a compliment if you were to refer the difficulty to him and congratulate him when he tells you that everything is provided for."

"I will."

In the short time that they had been upstairs, Mr. Puffett had evidently finished his chimney-sweeping, for the sitting-room had been cleared of dust-sheets and a fire kindled upon the hearth. A table had been drawn out into the centre of the room; on it stood a tray filled with plates and cutlery. Passing through into the passage, Harriet was aware of a good deal of activity in progress. Before the shut door of the cellar stood the uniformed figure of P.C. Sellon, like young Harry with his beaver on, prepared to resist any interference with the execution of his duty. In the kitchen, Mrs. Ruddle was cutting sand-wiches. In the scullery, Crutchley and Mr. Puffett were clearing a quantity of pots and pans and old flower-pots from a long deal dresser, preparatory (as appeared from the presence beside them of a steaming pail) to scrubbing it clean to receive the body of its late owner. In the back door stood Bunter, con-ducting some kind of financial transaction with two men who seemed to have arrived from nowhere in a motor van. Beyond them could be seen Mr. MacBride, strolling about the back-yard; he had the air of inventorying its contents with a view to assessing their value. And at that moment there came a heavy knock on the front door.

"That'll be the police," said Peter. He went to let them in, and at the same time Bunter finished paying the men, came in, and shut the back door sharply.

"Oh, Bunter," said Harriet, "I see you're giving us something to eat—?"

"Yes, my lady. I succeeded in intercepting the Home & Colonial and procuring some ham for sandwiches. There is also a portion of the foie gras and the Cheshire cheese which we brought from Town. The draught beer in the cellar being at the moment not readily available, I took the liberty of instructing Mrs. Ruddle to fetch a few bottles of Bass from the village. If anything further should be required, there is a jar of caviar in the hamper, but we have no lemons, I am sorry to say."

"Oh, I don't think caviar would strike the right note, Bunter, do you?"

"No, my lady. The heavy luggage has just arrived, per Carter Paterson; I instructed that it should be deposited in the oil-shed until we had leisure to attend to it."

"The luggage! I'd forgotten all about it."

"Very naturally, my lady, if I may say so. . . . The scullery," went on Bunter, with a touch of hesitation, "appeared a more suitable place than the kitchen for—ah—the medical gentleman to work in."

"Certainly," said Harriet, with emphasis.

"Yes, my lady. I inquired of his lordship whether, in view of all the circumstances, he would desire me to order in any coal. He said he would refer the matter to your ladyship."

"He has. You can order the coal."

"Very good, my lady. I fancy there will be time between lunch and dinner to effect a clearance of the kitchen chimney, provided there is no interference from the police. Would your ladyship wish me to instruct the sweep accordingly?"

"Yes, please. I don't know what we should do without your head for detail, Bunter."

"I am much obliged to your ladyship."

The police party had been taken into the sitting-room. Through the half-open door one could hear Peter's high, fluent voice giving a lucid account of the whole incredible business, with patient pauses for interrogation or to allow a deliberate constabulary pencil to catch up with him. Harriet sighed angrily.

"I do wish he hadn't to be worried like this! It's too bad."

"Yes, my lady." Bunter's face stirred, as though some human emotion were trying to break through. He made no further comment, but something which Harriet recognised as sympathy seemed to waft out of him. She said impulsively:

"I wonder. Do you think I'm right in ordering the coal?"

It was scarcely fair to push Bunter on to such delicate ground. He remained impassive:

"It is not for me to say, my lady."

She was determined not to be beaten.

"You have known him much longer than I have, Bunter. If his lordship had only himself to consider, do you suppose he would go or stay?"

"Under those circumstances, my lady, I fancy his lordship would decide to remain."

"That's what I wanted to know. You had better order enough coal for a month."

"Certainly, my lady."

The men were coming out of the sitting-room. They were introduced: Dr. Craven, Superintendent Kirk, Sergeant Blades. The cellar door was opened; somebody produced an electric torch and they all went down. Harriet, relegated to the woman's rôle of silence and waiting, went into the kitchen to help with the sandwiches. The rôle, though dull, was not a useless one, for Mrs. Ruddle, with a large knife in her hand, was standing at the scullery door as though prepared to carry out a butcherly kind of post-mortem upon whatever might be brought up from the cellar.

"Mrs. Ruddle!"

Mrs. Ruddle gave a violent start and dropped the knife.

"Law, m'lady! You did give me a turn."

"You want to cut the bread thinner. And please shut that door."

A slow, heavy shuffling. Then voices. Mrs. Ruddle broke off in the middle of a spirited piece of narrative to listen.

"Yes, Mrs. Ruddle?"

"Yes, m'lady. So I says to him, 'You needn't think you're going to ketch me that way, Joe Sellon,' I says. 'Like to make out you're somebody, don't you,' I says. 'I wonder you 'as the face, seein' what a fool you made of yourself over Aggie Twitterton's 'ens. No,' I says, 'when a proper policeman comes, 'e can ask all the questions 'e likes. But don't you think you can go ordering me about,' I says, 'an' me old enough to be your grandma. You can put away that there notebook,' I says, 'go on,' I says, 'it'd make me old cat laugh ter see yer,' I says. 'I'll tell 'em all I knows,' I says, 'don't you fret yourself w'en the time comes.' 'You ain't no right,' 'e says, 'to obstruct an orficer of the law.' 'Law?' I says, 'call yerself the law? If you're the law,' I says, 'I don't think much of it.' 'E got that red. 'You'll 'ear about this,' 'e says. And I says, 'And you'll ear summink, too. None o' yer sauce,' I says, 'they'll be glad enough to 'ear what I 'as to tell 'em, I dessay, without you goin' an' twistin' it all up afore they gets it,' I says. So 'e says—"

There was a peculiar mixture of malice and triumph in Mrs. Ruddle's voice which Harriet felt the episode of the hens did not altogether account for. But at this moment Bunter came in by the passage door.

"His lordship's compliments, my lady; and Superintendent Kirk would be glad to see you for a moment in the sitting-room if you can spare the time."

Superintendent Kirk was a large man with a mild and ruminative expression. He seemed already to have obtained from Peter most of the information he needed, asking only a few questions to confirm such points as the time of the party's arrival at Talboys and the appearance of the sitting-room and kitchen when they came in. What he really wanted to get from Harriet was a description of the bedroom. All Mr. Noakes's clothes had been there? His toilet articles? No suit-cases? No suggestion that he intended to leave the house at once? No? Well, that confirmed the idea that Mr. Noakes intended to get away, but was in no immediate hurry. Not, for example, particularly expecting any unpleasant interview that night. The Superintendent was much obliged to her ladyship; he should be sorry to disturb poor Miss Twitterton, and, after all, nothing much was to be gained by examining the bedroom at once, since its contents had already been disturbed. That applied, of course, to the other rooms as well. Unfortunate, but nobody could be blamed for that. They might be a bit further on when they had Dr. Craven's report. He would perhaps be able to tell them whether Noakes had been alive when he fell down the cellar steps or had been killed and thrown there afterwards. No bloodshed, that was the trouble, though the skull had been broken by the blow. And with so many people in and out of the house all night and morning, one could scarcely expect footprints or anything like that. At any rate, nothing had been seen to suggest a struggle? Nothing. Mr. Kirk was greatly obliged.

Harriet said, Not at all, and murmured something about lunch. The Superintendent said he saw no objection to that; he had finished with the sitting-room for the moment. He would just like a word with this fellow MacBride about the financial side of the business, but he would send him in as soon as he had done with him. He tactfully refused to join the party, but accepted the offer of a mouthful of bread-and-cheese in the kitchen. When the doctor had finished, he would finish the interrogations in the light of whatever the medical examination might reveal.

Years afterwards, Lady Peter Wimsey was accustomed to say that the first few days of her honeymoon remained in her memory as a long series of assorted surprises, punctuated by the most incredible meals. Her husband's impressions were even less coherent; he said he had had, all the time, the sensation of being slightly drunk and tossed in a blanket. The freakish and arbitrary fates must have given the blanket an especially energetic tweak, to have tossed him, towards the end of that strange, embarrassed luncheon, so high over the top of the world. He stood at the window, whistling. Bunter, hovering about the room, handing sandwiches and straightening out the last traces of the disorder left after the sweep's departure, recognised the tune. It was the one he had heard the night before in the woodshed. Nothing could have been less suited to the occasion, nothing should more deeply have offended his inborn sense of propriety; yet, like the poet Wordsworth, he heard it and rejoiced.

"Another sandwich, Mr. MacBride?"

(The new-wedded lady doing the honours at her own table for the first time. Curious, but true.)

"No more, thanks; much obliged to you." Mr. MacBride swallowed the last drop of his beer and polished his mouth and fingers politely with his handkerchief. Bunter swept down upon the empty plate and glass.

"I hope you've had something to eat, Bunter?"

(One must consider the servants. Only two fixed points in the universe: death, and the servants' dinner; and here they both were.)

"Yes, thank you, my lady."

"I suppose they'll be wanting this room in a minute. Is the doctor still there?"

"I believe he has concluded his examination, my lady."

"Nice job, I don't think," said Mr. MacBride.

> *"La caill', la tourterelle*
> *Et la joli' perdrix—*
> *Auprès de ma blonde*
> *Qu'il fait bon, fait bon, fait bon,*
> *Auprès de ma blonde—"*

Mr. MacBride looked round, scandalised. He had his own notions of propriety. Bunter darted hastily across the room and attracted the singer's wandering attention.

"Yes, Bunter?"

"Your lordship will excuse me. But in view of the melancholy occasion—"

"Eh, what? Oh, sorry. Was I making a noise?"

"My dear—" His swift, secret, reminiscent smile was a challenge; she beat it down, and achieved the right tone of wifely rebuke. "Poor Miss Twitterton's trying to get to sleep."

"Yes. Sorry. Dashed thoughtless of me. And in a house of bereavement and all that." His face darkened with a sudden odd impatience. "Though, if you ask me, I doubt whether anybody—I say, *anybody* feels particularly bereft."

"Except," said Mr. MacBride, "that chap Crutchley with his forty pound. I fancy that grief's genuine."

"From that point of view," said his lordship, "you should be the chief mourner."

"It won't keep *me* awake at night," retorted Mr. MacBride. "It ain't my money, you see," he added frankly. He rose, opened the door and glanced out into the passage. "I only hope they're getting a move on out there. I've got to toddle back to Town and see Mr. Abrahams. Pity you ain't on the telephone." He paused. "If I was you, I wouldn't let it worry me. Seems to me, deceased was a dashed unpleasant old gink and well out of the way."

He went out, leaving the atmosphere clearer, as though by the removal of funeral flowers.

"I'm afraid that's true," said Harriet.

"Just as well, isn't it?" Wimsey's tone was studiously light. "When I'm investigating a murder, I hate to have too much sympathy with the corpse. Personal feelings cramp the style."

"But, Peter—need you investigate this? It's rather rotten for you."

Bunter, piling plates on a tray, made for the door. This, of course, was bound to happen. Let them fight it out for themselves. He had delivered his own warning.

"No, I needn't. But I expect I shall. Murders go to my head like drink. I simply can't keep off them."

"Not even now? They can't expect you, surely! You've got a right to your own life sometimes. And it's such a beastly little crime—sordid and horrible."

"That's just it," he broke out, with unexpected passion. "That's why I can't leave it alone. It's not picturesque. It's not exciting. It's no fun at all. Just dirty, brutal bashing, like a butcher with a pole-axe. It makes me sick. But who the hell am I, to pick and choose what I'll meddle in?"

"I see. But after all, this was just wished on us. It's not as though you'd been called in to help."

"How often am I 'called in,' I wonder," he demanded, rather bitterly. "I call myself in, half the time, out of sheer mischief and inquisitiveness. Lord Peter Wimsey the aristocratic sleuth—my God! The idle rich gentleman who dabbles in detection. That's what they say—isn't it?"

"Sometimes. I lost my temper with somebody who said that, once. Before we were engaged. It made me wonder if I wasn't getting rather fond of you."

"Did it? Then perhaps I'd better not justify that view of myself. What do such fellows as I, crawling between heaven and earth? I can't wash my hands of a thing, merely because it's inconvenient to my lordship, as Bunter says of the sweep. I hate violence! I loathe wars and slaughter, and men quarrelling and fighting like beasts! Don't say it isn't my business. It's everybody's business."

"Of course it is, Peter. Go ahead. I was just being feminine, or something. I thought you looked as if you'd be better for a little peace and quiet. But you don't seem to shine as a lotos-eater."

"I can't eat lotos, even with you," he said, pathetically, "with murdered bodies popping up all over the place."

"You shan't, angel, you shan't. Have a nice mouthful of prickly cactus instead. And don't pay any attention to my imbecile efforts to strew your path with rose-leaves. It won't be the first time we've followed the footprints together. Only"—she faltered a moment, as another devastating matrimonial possibility loomed up like a nightmare—"whatever you do, you'll let me take a hand, won't you?"

To her relief, he laughed.

"All right, domina. I promise you that. Cactus for both or neither, and no lotos till we can share it. I won't play the good British husband—in spite of your alarming plunge into wifeliness. The Ethiopian shall stay black and leave the leopardess her spots."

He appeared satisfied, but Harriet cursed herself for a fool. This business of adjusting oneself was not so easy after all. Being preposterously fond of a person didn't prevent one from hurting him unintentionally. She had an uncomfortable feeling that his confidence had been shaken and that this was not the end of the misunderstanding. He wasn't the kind of man to whom you could say, "Darling, you're wonderful, and whatever you do is right"—whether you thought so or not. He would write you down a fool. Nor was he the sort who said, "I know what I'm doing and you must take my word for it." (Thank God for that, anyway!) He wanted you to agree with him intelligently or not at all. And her intelligence did agree with him. It was her own feelings that didn't seem to be quite pulling in double harness with her intelligence. But whether it was her feeling for Peter or her feeling for the deceased Mr. Noakes, butchered to make a busman's honeymoon for them, or a merely selfish feeling that she didn't want to be bothered at this moment with corpses and policemen, she was not sure.

"Cheer up, sweetheart," said Peter. "They may not want my kind assistance. Kirk may cut the Gordian knot by booting me out."

"Well, he'd be an idiot!" said Harriet, with prompt indignation.

Mr. Puffett entered suddenly without knocking.

"They're takin' Mr. Noakes away. Shall I be gettin' on with the kitchen chimney?" He walked across to the fireplace. "Draws beautiful now, don't she? I allus said there was nothing the matter with the flue. Ah! it's a good thing Mr. Noakes ain't alive to see all that 'eap of coal. That's a fire as does credit to any chimney."

"All right, Puffett," said Peter, absently. "Carry on."

Steps on the path, and a dismal little procession passing the window: a sergeant of police and another uniformed man, carrying a stretcher between them.

"Very good, me lord." Mr. Puffett glanced from the window and removed his bowler hat. "And where's all 'is cheeseparin' brought 'im now?" he demanded. "Nowhere."

He marched out.

"*De mortuis*," said Peter, "and then some."

"Yes, he seems to be getting a nice derangement of epitaphs, poor old creature."

Corpse and policemen—there they were, not to be got

rid of, whatever one's feelings might be. Much better to accept the situation and do one's best. Superintendent Kirk came in, followed by Joe Sellon.

"Well, well," said Peter. "All ready for the third degree?"

"'Tain't likely to come to that, my lord," replied Mr. Kirk, jovially. "You and your lady had something better to do last week than committing murders, I'll be bound. That's right, Joe, come along. Let's see what you can do with a bit o' shorthand. I'm sending my sergeant over to Broxford to pick up what he can there, so Joe can give me a hand with the statements. I'd like to use this room, if it's not inconvenient."

"Not at all." Seeing the Superintendent's eye fix modestly upon a spindly specimen of Edwardian craftsmanship, Peter promptly pushed forward a stout, high-backed chair with gouty arms and legs and an eruption of heavy scroll work about its head. "You'll find this about up to your weight, I fancy."

"Nice and imposing," said Harriet.

The village constable added his comment:

"That's old Noakes's chair, that was."

"So," said Peter, "Galahad will sit down in Merlin's seat."

Mr. Kirk, on the point of lowering his solid fifteen stone into the chair, jerked up abruptly.

"Alfred," said he, "Lord Tennyson."

"Got it in one," said Peter, mildly surprised. A glow of enthusiasm shone softly in the policeman's ox-like eyes. "You're a bit of a student, aren't you, Superintendent?"

"I like to do a bit o' reading in my off-duty," admitted Mr. Kirk, bashfully. "It mellows the mind." He sat down. "I often think as the rowtine of police dooty may tend to narrow a man and make him a bit hard, if you take my meaning. When I find that happening, I say to myself, what you need, Sam Kirk, is contact with a Great Mind or so, after supper. Reading maketh a full man—"

"Conference a ready man," said Harriet.

"And writing an exact man," said the Superintendent. "Mind that, Joe Sellon, and see you let me have them notes so as they can be read to make sense."

"Francis Bacon," said Peter, a trifle belatedly. "Mr. Kirk, you're a man after my own heart."

"Thank you, my lord. Bacon. You'd call him a Great Mind, wouldn't you? And what's more, he came to be Lord Chancellor of England, so he's a bit in the legal way, too. Ah! well, I suppose we'll have to get down to business."

"As another great mind so happily put it, 'However entrancing it is to wander through a garden of bright images, are we not enticing your mind from another subject of almost equal importance?'"

"What's that?" said the Superintendent. "That's a new one on me. 'Garden of bright images,' eh? That's pretty, that is."

"*Kai-Lung*," said Harriet.

"*Golden Hours of*," said Peter. "Ernest Bramah."

"Make a note 'o that for me, will you, Joe? 'Bright images'—That's just what you get in poetry, isn't it? Pictures, as you might say. And in a garden too—what you'd call flowers of fancy, I dessay. Well, now—" He pulled himself together and turned to Peter. "As I was saying, we mustn't waste time with the fancy-work. About this money we found on the body. What did you say you paid him for the house?"

"Six-fifty, altogether. Fifty at the beginning of the negotiations and the six hundred at quarter-day."

"That's right. That accounts for the six hundred he had in his pocket. He'd just about have cashed it the day he was put away."

"The quarter-day was a Sunday. The cheque was actually dated and sent on the 28th. It would have reached him Monday."

"That's right. We'll check the payment at the bank, but it's not really necessary. Wonder what *they* thought of him taking it away in cash instead of paying it in. H'm. It's a pity it ain't the bank's business to give us the office when people do things that look like bolting. But it wouldn't do, naturally."

"He must have had it in his pocket when he told poor Crutchley he'd no money to pay him his forty pounds. He could have given it him then."

"Course he could, my lady, if he'd wanted to. He was a proper old dodger, was Mr. Noakes, a regular Artful Dodger."

"Charles Dickens!"

"That's right. There's an author what knew a bit about crooks, didn't he? A pretty rough place London must have been in those days, if you go by what he says. Fagin and all. But we wouldn't hang a man for being a pickpocket, not now. Well—and having sent the cheque, you just came on here the next week and left it to him?"

"Yes. Here's his letter, you see, saying he'd have everything ready. It's addressed to my agent. We really ought to have sent someone ahead to see to things, but the fact is, as I told you before, what with newspaper reporters and one thing and another—"

"They give us a lot of trouble, them fellows," said Mr. Kirk, sympathetically.

"When," said Harriet, "they gate-crash your flat and try to bribe your servants—"

"Fortunately, Bunter is sea-green incorruptible—"

"Carlyle," said Mr. Kirk, with approval. "*French Revolution*. Seems a good man, that Bunter. Head screwed on the right way."

"But we needn't have troubled," said Harriet. "We'll have them all on our backs now."

"Ah!" said Mr. Kirk. "That's what comes of being a public character. You can't escape the fierce light that beats upon—"

"Here!" said Peter, "that's not fair. You can't have Tennyson twice. Anyway, there it is and what's done—no, I may want Shakespeare later on. The ironical part of it is that we expressly told Mr. Noakes we were coming for peace and quiet and didn't want the whole thing broadcast about the neighbourhood."

"Well, he saw to that all right," said the Superintendent. "By George, you were making it easy for him, weren't you? Easy as pie. Off he could go, and no inquiry. Don't suppose he meant to go quite so far as he did go, all the same."

"Meaning, there's no chance of it's being suicide?"

"Not likely, is it, with all that money on him? Besides, the doctor says there's not a chance of it. We'll come to that later. About them doors, now. You're sure they were both locked when you arrived?"

"Absolutely. The front we opened ourselves with the latch-key, and the back—let me see—"

"Bunter opened that, I think," said Harriet.

"Better have Bunter in," said Peter. "He'll know. He never forgets anything." He called Bunter, adding, "What we want here is a bell."

"And you saw no disturbance, except what you've mentioned. Eggshells and such. No marks no weapon? Nothing out of its place?"

"I'm sure I didn't notice anything," said Harriet. "But there wasn't much light, and of course, we weren't looking for anything. We didn't know there was anything to look for."

"Wait a bit," said Peter. "Wasn't there something struck me this morning? I—no, I don't know. It was all upset for the sweep, you see. I don't know what I thought I—If there was anything, it's gone now. . . . Oh, Bunter! Superintendent Kirk wants to know was the back door locked when we arrived last night."

"Locked and bolted, my lord, top and bottom."

"Did you notice anything funny about the place at all?"

"Apart," said Bunter, warmly, "from the absence of those conveniences that we were led to expect, such as lamps and coal and food and the key of the house and the beds made up and the chimneys swept, and allowing further for the soiled crockery in the kitchen and the presence of Mr. Noakes's personal impedimenta in the bedroom—no, my lord. The house presented no anomalies nor incongruities of any kind that I was able to observe. Except—"

"Yes?" said Mr. Kirk, hopefully.

"I attached no significance to it at the time," said Bunter, slowly, as though he were admitting to a slight defection from duty, "but there were two candlesticks in this room, upon the sideboard. Both candles were burnt down to the socket. Burnt out."

"So they were," said Peter. "I remember seeing you clean out the wax with a pen-knife. Night's candles are burnt out."

The Superintendent, absorbed in the implications of Bunter's statement, neglected the challenge till Peter poked him in the ribs and repeated it, adding, "I knew I should want Shakespeare again!"

"Eh?" said the Superintendent. "Night's candles? *Romeo and Juliet*—not much o' that about this here. Burnt out? Yes. They must a-been alight when he was killed. After dark, that means."

"He died by candle-light. Sounds like the title of a highbrow thriller. One of yours, Harriet. When found, make a note of."

"Captain Cuttle," said Mr. Kirk, not to be caught napping again. "October 2nd—sun would be setting about half-past five. No, it was Summer Time. Say half-past six. I dunno as that gets us much further. You didn't see nothing lying about as might have been used for a weapon? No mallet or bludgeon, eh? Nothing in the way of a—"

"He's going to say it!" said Peter to Harriet, in a whisper.

"—in the way of a blunt instrument?"

"He's said it!"

"I've never really believed they did say it."

"Well, now you know."

"No," said Bunter, after a short meditation. "Nothing beyond the customary household utensils in their appropriate situations."

"Have we any idea," inquired his lordship, "what kind of a jolly old blunt instrument we are looking for? How big? What shape?"

"Pretty heavy, my lord, that's all I can say. With a smooth, blunt head. Meaning, the skull was cracked like an eggshell, but the skin hardly broken. So there's no blood to help us, and the worst of it is, we don't know, no more than Adam, whereabouts it all 'appened. You see, Dr. Craven says deceased—Here, Joe, where's that letter Doctor wrote out for me to send to the coroner? Read it out to his lordship. Maybe he'll be able to make it out, seein' he's had a bit of experience and more eddication than you or me. Beats me what doctors want to use them long words for. Mind you, it's educational; I don't say it isn't. I'll have a go at it with the dictionary afore I goes to bed and I'll know I'm learning something. But to tell you the truth, we don't have many murders and violent deaths hereabouts, so I don't get much practice in the technical part, as you might say."

"All right, Bunter," said Peter, seeing that the Superintendent had finished with him. "You can go."

Harriet thought Bunter seemed a little disappointed. He would doubtless have appreciated the doctor's educational vocabulary.

P.C. Sellon cleared his throat and began: "'Dear Sir—It is my duty to notify—'"

"Not there," interrupted Kirk. "Where it begins about deceased."

P.C. Sellon found the place and cleared his throat again: "'I may state, as the result of a superficial examination'—is that it, sir?"

"That's it."

"'That deceased appears to 'ave been struck with a 'eavy blunt instrument of some considerable superficies'—"

"Meaning, he said, by that," explained the Superintendent, "as it wasn't a little fiddlin' thing like the beak of a 'ammer."

"'On the posterior part of the'—I can't rightly make this out, sir. Looks to me like 'onion,' and that makes sense all right, only it don't sound like doctor's language."

"It couldn't be that, Joe."

"Nor it ain't 'geranium' neither—leastways, there's no tail to the G."

"'Cranium,' perhaps," suggested Peter. "The back of the skull."

"That'll be it," said Kirk. "That's where it *is*, anyhow, never mind what the doctor calls it."

"Yes, sir. 'A little above and beyond the left ear, the apparent direction of the blow being from behind downwards. An extensive fracture'—"

"Hullo!" said Peter. "On the left, from behind downwards.

That looks like another of our old friends."

"The left-handed criminal," said Harriet.

"Yes. It's surprising how often you get them in detective fiction. A sort of sinister twist running right through the character."

"It might be a back-handed blow."

"Not likely. Who goes about swotting people left-handed? Unless the local tennis-champion wanted to show off. Or a navvy mistook old Noakes for a pile that needed driving."

"A navvy'd have hit him plumb centre. They always do. You think they're going to brain the man who holds the thing up, but it never happens. I've noticed that. But there's another thing. My recollection of Noakes is that he was awfully tall."

"Quite right," said Kirk, "so he was. Six foot four, only he stooped a bit. Call it six foot two or three."

"You'll want a pretty tall murderer," said Peter.

"Wouldn't a long-handled weapon do? Like a croquet-mallet? or a golf club?"

"Yes, or a cricket-bat. Or a beetle, of course—"

"Or a spade—the flat side—"

"Or a gun-stock. Possibly even a poker—"

"It'd have to be a long, heavy one with a thick knob. I think there's one in the kitchen. Or even a broom, I suppose—"

"Don't think it'd be heavy enough, though it's possible. How about an axe or a pick—"

"Not blunt enough. They've got square edges. What other long things are there? I've heard of a flail, but I've never seen one. A lead cosh, if it was long enough. Not a sand-bag—they bend."

"A lump of lead in an old stocking would be handy."

"Yes—but look here, Peter! Anything would do—even a rolling-pin, always supposing—"

"I've thought of that. He might have been sitting down."

"So it might be a stone or a paper-weight like that one on the window-sill there."

Mr. Kirk started.

"Strewth!" he observed, "you're quick, you two. Not much

you miss, is there? And the lady's as smart as the gentleman."

"It's her job," said Peter. "She writes detective stories."

"Does she now?" said the Superintendent. "I can't say I reads a lot o' them, though Mrs. Kirk, she likes a good Edgar Wallace now and again. But I couldn't rightly call 'em a mellering influence to a man in my line. I read an American story once, and the way the police carried on—well, it didn't seem right to me. Here, Joe, hand me that there paper-weight, would you? Hi! Not that way! Ain't you never heard of finger-prints?"

Sellon, his large hands clasped round the stone, stood awkwardly and scratched his head with his pencil. He was a big, fresh-faced young man, who looked as though he would be better at grappling with drunks than measuring prints and reconstructing the time-table of the crime. At length he opened his fingers and brought the paper-weight balanced on his open palm.

"That won't take finger-prints," said Peter. "It's too rough. Edinburgh granite, from the look of it."

"It might a-done the bashing, though," said Kirk, "leastways, the underneath part, or this here rounded end. Model of a building, ain't it?"

"Edinburgh Castle, I fancy. It shows no signs of skin or hair or anything about it. Just a minute." He picked it up by a convenient chimney, examined its surface with a lens, and said, definitely, "No."

"Humph. Well. That gets us nowhere. We'll have a look at the kitchen poker presently."

"You'll find lots of finger-prints on that. Bunter's and mine, and Mrs. Ruddle's—possibly Puffett's and Crutchley's."

"That's the devil of it," said the Superintendent, frankly. "But none the more for that, Joe, you keep your fingers off anything what looks like a weapon. If you sees any of them things what his lordship and her ladyship here mentioned laying about, you just leave 'em be and shout till I come. See?"

"Yes, sir."

"To go back," said Peter, "to the doctor's report. I take it Noakes can't have bashed the back of his own head falling down the steps? He was an oldish man, wasn't he?"

"Sixty-five, my lord. Sound as a bell, though, as far as you can judge now. Eh, Joe?"

"That's a fact, sir. Boasted of it, he did. Talked large as Doctor said 'e was good for another quarter of a century. You ask Frank Crutchley. 'E 'heard 'im. Over at Pagford, in the Pig and Whistle. And Mr. Roberts wot keeps the Crown in the village—he've heard him many a time."

"Ah! well, that's as may be. It ain't never safe to boast. The boast of heraldry—well, I take it that'd be more in your lordship's line, but it all leads to the grave as Gray's Elegy has it. Still, he wasn't killed falling down the stairs, because there's a bruise on his forehead where he went down and hit the bottom step—"

"Oh!" said Peter. "Then he was alive when he fell?"

"Yes," said Mr. Kirk, a little put out by being anticipated. "That's what I was leading up to. But there again, that don't prove nothing, because seemin'ly he didn't die straight off. Accordin' to what Dr. Craven makes out—"

"Shall I read that bit, sir?"

"Don't bother with it, Joe. It's only a lot of rigmarole. I can explain to his lordship without all your onions and geraniums. What it comes to is this. Somebody 'it him and bust his skull, and he'd likely tumble down and lose consciousness—concussed, as you might say. After a bit, he'd come to, like as not. But he'd never know what hit 'im. Wouldn't remember a thing about it."

"Nor he would," said Harriet, eagerly. She knew that bit—in fact she'd had to expound it in her latest detective novel but one. "There'd be complete forgetfulness of everything immediately preceding the blow. And he might even pick himself up and feel all right for some time."

"Except," put in Mr. Kirk, who liked a literal precision, "for a sore head. But, generally speaking, that's correct, according to Doctor. He might walk about and do quite a bit for himself—"

"Such as locking the door behind the murderer?"

"*Exactly,* there's the trouble."

"Then," pursued Harriet, "he'd get giddy and drowsy,

wouldn't he? Wander off to get a drink or call for help and—"

Memory suddenly showed her the open cellar-door, yawning between the back-door and the scullery.

"And pitch down the cellar-steps and die there. That door was standing open when we arrived, I remember Mrs. Ruddle telling her Bert to shut it."

"Pity they didn't happen to look inside," grunted the Superintendent. "Not as it'd have done the deceased any good—he'd been dead long enough—but if you'd a-known you could have kept the house *in statu quo*, as they say."

"We *could*," said Peter, with emphasis, "but I don't mind telling you frankly that we were in no mood to."

"No," said Mr. Kirk, meditatively, "I don't suppose you were. No. All things considered, it would have been inconvenient, I see that. But it's a pity, all the same. Because, you see, we've got very little to go on and that's a fact. The poor old chap might a-been killed anywhere—upstairs, downstairs, in my lady's chamber—"

"No, no, Mother Goose," said Peter, hastily. "Not there, not there, my child, Felicia Hemans. Let us pass on. How long did he live after he was hit?"

"Doctor says," put in the constable, "'from half an hour to one hour, judging by the—the—hem-something or other.'"

"Haemorrhage?" suggested Kirk, taking possession of the letter. "That's it. Haemorrhagic effusion into the cortex. That's a good one."

"Bleeding in the brain," said Peter. "Good Lord—he had plenty of time. He may have been coshed outside the house altogether."

"But when do you suppose it all happened?" demanded Harriet. She appreciated Peter's effort to exonerate the house from all share in the crime, and was annoyed with herself for having betrayed any sensibility on the subject. It was distracting for him. Her tone, in consequence, was determinedly off-hand and practical.

"That," said the Superintendent, "is what we've got to find out. Some time last Wednesday night, putting what the doctor says with the rest of the evidence. After dark, if them candles are anything to go by. And that means—H'm! We'd better have this chap Crutchley in. Seems like he might have been the last person to see deceased alive."

"Enter the obvious suspect," said Peter, lightly.

"The obvious suspect is always innocent," said Harriet in the same tone.

"In books, my lady," said Mr. Kirk, with a little indulgent bow towards her, as who should say, "The ladies. God bless them!"

"Come, come," said Peter, "we must not introduce our professional prejudices into the case. How about it, Superintendent? Shall we make ourselves scarce?"

"That's as you like, my lord. I'd be glad enough if you'd stay; you might give me a bit of help, seeing as you know the ropes, so to speak. Not but what it'll be a kind of busman's holiday for you," he finished up, rather dubiously.

"That's what I was thinking," said Harriet. "A busman's honeymoon. Butchered to make a—"

"Lord Byron!" cried Mr. Kirk, a little too promptly. "Butchered to make a busman's—No, that don't seem right somehow."

"Try Roman," said Peter. "All right, we'll do our best. No objection to smoking in court, I take it. Where the devil did I put the matches?"

"Here you are, my lord," said Sellon. He produced a box and struck a light. Peter eyed him curiously, and remarked:

"Hullo! You're left-handed."

"For some things, my lord. Not for writing."

"Only for striking matches—and handling Edinburgh rock?"

"Left-handed?" said Kirk. "Why, so you are, Joe. I hope you ain't this tall, left-handed murderer what we're looking out for?"

"No, sir," said the constable, briefly.

"A pretty thing that'ud be, wouldn't it?" said his superior, with a hearty guffaw. "We shouldn't never hear the last of that. Now, you hop out and get Crutchley. Nice lad he is," he went on, turning to Peter as Sellon left the room. "'Ard working, but no Sherlock 'Olmes, if you follow me. Slow in the uptake. I sometimes think his heart ain't rightly in his work these days. Married too young, that's what it is, and started a family, which is a handicap to a young officer."

"Ah!" said Peter, "all this matrimony is a sad mistake."

He laid his hand on his wife's shoulder, while Mr. Kirk tactfully studied his note-book.

CHAPTER VIII

◆

£ s. d.

SAILOR: *Faith, Dick Reede, it is to little end:*
His conscience is too liberal, and he too
niggardly
To part from anything may do thee good. . . .

REEDE: *If prayers and fair entreaties will not serve,*
Or make no battery in his flinty breast,
I'll curse the carle, and see what that will do.

—*Arden of Feversham*

The gardener walked up to the table with a slightly belligerent air, as though he had an idea that the police were there for the sole purpose of preventing him from exercising his lawful right to obtain payment of forty pounds. He admitted, briefly, when questioned, that his name was Frank Crutchley and that he was accustomed to attend to the garden one day a week at Talboys for a stipend of five shillings per diem, putting in the rest of his time doing odd jobs of lorry-driving and taxi-work for Mr. Hancock at the garage in Pagford.

"Saving up, I was," said Crutchley, with insistence, "to get a garridge of my own, only for that there forty pound Mr. Noakes had off of me."

"Never mind that now," said the Superintendent. "That's gone west, that has, and it's no use crying over spilt milk."

Crutchley was about as much convinced by this assurance as were the Allies, on being informed by Mr. Keynes, after the conclusion of the Peace Treaty, that they might whistle for their indemnities, since the money was not there. It is impossible for human nature to believe that money is not there. It seems so much more likely that the money is there and only needs bawling for.

"He promised," affirmed Frank Crutchley, in a dogged effort to overcome Mr. Kirk's extraordinary obtuseness, "that he'd let me have it when I came today."

"Well," said Kirk, "I dare say he might have done, if somebody hadn't butted in and brained him. You ought to a-been smarter and got it out of him last week."

This could be nothing but stupidity. Crutchley explained patiently: "He hadn't got it then."

"Oh, hadn't he though?" said the Superintendent. "That's all you know about it."

This was a staggerer. Crutchley turned white.

"Cripes! you don't mean to tell me—"

"Oh, yes, he had," said Kirk. This information, if he knew anything about it, was going to loosen his witness's tongue for him and save a deal of trouble. Crutchley turned with a frantic look at the other members of the party. Peter confirmed Kirk's statement with a nod. Harriet, who had known days when the loss of forty pounds would have meant greater catastrophe than Peter could ever suffer by the loss of forty thousand, said sympathetically:

"Yes, Crutchley. I'm afraid he had the money on him all the time."

"What! He had the money? You found it on him?"

"Well, we did," admitted the Superintendent. "There's no call to make a secret of it." He waited for the witness to draw the obvious conclusion.

"Mean to say, if he hadn't been killed, I might have had my money?"

"If you could have got in before Mr. MacBride," said Harriet, with more honesty than consideration for Kirk's tactics. Crutchley, however, was not troubling his head about Mr. MacBride. The murderer was the man who had robbed him of his own, and he took no pains to conceal his feelings.

"God! I'll—I'll—I'll—I'd like to—"

"Yes, yes," said the Superintendent, "we quite understand that. And now's your opportunity. Any facts you can give us—"

"Facts! I've been done, that's what it is, and I—"

"Look here, Crutchley," said Peter. "We know you've had a rotten deal, but that can't be helped. The man who killed Mr. Noakes has done you a bad turn, and he's the man we're after. Use your wits and see if you can't help us to get even with him."

The quiet, incisive tone had its effect. A kind of illumination spread over Crutchley's features.

"Thank you, my lord," said Kirk. "That's about the size of it, and put very plain. Now, my lad, we're sorry about your money, but it's up to you to give us a hand. See?"

"Yes," said Crutchley, with an almost savage eagerness. "All right. What d'you want to know?"

"Well, first of all—when did you last see Mr. Noakes?"

"Wednesday evening, same as I said. I finished up my work just before six and come in here to do the pots; and when I'd done 'em he give me five bob, same as usual, and that's when I started askin' him for my forty quid."

"Where was that? In here?"

"No, in the kitchen. He always sat in there. I come out of here with the steps in my 'and—"

"Steps? Why the steps?"

"Why, for that there cactus and the clock. I wind the clock every week—it's an eight-day. I can't reach either on 'em without the steps. I goes into the kitchen, like I was saying, to put the steps away, and there he was. He give me my money—'arf a crown, and a bob, and two tanners and sixpence in coppers, if you want to be perticler, all out of different pockets.

He liked to make out he couldn't 'ardly lay 'and on a 'apenny, but I was used to that. And when he'd finished play-actin', I asks him for my forty pound. I want that money, I says—"

"Just so. You wanted the money for the garage. What did he say to that?"

"Promised he'd let me have it next time I come—that's today. I might a-known 'e never meant it. Wasn't the first time he'd promised, and then always 'ad some excuse. But he promised faithful, this time—the dirty old swine, and well he might, and he all set to skip with 'is pockets stuffed full of bank-notes, the bleeder."

"Come, come," said Kirk, reprovingly, with a deprecatory glance at her ladyship. "Mustn't use language. Was he alone in the kitchen when you went out?"

"Yes. He wasn't the sort people dropped in for a chat with. I went off then, and that's the last I see of him."

"You went off," repeated the Superintendent, while Joe Sellon's right hand travelled laboriously among the pothooks, "and left him sitting in the kitchen. Now, when—"

"No, I didn't say that. He followed me down the passage, talkin' about givin' me the money first thing in the morning, and then I 'eard 'im lock and bolt the door be'ind me."

"Which door?"

"The back door. He mostly used that. The front door was allus kep' locked."

"Ah! is that a spring lock?"

"No; mortice lock. He didn't believe in them Yale things. Don't take much to bust *them* off with a jemmy, he'd say."

"That's a fact," said Kirk. "So that means the front door could only be opened with a key—from inside or out."

"That's right. I should a-thought you'd a-seen that for yourself, if you'd looked."

Mr. Kirk, who had indeed examined the fastenings of both doors with some care, merely inquired:

"Was the front-door key ever left in the lock?"

"No; he kept it on his bunch. It ain't a big one."

"It certainly wasn't in the lock last night," volunteered

Peter. "We got in that way with Miss Twitterton's key, and the lock was perfectly free."

"Just so," said the Superintendent. "Was there any other spare key that you know of?"

Crutchley shook his head.

"Mr. Noakes wouldn't go 'andin' out keys by the bushel. Somebody might a-got in, you see, and pinched something."

"Ah! Well now, to get back. You left the house last Wednesday night—what time?"

"Dunno," said Crutchley, thoughtfully. "Must a-been getting on for twenty-past, I reckon. Anyway, it was ten past when I wound that there clock. And it keeps good time."

"It's right now," said Kirk, glancing at his watch. Harriet's wrist-watch confirmed this, and so did Joe Sellon's. Peter, after a blank gaze at his own watch, said "Mine's stopped," in a tone which might have suggested that Newton's apple had been observed to fly upward or a B.B.C. announcer heard to use a bawdy expression.

"Perhaps," suggested Harriet, practically, "you forgot to wind it up."

"I never forget to wind it up," said her husband, indignantly. "You're quite right, though; I did. I must have been thinking of something else last night."

"Very natural, I'm sure, in all the excitement," said Kirk. "Can you remember whether that there clock was going when you arrived?"

The question distracted Peter from his own lapse of memory. He dropped his watch back into his pocket unwound and stared at the clock.

"Yes," he said, finally. "It was. I heard it ticking, when we were sitting here, it was the most comfortable thing in the house."

"It was right, too," said Harriet. "Because you said something about its being past midnight and I looked, and it said the same as my watch."

Peter said nothing, but whistled a couple of bars almost inaudibly. Harriet remained imperturbable; twenty-four hours of matrimony had taught her that, if one was going to be disturbed by sly allusions to Greenland's coast or anything else, one might live in a state of perpetual confusion.

Crutchley said:

"Of course it was going. It's an eight-day, I tell you. And it was right enough this morning when I wound it. What's the odds, anyhow?"

"Well, well," said Kirk. "We'll take it then that you left here some time after 6.10 by that clock, which was right as near as makes no difference. What did you do next?"

"Went straight to choir practice. See here—"

"Choir practice, eh? Ought to be easy enough to check up on that. What time's practice?"

"Six-thirty. I was in good time—you can ask anybody."

"Quite so," agreed Kirk. "All this is rowtine, you know—getting the times straight and so on. You left the house not earlier than 6.10 and not later than—say 6.25, to let you get to the church at 6.30. Right. Now, *as* a matter of rowtine, what did you do after that?"

"Vicar asked me to drive his car over to Pagford for him. He don't like driving himself after lighting-up. He ain't so young as he was. I had me supper over there at the Pig and Whistle and had a look-on at the darts match. Tom Puffett can tell you. He was there. Vicar give him a lift over."

"Puffett a darts player?" inquired Peter, pleasantly.

"Ex-champion. And still throws a tidy dart."

"Ah! it's the power he puts behind it, no doubt. Black he stood as night, Fierce as ten furies, terrible as hell, And shook a dreadful dart."

"Ha, ha!" cried Kirk, taken unaware and immensely tickled. "That's good. Hear that, Joe? That's good, that is. Black? He was black enough last time I saw him, halfway up the kitchen chimney. And shook a dreadful dart—I must tell him that. Worst of it is, I don't suppose he ever heard of Milton. Fierce as—well, there, poor old Tom Puffett!"

The Superintendent waited to roll the jest over again on his tongue before returning to his inquiry.

"We'll see Tom Puffett presently. Did you bring Mr. Goodacre back?"

"Yes," said Crutchley, impatiently; he was not interested in John Milton. "Half-past ten I got him home, or just after. Then I went back to Pagford on my bike. I got in just on eleven and went to bed."

"Where do you sleep? Hancock's garage?"

"That's right. Along of their other chap, Williams. He'll tell you."

Kirk was in the middle of extracting further particulars about Williams, when in through the door the sooty face of Mr. Puffett poked itself.

"Excuse me," said Mr. Puffett, "but I can't do nothing with this 'ere pot. Will you 'ave the reverend's gun, my lord? or shall I fetch the ladders afore it gets dark?"

Kirk opened his mouth to reprove the intruder, but was suddenly overcome. "Black he stood as night," he muttered, joyfully. This new way of applying quotations, not to edification, seemed to have caught his fancy.

"Oh, dear," said Harriet. She glanced at Peter. "I wonder if we'd better leave it till tomorrow?"

"I don't mind telling you, me lady," observed the sweep, "Mr. Bunter's fair put out, thinkin' he'll have to cook dinner on that there perishin' oil-stove."

"I'd better come and talk to Bunter," said Harriet. She felt she could not bear to see Bunter suffer any more. Besides, the men would probably get on better without her. As she went out, she heard Kirk call Puffett into the room.

"Just a moment," said Kirk. "Crutchley here says he was at choir practice last Wednesday night from half-past six on. Do you know anything about that?"

"That's right, Mr. Kirk. We was both there. 'Arf-past six to 'arf-past seven. 'Arvest anthem. 'For 'Is mercies still endure, Ever faithful, ever sure.'" Finding his notes less powerful than usual, Mr. Puffett cleared his throat. "Been swallowing of the sut, that's what I've been doing of. 'Ever faithful, ever sure.' That's quite correct."

"And you see me round at the Pig, too," said Crutchley.

"'Course I did. I'm not blind. You dropped me there and took vicar on to the Parish 'All and come back not five minutes arter for your supper. Bread and cheese, you 'ad, and four and 'arf pints, 'cause I counted 'em. Drahnd yourself one o' these days, I reckon."

"Was Crutchley there all the time?" asked Kirk.

"Till closin'. Ten o'clock. Then we 'ad to go round and pick up Mr. Goodacre again. Whist-drive was over at 10, but we 'ad to wait gettin' on ten minutes while he 'ad a chat with old Miss Moody. 'Ow that woman do clack on, to be sure! Then 'e come back with us. That's right, ain't it, Frank?"

"That's right."

"And," pursued Mr. Puffett, with a large wink, "if it's me you've got your eye on, you can ask Jinny wot time I got 'ome. George, too. Real vexed, Jinny was, at me settin' down to tell George about the match. But there! She's expectin' 'er fourth and it makes 'er fratchetty-like. I tell her, it ain't no good blamin' her dad, but I reckon she gotter take it outer George somehow."

"Very good," said the Superintendent, "that's all I want to know."

"Right," said Mr. Puffett. "I'll be seein' about them ladders, then."

He retired promptly, and Kirk again turned to Crutchley.

"Well, that seems straight enough. You left—call it 6.20—and didn't come back that night. You left deceased alone in the house, with the back door locked and bolted and the front locked, so far as you know. How about the windows?"

"Shut and locked 'em all afore I went. Burglar-proof catches you can see they have. Mr. Noakes didn't set much store by fresh air."

"H'm!" said Peter. "He seems to have been a careful bird. By the way, Superintendent, did you find the front-door key on the body?"

"Here's his bunch," said Kirk.

Peter pulled Miss Twitterton's key from his pocket, looked over the bunch, picked out its counterpart and said, "Yes; here you are." He laid the two side by side on his palm, examined them thoughtfully with a lens, and finally handed the whole thing over to Kirk, remarking, "Nothing there, so far as I can see."

Kirk scrutinised the keys silently and then asked Crutchley:

"Did you come back here any time during the week?"

"No. Wednesday's my day. Mr. 'Ancock gives me Wednesday from eleven o'clock on. And Sundays, of course. But I wasn't here Sunday. I went to London to see a young lady."

"Are you a London man?" asked Peter.

"No, my lord. But I worked there once and I got friends there."

Peter nodded.

"And you can't give us any further information? Can't think of anybody who might have come to see Mr. Noakes that night? Anybody who might have had a grudge against him?"

"I might think o' plenty o' *them*," said Crutchley, with emphasis. "But nobody what you might call special."

Kirk was about to make a gesture of dismissal, when Peter put in a question.

"Do you know anything about a note-case Mr. Noakes lost some time ago?"

Kirk, Crutchley and Sellon all stared at him. Peter grinned.

"No; I wasn't born with second sight. Mrs. Ruddle was eloquent on the subject. What can you tell us about that?"

"I know he made a hell of a fuss about it, that's all. Ten pound he had in it—or so he said. If 'e'd a-lost forty pound like me—"

"That'll do," said Kirk. "Have we any information about that, Joe?"

"No, sir. Except it wasn't found. We made out he must have dropped it out of his pocket in the road."

"All the same," put in Crutchley, "he had new locks put on the doors and the windows done too. Two years ago, that was. You ask Ma Ruddle about it."

"Two years ago," said Kirk. "Well—it don't seem to have much connection with this here."

"It explains, perhaps," said Peter, "why he was so careful about locking up."

"Oh, yes, of course," agreed the Superintendent. "Well, all right, Crutchley. That'll do for the moment. Stay about in case you're wanted."

"It's my day here," said Crutchley. "I'll be workin' in the garden."

Kirk watched the door close behind him.

"It don't seem as if it could be him. Him and Puffett are alibis for one another."

"Puffett? Puffett is his own best alibi. You've only got to look at him. The man of upright soul and humour placid needs no blunt instrument nor prussic acid. Horace; Wimsey's translation."

"Then Puffett's word is enough to let out Crutchley. Not but what he mightn't have done it later on. Doctor only says, 'Dead only a week.' Suppose Crutchley did it the next day—"

"Not very likely. When Mrs. Ruddle came in the morning she couldn't get in."

"That's true. We'll have to check up the alibi with this chap Williams at Pagford. He might have come back and done the job after eleven."

"He might. Only remember, Noakes hadn't gone to bed. How about earlier—say, 6 o'clock, before he left?"

"Don't fit in with the candles."

"I was forgetting them. But you know, you could light candles at six o'clock on purpose to create that alibi."

"I suppose you could," agreed Kirk, with deliberation. He was apparently unused to dealing with criminals of so much subtlety as that would imply. He ruminated for a moment, and then suggested:

"But them eggs and that cocoa?"

"I've known even that done, too. I've known a murderer sleep in two beds and eat two breakfasts in order to lend verisimilitude to an otherwise unconvincing narrative."

"Gilbert and Sullivan," said the Superintendent, a little hopelessly.

"Mostly Gilbert, I fancy. It's more likely, if Crutchley did it, that it was done then, because I don't see old Noakes letting in Crutchley after dark. Why should he? Unless Crutchley *did* have a key after all."

"Ah!" said Kirk. He swivelled round heavily in his chair and looked Peter in the face:

"What was you looking for on them keys, my lord?"

"Traces of wax in the wards."

"Oh!" said Kirk.

"If a duplicate was made," went on Peter, "it was made within the last two years. Difficult to trace, but not impossible. Especially when people have friends in London."

Kirk scratched his head.

"That'll be a nice job," he said. "But see here. The way I look at it is this. If Crutchley did it, how did he come to miss all that money? That's the thing I can't get over. That don't look reasonable to me."

"You're quite right. It's the most puzzling thing about the case, whoever committed the murder. It almost looks as though it wasn't done for money. But it's not easy to see any other motive."

"That's the funny thing about it," said Kirk.

"By the way, if Mr. Noakes had had any money to leave, who would have come in for it?"

"Ah!" The Superintendent's face brightened. "We've got that. Found this bit of a will in that old desk in the kitchen." He produced the paper from his pocket and spread it out. "'After payment of my just debts—'"

"Cynical blighter! A fine fat legacy to leave anyone."

"'All I die possessed of to my niece and sole surviving relative, Agnes Twitterton.' That surprise you?"

"Not at all. Why should it?" But Kirk, slow as he seemed, had seen Peter's quick frown and now pressed home his advantage.

"When this Jew-bird, MacBride, started blowing the gaff, what did Miss Twitterton say?"

"Er—well!" said Peter, "she went off the deep end—naturally."

"Naturally. Seemed a bit of a blow to her, eh?"

"Not more than you might expect. Who witnessed the will, by the way?"

"Simon Goodacre and John Jellyfield. He's the doctor from Pagford. It's all in order. What did Miss Twitterton say when your man discovered the body?"

"Well, she shrieked a bit and so on, and went off into hysterics."

"Did she say anything particular, besides shrieking?"

Peter was conscious of a curious reluctance. Theoretically, he was quite as ready to hang a woman as a man, but the memory of Miss Twitterton, frenziedly clinging to Harriet, was disturbing to him. He was tempted to feel, with Kirk, that marriage was a handicap to a young officer.

"See here, my lord," said Kirk, his ox-eyes mild but implacable, "I've heard one or two things from these other people."

"Then," retorted Peter, "why don't you ask them?"

"I'm going to. Joe, ask Mr. MacBride to step here a minute. Now, my lord, you're a gentleman and you've got your feelings. I know all that, and it does you credit. But I'm a police-officer, and I can't afford to indulge in feelings. They're a privilege of the upper classes."

"Upper classes be damned!" said Peter. This stung him, all the more that he knew he deserved it.

"Now, MacBride," went on Kirk, cheerfully, "he's no class at all. If I asked you, you'd tell the truth, but it might 'urt you. Now I can get it out of MacBride, and it won't 'urt him in the least."

"I see," said Peter. "Painless extractions a specialty."

He walked up to the fire and kicked the logs moodily.

Mr. MacBride came in with great alacrity; his face expressed that the sooner all this was over, the sooner to Town. He had already given the police the details of the financial situation and was straining like a greyhound at the official leash.

"Oh, Mr. MacBride, there's just one other thing. Did you happen to notice what sort of effect the discovery of the body had upon the family and friends, so to speak?"

"Well," said Mr. MacBride, "they were upset. Who wouldn't be?" (A silly question to keep a man waiting about for.)

"Remember anything special said?"

"Oh, ah!" said Mr. MacBride. "I get you. Well, now, the gardener chap—he went as white as a sheet, he did—and the old gentleman was badly put about. The niece had hysterics—but *she* didn't seem as much surprised as the rest, did she?"

He appealed to Peter, who avoided his sharp eye by strolling over to the window and gazing out at the dahlias.

"What do you mean by that?"

"Well, when the servant came in and said they'd found Mr. Noakes, she yelled out at once, 'Oh! Uncle's dead!'"

"Did she now?" said Kirk.

Peter swung round on his heel.

"That's not quite fair, MacBride. Anybody could have told that from Bunter's manner. I know *I* could."

"Could you?" said MacBride. "You didn't seem in any hurry to believe it." He glanced at Kirk, who asked:

"Did Miss Twitterton say anything else?"

"She said, 'Uncle's dead and all the money's gone!' just like that. Then she had the jim-jams. Nothing like £ s. d. for going straight to the heart, is there?"

"Nothing," said Peter. "You, if I recollect rightly, asked whether they'd found any money on the corpse."

"Quite right," admitted Mr. MacBride. "He was no relation of mine, you see, was he?"

Peter, worsted at every thrust, lowered his weapon and admitted defeat.

"The legal profession," he said, "must present you with a comprehensive picture of Christian family life. What do you think of it?"

"Not much," replied Mr. MacBride, succinctly. He turned back to the table. "I say, Mr. Superintendent, are you going to want me any more? I've got to get back to Town."

"That's O.K. We've got your address. Good morning, Mr.

MacBride, and thanks very much."

As the door shut behind him, Kirk transferred his glance to Peter. "That right, my lord?"

"Quite right."

"Ah! well, I think we'll have to see Miss Twitterton."

"I'll get my wife to fetch her down," said Peter, and escaped. Mr. Kirk sat back in Merlin's seat and rubbed his hands thoughtfully.

"That's a real nice gentleman, Joe," said Mr. Kirk. "Straight out o' the top drawer. Pleasant and easy as kiss-me-'and. Well eddicated, too. But he sees which way the wind's blowing, and he don't like it. Small blame to him."

"But," objected the constable, "he can't think Aggie Twitterton coshed old Noakes on the 'ead with a mallet. She's a little slip of a thing."

"You never know, me lad. The female of the species is deadlier than the male. That's Rudyard Kipling. He knows that, though it's agin his upbringing to say so. Not but what he'd a-made it sound a lot better if he *had* said it, instead of leaving it to MacBride. But there! he couldn't lay tongue to it, I suppose. Besides, he knew well enough I'd have it out of MacBride in the end."

"Well, he ain't done her much good, as I can see."

"Them sort of feelings," pronounced Mr. Kirk, "commonly don't do much good, except to complicate things. But they're pretty, and, if taken the right way, 'armless. You got to learn to get round 'em, when you're dealing with gentry. And remember this: what they *don't* say is more important than what they *do* say, especially when they've got good brains, like this here gentleman has. He sees well enough that if Noakes was killed for what he had to leave—"

"But he hadn't nothing to leave."

"I know that. But *she* didn't. Aggie Twitterton didn't know. And *if* he was murdered for what he had to *leave*, that 'ud explain why the £600 wasn't took off the body. Maybe she didn't know it was there, and if she did, she didn't have to take it, because it'ud all be hers in the end. Use your 'ead, Joe Sellon."

* * *

Peter in the meantime had caught Mr. MacBride on the doorstep.

"How do you get back?"

"Lord knows," said Mr. MacBride, frankly. "I *came* by train to Great Pagford and took the bus on. If there's no bus handy I'll have to get a lift. I wouldn't have believed there were places like this, within fifty mile of London. Beats me how people can live in 'em. But it's all a matter of taste, ain't it?"

"Bunter can take you in the car to Pagford," said Peter. "They won't want him again for a bit. Sorry you should have been dumped into all this."

Mr. MacBride was grateful, and said so. "It's all in the day's work," he added. "You're the ones that come off worst, in one way, you and her ladyship. I never saw much to fancy in these three-by-four villages myself. Think it's the little woman, do you? Well, you can't be sure; but in our way of business we do have to keep our eyes peeled when it comes to relations, particularly if there's money in it. There's some people won't ever make a will—say it's like signing their own death-warrant. And they ain't so far out. But look here! This chap Noakes was pretty well up against it, wasn't he? He may have been doing some funny stuff on the side. I've known men get bumped off for other things besides money. Well, so long. My respects to her ladyship, and much obliged."

Bunter brought round the car and he hopped in, waving a friendly gesture. Peter caught Harriet, and explained what was wanted.

"Poor little Twitters," said Harriet. "Are you going to be there?"

"No. I'm going out for a breath of air. I'll come back presently."

"What's the matter? Kirk hasn't been unpleasant, surely?"

"Oh, no. He handled me with kid gloves on. Showed all the proper consideration for my rank and refinement and other inferiorities. My own fault, I asked for it. Oh, golly, here's the vicar. What does he want?"

"They asked him to come back. Go on out the back way, Peter. I'll tackle him."

Kirk and Sellon, from the window, had watched Mr. MacBride's departure.

"Hadn't I ought to fetch Aggie Twitterton down myself?" suggested Sellon. "His lordship will maybe tell his wife to give her the tip."

"The trouble with you, Joe," replied the Superintendent, "is, you ain't got no pussychology, as they call it. They wouldn't do a thing like that, neither of them. They ain't compounding no felonies nor yet obstructing the law. All that's the matter is, *he* don't like 'urting women and *she* don't like 'urting him. But they won't either on 'em put out a finger to stop it, because that sort of thing ain't done. And when things ain't done, they won't do 'em—and that's the long and the short of it."

Having thus laid down the code of behaviour for the nobility and gentry, Mr. Kirk blew his nose, and resumed his seat; whereupon the door opened to admit Harriet and Mr. Goodacre.

CHAPTER IX

◆

Times and Seasons

> *—Dost thou know what reputation is?*
> *I'll tell thee—to small purpose, since the instruction*
> *Comes now too late. . . .*
> *You have shook hands with Reputation,*
> *And made him invisible.*
>
> —John Webster, *The Duchess of Malfi*

The Rev. Simon Goodacre blinked nervously when confronted by the two officers drawn up, as it were, in battle-array, and

Harriet's brief announcement on her way upstairs that he had "something to say to you, Superintendent," did little to set him at ease.

"Dear me! Well. Yes. I came back to see if you wanted me for anything. As you suggested, you know, as you suggested. And to tell Miss Twitterton—but I see she is not here—Well, only that I had seen Lugg about the—er, dear me, the coffin. There must be a coffin, of course—I am not acquainted with the official procedure in such circumstances, but no doubt a coffin will have to be provided?"

"Certainly," said Kirk.

"Oh, yes, thank you. I had supposed so. I have referred Lugg to you, because I imagine the—the body is no longer in the house."

"It's over at the Crown," said the Superintendent. "The inquest will have to be held there."

"Oh, dear!" said Mr. Goodacre. "The inquest—oh, yes."

"The coroner's office will give all the usual facilities."

"Yes, thank you, thank you. Er—Crutchley spoke to me as I came up the path."

"What did he say?"

"Well—I think he thinks he might be suspected."

"What makes him think that?"

"Dear me!" said Mr. Goodacre. "I fear I am putting my foot in it. He didn't say he did think it. I only thought he might think it from what he said. But I assure you, Superintendent, that I can confirm his alibi in every particular. He was at choir practice from 6.30 to 7.30, and then he took me over to Pagford for the whist-drive and brought me back here at 10.30. So, you see—"

"That's all right, sir. If an alibi's wanted for them times, you and him's out of it."

"I'm out of it?" exclaimed Mr. Goodacre. "Bless my soul, Superintendent—"

"Only my joke, sir."

Mr. Goodacre seemed to find the joke in but poor taste. He replied, however, mildly:

"Yes, yes. Well, I hope I may assure Crutchley that it's all right. He's a young man of whom I have a very high opinion. So keen and industrious. You mustn't attach too much importance to his chagrin about the forty pounds. It's a considerable sum for a man in his position."

"Don't you worry about that, sir," said Kirk. "Very glad to have your confirmation of those times."

"Yes, yes. I thought I'd better mention it. Now, is there anything else I can do to help?"

"Thank you very much, sir; I don't know as there is. You spent Wednesday night at home, I take it, after 10.30?"

"Why, of course," said the vicar, not at all relishing this tendency to harp upon his movements. "My wife and my servant can substantiate my statement. But you scarcely suppose—"

"We ain't got to supposing things yet, sir. That comes later. This is all rowtine. You didn't call here at any time during the last week, by any chance?"

"Oh, no. Mr. Noakes was away."

"Oh! you knew he was away, did you, sir?"

"No, no. At least I supposed so. That is to say, yes. I called here on the Thursday morning, but got no answer, so I supposed he was away, as he sometimes was. In fact I fancy Mrs. Ruddle told me so. Yes, that was it."

"That the only time you called?"

"Dear me, yes. It was only a little matter of a subscription—in fact, that was what I came about today. I was passing by, and saw a notice on the gate asking for bread and milk to be delivered, so I supposed he had returned."

"Ah, yes. When you came on Thursday, you didn't notice anything funny about the house?"

"Goodness me, no. Nothing unusual at all. What would there be to notice?"

"Well—" began Kirk; but, after all, what could he expect this short-sighted old gentleman to notice? Signs of a struggle? Finger-prints on a door? Footmarks on the path? Scarcely. Mr. Goodacre would possibly have noticed a full-sized corpse, if he had happened to trip over it, but probably nothing smaller.

He accordingly thanked and dismissed the vicar, who, once more observing that he could fully account for Crutchley's movements and his own after half-past six, blundered vaguely out again, murmuring a series of agitated "Good afternoons" as he went.

"Well, well," said Kirk. He frowned. "What makes the old gentleman so sure those *are* the essential times. *We* don't know they are."

"No, sir," said Sellon.

"Seems very excited about it. It can't 'ardly be him, though, come to think of it, he's tall enough. He's taller nor what you are—pretty well as tall as Mr. Noakes was I reckon."

"I'm sure," said the constable, "it couldn't be vicar, sir."

"Isn't that just what I'm saying? I suppose Crutchley must a-got the idea of the times being important from us questioning him so close about them. It's a hard life," added Mr. Kirk, plaintively. "If you ask questions, you tell the witness what you're after; if you don't ask 'em, you can't find out anything. And just when you think you're getting on to something you come slap up against the Judges' Rules."

"Yes, sir," said Sellon, respectfully. He rose as Harriet led Miss Twitterton in, and brought forward another chair.

"Oh, please!" exclaimed Miss Twitterton, faintly. "Please don't leave me, Lady Peter."

"No, no," said Harriet. Mr. Kirk hastened to reassure the witness.

"Sit down, Miss Twitterton; there's nothing to be alarmed about. Now, first of all, I understand you know nothing about your uncle's arrangement with Lord Peter Wimsey—selling the house, I mean, and so on. No. Just so. Now, when had you seen him last?"

"Oh! not for—" Miss Twitterton paused and counted the fingers of both hands carefully—"not for about ten days. I looked in last Sunday after morning service. I mean, of course, last Sunday *week*. I came over you see, to play the organ for the dear vicar. It's a tiny church, of course, and *not* many people—nobody in Paggleham plays the organ, and of course

I'm delighted to help in any way—and I called on Uncle then and he seemed *quite* as usual, and—and that's the—the last time I saw him. Oh, dear!"

"Were you aware that he was absent from home ever since last Wednesday?"

"But he wasn't absent!" exclaimed Miss Twitterton. "He was here all the time."

"Quite so," said the Superintendent. "Did you know he was here, and not absent?"

"Of course not. He often goes away. He usually tells—I meant, told me. But it was quite an ordinary thing for him to be at Broxford. I mean, if I had known, I shouldn't have thought anything of it. But I didn't know anything about it."

"Anything about what?"

"About anything. I mean, nobody told me he wasn't here, so I thought he was here—and so he was, of course."

"If you'd been told the house was shut up and Mrs. Ruddle couldn't get in, you wouldn't have been surprised or uneasy?"

"Oh, no. It often happened. I should have thought he was at Broxford."

"You have a key for the front door, haven't you?"

"Oh, yes. And the back door, too." Miss Twitterton fumbled in a capacious pocket of the old-fashioned sort. "But I never use the back-door key because it's always bolted—the door, I mean." She pulled out a large key-ring. "I gave them both to Lord Peter last night—off this bunch. I always keep them on the ring with my own. They *never* leave me. Except last night, of course, when Lord Peter had them."

"H'm!" said Kirk. He produced Peter's two keys. "Are these the ones?"

"Well, they must be, mustn't they, if Lord Peter gave them to you."

"You haven't ever lent the front-door key to anybody?"

"Oh, *dear*, no!" protested Miss Twitterton. "Not *anybody*. If Uncle was away and Frank Crutchley wanted to get in on Wednesday morning, he *always* came to me and I went over with him and unlocked the door for him. Uncle was *ever* so particular. And besides, I should want to go myself and see that the rooms were all right. In fact, if Uncle William was at Broxford I used to come over *most* days."

"But on this occasion, you didn't know he was away?"

"No, I didn't. That's what I keep on telling you. I didn't know. So of course I didn't come. And he *wasn't* away."

"Exactly. Now, you're sure you've never left these keys about where they might be pinched or borrowed?"

"No, never," replied Miss Twitterton, earnestly—as though, thought Harriet, she asked nothing better than to twist a rope for her own neck. Surely she must see that the key to the house was the key to the problem; was it possible for any innocent person to be quite as innocent as that? The Superintendent ploughed on with his questions unmoved.

"Where do you keep them at night?"

"*Always* in my bedroom. The keys, and dear Mother's silver tea-pot and Aunt Sophy's cruet that was a wedding-present to grandpa and grandma. I take them up with me *every* night and put them on the little table by my bed, with the dinner-bell handy in case of fire. And I'm *sure* nobody could come in when I was asleep, because I always put a deck-chair across the head of the staircase."

"You brought the dinner-bell down when you came to let us in," said Harriet, vaguely corroborative. Her attention was distracted by the sight of Peter's face, peering in through the diamond panes of the lattice. She waved him a friendly gesture. Presumably he had walked off his attack of self-consciousness and was getting interested again.

"A deck-chair?" Kirk was asking.

"To trip up a burglar," explained Miss Twitterton, very seriously. "It's a *splendid* thing. You see, while he was getting all tangled up and making a noise, I should hear him and ring the dinner-bell out of the window for the police."

"Dear me!" said Harriet. (Peter's face had vanished—perhaps he was coming in.) "How dreadfully ruthless of you, Miss Twitterton. The poor man might have fallen over it and broken his neck."

"What man?"

"The burglar."

"But, dear Lady Peter, I'm trying to explain—there never *was* a burglar."

"Well," said Kirk, "it doesn't look as if anybody else could have got at the keys. Now, Miss Twitterton—about these money difficulties of your uncle's—"

"Oh, dear, oh, dear!" broke in Miss Twitterton, with unfeigned emotion. "I know *nothing* about those. It's terrible. It gave me *such* a shock. I thought—we *all* thought—Uncle was ever so well off."

Peter had come in so quietly that only Harriet noticed him. He remained near the door, winding his watch and setting it by the clock on the wall. Obviously he had come back to normal, for his face expressed only an alert intelligence.

"Did he make a will, do you know?" Kirk dropped the question out casually; the tell-tale sheet of paper lay concealed under his note-book.

"Oh, yes," said Miss Twitterton. "I'm sure he made a will. Not that it would have mattered, I suppose, because I'm the only one of the family left. But I'm certain he told me he'd made one. He always said, when I was worried about things—of course I'm *not* very well off—he always said, Now, don't you be in a hurry, Aggie. I can't help you now, because it's all tied up in the business, but it'll come to you after I'm dead."

"I see. You never thought he might change his mind?"

"Why, no. Who else *should* he leave it to? I'm the only one. I suppose now there won't be anything?"

"I'm afraid it doesn't look like it."

"Oh, dear! Was that what he meant when he said it was tied up in the business? That there wasn't any?"

"That's what it very often does mean," said Harriet.

"Then that's what—" began Miss Twitterton, and stopped.

"That's what, what?" prompted the Superintendent.

"Nothing," said Miss Twitterton, miserably. "Only something I thought of. Something private. But he said once something about being short and people not paying their bills. . . . Oh, what *have* I done? How ever can I explain—?"

"What?" demanded Kirk again.

"Nothing," repeated Miss Twitterton, hastily. "Only it sounds so silly of me." Harriet received the impression that this was not what Miss Twitterton had originally meant to say. "He borrowed a little sum of me once—not much—but of course I hadn't *got* much. Oh, dear! I'm afraid it looks dreadful to be thinking about money just now, but . . . I *did* think I'd have a little for my old age . . . and times are so hard . . . and . . . and . . . there's the rent of my cottage . . . and . . ."

She quavered on the verge of tears. Harriet said, confusedly:

"Don't worry. I'm sure something will turn up."

Kirk could not resist it. "Mr. Micawber!" he said, with a sort of relief. A faint echo behind him drew his attention to Peter, and he glanced round. Miss Twitterton hunted wildly for a handkerchief amid a pocketful of bast, pencils and celluloid rings for chickens' legs, which came popping out in a small shower.

"I'd counted on it—rather specially," sobbed Miss Twitterton. "Oh, I'm sorry. Please don't pay any attention."

Kirk cleared his throat. Harriet, who was as a rule good at handkerchiefs, discovered to her annoyance that on this particular morning she had provided herself only with an elegant square of linen, suitable for receiving such rare and joyful drops as might be expected on one's honeymoon. Peter came to the rescue with what might have been a young flag of truce.

"It's quite clean," he said, cheerfully. "I always carry a spare."

(The devil you do, said Harriet to herself; you are too well trained by half.)

Miss Twitterton buried her face in the silk and snuffled in a dismal manner, while Joe Sellon studiously consulted the back pages of his shorthand notes. The situation threatened to prolong itself.

"Shall you want Miss Twitterton any more, Mr. Kirk?" Harriet ventured, at length. "Because I really think—"

"Er—well," said the Superintendent. "If Miss Twitterton wouldn't mind telling us—just as a matter of form, you understand—where she was last Wednesday evening."

Miss Twitterton came quite briskly out of the handkerchief.

"But Wednesday is *always* choir practice," she announced, with an air of astonishment that anyone should ask so simple a question.

"Ah, yes," agreed Kirk. "And I suppose you'd quite naturally pop in on your uncle when that was over?"

"Oh, no!" said Miss Twitterton. "Indeed I didn't. I went home to supper. Wednesday's my busy night, you know."

"That so?" said Kirk.

"Yes, of course—because of market on Thursday. Why, I had half a dozen fowls to kill and pluck before I went to bed. It made me ever so late. Mr. Goodacre—he's always so kind—he's often said he knew it was inconvenient having the practice on Wednesday, but it happens to suit some of the men better, and so you see—"

"Six to kill and pluck," said Kirk, thoughtfully, as though estimating the time that this would take. Harriet looked at the meek Miss Twitterton in consternation.

"You don't mean to say you kill them yourself?"

"Oh, yes," said Miss Twitterton, brightly. "It's *so* much easier than you would think, when you're used to it."

Kirk burst into a guffaw, and Peter—seeing that his wife was disposed to attach overmuch importance to the matter—said in an amused tone:

"My dear girl, wringing necks is only a knack. It doesn't need strength."

He twisted his hands in quick pantomime, and Kirk, either genuinely forgetting the errand he was on, or of malice prepense, added:

"That's right." He tightened an imaginary noose about his own bull neck. "Wring 'em or string 'em up—it's the sharp jerk does it."

His head flopped sideways suddenly, sickeningly. Miss Twitterton gave a squeak of alarm; for the first time, perhaps, she realised where all this had to end. Harriet was angry, and her face showed it. Men; when they got together they were all alike—even Peter. For a moment he and Kirk stood together on the far side of a chasm, and she hated them both.

"Steady on, Super," said Wimsey; "we're alarming the ladies."

"Dear, dear, that'll never do." Kirk was jovial; but the brown ox-eyes were as watchful as the gray. "Well, thank you, Miss Twitterton. I think that's all for the moment."

"That's all right then." Harriet got up. "It's all over. Come along and see how Mr. Puffett is getting on with the kitchen chimney." She pulled Miss Twitterton to her feet and steered her out of the room. As Peter opened the door for them, she darted a reproachful glance at him, but, as with Lancelot and Guinevere, their eyes met and hers fell.

"Oh, and my lady!" said the Superintendent, unmoved, "would you be so kind as to tell Mrs. Ruddle she's wanted? We must get those times straightened out a bit," he went on, addressing himself to Sellon, who grunted and took out a knife to sharpen his pencil.

"Well," said Peter, in a tone almost of challenge, "she was quite frank about that."

"Yes, my lord. She knew about it all right. A little knowledge is a dangerous thing."

"Not knowledge—learning!" Peter corrected him peevishly. "A little *learning*—Alexander Pope."

"Is that so?" replied Mr. Kirk, not at all perturbed. "I must make a note of that. Ah! it don't look as though anybody else could have got hold of the keys, but you never know."

"I think she was telling the truth."

"Reckon there's several kinds of truth, my lord. There's truth as far as you knows it; and there's truth as far as you're asked for it. But they don't represent the whole truth—not necess*ar*ily. F'rinstance, I never asked that little lady if she locked up the house after someone else, did I? All I said was, When did you last see your fa—your uncle? See?"

"Yes, I see. Personally, I always prefer *not* to have a key to the house in which they've discovered the body."

"There's that about it," admitted Kirk. "But there's circumstances in which you might rather it was you than somebody else, if you take my meaning. And there's times when—What do you suppose she meant when she said, what had she done? Eh? Maybe it come to her then as she might have left them keys about, accidental on purpose. Or maybe—"

"That was about the money."

"So it was. And maybe she thought of something else she'd done as wasn't much use to her nor anybody, as it turned out. Something she was hiding there, if you ask me. If she'd been a man, I'd a-got it out of her fast enough—but women! They get howling and sniffing and you can't do nothing with them."

"True," said Peter; and felt in his turn a momentary resentment against the whole sex, including his wife. After all, hadn't she, more or less, ticked him off in the matter of neck-wringing? And the lady who now entered rubbing her hands on her apron and crying in self-important tones, "Did you want me, mister?"—there was nothing in *her* to thrill to music the silent string of chivalry. Kirk, however, knew where he was with the Mrs. Ruddles of this life and attacked the position confidently.

"Yes. We wanted to fix up a bit more exactly about the time of this murder. Now, Crutchley says he saw Mr. Noakes alive and well on Wednesday evening about twenty-past six. You'd gone home by then, I suppose?"

"Yes, I had. I only came to Mr. Noakes mornings. I wasn't in the 'ouse after dinner-time."

"And you came up next morning and found the place shut up?"

"That's right. I knocks 'ard on both doors—'im bein' a bit deaf I allus knocks 'ard, and then I gives a shout, like, under 'is bedroom winder, and then I knocks again and nothing come of it, and I says, Drat the man, I says, 'e's gone off to Broxford. Thinkin' he'd took the 10 o'clock bus the night before. There! I says, 'e might a-told me, and me not paid for last week, neither."

"What else did you do?"

"Nothing. There wasn't nothing *to* do. Only tell the baker and milkman not to call. And the noospaper. And leave word at the post-office to bring 'is letters down to me. Only there wasn't no letters, only two, and they was bills, so I didn't send 'em on."

"Ah!" said Peter. "That's the right way with bills. There, as the poet ungrammatically observes, there let them lay, like the goose with the golden eggs."

Mr. Kirk found this quotation confusing and refused to pursue it.

"Didn't you think of sending over to Miss Twitterton? She usually came down when Mr. Noakes was away. You must have been surprised not to see her."

"It ain't my place to go sendin' for people if they don't choose to come," said Mrs. Ruddle. "If Mr. Noakes 'ad wanted Aggie Twitterton, he could a-told her. Leastways, that's how I thought about it. 'Im bein' dead, I see now, o' course, he couldn't, but I wasn't to know that, was I? And I was inconvenienced enough, not 'avin' 'ad me money—you don't expect me to go sendin' two miles for people, as if I 'adn't enough to do without that. Nor wasting good stamps on 'em, neither. And what's more," said Mrs. Ruddle, with some energy, "I says to meself, if 'e ain't said nothing to me about goin', maybe 'e ain't told Aggie Twitterton, neither—and I ain't one to interfere in other folks' business, and don't you think it."

"Oh!" said Kirk. "Mean to say you thought he might have had some reason for wanting to leave the place quiet like?"

"Well, he might and he mightn't. That's the way I looked at it. See? Of course, there was my week's money—but there wasn't no 'urry for that. Aggie Twitterton 'ud a-paid me if I arst 'er."

"Of course," said Kirk. "I suppose you didn't think of asking her on Sunday when she came over to play the organ in church?"

"Me?" said Mrs. Ruddle, quite affronted. "I'm chapel. They're out and gone by the time we finish. Not but what I '*ave* been to church now and again, but there ain't nothing to show for it. Up and down, up and down, as if one's knees wasn't wore out with scrubbing on week-days, and a pore little bit of a sermon with no 'eart in it. Mr. Goodacre's a very kind gentleman and friendly to all, I ain't sayin' a word agin' 'im, but I'm chapel and always was, and that's the other end of the village, which by the time I was back here, they've all gone 'ome and Aggie Twitterton on 'er bicycle. So you see, I couldn't ketch 'er, not if I wanted ever so."

"Of course you couldn't," said Kirk. "All right. Well, you didn't try to let Miss Twitterton know. I suppose you mentioned in the village that Mr. Noakes was away?"

"I dare say I did," admitted Mrs. Ruddle. "It wasn't nothing out o' the way."

"You told us," put in Peter, "that he'd gone by the bus at 10 o'clock."

"So I thought 'e 'ad," said Mrs. Ruddle.

"And that would seem natural, so there would be no inquiries. Did anybody call for Mr. Noakes during the week?"

"Only Mr. Goodacre. I see him on Thursday morning, poking about the place, and he sees me and hollers out, 'Is Mr. Noakes away?' 'That's right,' I says, 'gone over to Broxford,' I says. And he says, 'I'll call another day,' he says. I don't remember as nobody come after him."

"Then last night," resumed Kirk, "when you let this lady and gentleman in, did you find everything as usual?"

"That's right. Exceptin' 'is dirty supper things on the table where 'e'd left them. 'E allus 'ad 'is supper at ar-par-seven reg'lar. Then 'e'd set in the kitchen with the paper till 'e come in 'ere for the noos at 9.30. Very reg'lar 'e was, a very reg'lar sort of man."

Kirk beamed. This was the kind of information he was looking for.

"So he'd had his supper. But his bed hadn't been slept in?"

"No, it 'adn't. But of course I put on clean sheets for the lady and gentleman. I 'ope I knows what's proper. Them," explained Mrs. Ruddle, anxious to make things clear, "wos the week-before's sheets, wot wos all dried and ready Wednesday, but I couldn't take 'em in, along of the 'ouse bein' shet up. So I 'ad them all put aside neat in me kitchen, and I didn't 'ave to do more than put them to the fire a minnit and there they wos, all aired and fit for the King and Queen of England."

"That helps us a lot," said Kirk. "Mr. Noakes ate his supper at 7.30, so presumably he was alive then." He glanced at Peter, but Peter was offering no further embarrassing suggestions about murderers who ate their victims' suppers, and the Superintendent was encouraged to proceed. "He didn't go to bed, so that gives us—When did he usually go to bed, Mrs. Ruddle, do you know?"

"Eleven o'clock, Mr. Kirk, reg'lar as clockwork, 'e'd switch off the wireless and I'd see 'is candle go upstairs to bed. I can see 'is bedroom from my back winder, plain enough."

"Ah! now, Mrs. Ruddle, just you cast your mind back to Wednesday night. Do you recollect seeing his candle go upstairs to bed?"

"Well, there!" exclaimed Mrs. Ruddle, "now you comes to mention of it, Mr. Kirk, I did not. Which I remember saying to my Bert only the next day, 'There,' I says, 'if I'd only kep' awake, I mighter known 'e'd gone off, alonger seein' 'is bedroom winder dark. But there!' I says, 'I was that wore out, I dropped off the moment me 'ead was on the piller."

"Oh, well," said Kirk, disappointed, "it don't really matter. Seeing as his bed wasn't slept in, it's likely he was downstairs when—"

(Thank God! thought Peter. Not in my lady's chamber.)

Mrs. Ruddle interrupted with a sharp screech.

"Oh, lor', Mr. Kirk! There now!"

"Have you thought of something?"

Mrs. Ruddle had, and her expression, as her eyes wandered from Kirk to Sellon and then to Peter, indicated that it was not only important but alarming.

"Why, of course. I dunno how it didn't come into me 'ead before, but I been that moithered with all these dretful things a-'appenin'. 'Course, come to think of it, if 'e wasn't off by the 'bus, then 'e must a-been dead afore 'ar-pas'-nine."

The constable's hand paused in its note-taking. Kirk said sharply:

"What makes you think that?"

"W'y, 'is wireless wasn't a-workin', and I says to Bert—"

"Just a minute. What's all this about the wireless?"

"W'y, Mr. Kirk, if Mr. Noakes 'ad been 'ere alive, 'e

wouldn't a-missed the 9.30 noos, not if it wos ever so. 'E set great store by the last noos, pore soul—though wot good it done 'im I *don't* know. And I recollects sayin' to Bert last Wednesday night as ever was, 'Funny thing,' I says, 'Mr. Noakes ain't got 'is wireless goin' tonight. That ain't like 'im,' I says."

"But you couldn't hear his wireless from your cottage with all these doors and windows shut?"

Mrs. Ruddle licked her lips.

"Well, I won't deceive you, Mr. Kirk." She swallowed, and then went on as volubly as ever; her eye avoided the Superintendent's and fixed itself on Joe Sellon's pencil. "I did jest run over 'ere a few minutes arter the 'arf-hour to borrer a drop of paraffin from 'is shed. And if the wireless 'ad bin on then I couldn't a-'elped 'earin' of it, for them walls at the back ain't only plaster, and 'e allus 'ad it a-roarin' powerful 'ard on account of bein' 'ard of 'earin'."

"I see," said Mr. Kirk.

"No 'arm," said Mrs. Ruddle, backing away from the table, "no 'arm in borrowin' a drop o' paraffin."

"Well," replied Kirk, cautiously, "that's neether here nor there. Nine-thirty news. That's on the National."

"That's right. He never troubled with the 6 o'clock."

Peter consulted Kirk with a glance, stepped over to the radio cabinet and raised the lid.

"The pointer," he observed, "is set to Regional."

"Well, if you ain't altered it since—" Peter shook his head, and Kirk continued. "Looks like he didn't have it on—not for the 9.30. H'm. We're getting there, aren't we? Whittling the time down. Line upon line, line upon line, here a little and there a little—"

"Isaiah," said Peter, shutting down the lid. "Or is it, more appropriately, Jeremiah?"

"Isaiah, my lord—and no call for Lamentations that I can see. That's pretty satisfactory, that is. Dead or unconscious at 9.30—last seen alive about 6.20—ate his supper at—"

"Six-twenty?" cried Mrs. Ruddle. "Go on! He was alive and kicking at 9 o'clock."

"What! How do you know? Why didn't you say so before?"

"Well, I thought you knowed it. You didn't ask. And 'ow do I know? 'Cause I seen 'im, that's why. 'Ere! wotter you gettin' at? Tryin' to put summat on me? You knows as well as I do 'e was alive at nine. Joe Sellon 'ere was a-talkin' to 'im."

Kirk gaped dumbfounded. "Eh?" he said, staring at the constable.

"Yes," muttered Sellon, dully, "that's right."

"'Course it is," said Mrs. Ruddle. Her small eyes gleamed with malicious triumph, behind which lurked an uneasy horror. "You don't catch me that way, Joe Sellon. I come in 9 o'clock from fetchin' a pail o' water, and I sees you plain as the nose on my face a-talkin' to him at this very winder. Ah! and I 'eard you, too. Usin' language—you did oughter be ashamed of yourself—not fit for a decent woman to listen to. I come up the yard—which you know where the pump is, and the only water fit to drink, bar you goes down to the village, Mr. Kirk, and always free permission to use the pump in the yard, without it's for washin', what I always uses rainwater on account of the woollens, and I 'ears you from the pump—yes, you may look! And I says to meself, 'Lor',' I ses, 'wotever is a-going on?' And I comes round the corner of the 'ouse and I sees you—*and* your 'elmet, so don't you go a-denying of it."

"All right, Ma," said Kirk, shaken, but sticking loyally by his subordinate. "Much obliged. That brings us pretty near the time. Nine o'clock, you say it was?"

"Near as makes no difference. My clock said ten past, but it gains a bit. But you ask Joe Sellon. If yer want to know the time, ask a p'leeceman!"

"Very good," replied the Superintendent. "We just wanted a bit of confirmation on that there point. Two witnesses are better than one. That'll do. Now, just you run along and—see here—don't you get shooting your mouth off."

"I'm sure," said Mrs. Ruddle, bridling, "I ain't one to talk."

"Certainly not," said Peter. "That's the last thing anybody would accuse you of. But you see, you're a very important witness—you and Sellon here—and there might be all sorts of people, reporters and so on, trying to wheedle things out of you. So you must be very discreet—just like Sellon—and come down sharp on them. Otherwise, you might make things difficult for Mr. Kirk."

"Joe Sellon, indeed!" said Mrs. Ruddle, contemptuously. "I can do as well as 'im any day. I 'ope I knows better than to go talking to newspaper fellows. A nasty, vulgar lot."

"Most unpleasant people," said Peter. He made for the door, driving her gently before him like a straying hen. "We know we can rely on you, Mrs. Ruddle, thou foster-child of Silence and slow Time. Whatever you do," he added earnestly, as he propelled her over the threshold, "don't say anything to Bunter—he's the world's worst chatterbox."

"Certainly not, my lord," said Mrs. Ruddle. The door closed. Kirk drew himself up in the big chair; his subordinate sat huddled, waiting for the explosion.

"Now, Joe Sellon. What's the meaning of this?"

"Well, sir—"

"I'm disappointed in you, Joe," went on Kirk, with more distress than anger in his puzzled voice. "I'm astonished. Mean to say you was there at nine o'clock talking to Mr. Noakes and you said nothin' about it. Ain't you got no sense of duty?"

"I'm sure I'm very sorry, sir."

Lord Peter Wimsey strolled over to the window. One does not interfere with another man ticking off his subordinate. All the same—

"*Sorry?* That's a nice word to use. You—a police-officer? With'oldin' important evidence? And say you're sorry?"

(Dereliction of duty. Yes—that was the first way it would strike one.)

"I didn't mean—" began Sellon. Then, furiously: "I didn't know that old cat had seen me."

"What the hell does it matter who saw you?" cried Kirk, with rising exasperation. "You ought to have told me first thing. . . . My God, Joe Sellon, I don't know what to make of you. Upon my word I don't. . . . You're *for* it, my lad."

The wretched Sellon sat twisting his hands together, finding no answer but a miserable mumble:

"I'm sorry."

"Now, look here," said Kirk, with a dangerous note in his voice. "What were you doing there, that you didn't want anybody to know about? . . . Speak up! . . . Wait a minute. Wait a minute." (He's seen it, thought Peter, and turned round.) "You're left-handed, ain't you?"

"Oh, my God, sir, my God! I never done it! I swear I never done it! 'Eaven knows I 'ad cause enough, but I never done it—I never laid a 'and on 'im—"

"Cause? What cause? . . . Come on, now. Out with it! What were you doing with Mr. Noakes?"

Sellon looked round wildly. At his shoulder stood Peter Wimsey with an inscrutable face.

"I never touched 'im. I never done nothing to 'im. If I was to die the next minute, sir, I'm innocent!"

Kirk shook his massive head, like a bull teased by gadflies.

"What were you doing up here at nine o'clock?"

"Nothin'," said Sellon, stubbornly. The excitement died out of him. "Only to pass the time of day."

"Time o' day!" echoed Kirk, with so much contempt and irritation that Peter nerved himself to interfere.

"Look here, Sellon," he said, in the voice that had induced many a troubled private to disclose his pitiful secrets. "You'd much better make a clean breast of it to Mr. Kirk. Whatever it is."

"This," growled Kirk, "is a nice thing, this is. A police-officer—"

"Go easy with him, Superintendent," said Peter. "He's only a youngster." He hesitated. Perhaps it would be easier for Sellon without an outside witness. "I'll push along into the garden," he said, reassuringly. Sellon turned in a flash.

"No, no! I'll come clean. Oh, my God, sir!—Don't go, my lord. Don't *you* go! . . . I've made a damn bloody fool of myself."

"We all do that at times," said Peter, softly.

"*You*'ll believe me, my lord. . . . Oh, God—this'll break me."

"I shouldn't wonder," said Kirk, grimly.

Peter glanced at the Superintendent, saw that he, too,

recognised the appeal to an authority older than his own, and sat down on the edge of the table.

"Pull yourself together, Sellon. Mr. Kirk's not the man to be hard or unjust to anybody. Now, what was it all about?"

"Well . . . that there note-case of Mr. Noakes's—what he lost—"

"Two years ago—well, yes, what happened to it?"

"I found it . . . I—I—he'd dropped it in the road—ten pound it had in it. I—my wife was desperate bad after the baby—doctor said she ought to have special treatment—I hadn't saved nothing—and the pay's not much, nor the allowance—I been a damned fool—I meant to put it back right away. I thought he could spare it, being well off. I know we're supposed to be honest, but it's a dreadful temptation in a man's way."

"Yes," said Peter. "A generous country expects a lot of honesty for two or three pounds a week." Kirk seemed incapable of speech, so he went on:

"And what happened about it?"

"He found out, my lord. I dunno how, but he did. Threatened to report me. Well, of course, that'd have been the end of me. Out of a job, and who'd a-given me work after that? So I 'ad to pay him what he said, to stop his tongue."

"Pay him?"

"That's blackmail," said Kirk, coming out of his stupefaction with a pounce. He spoke the words as though they were, somehow, a solution of this incredible situation. "It's an indictable offence. Blackmail. And compounding a felony."

"Call it what you like, sir—it was life and death to me. Five bob a week he been bleeding me for these last two years."

"Good God!" said Peter, disgusted.

"And I tell you, my lord, when I came in this room this morning and 'eard as he was dead, it was like a breath of 'Eaven to me. . . . But I didn't kill him—I swear I didn't. You do believe me? My lord, *you* believe me. I didn't do it."

"I don't know that I could blame you if you had."

"But I didn't," said Sellon, eagerly. Peter's face was noncommittal and he turned to Kirk again. "It's all right, sir. I know I been a fool—and worse—and I'll take my medicine;

but as sure as I stand here, I didn't kill Mr. Noakes."

"Well, Joe," said the Superintendent, heavily, "it's bad enough without that. You've been a fool and no mistake. We'll have to see about that later. You'd better tell us now what *did* happen."

"I came up to see him, to tell him I hadn't got the money that week. He laughed in my face, the old devil. I—"

"What time was this?"

"I came up here by the path and I looked in at that there window. The curtains wasn't drawn, and it was all dark. Only then I see him coming in from the kitchen with a candle in his hand. He holds the candle up to the clock there, and I see it was five minutes past nine."

Peter shifted his position and spoke quickly:

"You saw the clock from the window. You're sure?"

The witness failed to catch the note of warning, and said briefly: "Yes, my lord." He licked his lips nervously and went on:

"Then I taps on the window and he comes over and opens it. I tells him I ain't got the money and he laughs at me, nasty-like. 'All right,' he says, 'I'll report you in the morning.' So then I plucks up 'eart and says to him, 'You can't. It's blackmail. All this money you've been takin' off of me is blackmail, and I'll see you in the dock for it.' And he says, 'Money? you can't prove you ever paid me money. Where's your receipts? You got nothing on paper.' So I swears at him."

"No wonder," said Peter.

"'Get out,' he says, and slams the window shut. I tried the doors, but they was locked. So I gets out, and that's the last I seen of him."

Kirk drew a long breath.

"You didn't go into the house?"

"No, sir."

"Are you telling all the truth?"

"Honest to God, I am, sir."

"Sellon, are you sure?"

This time, the warning was unmistakable.

"It's God's truth, my lord."

Peter's face changed. He got up and walked slowly over to the fireplace.

"H'm, well," said Kirk. "I don't rightly know *what* to say. See here, Joe; you better go over straight away to Pagford and check up that alibi for Crutchley. See this man Williams at the garage and get a statement from him."

"Very good, sir," said Sellon in a subdued tone.

"I'll talk to you when you come back."

Sellon said again, "Very good, sir." He looked at Peter, who was gazing down at the burning logs and made no movement. "I hope you won't be too hard on me, sir."

"That's as may be," said Kirk, not unkindly. The constable went out, his big shoulders drooping.

"Well," said the Superintendent, "and what do you think of that?"

"It sounded straight enough—so far as the note-case was concerned. So there's a motive for you—a nice new motive, all a-growing and a-blowing. Widens the field a bit, doesn't it? Blackmailers don't as a rule stop at a single victim."

Kirk scarcely noticed this ingenious attempt to divert him from his natural suspicions. It was the breach of duty by one of his own officers that hurt him. Theft and the concealment of evidence—! He hammered on at this wretched worry, the angrier because it was the kind of thing that need not ever have occurred.

"Why couldn't the young fool have come to his sergeant, if he was short—or to me? This is the devil and all. Beats me altogether. I wouldn't have believed it."

"There are more things in heaven and earth," said Peter, with a kind of melancholy amusement.

"That's so, my lord. There's a lot of truth in *Hamlet*."

"Hamlet?" Peter's bark of harsh laughter astonished the Superintendent. "By God, you're right. Village or hamlet of this merry land. Stir up the mud of the village pond and the stink will surprise you." He paced the room restlessly. The light thrown on Mr. Noakes's activities had only confirmed his own suspicions, and if there was one sort of criminal whom he would have been ready to strangle with his bare hands, it was the blackmailer. Five shillings a week for two years. He could not doubt that part of the story; no man would so pile up the evidence against himself unless he were telling the truth. All the same—He stopped abruptly at Kirk's side.

"Look here!" he said. "You've had no *official* information about that theft, have you? And the money's been paid back—twice over."

Kirk fixed him with a steady eye. "It's easy enough for *you* to be soft-'earted, my lord. It ain't your responsibility."

This time the kid gloves were off, and Peter took it on the chin.

"Coo!" added Kirk, reflectively. "That there Noakes he must have been a proper old twister."

"It's a damned ugly story. It's enough to make a man—"

But it was not. Nothing was enough for that. "Oh, hell!" said Peter, beaten and exasperated.

"What's up?"

"Superintendent, I'm sorry for that poor devil, but—curse it—I suppose I've got to say it—"

"Well?"

Kirk knew that something was coming and braced himself to meet it. Force Peter's sort to the wall, and they will tell the truth. He had said so, and now his words were to be proved upon him, and he had got to take the punishment.

"That story of his. It sounded all right. . . . But it wasn't. . . . One bit of it was a lie."

"A lie?"

"Yes. . . . He said he never came into the house. . . . He said he saw the clock from that window. . . ."

"Well?"

"Well, I tried to do the same thing just now, when I was out in the garden. I wanted to set my watch. Well . . . it can't be done, that's all. . . . That damned awful cactus is in the way."

"What!"

Kirk sprang to his feet.

"I say, that infernal bloody cactus is in the way. It covers the face of the clock. You can't see the time from that window."

"You can't?"

Kirk darted towards the window, knowing only too well what he would find there.

"You can try it," said Peter, "from any point you like. It's absolutely and definitely impossible. You can *not* see the clock from that window."

CHAPTER X

♦

Four-Ale Bar

> *"What should I have done?" I cried, with some heat.*
> *"Gone to the nearest public-house. That is the centre of country gossip."*
>
> —Arthur Conan Doyle, *The Solitary Cyclist*

The police were out of the house by tea-time. Indeed the unhappy Kirk, having ascertained that by no dodging, stooping or standing on tip-toe could anyone obtain a sight of the clock-face from the window, found himself with but little zest to prolong his inquiries. He made the half-hearted suggestion that Noakes might have temporarily removed the cactus from its pot after 6.20 and replaced it before 9.30; but he could offer himself no plausible explanation of any such aimless proceeding. There was, of course, only Crutchley's word for it that the plant had been there at 6.20—if there was even that; Crutchley had mentioned watering it—he might have taken it down and left it for Noakes to put back. One could ask—but even as he made a note of this intention, Kirk felt little hope of any result. He examined the bedrooms in a dispirited way, impounded a number of books and papers from a cupboard and again examined Mrs. Ruddle about Sellon's interview with Noakes.

The result of all this was not very satisfactory. A note-book was discovered, containing, among other entries, a list of weekly payments, five shillings at a time, under the initials "J.S." This corroborated a story that scarcely needed corroboration. It also suggested that Sellon's frankness might be less a virtue than a necessity, since, had he suspected the existence of such a document, he would have realised that it was better to confess before being confronted with it. Peter's comment was, Why, if Sellon were the murderer, had he not searched the house for compromising papers? With this consideration Kirk tried hard to comfort himself.

There was nothing else that could be interpreted as evidence of blackmailing payments from anybody, though plenty of testimony going to show that Noakes's affairs were in an even worse state of confusion than had hitherto appeared. An interesting item was a bundle of newspaper cuttings and jottings in Noakes's hand, concerning cheap cottages on the west coast of Scotland—a country in which it is notoriously difficult to proceed for the recovery of civil debts contracted elsewhere. That Noakes had been the "proper twister" Kirk had supposed him was clear enough; unhappily, it was not *his* misdoings that needed proof.

Mrs. Ruddle was unhelpful. She had heard Noakes slam the window shut and seen Sellon retreat in the direction of the front door. Supposing that the show was over, she had hastened home with her pail of water. She thought she had heard a knocking at the doors a few minutes later, and thought, 'He's got some hopes!' Asked whether she had heard what the quarrel was about, she admitted with regret, that she had not, but (with a malicious grin) "supposed as Joe Sellon knew all about it." Sellon, she added, "often came up to see Mr. Noakes"—her own opinion, if Kirk wanted it, was that he was "a-trying to borrer money" and that Noakes had refused to lend any more. Mrs. Sellon was thriftless, everybody knew that. Kirk would have liked to ask her whether, having last seen Mr. Noakes engaged in a violent quarrel, she had had no qualms about his subsequent disappearance; but the question stuck in his throat. He would be saying in so many words that an officer of the law could be suspected of a murder; without better evidence he could not bring himself to do it. His next dreary job was to question the Sellons, and he was not looking forward to that.

In a mood of the blackest depression, he went off to interview the coroner.

In the meantime, Mr. Puffett, having cleared the kitchen chimney from above and assisted at the lighting of the fire, had taken his fee and gone home, uttering many expressions of sympathy and good will. Finally, Miss Twitterton, tearful but flattered, was conveyed to Pagford by Bunter in the car, with her bicycle perched "high and disposedly" upon the back seat. Harriet saw her off and returned to the sitting-room, where her lord and master was gloomily building a house of cards with a greasy old pack which he had unearthed from the what-not.

"Well!" said Harriet, in unnaturally cheerful tones, "they've gone. At last we are alone!"

"That's a blessing," said he, glumly.

"Yes; I couldn't have stood much more. Could you?"

"Not any more. . . . And I can't stand it now."

The words were not said rudely; he sounded merely helpless and exhausted.

"I wasn't going to," said Harriet.

He made no reply, seeming absorbed in adding the fourth storey to his structure. She watched him for a few moments, then decided he was best left alone and wandered upstairs to fetch pen and paper. She thought it might be a good thing to write a few lines to the Dowager Duchess.

Passing through Peter's dressing-room, she found that somebody had been at work there. The curtains had been hung, the rugs put down and the bed made up. She paused to wonder what might be the significance of this—if any. In her own room, the traces of Miss Twitterton's brief occupation had been removed—the eiderdown shaken, the pillows made smooth, the hot-water bottle taken away, the disorder of washstand and dressing-table set to rights. The doors and drawers left open by Kirk had been shut, and a bowl of chrysanthemums stood on the window-sill. Bunter, like a steam-roller, had passed over everything, flattening out all traces of upheaval. She got the things she needed and carried them down. The card house had reached the sixth storey. At the sound of her step, Peter started, his hand shook, and the whole flimsy fabric dissolved into ruins. He muttered something and began doggedly to rebuild it.

Harriet glanced at the clock; it was nearly five, and she felt she could do with some tea. She had coerced Mrs. Ruddle into putting the kettle on and doing some work; it could not take very long now. She sat down on the settle and began her letter. The news was not exactly what the Duchess would expect to receive, but it was urgently necessary to write something that she might get before the headlines broke out in the London papers. Besides, there were things Harriet wanted to tell her—things she would have told her in any case. She finished the first page and looked up. Peter was frowning; the house, risen once again to the fourth storey, was showing signs of imminent collapse. Without meaning to, she began to laugh.

"What's the joke?" said Peter. The tottering cards immediately slid apart, and he damned them fretfully. Then his face suddenly relaxed, and the familiar, sidelong smile lifted the corner of his mouth.

"I was seeing the funny side of it," said Harriet, apologetically. "This looks not like a nuptial."

"True, O God!" said he, ruefully. He got up and came over to her. "I rather think," he observed in a detached and dubious manner, "I am behaving like a lout."

"Do you? Then all I can say is, your notion of loutishness is exceedingly feeble and limited. You simply don't know how to begin."

He was not comforted by her mockery. "I didn't mean things to be like this," he said, lamely.

"My dear cuckoo—"

"I wanted it all to be wonderful for you."

She waited for him to find his own answer to this, which he did with disarming swiftness.

"That's vanity, I suppose. Take pen and ink and write it down. His lordship is in the enjoyment of very low spirits, owing to his inexplicable inability to bend Providence to his own designs."

"Shall I tell your mother so?"

"Are you writing to her? Good Lord, I never thought about it, but I'm dashed glad you did. Poor old Mater, she'll be horribly upset about it all. She's got it firmly into her head that to be married to her white-headed boy meant an untroubled elysium, world without end, amen. Strange, that one's own mother should know so little about one."

"Your mother is the most sensible woman I ever met. She has a much better grasp of the facts of life than you have."

"Has she?"

"Yes, of course. By the way, you don't insist on a husband's right to read his wife's letters?"

"Great heavens, no!" said Peter, horrified.

"I'm glad of that. It mightn't be good for you. Here's Bunter coming back; we may get some tea. Mrs. Ruddle is in such a state of excitement that she has probably boiled the milk and put the tea-leaves into the sandwiches. I ought to have stood over her till she'd finished."

"Blow Mrs. Ruddle!"

"By all means—but I expect Bunter is doing that already."

The precipitate entry of Mrs. Ruddle with the tea-tray gave weight to the supposition.

"Which," said Mrs. Ruddle, setting down her burden with a rattle on a small table before the fire, "I'd a-brought it before, if it wasn't the policeman from Broxford come a-busting in, jest as I was makin' of the toast. Me 'eart come into me mouth, thinkin' summink 'orrible 'ad 'appened. But it ain't only summingses from the coroner. Quite a bunch of 'em 'e 'ad in 'is 'and, and these 'ere is yours."

"Oh, yes," said Peter, breaking the seal. "They've been pretty quick. 'To wit—To Lord Peter Death Bredon Wimsey, By virtue of a Warrant under the Hand and Seal of John Perkins'—all right, Mrs. Ruddle, you needn't wait."

"Mr. Perkins the lawyer, that is," explained Mrs. Ruddle. "A very nice gentleman, so I'm told, though I ain't never seen 'im to speak to."

"'. . . one of His Majesty's coroners for the said county of Hertfordshire to be and appear before him on Thursday the tenth day of October' . . . you'll see him and hear him tomorrow all right, Mrs. Ruddle . . . 'at 11 o'clock in the forenoon precisely at the Coroner's Court at the Crown Inn situate in the parish of Paggleham in the said County; then and there to give Evidence and be examined on His Majesty's behalf, touching the death of William Noakes, and not to depart without leave.'"

"That's all very fine," observed Mrs. Ruddle, "but 'oo's to give my Bert 'is dinner? Twelve o'clock's 'is time, and I ain't a-goin' to see my Bert go 'ungry, not for King George nor nobody."

"Bert will have to get on without you, I'm afraid," said Peter, solemnly. "You see what it says: 'Herein fail not at your peril.'"

"Lor', now," said Mrs. Ruddle. "Peril of what, I should like to know?"

"Prison," said Peter, in an awful voice.

"Me go to prison?" cried Mrs. Ruddle, in great indignation. "That's a nice thing for a respectable woman."

"Surely you could get a friend to see to Bert's dinner," suggested Harriet.

"Well," said Mrs. Ruddle, dubiously, "maybe Mrs. 'Odges would oblige. But I'm thinkin' she'll want to come and 'ear wot's going on at the 'quest. But there! I dessay I could make a pie tonight and leave it out for Bert." She retreated thoughtfully to the door, returning to say, in a hoarse whisper:

"Will I 'ave to tell 'im about the paraffin?"

"I shouldn't think so."

"Oh!" said Mrs. Ruddle. "Not as there's anything wrong in borrowin' a drop of paraffin, w'en it's easy replaced. But them there pleecemen do twist a woman's words so."

"I shouldn't think you need worry," said Harriet. "Shut the door, please, as you go out."

"Yes, my lady," said Mrs. Ruddle; and vanished with unexpected docility.

"If I know anything about Kirk," said Peter, "they'll adjourn the inquest, so it shouldn't take very long."

"No. I'm glad John Perkins has been so prompt—we shan't get such a crowd of reporters and people."

"Shall you mind the reporters very much?"

"Not nearly as much as you will. Don't be so tragic about it, Peter. Make up your mind that the joke's on us, this time."

"It's that, right enough. Helen's going to make a grand cockadoodle over this."

"Well, let her. She doesn't look as though she got much fun out of life, poor woman. After all, she can't alter the facts. I mean, here I am, you know, pouring out tea for you—from a chipped spout, admittedly—but I'm here."

"I don't suppose she envies you that job. I'm not exactly Helen's cup of tea."

"She'd never enjoy any tea—she'd always be thinking about the chips."

"Helen doesn't allow chips."

"No—she'd insist on silver—even if the pot was empty. Have some more tea. I can't help its dribbling into the saucer. It's the sign of a generous nature, or an overflowing heart, or something."

Peter accepted the tea and drank it in silence. He was still dissatisfied with himself. It was as though he had invited the woman of his choice to sit down with him at the feast of life, only to discover that his table had not been reserved for him. Men, in these mortifying circumstances, commonly find fault with the waiter, grumble at the food and irritably reject every effort to restore pleasantness to the occasion. From the worst exhibitions of injured self-conceit, his good manners were sufficient to restrain him, but the mere fact that he knew himself to be in fault made it all the more difficult for him to recover spontaneity. Harriet watched his inner conflict sympathetically. If both of them had been ten years younger, the situation would have resolved itself in a row, tears and reconciling embraces; but for them, that path was plainly marked, NO EXIT. There was no help for it; he must get out of his sulks as best he could. Having inflicted her own savage moods upon him for a good five years, she was in no position to feel aggrieved; compared with herself, indeed, he was making a pretty good showing.

He pushed the tea-things aside and lit cigarettes for both of them. Then, rubbing fretfully upon the old sore, he said:

"You show commendable patience with my bad temper."

"Is that what you call it? *I've* seen tempers in comparison with which you'd call that a burst of heavenly harmony."

"Whatever it is, you are trying to flatter me out of it."

"Not at all." (Very well, he was asking for it; better use shock tactics and carry the place by assault.) "I'm only trying to tell you, in the nicest possible manner, that provided I were with you, I shouldn't *greatly* mind being deaf, dumb, halt, blind and imbecile, afflicted with shingles and whooping-cough, in an open boat without clothes or food, with a thunderstorm coming on. But you're being painfully stupid about it."

"Oh, my dear!" he said, desperately, and with a very red face, "what the devil am I to say to that? Except that I shouldn't mind anything either. Only I can't help feeling that it's I that have somehow been idiot enough to launch the infernal boat, call up the storm, strip you naked, jettison the cargo, strike you lame and senseless and infect you with whooping-cough and—what was the other thing?"

"Shingles," said Harriet, drily; "and it isn't infectious."

"Crushed again." His eyes danced, and all of a sudden her heart seemed to turn right over. "O ye gods! render me worthy of this noble wife. All the same, I have a strong suspicion that I am being managed. I should resent it very much, if I were not full of buttered toast and sentiment—two things which, as you may have noticed, tend to go together. And that reminds me—hadn't we better get the car out and run over to Broxford for dinner? There's sure to be some sort of pub there, and a little fresh air may help to blow the bats out of my belfry."

"That's rather a good idea. And can't we take Bunter? I don't believe he's had anything to eat for years."

"Still harping on my Bunter! I myself have suffered many things for love, very like this. You may have Bunter, but I draw the line at a *partie carrée*. Mrs. Ruddle shall not come tonight. I observe the Round Table rule—to love one only and cleave to her. One at a time, I mean, of course. I will not pretend that I have never been linked up before, but I absolutely refuse to be coupled in parallel."

"Mrs. Ruddle can go home to bake her pies. I'll just finish my letter and then we can post it in Broxford."

But Bunter respectfully requested to be omitted from the party—unless, of course, his lordship required his services. He would prefer, if permitted, to utilise the leisure so kindly placed at his disposal in a visit to the Crown. He should be interested to make the acquaintance of some of the local inhabitants, and, as for his supper, Mr. Puffett had been so good as to hint that there was pot luck waiting for him at his house whenever he might care to step in and partake of it.

"Which means," said Peter, interpreting the decision to Harriet, "that Bunter wants to get a side-line through the local gossip on the late Noakes and all his household. In addition, he would like to establish diplomatic relations with the publican, the coal-merchant, the man who grows the best vegetables, the farmer who happens to have cut down a tree and can oblige with logs, the butcher who hangs his meat longest, the village carpenter and the man who does a job about the drains. You'll have to put up with me. Nothing is ever gained by diverting Bunter from his own mysterious ends."

The bar of the Crown was remarkably full when Bunter made his way in. No doubt the unobtrusive presence of the late Mr. Noakes behind a locked door lent a special body to the mild and bitter. At the entrance of the stranger, the voices, which had been busy, fell silent, and glances, at first directed to the door, were swiftly averted and screened behind lifted tankards. This was fully in accordance with etiquette. Bunter saluted the company with a polite "Good evening," and asked for a pint of old ale and a packet of Players. Mr. Gudgeon the landlord fulfilled the order with a dignified leisure, observing, as he changed a ten-shilling note, that the day had been fine. Bunter assented to this proposition, saying further that the country air was agreeable after Town. Mr. Gudgeon remarked that a-many London gentlemen had been known to say the same thing, and inquired whether this was his customer's first visit to that part of the country. Bunter said that though he had frequently passed through the district he had never stayed there before, and that Paggleham seemed to be a pretty spot. He also volunteered the information that he was Kentish by birth. Mr. Gudgeon said, Indeed? they grew hops there, he believed. Bunter admitted that this was so. A very stout man with one eye intervened at this point to say that his wife's cousin lived in Kent and that it was all 'ops where he was. Bunter said there were hops where his mother lived; he himself knew little about hops, having been brought up in London from the age of five. A thin man with a lugubrious countenance said he supposed that there gallon of beer he'd had off Mr. Gudgeon last June came from Kent. This appeared to be a reference to some standing jest, for the bar laughed appreciatively, and much chaff was bandied about, till the thin man closed the discussion by saying, "All right, Jim; call it 'ops if it makes you feel any better."

During this exchange the customer from London had quietly retired to a window-seat, taking his pint with him. The conversation turned upon football. At length, however, a plump woman (who was, in fact, no other than Mrs. Ruddle's friend, Mrs. Hodges) remarked, with that feminine impulsiveness which rushes in where the lords of creation fear to tread:

"You lost a customer, seemin'ly, Mr. Gudgeon."

"Ah!" said Mr. Gudgeon. He darted a look towards the window-seat, but it encountered only the back of the stranger's head. "Where one goes another comes, Mrs. Hodges. 'Tain't much I'll be losing on the beer."

"You're right," said Mrs. Hodges. "Nor nobody else, neither. But is it true as 'e was put away a-purpose?"

"That's as may be," replied Mr. Gudgeon, cautiously. "We'll be hearin' tomorrow."

"And *that* won't do no 'arm to the trade, I reckon," observed the one-eyed man.

"Dunno about that," retorted the landlord. "We'll 'ave to close the 'ouse till it's over. 'Tis only decent. And Mr. Kirk's particular."

A scrawny woman of uncertain age piped up suddenly:

"Wot's 'e look like, George? Can't you let us 'ave a peep at 'im?"

"'Ark at Katie!" exclaimed the lugubrious man, as the landlord shook his head. "Can't let a man alone, dead or alive."

"Go on, Mr. Puddock!" said Katie; and the bar laughed again. "You're on the jury, ain't you? You gets a front seat free."

"We don't 'ave to view the body these days," Mr. Puddock corrected her. "Not without we ask to. 'Ere's George Lugg; you better ask 'im."

The undertaker came out of the inner room, and all eyes were turned to him.

"When's the funeral to be, George?"

"Friday," said Mr. Lugg. He ordered a tankard of bitter and added to a young man who now came out, locking the door behind him and handing the key to Mr. Gudgeon:

"You better get started, Harry. I'll be along in two ticks. We'll want to close him down after the inquest. He'll go till then."

"Ay," said Harry. "'Tis fine, sharp weather." He called for a half-pint, took it down briskly, and went out, saying, "See you presently, then, Dad."

The undertaker became the centre of a small circle, ghoulishly intent upon descriptive detail. Presently the voice of the irrepressible Mrs. Hodges was raised:

"And by what Martha Ruddle says, them as didn't 'ave 'is custom 'ull lose least by 'im."

"Ah!" said a small man with a fringe of sandy hair and a shrewd eye. "I've 'ad me doubts. Too many irons in that fire, I reckon. Not as I've a lot to grumble at. I don't let no books run beyond the month, and I got me money—allus exceptin' that there collar of bacon as 'e made trouble about. But it's like that there 'Atry and these other big companies as goes bust—you puts money out o' one thing into another, till you don't rightly know wot you've got."

"That's right," said the one-eyed man. "Allus investin' in things, 'e wos. Too clever be 'alf."

"And a 'ard bargain 'e did drive," said Mrs. Hodges. "Dear, oh, dear! Remember when 'e lent my poor sister that bit o' money? Crool, it was, wot she 'ad to pay. And makin' 'er sign away all her furniture."

"Well, 'e never made much on the furniture," said the sandy man. "A soakin' wet day that was, w'en they come up for sale. Tom Dudden 'ad 'em over at Pagford, and there wasn't a soul there but the dealers."

An ancient man with long grey whiskers raised his voice for the first time:

"Ill-gotten goods never thrive. 'Tis in Scripture. Because he hath oppressed and forsaken the poor, because he hath violently taken away a house which he builded not—ah! and the furniture, too—therefore shall no man look for his goods. In the fulness of his sufficiency shall he be in straits—ain't that so, Mr. Gudgeon?—He shall flee from the iron weapon—ay—but there ain't no good fleein' when the 'and of the Lord is agin the wicked man. There's a curse upon 'im, and we 'ave lived to see it fulfilled. Wasn't there a gentleman came down from London this morning with a writ agin 'im? In the same pit that 'e digged for others is 'is foot taken. Let the extortioner consume all that he hath—'tis writ so—Ah! let 'is children be vagabonds and beg their bread—"

"There, there, Dad!" said the innkeeper, seeing that the old gentleman was becoming excited, "'e ain't got no children, praise be."

"That's true," said the one-eyed man "but 'e 'ave got a niece. It'll be a sad come-down for Aggie Twitterton. Wonderful set up, she allus wos, thinkin' there was money comin' to 'er."

"Well," said Mrs. Hodges, "them as gives themselves airs above other folks don't deserve nothin' but disappointments. 'Er dad wasn't only Ted Baker's cowman when all's said and done, and a dirty, noisy, foul-mouthed fellow in 'is drink, wot's more, as there ain't no call to be proud on."

"That's right," said the old man. "A very violent man. Beat 'is pore wife something crool, 'e did."

"If you treat a man like dirt," opined the one-eyed man, "'e'll act dirty. Dick Twitterton was a decent sort enough till 'e tuk it into 'is 'ead to marry the schoolmistress, with 'er airs and lah-di-dah ways. 'Wipe yer boots on the mat,' she says to 'im, 'afore you comes into the parlour.' Wot's the good of a wife like that to a man w'en 'e comes in mucky from the beasts an' wantin' 'is supper?"

"Good-lookin' feller, too, wasn't he?" said Katie.

"Now, Katie!" said the lachrymose man, reprovingly. "Yes, 'e wos a well set-up man, wos Dick Twitterton. That's wot the schoolmistress fell for, you see. You be keerful o' that soft 'eart o' yours, or it'll get you into trouble."

More chaff followed upon this. Then the undertaker said:

"None the more for that, I'm sorry for Aggie Twitterton."

"Bah!" said the lachrymose man, "*she's* all right. She've got 'er 'ens an' the church organ, and she don't do so bad. Gettin' a bit long in the tooth now, but a man might go farther and fare wuss."

"Well, there, Mr. Puddock!" cried Mrs. Hodges. "Don't say as you're thinkin' o' makin' an offer."

"'E's a one to talk, ain't he?" said Katie, delighted to get her own back. The old man chimed in solemnly:

"Now, do 'ee look where you're goin', Ted Puddock. There's bad blood o' both sides in Aggie Twitterton. 'Er mother was Willium Noakes's sister, don't 'ee forgit that; and Dick Twitterton, 'e was a violent, God-forsaking man, a swearer and a sabbath-breaker—"

The door opened to admit Frank Crutchley. He had a girl with him. Bunter, forgotten in his corner, summed her up as a lively young person, with an up-and-coming eye. The couple appeared to be on affectionate, not to say intimate terms, and Bunter gained the impression that Crutchley was seeking consolation for his losses in the linked arms of Bacchus and Aphrodite. He stood the young lady a large port (Bunter shuddered delicately) and submitted with good humour to a certain amount of chaff when he offered drinks all around.

"Come into a fortune, 'ave you, Frank?"

"Mr. Noakes 'ave left 'im 'is share of liabilities, that's what it is."

"Thought you said your speckilations 'ad gone wrong."

"Ah, that's the way wi' these 'ere capitalists. Every time they loses a million they orders a case o' champagne."

"'Ere, Polly, don't you know better 'a to go about with a chap wot speckilates?"

"She thinks she'll learn 'im better w'en 'e's bringin' the money 'ome to 'er."

"And so I would," said Polly, with some vigour.

"Ah! thinkin' o' gettin' spliced, you two?"

"No charge for thinkin'," said Crutchley.

"'Ow about the young lady in London, Frank?"

"Which one's that?" retorted Crutchley.

"'Ark at 'im! 'E've got so many 'e don't know 'ow to keep count on 'em."

"You watch your step, Polly. Maybe 'e's married three times a'ready."

"I *should* worry," said the girl, with a toss of the head.

"Well, well, after buryin' comes a weddin'. Tell us w'en it's to be, Frank."

"I'll 'ave ter save up for the parson's fee," said Crutchley, good temperedly, "seein' me forty pounds gone west. But it was almost worth it, to see old Aggie Twitterton's face. 'Ow! Uncle's dead and the money's gone!' she said. 'Ow, and 'im that rich—'oo'd a-thought it?' Silly old cow!" Crutchley laughed contemptuously. "'Urry up with your port, Polly, if you want us to get over in time for the big picture."

"So that's what you're after. Ain't.goin' into no mourning for old Mr. Noakes, is yer, from the looks of it?"

"'Im?" said Crutchley. "No fear, the dirty old twister. There'll be more pickings out o' me lord than ever there was out of '*im*. Pocket full o' bank-notes and a nose like a cheese-faced rabbit—"

"Hey!" said Mr. Gudgeon, with a warning glance.

"His lordship will be much obliged to you, Mr. Crutchley," said Bunter, emerging from the window-seat.

"Sorry," said Crutchley, "didn't see you was there. No offence meant. A joke's a joke. What'll you take, Bunter?"

"I'll take no liberties from anyone," said that gentleman, with dignity. "Mr. Bunter to you, if you please. And by the way, Mr. Gudgeon, I was to ask you kindly to send up a fresh nine-gallon cask to Talboys, the one that's there being the property of the creditors, as we understand."

"Right you are," said the landlord, with alacrity. "When would you like it?"

"First thing tomorrow," replied Bunter, "and another dozen of Bass while it settles. . . . Ah, Mr. Puffett, good evening! I was just thinking of looking you up."

"You're welcome," said Mr. Puffett, heartily. "I jest came along to fetch up the supper-ale, George being called out. There's a cold pie in the 'ouse and Jinny'll be glad to see you. Make it a quart, then, Mr. Gudgeon, if you please."

He handed a jug over the counter, which the landlord filled, saying as he did so to Bunter:

"That's all right, then. It'll be up at ten o'clock and I'll step round and tap it for you."

"I am much obliged to you, Mr. Gudgeon. I shall attend personally to its reception."

Crutchley had seized the opportunity to go out with his young woman. Mr. Puffett shook his head.

"Off to them pictures again. Wot I says is, they things are unsettlin' the girls' minds nowadays. Silk stockin's and all. You wouldn't a-seen that in my young days."

"Ah! come now," said Mrs. Hodges. "Polly hev' been walkin' out wi' Frank a good while now. 'Tis time 'twere settled between 'em. She's a good girl, for all she's saucy in her ways."

"Made up 'is mind, hev' he?" said Mr. Puffett. "Thought 'e was set on 'avin' a wife from London. But there! maybe 'e thinks she won't 'ave 'im, now 'e's lost 'is forty pound. Ketch 'em on the rebound, as they say—that's 'ow they makes marriages these days. A man may do all 'e likes, there's some lass gets 'im in the end, for all 'is runnin' and dodgin' like a pig in a lane. But I likes to see a bit o' money into the bargain—there's more to marriage, as they say, than four bare legs in a bed."

"'Ark at 'im!" said Katie.

"Or legs in silk stockings, neither," said Mr. Puffett.

"Well, Tom," said Mrs. Hodges, comfortably, "you're a

widow-man with a bit o' money, so there's a chance for some on us yet."

"Is there?" retorted Mr. Puffett. "Well, I give yer leave to try. Now, Mr. Bunter, if you're ready."

"Is Frank Crutchley a native of Paggleham?" inquired Bunter, as they walked away up the road, slowly, so as not to set the beer all of a froth.

"No," said Mr. Puffett. "He came here from London. Answered an advertisement of Mr. 'Ancock's. Been here six or seven year now. I don't fancy 'e's got no parents. But 'e's a pushin' young fellow, only all the girls is arter 'im, which makes it 'ard for 'im to settle. I'd a-thought 'e'd more sense than to take up with Polly Mason—serious-like, I mean. 'E was allus set to look for a wife as could bring 'im a bit. But there! Say what you like before'and, a man proposes and a woman disposes on 'im for good an' all, and then it's too late to be careful. Look at your good gentleman—I dessay, now, there was a-many rich young ladies arter 'im. And maybe he said he didn't want none on 'em. And 'ere 'e is on 'is 'oneymoon, and from what they was a-tellin' the Reverend, not a wealthy young lady neither."

"His lordship," said Mr. Bunter, "married for love."

"I thought as much," said Mr. Puffett, shifting the jug to his other hand. "Ah, well—he can afford it, I dessay."

At the conclusion of a pleasant and, on the whole, profitable evening, Mr. Bunter congratulated himself on a number of things attempted and done. He had ordered the beer; he had put (through Mr. Puffett's Jinny) a nice duck in hand for the following day, and Mr. Puffett knew a man who could send round three pound of late peas in the morning. He had also engaged Mr. Puffett's son-in-law to deal with the leak in the copper and mend two broken panes in the scullery. He had found out the name of a farmer who cured his own bacon and had written and posted to London an order about coffee, potted meats and preserves. Before leaving Talboys he had assisted Mrs. Ruddle's Bert to bring the luggage upstairs, and he now had his lordship's wardrobe arranged, as fittingly as might be, in the cupboards at his disposal. Mrs. Ruddle had made up a bed for him in one of the back rooms, and this, though of minor importance, brought with it a certain satisfaction. He went round stoking all the fires (observing with pleasure that Mrs. Ruddle's friend's husband, Mr. Hodges, had delivered the logs as requested). He laid out his lordship's pyjamas, gave a stir to the bowl of lavender in her ladyship's bedroom, and straightened the trifling disorder which she had left on the toilet-table, whisking away a few grains of powder and putting the nail-scissors back in their case. He noticed, with approval, an absence of lipstick; his lordship had a particular dislike of pink-stained cigarette-ends. Nor, as he had before thankfully observed, did her ladyship enamel her nails to the likeness of blood-stained talons; a bottle of varnish there was, but it was barely tinted. Quite good style, thought Bunter, and gathered up a pair of stout shoes for cleaning. Down below, he heard the car draw up to the door and stand panting. He slipped out by the Privy Stair.

"Tired, Domina?"

"Rather tired—but much better for the run. Such a terrific lot seems to have happened lately, hasn't it?"

"Like a drink?"

"No, thanks. I think I'll go straight up."

"Right you are. I'm only going to put the car away."

Bunter, however, was already dealing with this. Peter walked round to the shed and listened to what he had to say.

"Yes; we saw Crutchley and his young woman in Broxford. When the heart of a man is oppressed with cares, and so on. Have you taken up the hot water?"

"Yes, my lord."

"Then cut along to bed. I can look after myself for once. The grey suit tomorrow, with your permission and approval."

"Entirely appropriate, my lord, if I may say so."

"And will you lock up? We must learn to be householders, Bunter. We will presently purchase a cat and put it out."

"Very good, my lord."

"That's all then. Good night, Bunter."

"Good night, my lord, and thank you."

When Peter knocked at the door, his wife was sitting by the fire, thoughtfully polishing her nails.

"I say, Harriet, would you rather sleep with me tonight?"

"Well—"

"I'm sorry; that sounded a little ambiguous. I mean, do you feel any preference for the other room? I won't make a nuisance of myself if you're feeling fagged. Or I'll change rooms with you if you'd rather."

"That's very sweet of you, Peter. But I don't think you ought to give way to me when I'm merely being foolish. Are you going to turn out one of these indulgent husbands?"

"Heaven forbid! Arbitrary and tyrannical to the last degree. But I have my softer moments—and my share of human folly."

Harriet rose up, extinguished the candles and came out to him, shutting the door behind her.

"Folly seems to be its own reward," said he. "Very well. Let us be foolish together."

CHAPTER XI

♦

Policeman's Lot

ELBOW: *What is't your worship's pleasure I shall do with this wicked caitiff?*

ESCALUS: *Truly, Officer, because he hath some offences in him that thou wouldest discover if thou couldst, let him continue in his courses till thou knowest what they are.*

—William Shakespeare, *Measure for Measure*

The distressful Mr. Kirk had in the meantime spent a strenuous evening. He was a slow-thinking man and a kindly one, and it was with reluctance and expenditure of severe mental labour that he hammered out a procedure for himself in this unusual situation.

His sergeant having returned to drive him over to Broxford, he sank back in the passenger's seat, his hat pulled over his eyes and his thoughts revolving silently in this squirrel-cage of mystification. One thing he saw clearly: the coroner must be persuaded to take as little evidence as possible at the inquest and adjourn *sine die* pending further investigation. Fortunately, the law now provided for such a course, and if only Mr. Perkins would not be sticky, everything might pass off very well. The wretched Joe Sellon would have, of course, to speak of seeing Mr. Noakes alive at nine o'clock; but with luck he would not have to go into details about the conversation. Mrs. Ruddle was the stumbling-block: she liked to use her tongue—and then, there was that unfortunate business of Aggie Twitterton's hens, which had left her with a grudge against the police. Also, of course, there was the awkward fact that one or two people in the village had wagged their heads when Mr. Noakes lost his pocketbook, and had hinted that Martha Ruddle might know something about it; she would not readily forgive Joe Sellon for that misunderstanding. Could one, without actually uttering threats or using improper methods, suggest that over-informativeness in the witness-box might involve an inquiry into the matter of paraffin? Or was it safer merely to hint to the coroner that too much talk from Martha would tend to hamper the police in the execution of their duty?

("Half a mo', Blades," said the Superintendent, aloud, at this point in his meditations. "What's that chap doing, obstructing the traffic like that?—Here, you! don't you know better than to park that lorry of yours on a blind corner? If you want to change your wheel you must go further along and get her onto the verge. . . . All right my lad, that's quite enough of that. . . . Let's have a look at your license. . . .")

As for Joe Sellon . . . This business of parking on bends, now, he wouldn't have it. A dashed sight more dangerous than fast driving by a man who knew how to drive. The police liked to be fair; it was the magistrates who were obsessed by miles per hour. All corners should be approached dead slow—all right, because there might be some fool sitting in the middle of the road; but equally, nobody should sit in the middle of the road, because there might be some fool coming round the corner. The thing was fifty-fifty, and the blame should be distributed fifty-fifty; that was only just. In a routine matter like that, it was easy to see one's way. But Joe Sellon, now . . . Well, whatever happened, Joe must be taken off the Noakes case p.d.q. It wasn't proper to have him investigating it as things were. Why, come to think of it, Mrs. Kirk had been reading a book only the other day, in which one of the police in charge of the case turned out actually to have done the murder. He distinctly remembered laughing, and saying, "It's wonderful what these writer-fellows think of." That Lady Peter Wimsey, who wrote these books—she'd be ready enough to believe a tale like that. So, no doubt, would other people.

("Was that Bill Skipton getting over the stile, Blades? Seemed a bit anxious to avoid notice. Better keep your eye on him. Mr. Raikes has been complaining about his birds—shouldn't wonder if Bill was up to his old tricks again."

"Yes, sir.")

It all went to show that an officer couldn't take too much trouble about getting to know his men. A kindly inquiry—a word in season—and Sellon wouldn't have got himself into this jam. How much did Sergeant Foster know about Sellon? One must look into that. Rather a pity in a way, that Foster was a bachelor and a tee-totaller and belonged to a rather strict sect of Plymouth Brethren or something. A most trustworthy officer, but not very easy for a young fellow to confide in. Perhaps one ought to give more attention to these traits of character. Handling men was born in some people—this Lord Peter, for instance. Sellon had never seen him before, yet he was readier to explain himself to *him* than to his own superior officer. One couldn't resent that, of course; it was only natural. What was a gentleman for, except to take your difficulties to? Why, look at the old squire and his lady, when Kirk was a lad—everybody in and out of the big house all day with their troubles. That sort was dying out, more's the pity. Nobody could go to this new man that had the place now—for one thing, half the time he wasn't there, and for another, he'd always lived in a town and didn't understand the way things worked in the country. . . . But how Joe could be such a blamed fool as to tell his lordship a lie—which was the one thing that sort of gentleman would never overlook; you could see his face change when he heard it. You needed a pretty good reason for telling a lie to a gentleman that was taking an interest in you—and, well, the reason you might have didn't bear thinking of.

The car drew up before Mr. Perkins's house, and Kirk heaved himself out with a deep sigh. Maybe Joe was telling the truth after all; he must look into that. Meanwhile, do the thing that's nearest—was that Charles Kingsley or Longfellow?—and, dear, dear, it just showed you what happened when lame dogs were left to get over stiles on their own three legs.

The coroner proved amenable to the suggestion that, in view of investigations now proceeding, based on information received, the inquest should be kept as formal as possible. Kirk was glad Mr. Perkins was a lawyer; medical coroners sometimes took the oddest views of their own importance and legal powers. Not that the police were anxious for any curtailing of the coroner's privileges; there were times when an inquest came in very handy to elicit information which couldn't be got any other way. The silly public liked to make a fuss about the feelings of witnesses, but that was the public all over—always shouting they wanted to be protected and always getting in your way when you tried to do it for them. Wanting it both ways. No, there was no harm in coroners, only they ought to put themselves under police guidance, that was the way Kirk looked at it. Anyhow, Mr. Perkins didn't seem eager to cause trouble; he had a bad cold, too, and would be all the better pleased to keep things short. Well, that was that. Now about Joe Sellon. Better look in at the station first and see if there was anything special needed attending to.

The first thing handed to him when he got there was Joe

Sellon's own report. He had interviewed the man Williams, who asserted positively that Crutchley had come in to the garage just before eleven and gone immediately to bed. The two men shared a room, and Williams's bed was between Crutchley's and the door. Williams said he didn't think he could have failed to wake up if Crutchley had gone out during the night, because the door squeaked badly on its hinges. He was a light sleeper. As a matter of fact he had woken up, about 1 o'clock, with a fellow blowing his horn and knocking at the garage door. Turned out to be a commercial vehicle with a leaking feed, called for repairs and petrol. Crutchley had been asleep then, because Williams saw him when he lit his candle and went down to deal with the vehicle. The window was a small dormer—nobody could get out and down that way, and there were no marks of anybody's having done so.

That seemed all right—but in any case, it didn't amount to anything, since Noakes *must* have been dead before 9.30, as it seemed. Unless Mrs. Ruddle was lying. And she had no cause to lie, so far as Kirk could see. She had gone out of her way to mention her presence in the paraffin-shed, and she wouldn't do that for nothing. Unless she was telling lies on purpose to get Sellon into trouble. Kirk shook his head: that would be a big assumption to make. Still, lies or no lies, it was a good thing to check all alibis as closely as possible, and this one appeared to be sound. Always supposing Joe Sellon wasn't lying again. Confound it! when it came to not being able to trust your own men. . . . No doubt about it, Joe must come off this case. And what was more, for form's sake he would have to get Williams's evidence checked again and confirmed—a nuisance, and a waste of time. He asked where Sellon was and learned that, having waited a little in the hope of seeing the Superintendent, he had gone off back to Paggleham about an hour ago. They must have missed him on the road, then, somehow. Why hadn't he come to Talboys?—oh, drat Joe Sellon!

Anything else? Nothing much. P.C. Jordan had been called on to deal with a customer at the Royal Oak, who had used insulting language and behaviour to the landlord with conduct tending to provoke a breach of the peace; a woman had reported the loss of a handbag containing 9*s.* 4*d.*, the return half of a ticket, and a latch-key; the sanitary inspector had been in about a case of swine-fever at Datchett's farm; a child had fallen into the river off the Old Bridge, and been dexterously retrieved by Inspector Goudy, who happened to be passing at the time; P.C. Norman had been knocked off his bicycle by a Great Dane under insufficient control and had sprained his thumb; the Noakes affair had been reported by telephone to the Chief Constable, who was in bed with influenza, but wanted an immediate and detailed report in writing; instructions had come through from headquarters that the Essex County Constabulary wanted a sharp lookout kept for a tramping youth aged about seventeen (description) suspected of breaking and entering a house at Saffron Walden (particulars) and stealing a piece of cheese, an Ingersoll watch and a pair of garden-shears valued at three shillings and sixpence, and thought to be making his way through Herts; there was a summons wanted for a chimney afire in South Avenue; a householder had complained about a barking dog; two lads had been brought in for playing at crown and anchor on the steps of the Wesleyan Chapel, and Sergeant Jakes had very competently tracked down and brought to book the miscreant who had improperly rung the fire-alarm on Monday evening: a nice, quiet day. Mr. Kirk listened patiently, distributed sympathy and praise where they were due, and then rang up Pagford and asked for Sergeant Foster. He was out at Snettisley, about that little burglary. Yes, of course. Well, thought Kirk, as he appended his careful signature to a number of routine documents, Datchett's farm was in the Paggleham district; he'd put young Sellon on to that; he couldn't do himself much harm over swine-fever. He telephoned instructions that Sergeant Foster was to report to him as soon as he returned and then, feeling empty, went over to his own quarters to enjoy, as best he might, a supper of beefsteak pie, plum-cake and a pint of mild ale.

He was just finishing, and feeling a little better, when Sergeant Foster arrived, self-congratulatory about the progress of the burglary, righteously dutiful about being summoned to

Broxford when he ought to have been partaking of his evening meal, and coldly critical of his superior's taste in liquor. Kirk never found it easy to get on with Foster. There was, to begin with, this air of teetotal virtue; he disliked having his evening pint referred to as "alcohol." Then, Foster, though much subordinate to him in rank, was more refined in speech; he had been educated at a bad grammar-school instead of a good elementary school, and never misplaced his h's—though, as for reading good literature or quoting the poets, he couldn't do it and didn't want to. Thirdly, Foster was disappointed; he had, somehow, always missed the promotion he felt to be his due—an excellent officer, but just somehow lacking in something or the other, he could not understand his comparative failure, and suspected Kirk of having a down on him. And fourthly, Foster never did anything that was not absolutely correct; this, perhaps, was his real weakness, for it meant that he lacked imagination, both in his work and in handling the men under him.

Kirk, feeling oddly at a disadvantage, in spite of his age and position, waited till Foster had said all he had to say about the Snettisley burglary, and then laid before him the full details of the Talboys affair. The outline of it, Foster of course knew already, since Paggleham was in the Pagford district. In fact, Sellon's original report had come through to him, only ten minutes after the report from Snettisley. Being unable to be in two places at once, he had then rung up Broxford and asked for instructions. Kirk had told him to proceed to Snettisley; he (Kirk) would personally take charge of the murder. This was just the way Kirk was always standing between him and anything important. On his return to Pagford, he had found a curiously unsatisfactory report from Sellon—and no Sellon, nor any news of him. While he had been digesting this, Kirk had sent for him. Well, here he was: he was ready to listen to anything the Superintendent had to tell him. Indeed, it was really time he *was* told something.

He did not, however, like what he was told. And it seemed to him, as the disgraceful narrative boomed on, that he was being blamed—for what? For not acting as a wet-nurse to Joe

Sellon's baby, apparently. That was very unfair. Did the Superintendent expect him personally to examine the household budget of every village constable in the Pagford area? He ought to have seen that this young man had "something on his mind"—well, he liked that. Constables were always getting things on their minds—mostly young women, if it wasn't professional jealousies. He had quite enough to do with the men at the Pagford police-station; when it came to married police-officers in small villages, they ought surely to be supposed capable of looking after themselves. If they couldn't keep themselves and their families on the very generous pay and allowance then they ought not to have families. He had seen Mrs. Sellon—a shiftless girl, he thought, pretty before she was married, and dressed in cheap finery. He distinctly remembered warning Sellon against wedding her. If, when Sellon got into financial difficulties he had come to him (as, he quite agreed, he should have done) he would have reminded Sellon that nothing else was to be expected when one flouted the advice of one's superior officer. He would also have pointed out that, by knocking off beer and tobacco, a considerable saving of money might be effected, in addition to the saving of one's soul—always supposing Sellon took any interest in that immortal part of himself. When he (Foster) had been a constable, he had put away a considerable sum of his pay every week.

"Kind hearts," Kirk was saying, "are more than coronets; him as said that lived to wear a coronet himself. Mind you, I ain't saying as you been any way neglectful of your dooty—but it do seem a pity as a young fellow should have his career broke, all for want of a bit of 'elp and guidance. Not to speak of this other suspicion which it's to be hoped won't come to anything."

This was more than Foster could stomach in silence. He explained that he had offered help and guidance at the time of Sellon's marriage; it had not been well received. "I told him he was doing a foolish thing and that that girl would be the ruin of him."

"Did you?" said Kirk, mildly. "Well, then, perhaps it's no wonder he didn't turn to you when he was in a fix. I dunno as I would myself in his place. You see, Foster, when a young fellow's made up his mind, it ain't no good calling the young woman names. You only alienates him and puts yourself in a position where you can't do no good. When I was courtin' Mrs. K., you don't think I'd have 'eard a word agen her, not from the Chief Constable himself. Not likely. Just you put yourself in his place."

Sergeant Foster said briefly that he couldn't put himself in the place of making a fool of himself over a bit of skirt—still less could he understand taking other people's money, defection from duty and failure to make proper reports to one's superior officer.

"I couldn't make head or tail of the report Sellon sent in. He dropped it in, didn't seem able to give a proper account of himself to Davidson, who was on duty at the station, and now he's off somewhere and can't be found."

"What's that?"

"He's not been back home," said Sergeant Foster, "and he's neither rung up nor left a message. I shouldn't be surprised if he'd made tracks."

"He was over here, looking for me at 5 o'clock," said Kirk unhappily. "He brought a report from Pagford."

"He wrote that out in the station, I'm told," said Foster. "And he left a bunch of shorthand stuff; they're typing it now. Davidson says it doesn't seem to be complete. I suppose it breaks off at the point where—"

"What do you expect?" retorted Kirk. "You don't suppose he'd go on taking down his own confession, do you? Be reasonable. . . . What's worrying me is, that if he was here at five, we ought to have passed him between here and Paggleham, if he was a-going home. I hope he ain't rushed off to do something rash. That 'ud be a nice thing, wouldn't it? Maybe he took the 'bus—but if he did, where's his bike?"

"If he took the 'bus he didn't get home by it," said the Sergeant, grimly.

"His wife must be worrying. I think we'd better have a look-see into this. We don't want nothing of an unfort'nate nature to 'appen. Now—where could 'e a-got to? You take your bike—no, that won't do—takes too long, and you've had a pretty hard day. I'll send Hart on his motor-bike, to see if anybody's seen Sellon round Pillington way—it's all woods round there—and the river—"

"You don't really think—?"

"I don't know what to think. I'm going over to see his wife. Shall I give you a lift over? Your bike can be sent back tomorrow. You'll get the 'bus at Paggleham."

Sergeant Foster could find nothing to resent in this offer, though his voice sounded injured in accepting it. As far as he could see, there was going to be an unholy row about Joe Sellon, and Kirk, characteristically, was taking steps to see that whatever happened he, Foster, should get the blame. Kirk was relieved when they overtook the local omnibus just outside Paggleham; he could drop his austere companion at once, without suggesting that they should go to Sellon's place together.

He found Mrs. Sellon in what Mrs. Ruddle would have called "a state of mind." She looked ready to drop with fright when she opened the door to him, and had evidently been crying. She was fair, pretty in a helpless sort of way, and delicate looking; Kirk noticed, with irritation as well as sympathy, that there was another baby coming. She asked him in, apologising for the state of the room, which was indeed somewhat disorderly. The two-year-old whose arrival in the world was the indirect cause of all Sellon's misfortunes, was ramping noisily about, dragging a wooden horse, whose wheels squeaked. The table was laid for a tea now long overdue.

"Joe not come in yet?" said Kirk, pleasantly enough.

"No," said Mrs. Sellon. "I don't know what's gone of him. Oh, be quiet, Arthur, do!—He's not been in all day and his supper's spoiling. . . . Oh, Mr. Kirk! Joe ain't in any trouble, is he? Martha Ruddle's been saying such things—Arthur! you bad boy—if you don't give over I'll take that horse away from you."

Kirk captured Arthur and stood him firmly between his own massive knees.

"Now, you be a good boy," he admonished him. "Grown

a lot, ain't he? He'll be getting quite a handful for you. Well, now, Mrs. Sellon—I wanted to have a bit of a talk with you about Joe."

Kirk had the advantage of being a local man, having in fact been born at Great Pagford. He had not seen Mrs. Sellon more than twice or thrice before; but he was at least not completely strange and therefore not completely awe-inspiring. Mrs. Sellon was induced to pour out her fears and troubles. As Kirk had suspected, she knew about Mr. Noakes and his missing note-case. She had not been told of it at the time, naturally; but later, when the weekly payments to Noakes had begun to press heavily on the exchequer, she had "wormed it out of" Joe. She had gone about in a state of anxiety ever since, fearing that something dreadful would happen. And then, a week ago today, Joe had had to go and tell Mr. Noakes he couldn't pay that week, and came back "looking awful," and saying "they were done for now for good and all." He'd been "very queer in his ways" all the week, and now Mr. Noakes was dead and Joe was missing and Martha Ruddle told her there'd been a dreadful quarrel and, "oh, I dunno, Mr. Kirk, I'm that terrified he may have done something rash."

Kirk, as delicately as he could, asked whether Joe had said anything to his wife about his quarrel with Noakes. Well, no, not exactly. All he'd said was, that Mr. Noakes wouldn't listen to nothing and it was all up. He wouldn't answer no questions—seemed regular fed-up like. Then he'd suddenly said he thought the best thing would be to chuck everything and go out to his elder brother in Canada, and would she go with him? She'd said, Why goodness gracious, Joe, surely Mr. Noakes wasn't going to tell on him after all this long while—it'd be a wicked shame, and after he'd paid all that money! Joe had only said gloomily, Well, you'll see tomorrow. And then he'd sat with his head in his hands, and there wasn't nothing to be got out of him. Next day they heard that Mr. Noakes had gone away. She had been afraid he'd gone to Broxford to tell on Joe; but nothing happened, and Joe cheered up a bit. And then this morning, she heard Noakes was dead, and she was that thankful, you couldn't think. But now Joe had gone off somewhere and Martha Ruddle came in with her talk—and since Mr. Kirk had found out about the note-case, she supposed it had all come out, and oh, dear, what *was* she to do and where was Joe?

None of this was very comforting to Kirk. It would have cheered him up a good deal to learn that Sellon had spoken frankly to his wife about the quarrel. And he didn't at all like the reference to the brother in Canada. If Sellon really had done away with Noakes, he would have had about as much chance of escaping to Canada as of being made king of the Cannibal Islands, and reflection must have told him so; but that his first blind impulse should have been to flee the country was unpleasantly significant. It occurred to Kirk, incidentally, that whoever did the murder must have been going through a pretty trying time. For it seemed very unlikely that he or she had thrown Noakes down the cellar steps—else why was the door left open? The murderer, having clubbed Noakes and left him for dead, would have expected—what? Well, if he had done it in the sitting-room or the kitchen or any room downstairs, the body might have been seen the next time anyone happened to look in at the windows—Mrs. Ruddle, or the postman, or an inquisitive lad from the village, or the vicar, on one of his visits. Or Aggie Twitterton might have come over to see her uncle. At any moment the discovery might have been made. Some poor devil (Kirk really felt a passing twinge of pity for the culprit) had been sitting for a whole week on the safety-valve, wondering! At any rate, the body *must* have been found the next Wednesday (that was today) because of Crutchley's weekly attendance. If, of course, the murderer knew about that, as he or she was bound to do; unless the crime could be traced to a passing tramp or somebody—and what a good thing if it could!

(While thinking this out, Kirk was talking soothingly in his slow speech, saying that something unexpected might have called Joe away; he had sent a man out to hunt him up; a constable in uniform couldn't very well get lost; it didn't do to imagine things.)

It was queer that Sellon . . .

Yes, by God, thought Kirk, that *was* queer; queerer than he cared to think about. He must take that away and chew it over. He couldn't think properly, with Mrs. Sellon's lamenting voice in his ear. . . . And the time didn't fit, because Crutchley had been over an hour in the house before the body was discovered. If Joe Sellon had been hanging round there at, say, eleven o'clock instead of past twelve. . . . Coincidence. He breathed again.

Mrs. Sellon was wailing on.

"We were that surprised when Willy Abbot come up with the milk this morning, to hear as a gentleman had taken Talboys. We didn't know rightly what to make of it. I said to Joe, 'Surely,' I said, 'Mr. Noakes wouldn't go away like that and let the house'—because, of course, we thought he'd let it like he often done before—'not without letting someone know,' I said. And Joe looked awful excited. I said, 'D'you suppose he's gone off somewhere,' I said, 'it looks queer to me,' I said, and he said, 'I don't know, but I'll soon find out.' And off he went. And he came in afterwards and wouldn't hardly swallow his breakfast, and he said, 'I can't hear nothing,' he said, 'only there's a lady and gentleman come and Noakes ain't turned up,' he said. And he went out again, and that's the last I see of him."

Well, thought Kirk, that puts the lid on. He'd forgotten the Wimseys, coming in and upsetting everything. Though he was not an imaginative man, he could see Sellon, startled by hearing that there was someone in the house, rushing out to learn the news, perplexed beyond expression by the fact that no body had been found, not daring to go and make open inquiries, but hovering round the house, manufacturing excuses for talking to Bert Ruddle—and he didn't like the Ruddles—waiting, waiting for the summons he knew must come, to him, to the only man with authority, hoping that the people in the house would leave it to him to examine the corpse, remove all evidences—

Kirk wiped his forehead, saying apologetically that he felt

the room a little hot. He did not hear Mrs. Sellon's reply; he was imagining again.

What the murderer (better not call him Sellon), what the murderer found in that house was—not a helpless pair of London holiday-makers, not some vague artistic couple without practical common-sense, not some pleasant retired schoolmistress coming to the country to enjoy a few weeks of fresh air and fresh eggs, but—a duke's son who cared for no man and knew exactly where the local bobby got off, who had investigated more murders than Paggleham had known in four centuries, whose wife wrote detective stories, and whose manservant was here, there and everywhere on swift and silent feet. But supposing, just supposing, the first people who arrived had been Aggie Twitterton and Frank Crutchley—as in rights they ought to have been? Even a local bobby could do as he liked with them; take charge, turn them out of the house, arrange things as he chose—

Kirk's wits were slow-moving, but when they took hold of a thing they worked with an efficiency which dismayed their owner.

He was trying to make some sort of commonplace rejoinder to Mrs. Sellon, when there was the sound of a motor-cycle drawing up at the gate. Looking out of the window, he saw it was Police-Sergeant Hart with Joe Sellon behind him, like two knights templars on one mount.

"Well!" said Kirk, with a cheerfulness he was far from feeling, "here's Joe back, anyhow, safe and sound."

But he didn't like the beaten, exhausted look on Sellon's face as Hart steered him up the little garden path. And he didn't look forward to questioning him.

CHAPTER XII

♦

Pot-Luck

Why, how now, friends! what saucy mates are you
That know nor duty nor civility?
Are we a person fit to be your host;
Or is our house become your common inn
To beat our doors at pleasure? What such haste
Is yours, as that it cannot wait fit times?
Are you the masters of this commonwealth
And know no more discretion?
—John Ford, *'Tis Pity She's a Whore*

Superintendent Kirk was spared the greater part of his ordeal; Sellon was in no fit state for undergoing a long interrogation. Sergeant Hart had picked up his trail in Pillington, where he had ridden through on his bicycle about half-past six. Then a girl was found who had seen a policeman following the field path on foot in the direction of Blackraven Wood—a favourite resort of ramblers and children during the summer months. She had particularly noticed him, because it was an unusual place in which to see a uniformed policeman. Following, as he said, this indication, Hart had found Sellon's bicycle propped against a hedge near the entrance to the path. He had hastened in pursuit—rather uneasy when he remembered that the little wood ran down to the bank of the Pagg. It was darkish by that time, and quite dark among the trees. With the aid of his torch, he had searched about for some time, calling as loudly as he could. After about three-quarters of an hour (he admitted that it had seemed a lot longer) he came upon Sellon, sitting on a fallen tree. He wasn't doing anything—just sitting. Seemed dazed-like. Hart asked him what on earth he thought he was about, but could get no sense out of him. He told him, pretty sharply, that he must come along at once—the Super was asking for him. Sellon offered no objection, but came without protest. Asked again what brought him there, he said he was "trying to think things out." Hart—who knew no details of the Paggleham affair—could make neither head nor tail of him; he didn't think he was fit to be trusted to ride back alone, and therefore took him up on the carrier and brought him straight home. Kirk said he couldn't have done better.

This explanation took place in the sitting-room. Mrs. Sellon had got Joe into the kitchen and was trying to coax him into eating a bit of something. Kirk sent Hart back to Broxford, explaining that Sellon was unwell and in a spot of trouble, and warning him not to say too much about it to the other men. He then went in to tackle his black sheep.

He soon came to the conclusion that Sellon's chief trouble, beside worry, was sheer exhaustion and lack of food. (He remembered now that he had had practically no lunch, though ham sandwiches and bread-and-cheese had been liberally provided at Talboys.) Sellon's account of himself, when Kirk got it out of him, was that, after interviewing Williams and writing his report, he had gone straight over to Broxford, expecting to find Kirk already there. He hadn't liked to go back to Talboys, on account of what had happened—seemed to him he was better out of the way. He'd waited about half an hour for Kirk; but the men kept asking him about the murder, and what with one thing and another he couldn't stick it. So he'd left the station and gone down to the canal and walked about a bit by the gas-works, meaning to come back later. But then it "came over him" how he'd been and gone and done for himself, and even if he could clear himself of the murder charge there were no hopes for him. So he'd taken his bike again and gone off, he couldn't rightly remember where or why, because he couldn't get his mind clear, and he thought if he could just go and walk about somewhere, maybe he could think better. He remembered going through Pillington and walking over the fields. He didn't think he'd had any special reason for going to Blackraven Wood—he'd only wandered about. He might have fallen asleep. He had had a sort of notion about chucking himself into the river, but he was afraid it would upset his wife. And he was very sorry, sir, but he couldn't say no more than that, only that he didn't do the murder. But, he added, oddly, if his lordship didn't believe him, then nobody else would.

This didn't seem quite the moment for going into his lordship's reasons for disbelief. Kirk told Sellon he was a young fool to go rambling away like that, and that everybody was ready to believe him so long as he was telling the truth. And he'd better go to bed and try and wake up more sensible; he'd frightened his wife quite enough as it was, and here it was close on 10 o'clock (Crumbs! and the Chief Constable's report not written yet!); he would be over in the morning and would see him before the inquest.

"You'll have to give evidence, you know," said Kirk, "but I've seen the coroner and maybe he won't press you too hard, on account of the investigation being in progress."

Sellon only put his head in his hands, and Kirk, really feeling that there was little to be done with him in this state, left him. As he went out, he said what cheering things he could to Mrs. Sellon, and advised her not to fidget her husband with too many questions, but to let him rest and try to keep in good heart.

All the way back to Broxford, his mind was churning over his new ideas. He couldn't get out of his head that picture of Sellon, standing at Martha Ruddle's cottage door, waiting—

There was only one thing that gave him comfort—a comfort altogether irrational: that one curious sentence, "If his lordship won't believe me, then nobody else will." There was no reason why Wimsey should believe Sellon, if it came to that—there was no sense in it at all—but it had sounded, well, genuine. He could hear again Sellon's desperate cry: "Don't *you* go, my lord! My lord, *you*'ll believe me!" Kirk, rummaging the filing-cabinet of his mind, found words which seemed to him apt. Thou hast appealed unto Caesar; unto Caesar thou shalt go. But Caesar had disallowed the appeal.

Not till Kirk, weary and patient, was writing out his report to the Chief Constable did the great illumination come upon him. He stopped, pen in hand, staring at the wall. Something like an idea, that was. And he'd been on to it before, as near as nothing, only he hadn't properly followed it up. But of course, it explained everything. It explained Sellon's statement and exonerated him; it explained how he had seen the clock from the window; it explained how Noakes came to be killed behind locked doors; it explained why the body hadn't been robbed; and it explained the murder—explained it right away. Because, Kirk told himself with triumph, there had never been any murder!

Wait a bit, thought the Superintendent, figuring the thing out in his careful way; mustn't go too fast. There's a big snag at the start. How can we get over that, I wonder?

The snag was that, to make the theory work, one had to assume that the cactus had been removed from its place. Kirk had already dismissed this idea as silly; but he hadn't seen then what a lot it would explain. He had gone so far as to have a word with Crutchley, among the chrysanthemums, just as he left Talboys. He had managed the inquiry pretty well, he thought. He had been careful not to ask straight out: "Did you put the cactus back before you left?" That would have drawn attention to a point which was at present a secret between himself and his lordship. He didn't want any talk about that to get round to Sellon before he himself confronted him with it in his own way. So he had merely pretended to have misremembered what Crutchley had said about his final interview with Noakes. It took place in the kitchen? Yes. Had either of them gone back into the sitting-room after that? No. But he thought Crutchley said he was watering them plants at the time. No, he'd finished watering the plants and was putting back the steps. Oh! then Kirk had got that wrong. Sorry. He just really wanted to get at how long the altercation with Noakes had lasted. Had Noakes been there while Crutchley was seeing to the plants? No, he was in the kitchen. But didn't Crutchley take the plants out to the kitchen to water them? No, he watered them just where they were, and wound the clock and came out with the steps, and it wasn't till he'd done that that Noakes gave him his day's money and the argument started. It hadn't lasted more'n maybe ten minutes or so—not the argument. Well, possibly fifteen. Six o'clock was rightly Crutchley's time to stop work—he charged five bob for an eight-hour day, barrin' time off for lunch. Kirk apologised for his mistake: the step-ladder had confused him; he had thought Crutchley meant he needed the step-ladder to get the hanging plants out of their pots. No; the step-ladder was to get up to water them, same as he'd done this morning—they was above his head—and to wind the clock, like he said. That was all. It was quite ordinary, him using the step-ladder, he always did, and put it back in the kitchen afterwards. "You ain't tryin' to make out," added Crutchley, a little belligerently, "as I stood on them steps with a 'ammer to cosh the old bird over the 'ead?" That was an ingenious idea nobody had yet thought of. Kirk replied that he wasn't thinking anything particular; only trying to get the times clear in his head. He was glad to have given the impression that his suspicions were directed to the step-ladder.

Unfortunately, then, he couldn't begin by substantiating that the cactus had been out of its pot at 6.20. But now—suppose Noakes had taken it out himself for some purpose or the other. What purpose? Well, it was difficult to say. But suppose Noakes had seen something wrong with it—a spot of mildew, maybe, or whatever these ugly things suffered from. He might have taken it down to wipe it or—But he could have done that easy enough, standing on the steps or, as he was so tall, on a chair. Not good enough. What other things could happen to plants? Well, they might become pot-bound. Kirk didn't know whether that happened to cactuses (or was it cacti?), but suppose you wanted to look and see if its roots were growing out through the bottom of the pot. You'd have to take it out for that. Or to tap the pot to see if—no; it had been given water. But wait! Noakes hadn't *seen* Crutchley do that. He might have suspected Crutchley was neglecting it. Perhaps he felt at the top and it didn't seem wet enough, and then—Or, more likely, he thought it was being over-watered. These spiky cactus-affairs didn't like too much damp. Or did they? It was annoying not to know their habits; Kirk's own gardening was of the straight-forward flowerbed-and-kitchen-stuff variety.

Anyhow, it wasn't outside the bounds of possibility that Noakes had removed the cactus for some purpose of his own. You couldn't prove he hadn't. Say he did. All right. Then, at 9 o'clock, up comes Sellon, and sees Noakes coming into the parlour. . . . Here Kirk paused to consider again. If Noakes was coming for the 9.30 News as usual, he was before his time. He came in (said Sellon) and looked at the clock. The dead man had worn no watch, and Kirk had taken it for granted that he had come in merely to see how near it was to news-bulletin time. But he might also have been meaning to put the cactus back and come in a bit early on that account. That was all right. He comes in. He thinks, Now, have I got time to fetch that there plant in from the scullery, or wherever it is, before the News comes on? He looks at the clock. Then Joe Sellon taps at the window and he comes over. They have their talk and Joe goes away. The old boy fetches in his plant and gets up on a chair or something to put it back. Or maybe he gets the steps. Then, while he's doing that, he sees it's getting on for half-past nine, and that flurries him a bit. He leans over too far, or the steps slip, or he ain't careful getting down, and over he goes backwards and gives his head a crack on the floor—or, better still, on the corner of the settle. He's knocked out. Then presently he comes to, puts away the chair or the steps or whatever it was and after that—well, after that, we know what happened to him. So there you are. Simple as pie. No cutting or stealing keys or hiding blunt instruments or telling lies—nothing at all but a plain accident and everybody telling the truth.

Kirk was as much overcome by the beauty, simplicity and economy of this solution as Copernicus must have been when he first thought of putting the sun in the centre of the Solar System and saw all the planets, instead of describing complicated and ugly geometrical capers, move onward in orderly and dignified circles. He sat and contemplated it with affection for nearly ten minutes before venturing to examine it. He was afraid of knocking the bloom off it.

Still, a theory was only a theory; one had got to find evidence to support it. One must at any rate be sure there was no evidence against it. First of all, could a man kill himself like that, simply by falling off a pair of steps?

Side by side with half-crown editions of English poets and philosophers, flanked on the right by Bartlett's *Familiar Quotations* and on the left by that handy police publication which dissects and catalogues crimes according to the method of their commission, stood, tall and menacing, the two blue volumes of Taylor's *Medical Jurisprudence*, that canon of uncanonical practice and Baedeker of the back doors to death. Kirk had often studied it in a dutiful readiness for the unexpected. Now he took it down and turned the pages of Volume I, till he came to the running head: "Intercranial Haemorrhage—Violence or Disease." He was looking for the story of the gentleman who fell out of a chaise. Yes, here he was: he emerged with a kind of personality from the Report of Guy's Hospital for 1859:

> A gentleman was thrown out of a chaise, and fell upon his head with such violence as to stun him. After a short time he recovered his senses, and felt so much better that he entered the chaise again, and was driven to his father's house by a companion. He attempted to pass off the accident as of a trivial nature, but he soon began to feel heavy and drowsy, so that he was obliged to go to bed. His symptoms became more alarming, and he died in about an hour from effusion of blood in the brain.

Excellent and unfortunate gentleman, his name unknown, his features a blank, his life a mystery; embalmed for ever in a fame outlasting the gilded monuments of princes! He lived in his father's house, so was presumably unmarried and young—a bit of a swell, perhaps, wearing the fashionable new Inverness cape and the luxuriant silky side-whiskers which were just coming into favour. How did he come to be thrown out of the chaise? Did the horse bolt with him? Had he looked on the wine when it was red? The vehicle, we observe, was undamaged, and his companion at any rate sober enough to drive him home. A courageous gentleman (since he was resolute to enter the chaise again), a considerate gentleman (since he made light of the accident in order to spare his parents anxiety); his premature death must have occasioned much lamentation among the crinolines. No one could have guessed that, nearly eighty years later, a police superintendent in a rural district would be reading his brief epitaph: "A gentleman was thrown out of a chaise. . . ."

Not that Superintendent Kirk troubled his head with these biographical conjectures. What exasperated him was that the book did not mention the height of the chaise from the ground or the rate at which the vehicle was proceeding. How would the fall compare in violence with that of an elderly man from a step-ladder on to an oak floor? The next case quoted was even less to the point: this was a youth of eighteen, who was hit on the head in a fight, went about his business for ten days, had a headache on the eleventh day and died in the night. Then came a drunken carter, aged fifty, who fell from the shafts of his cart and was killed. This seemed more hopeful; except that the wretched creature had fallen three or four times, the last time being thrown under the wheels of the cart by the bolting horse. Still, it did seem to show that a short fall would do quite a lot of damage. Kirk pondered a little, and then went to the telephone.

Dr. Craven listened with patience to Kirk's theory, and agreed that it was an attractive one. "Only," said he, "if you want me to tell the coroner that the man fell on his back, I can't do it. There is no bruising whatever on the back, or on the left-hand side of the body. If you looked at my report to the coroner you must have seen that all the marks were on the right-hand side and in front, except the actual blow that caused death. I'll tell you again what they are. The right forearm and elbow show heavy bruises, with considerable extravasation from the surface vessels, showing that they were inflicted some time before death. I should say that when he was hit behind the left ear, he was flung over forwards on to his right side with the force of the blow. The only other marks are bruises and slight abrasions on the shins, hands and forehead. The hands and forehead are marked with dust, and this suggests, I think, that he got the injuries in falling forwards down the cellar steps. He died shortly after that, for there is very little extravasation from these injuries. I am, of course, excluding the hypostasis produced by his having lain a whole week face downwards in the cellar. That, naturally, is all in the front part of the body."

Kirk had forgotten the meaning of "hypostasis," which the doctor pronounced in a very unlikely way; but he gathered that it wasn't a thing that could be made to support the theory. He asked whether Noakes could have been killed by hitting his head in a fall.

"Oh, certainly," said Dr. Craven; "but you'll have to explain how he hit the back of his head in falling and yet came down on his face."

With this Kirk had to be content. It looked rather as though a flaw might be developing in his beautiful rounded theory. It is the little rift within the lute, he thought, mournfully, that by and by will make the music mute. But he shook his head angrily. Tennyson or no Tennyson, he wasn't going to abandon the position without a struggle. He called to his assistance a more robust and comforting poet—one who held "we fall to rise, are baffled to fight better"—called to his wife that he was going out, and reached for his hat and overcoat. If only he could have another look at the sitting-room, he might be able to see how that fall could have come about.

At Talboys the sitting-room was dark, though a light still burned in the casement above it and in the kitchen. Kirk knocked at the door, which was presently opened by Bunter in his shirt-sleeves.

"I'm very sorry to disturb his lordship so late," began Kirk, only then realising that it was past eleven.

"His lordship," said Bunter, "is in bed."

Kirk explained that, unexpectedly, a necessity had arisen to re-examine the sitting-room, and that he was anxious to get this done before the inquest. There was no need for his lordship to come down in person. Nothing was sought but permission to enter.

"We should be most unwilling," replied Bunter, "to obstruct the officers of the law in the execution of their duty; but you will permit me to point out that the hour is somewhat advanced and the available illumination inadequate. Besides that, the sitting-room is situated exactly underneath his lordship's—"

"Superintendent! Superintendent!" called a soft and mocking voice from the window above.

"My lord?" Mr. Kirk stepped out of the porch to get a view of the speaker.

"Merchant of Venice, Act V, Scene 1. Peace, ho! the moon sleeps with Endymion, and would not be awak'd."

"I beg your pardon, my lord," said Kirk, devoutly thankful that the mask of night was on his face. And the lady listening, too!

"Don't mention it. Is there anything I can do for you?"

"Only to let me take another look round downstairs," pleaded Kirk, apologetically.

"Had we but world enough and time that trifling request, Superintendent, were no crime. But take whatever you like. Only do, as the poet sings, come and go on lissome, clerical, printless toe. The first is Marvell and the second, Rupert Brooke."

"I'm very much obliged," said Mr. Kirk, generally, to cover the permission and the information. "The fact is, I got an idea."

"I only wish I had half your complaint. Do you want to unfold your tale now, or will it do in the morning?"

Mr. Kirk earnestly begged his lordship not to disturb himself.

"Well, good luck to it and good night."

Nevertheless, Peter hesitated. His natural inquisitiveness wrestled with a right and proper feeling that he should credit Kirk with intelligence enough to pursue his own inquiries. Proper feeling prevailed, but he remained for fifteen minutes perched on the window-sill, while soft scrapes and bumpings sounded from below. Then came the shutting of the front door and steps along the path.

"His shoulders are disappointed," said Peter aloud to his wife. "He has found a mare's-nest, full of cockatrice's eggs."

That was perfectly true. The rift in Kirk's theory had widened and with alarming rapidity silenced all that he could find to say for Joe Sellon. Not only was it extremely hard to visualise any way by which Noakes could have fallen so as to injure himself on both sides at once, but it was now plainly evident that the cactus had remained all the while solidly in its place.

Kirk had thought of two possibilities: the outer pot might have been unhooked from the chain, or the inner pot removed from the outer. On careful examination, he discounted the first alternative. The brass pot had a conical base, which would prevent it from standing upright when taken down; moreover, in order to relieve the strain on the hook, the ring which untied the three chains that rose from the sides of the pot itself had been secured to the first link above the hook by a sixfold twist of stout wire, the ends of which had been neatly turned in with the pliers. No one in his senses would have gone to the trouble of undoing that when he could more readily remove the inner pot. But here Kirk made a discovery which, while it did credit to his detective ability, destroyed all possibility of any such removal. Round the top of the shining brass pot ran a band of pierced work forming a complicated pattern, and within the openings the earthenware of the inner flower-pot was blackened with the unmistakable stain of brass-polish. If the flower-pot had been removed since the last cleaning, it was inconceivable that it should have been replaced with such mathematical exactness as to show no thin red line of earthenware at the edges of that band of open-work. Kirk, disappointed, called Bunter to give his opinion. Bunter, disapproving but correctly ready to assist, agreed absolutely. What was more, when they tried, together, to shift the inner pot in the outer, it proved to be an exceedingly tight fit. Nobody, unaided, could have turned it after wedging it in so as to make the pierced band coincide with the outlines stencilled on the earthenware—certainly not an elderly man in a hurry by the light of a distant candle. As a forlorn hope, Kirk asked:

"Did Crutchley polish the brass this morning?"

"I fancy not; he brought no brass-polish with him, nor did he use the materials contained in the kitchen cupboard. Will there be anything further tonight?"

Kirk gazed blankly about the room.

"I suppose," he suggested, despairingly, "the clock couldn't have been moved?"

"See for yourself," said Bunter.

But the plastered wall showed no trace of any hook or nail to which the clock might have been temporarily transferred. The nearest landmark to the east was the nail supporting "The Soul's Awakening" and that to the west, a fretwork bracket with a plaster image on it—both too light to take the clock and in the wrong line of sight from the window. Kirk gave it up.

"Well, that seems to settle it. Thanks very much."

"Thank *you*," retorted Bunter, austerely. Still dignified, in spite of his shirt-sleeves, he conducted the unwelcome guest to the door, as though ushering out a duchess.

Being human, Kirk could not but wish he had left his theory alone till after the inquest. All that he had done was to rule it definitely out of court, so that he could not now, in honesty, even hint at such a possibility.

CHAPTER XIII

This Way and That Way

"Serpent, I say again!" repeated the Pigeon . . . and added with a kind of sob, "I've tried every way, and nothing seems to suit them!"

"I haven't the least idea what you're talking about," said Alice.

"I've tried the roots of trees, and I've tried banks, and I've tried hedges," the Pigeon went on without attending to her; "but those serpents! There's no pleasing them!"

—Lewis Carroll, *Alice in Wonderland*

"And what," inquired Lord Peter Wimsey of Bunter the following morning, "did the Superintendent want last night?"

"He wished to ascertain, my lord, whether the hanging cactus could have been removed from its containing pot during the events of last week."

"What, again? I thought he'd realised that it couldn't. The marks of the brass polish should have told him that with half an eye. No need to get the step-ladder and bump round at midnight like a bumble-bee in a bottle."

"Quite so, my lord. But I thought it better not to intervene, and your lordship wished him to have every facility."

"Oh, quite. His brain works like the mills of God. But he has some other divine qualities; I know him to be magnanimous and suspect him of being merciful. He is trying hard to exonerate Sellon. That's natural enough. But he's attacking the strong side instead of the weak side of the case against him."

"What do you think about Sellon yourself, Peter?"

They had breakfast upstairs. Harriet was dressed, smoking a cigarette in the window. Peter, in the half-way dressing-gown stage, was warming the back of his legs at the fire. The ginger cat had arrived to pay its morning compliment, and had taken up a position on his shoulder.

"I don't know what to think. The fact is, we've got dashed little material for thinking with. It's probably too early for thinking."

"Sellon doesn't look like a murderer."

"They very often don't, you know. He didn't look, either, like the sort of man who would tell me a thundering great lie, except for a very good reason. But people do tell lies when they're frightened."

"I suppose he didn't notice till after he'd said that about the clock that it implied having been inside the house."

"No. You've got to be a very sharp-witted person to see ahead when you're telling half-truths. A story that's a lie from beginning to end will be consistent. And since he obviously hadn't meant to tell the story of the quarrel at all, he had to make up his mind on the spur of the moment. The thing that's bothering me is, how did Sellon get into the house?"

"Noakes must have let him in."

"Just so. Here's an elderly man, locked up alone in a house. Up comes a young man, big and strong and in a murderous rage, and quarrels with him, using strong language and possibly threats. The old man tells him to be off, and bangs the window shut. The young man goes on knocking at the doors and trying to get in. The old man has nothing to gain by admitting him; yet he does it, and obligingly turns his back to him, on purpose that the angry young man may attack him with a blunt instrument. It is possible, but, as Aristotle might say, it is an improbable-possible."

"Suppose Sellon said he *had* got the money after all, and Noakes let him in and sat down to write a—No, he wouldn't write a receipt, of course. Nothing on paper. Unless Sellon threatened him."

"If Sellon had the money, Noakes could have told him to hand it in through the window."

"Well, suppose he did hand it in—or said he was going to. Then, when Noakes opened the window, Sellon could have climbed in himself. Or could he? Those mullions are pretty narrow."

"You can have no idea," said Peter, irrelevantly, "how refreshing it is to talk to somebody who has a grasp of method. The police are excellent fellows, but the only principle of detection they have really grasped is that wretched phrase, *Cui bono?* They *will* hare off after motive, which is a matter for psychologists. Juries are just the same. If they can see a motive they tend to convict, however often the judge may tell them that there's no need to prove motive, and that motive by itself will never make a case. You've got to show

how the thing was done, and then, if you like, bring in motive to back up your proof. If a thing could only have been done one way, and if only one person could have done it that way, then you've got your criminal, motive or no motive. There's How, When, Where, Why and Who—and when you've got How, you've got Who. Thus spake Zarathustra."

"I seem to have married my only intelligent reader. That's the way you construct it from the other end, of course. Artistically, it's absolutely right."

"I have noticed that what's right in art is usually right in practice. In fact, nature is a confirmed plagiarist of art, as somebody has observed. Go on with your theory—only do remember that to guess how a job *might* have been done isn't the same thing as proving that it *was* done that way. If you will allow me to say so, that is a distinction which people of your profession are very liable to overlook. They will confuse moral certainty with legal proof."

"I shall throw something at you in a minute. . . . I say, do you think something might have been *thrown* at Noakes? Through the window? Bother! now I've got two theories at once. No—wait! . . . Sellon gets Noakes to open the window and then starts to climb in. You didn't answer about those mullions."

"I think I could climb in through them; but then I'm rather narrow in the shoulders compared with Sellon. But on the principle that where your head can go your body can follow I dare say he could manage it. Not very quickly, and not without giving Noakes plenty of warning of his intentions."

"That's where the throwing comes in. Suppose Sellon started to climb and Noakes got alarmed and made for the door. Then Sellon might snatch up something—"

"What?"

"That's true. He would scarcely have brought a stone or anything on purpose. He might have picked one up in the garden before he came back to the window. Or—I know! That paper-weight on the sill. He could have snatched that up, and chucked it at Noakes's retreating back. Would that work? I'm not good at trajectories and things."

"Very likely it would. I'd have to go and look."

"Well, then. Oh, yes. Then he'd only have to finish scrambling in, pick up the paper-weight and put it back and go out through the window again."

"Really?"

"Of course not; it was locked inside. No. He'd shut and lock the window, get Noakes's keys from his pocket, open the front door, put back the keys and—Well, then he'd have to go out leaving the door unlocked. And when Noakes came to, he obligingly locked it behind him. We've got to allow for that possibility, whoever did the murder."

"That's really brilliant, Harriet. It's very difficult to find a flaw in it. And I'll tell you another thing. Sellon was the only person who could, with comparative safety, leave the door unlocked. In fact, it would be an advantage."

"You've got ahead of me there. Why?"

"Why, because he was the village policeman. Look what happens next. In the middle of the night, he takes it into his head to go on a round of inspection. His attention, as he would put it in his report, is directed to the house by the circumstance of the candles being still alight in the sitting-room. That's why he left them burning, which no other murderer would be likely to do. He tries the door and finds it open. He goes in, sees that everything looks nice and natural, and then hurries out to call up the neighbours with the announcement that some tramp or other has been in and knocked Mr. Noakes on the head. It's a nuisance to be the last man to see the deceased alive, but it's a hell of a good wheeze to be the first to discover the body. It must have been a nasty shock to find that door locked after all."

"Yes. I suppose that would make him give up his idea. Especially if he looked in through the window and saw that Noakes wasn't lying where he'd left him. The curtains weren't drawn, were they? No—I remember—they were open when we arrived. What *would* he think?"

"He'd think Noakes wasn't killed after all, and would wait for the morning, wondering when—and how—"

"Poor man!—And then, when nothing happened after all, and Noakes didn't turn up—why, it was enough to drive him dotty."

"If it happened that way."

"And then we came and—I suppose he was hanging about here all morning, waiting to hear the worst. He was right on the spot when the body was found, wasn't he?... I say, Peter, all this is a bit grim."

"It's only a theory, after all. We haven't proved a word of it. That's the worst of you mystery-mongers. Anything's a solution so long as it holds together. Let's make a theory about somebody else. Whom shall we have? How about Mrs. Ruddle? She's a tough old lady and not an altogether sympathetic character."

"Why on earth should Mrs. Ruddle—?"

"Never mind Why. Why never gets you anywhere. Mrs. Ruddle came to borrow a drop of paraffin. Noakes was sniffing round and heard her. He invited her to step in and explain herself. He said he had often had doubts of her honesty. She said he owed her a week's money. High words passed. He made for her. She snatched up the poker. He ran away and she threw the poker at him and caught him on the back of the head. That's Why enough, when people lose their tempers. Unless you prefer to believe that Noakes made improper advances to Mrs. Ruddle and she dotted him one accordingly."

"Idiot!"

"Well, I don't know. Look at old James Fleming and Jessie MacPherson. I shouldn't fancy Mrs. Ruddle myself, but then, my standard is high. Very well. Mrs. Ruddle knocks Noakes on the head, and—Wait a minute; this is coming rather pretty. She runs over to the cottage in a terrible stew, crying, 'Bert! Bert! I've killed Mr. Noakes!' Bert says, 'Oh, nonsense,' and they come back to the house together, just in time to see Noakes go tumbling down the cellar steps. Bert goes down—"

"Leaving no footprints?"

"He'd taken off his boots for the night and ran over in his slippers—it's all grass over the field to the cottage. Bert says, 'He's dead this time, all right.' Then Mrs. Ruddle goes to fetch a ladder, while Bert locks the door and puts the key back in the dead man's pocket. He goes upstairs, through the trap-door on to the roof, and Mrs. Ruddle holds the ladder while he gets down."

"Do you mean that seriously, Peter?"

"I can't mean it seriously till I've had a look at the roof. But there's one thing they remember afterwards—Bert has left the cellar-door open—hoping it will look as though Noakes had had an accident. But when we arrive, they are a bit put out. We were not the people who were intended to discover the body. That was to be Miss Twitterton's job. They know *she's* easily hoodwinked, but they know nothing about *us*. First of all, Mrs. Ruddle isn't keen to have us here at all—but when we insist on getting the key and coming in, she makes the best of it. *Only*—she calls out to Bert, 'Shut the cellar-door, Bert! It's perishing cold.' Thinking to postpone matters a little, you see, and take stock of us first. And by the way, we've only got Mrs. Ruddle's word for it that Noakes died at that particular time, or that he didn't go to bed, or anything. It might all have happened much later at night, or, better still when she came in the morning; because then he'd be ready dressed, and she'd only have to make the bed again."

"What? In the morning? All that business on the roof? Suppose anybody came by?"

"Bert on a ladder, cleaning out the gutters. No 'arm in cleaning out a gutter."

"Gutter? . . . What does that? . . . gutter—guttered—the candles! Don't they prove it happened at night?"

"They don't prove it; they suggest it. We don't know how long the candles were to start with. Noakes may have sat listening to the wireless till they burnt themselves out in the sockets. Thrift, thrift, Horatio. It was Mrs. Ruddle who said the wireless wasn't going—who put the time at between 9 and 9.30—just after Sellon and Noakes had been quarrelling. It's not awfully like Mrs. Ruddle to have gone away without hearing the end of the row, when you come to think of it.

If you look at the thing in a prejudiced way, all her actions seem odd. And she had it in for Sellon, and sprang it on him beautifully."

"Yes," said Harriet, thoughtfully. "And, you know, she kept on sort of hinting things to me when we were doing the sandwiches for lunch. And she was very artful about refusing to answer Sellon's questions before the Superintendent came. But, honestly, Peter, do you think she and Bert have brains enough between them to work out that business with the keys? And would they have had the sense and self-restraint to keep their hands off the money?"

"Now you're asking something. But one thing I do know. Yesterday afternoon, Bert fetched a long ladder from the out-house and went up on the roof with Puffett."

"Oh, Peter! so he did!"

"Another good clue gone west. We do at least know there was a ladder, but how are we to tell now what marks were made when?"

"The trap-door."

Peter laughed ruefully.

"Puffett informed me when I met them fetching the ladder that Bert had just been up to the roof that way, to see if there was a 'sut-lid' anywhere in the chimney for cleaning the flue. He went up by the Privy Stair and through your bedroom when Miss Twitterton was being questioned down here. Didn't you hear him? You brought Miss Twitterton down, and up he nipped, pronto."

Harriet lit a fresh cigarette.

"Now let's hear the case against Crutchley and the vicar."

"Well—they're a bit more difficult, because of the alibi. Unless one of them was in league with Mrs. Ruddle, we've got to explain away the silence of the wireless. Take Crutchley first. If he did it, we can't very well make up a story about his climbing in at the window, because he couldn't have got there till after Noakes was in bed. He deposited the vicar at the parsonage at 10.30 and was back in Pagford before eleven. There'd be no time for long parleyings at windows and clever business with keys. I'm assuming, of course, that Crutchley's times at the garage have been confirmed; if he's guilty, of course, they will be, because they're part of the plan. If it was Crutchley, it must have been premeditated—which means that he might somehow have stolen a key or had one cut. Very early in the morning is Crutchley's time, I fancy—taking out a taxi for a non-existent customer or something of that kind. He leaves the car somewhere, walks up to the house and lets himself in—um! yes, it's awkward after that. Noakes would be upstairs, undressed and in bed. I can't see the point of it. If he attacked him, it would be to rob him—and he didn't rob him."

"Now it's you who are asking Why. But suppose Crutchley came to rob the house, and was rummaging in a bureau or something—in the kitchen, where the will was found—and Noakes heard him and came downstairs—"

"Stopping to put on his collar and tie, and carefully taking all his precious bank-notes with him?"

"Of course not. In his night-things. He interrupts Crutchley, who goes for him. He runs away, Crutchley hits him, thinks he's dead, gets the wind up and runs off, locking the door after him from outside. Then Noakes comes to, wonders what he's doing down there, goes back to his room, dresses, feels queer, goes towards the back door, meaning to fetch Mrs. Ruddle, and falls down the stairs."

"Excellent. But who made the bed?"

"Oh, bother! Yes—and we haven't explained about the wireless."

"No. My idea was that Crutchley had put the wireless out of action, meaning to establish his alibi for the night before the murder. I meant it to be a murder—but you put me off with your theory about robbing a bureau."

"I'm sorry. I was starting two hares at once. The Crutchley red herring does seem to be rather a mild one. Is the wireless working now, by the way?"

"We'll find out. Supposing it isn't, does that prove anything?"

"Not unless it looks as though it had been deliberately put out of order. I suppose it works from batteries. Nothing's easier than to loosen a terminal in an accidental-looking manner."

"Old Noakes could easily put a thing like that right for himself."

"So he could. Shall I run down and see whether it's working now or not?"

"Ask Bunter. He'll know."

Harriet called down the stairs to Bunter, and returned to say:

"Working perfectly. Bunter tried it yesterday evening after we'd gone."

"Ah! Then that proves nothing, one way or the other. Noakes may have tried to turn it on, failed to spot the trouble till the news-bulletin was over, put it right and left it at that."

"He may have done that in any case."

"And so the time-scheme goes west again."

"This is very discouraging."

"Isn't it? It now leaves the way open for a murderous attack by the vicar, between 10.30 and 11 o'clock."

"Why should the—? Sorry! I keep on asking why."

"There's an awful strain of inquisitiveness on both sides of the family. You'd better reconsider those children, Harriet; they'll be intolerable pests from the cradle."

"So they will. Frightful. All the same, I do think it looks neater to have a comprehensible motive. Murder for the fun of it breaks all the rules of detective fiction."

"All right. Well, then. Mr. Goodacre shall have a motive. I'll think of one presently. He walks over from the vicarage at about 10.35 and knocks at the door. Noakes lets him in—there's no reason why he shouldn't let in the vicar, who has always appeared mild and friendly. But the vicar, underneath his professional austerity, conceals one of those dreadful repressions so common among clergymen as depicted by our realistic novelists. So, of course, does Noakes. The vicar, under cover of a purity campaign, accuses Noakes of corrupting the village maiden whom sub-consciously he wants for himself."

"Of course!" said Harriet, cheerfully. "How silly of me not to think of it. Nothing could be more obvious. They have one of those squalid senile rows—and the vicar ends up with a brain-storm and imagines he's the hammer of God, like the parson in Chesterton's story. He lays Noakes out with the poker and departs. Noakes recovers his senses—and we go on from there. That accounts beautifully for the money's having been left on the body; Mr. Goodacre wouldn't want that."

"Exactly. And the reason why the vicar is so pleasant and innocent about it all now, is that the brain-storm has passed, and he has forgotten the whole thing."

"Dissociated personality. I think that's our best effort yet. We only need now to put a name to the village maiden."

"It need not even be that. The vicar may have had a morbid fancy for something else—a passion *á la* Plato for an aspidistra, or a strange, covetous longing for a cactus. He's a great gardener, you know, and these vegetable and mineral loves can be very sinister indeed. Remember the man in the Eden Phillpotts story who set his heart on an iron pineapple and brained a fellow with it? Believe me or believe me not, the vicar came prowling round for no good, and when old Noakes flung himself on his knees, crying, 'Take my life but spare the honour of my cactus!' he upped with the aspidistra-pot—"

"It's all very well, Peter—but the poor old thing was really killed."

"My heart, I know it. But until we find out *how*, one theory's as fanciful as another. We've got to laugh or break our hearts in this damnable world. It makes me sick to think that I didn't go down into the cellar the night we came. We might have made a job of it then, with the place left just as it was, no clues disturbed, no Ruddles and Puffetts and Wimseys tramping round and upsetting everything— My God! that was the worst night's work I ever put in!"

If he had been wanting to make her laugh, this time he succeeded beyond hope or desire.

"It's no good," said Harriet, when she had recovered. "Never, never, never shall we do anything like other people. We shall always laugh when we ought to cry and love when we ought to work, and make ourselves a scandal and a hissing. Don't do that! What ever will Bunter say if he sees you with your hair full of ashes? You'd better finish dressing and face the situation." She wandered back to the window. "Look! there are two men coming up the path, one of them with a camera."

"Hell!"

"I'll go and entertain them."

"Not alone," said Peter, chivalrously; and followed her down.

Bunter, in the doorway, was fighting a desperate verbal battle. "It's no good," said Peter. "Murder will in. Hullo! it's you, Sally, is it? Well, well! Are you sober?"

"Unfortunately," said Mr. Salcombe Hardy, who was a personal friend, "I am. Have you got anything in the place, old man? You owe us something, after the way we were treated on Tuesday."

"Whisky for these gentlemen, Bunter; and put some laudanum in it. Now, children, make it snappy, because the inquest's at eleven and I can't turn up in a dressing-gown. What are you after? Romance in High Life? Or mysterious Death in Honeymoon House?"

"Both," said Mr. Hardy, with a grin. "I suppose we'd better begin by offering our mingled congratulations and condolences. Do we mention that you are both in a state of collapse? Or is the message to the Great British Public that you are marvellously happy in spite of this untoward occurrence?"

"Be original, Sally. Say we are fighting like cat and dog, and only relieved from irritable boredom by the prospect of a little detective occupation."

"That would make a grand story," said Salcombe Hardy, with a regretful shake of the head. "You're conducting an investigation in double harness, I take it?"

"Not at all; the police are doing that. Say when."

"Thanks very much. Well, cheerio! The police, of course, officially. But, dash it all, you must have some personal angle on the thing. Come on, Wimsey, look at it from our point of view. It's the story of the century. Famous amateur sleuth weds mystery-writer, finds corpse on bridal night."

"We didn't. That's the snag."

"Ah! Why, now?"

"Because we had the sweep in next morning and all the

clues got destroyed in the muddle," said Harriet. "We'd better tell you, I suppose."

She glanced at Peter, who nodded. "Better we than Mrs. Ruddle," was in both their minds. They told the story as briefly as possible.

"Can I say you've got a theory of the crime?"

"Yes," said Peter.

"Fine!" said Salcombe Hardy.

"My theory is that you put the corpse there yourself, Sally, to make a good headline."

"I only wish I'd thought of it. Nothing else?"

"I tell you," said Peter, "the evidence is destroyed. You can't have a theory without evidence to go on."

"The fact is," said Harriet, "he's completely baffled."

"As baffled as a bathroom geyser," agreed her husband. "My wife's baffled too. It's the only point on which we are at one. When we're tired of heaving crockery about we sit and sneer at one another's bafflement. The police are baffled too. Or else they confidently expect to make an arrest. One or other. You can take your choice."

"Well," said Sally, "it's a devil of a nuisance for you, and I'm a nuisance too, but I can't help myself. D'you mind if we take a photograph? Quaint Tudor farmhouse with genuine rafters—bride delightfully workmanlike in tweed costume and bridegroom in full Sherlock Holmes rig-out—you ought to have a pipe and an ounce of shag."

"Or a fiddle and cocaine? Be quick, Sally, and get it over. And see here, old man—I suppose you've got to earn your living, but for God's sake use a little tact."

Salcombe Hardy, his violet eyes luminous with sincerity, promised that he would. But Harriet felt that the interview had left both her and Peter badly mauled, and that, of the two, Peter had come off the worse. He had picked his words carefully, and his light tone rang brittle as glass. There was going to be more of this—much more. With sudden determination she followed the pressmen out of the room and shut the door.

"Mr. Hardy—listen! I know one's absolutely helpless. One

has to put up with what newspapers choose to say. I've reason to know it. I've had it before. But if you put in anything sickening about Peter and me—you know what I mean—any of the sort of things that make one writhe and wish one was dead, it'll be pretty rotten for us and pretty rotten of you. Peter—isn't exactly a rhinoceros, you know."

"My dear Miss Vane—I'm sorry—Lady Peter. . . . Oh, and by the way, I forgot to ask, do you intend to go on writing now you are married?"

"Yes, of course."

"Under the same name?"

"Naturally."

"Can I say that?"

"Oh, yes, you can say that. You can say *anything* except all that awful matrimonial tripe about 'said he with a laughing glance at his brand-new wife,' and the rest of the romantic bilge-water. I mean, it's all quite trying enough; do leave us a little human dignity, if you possibly can. Look here! If you'll be reasonably restrained, and try to keep the other reporters reasonable, you've much more chance of getting stories out of us. After all, we're both News—and it's no good offending News, is it? Peter's been very decent; he's given you all the facts he can. Don't make his life a burden to him."

"Honestly," said Sally, "I'll try not. But editors are editors—"

"Editors are ghouls and cannibals."

"They are. But I'll really do my best. About this writing story—can you give me anything exclusive on that? Your husband eager you should continue your professional career—that kind of thing? Doesn't think women should be confined to domestic interests? You look forward to getting hints from his experience for use in your detective novels?"

"Oh, damn!" said Harriet. "Must you have the personal angle on everything? Well, I'm certainly going on writing, and he certainly doesn't object—in fact, I think he entirely approves. But don't make him say it with a proud and tender look, or anything sick-making, will you?"

"No, no. Are you writing anything now?"

"No—I've only just finished a book. But I've got a new one in my head. In fact, it's just come there."

"Good!" said Salcombe Hardy.

"It's about the murder of a journalist—and the title is, *Curiosity Killed the Cat*."

"Fine!" said Sally, quite unperturbed.

"And," said Harriet, as they passed along the path between the chrysanthemums, "we told you that I knew this place when I was a child, but we didn't mention that a dear old couple lived here who used to ask me in and give me seedy-cake and strawberries. That's very pretty and human, and they're dead, so it can't hurt them."

"Splendid!"

"And all the ugly furniture and aspidistras were put there by Noakes, so don't blame us for them. And he was a grasping sort of man, who sold the Tudor chimney-pots to make sun-dials." Harriet opened the gate and Sally and the photographer walked meekly through.

"And *that*," continued Harriet, triumphantly, "is some-body's ginger cat. He has adopted us. He sits on Peter's shoulder at breakfast. Everybody likes an animal story. You can have the ginger cat."

She shut the gate and smiled over it at them.

Salcombe Hardy reflected that Peter Wimsey's wife was almost handsome when she was excited. He sympathised with her anxiety about Peter's feelings. He really thought she must be fond of the old blighter. He was deeply moved, for the whisky had been generously measured. He determined to do all he could to keep the human story dignified.

Half way down the lane, he remembered that he had somehow omitted to interview the servants. He looked back; but Harriet was still leaning over the gate.

Mr. Hector Puncheon of the *Morning Star* was less lucky. He arrived five minutes after Salcombe Hardy's departure, and found Lady Peter Wimsey still leaning over the gate. Since he could scarcely force his way past her, he was obliged to take his story then and there, as she chose to give it to him. Half way through, he felt something blow warmly upon his neck, and turned round with a start.

"It's only a bull," said Harriet, sweetly.

Mr. Puncheon, who was town-bred, turned pale. The bull was accompanied by six cows, all inquisitive. Had he known it, their presence was the best guarantee of the bull's good conduct; but to him they were all, equally, large beasts with horns. He could not with courtesy drive them away, because Lady Peter was thoughtfully scratching the bull's forehead while contributing some interesting and exclusive details about her own early life at Great Pagford. Manfully—for a reporter must accept all risks in the execution of his duty—he stuck to his post, listening with (he could not help it) a divided attention. "You are fond of animals?" he inquired. "Oh, very," said Harriet; "you must tell your readers that; it's a sympathetic trait, isn't it?" "Sure thing," replied Hector Puncheon. All very well; but the bull was on his side of the gate and she was on the other. A friendly cow all red and white licked his ear—he was astonished to find its tongue so rough.

"You'll excuse my not opening the gate," said Harriet, with an engaging smile. "I love cows—but not in the garden." To his embarrassment, she climbed over and escorted him with a firm hand to his car. The interview was over, and he had had very little opportunity of getting a personal angle on the murder. The cows scattered, with lowered heads, from before his moving wheels.

By a remarkable coincidence, no sooner had he gone than the invisible guardian of the cattle rose up from nowhere and began to collect the herd. On seeing Harriet, he grinned and touched his cap. She strolled back to the house, and before she had got there the cows were gathered round the gate again. At the open kitchen window stood Bunter, polishing glasses.

"Rather convenient, " said Harriet, "all those cows in the lane."

"Yes, my lady," agreed Bunter demurely. "They graze upon the grass verge, I understand. A very satisfactory arrangement if I may say so."

Harriet opened her mouth, and shut it again as a thought struck her. She went down the passage and opened the back door. She was not really surprised to see an extraordinarily ugly bull-mastiff tied by a rope to the scraper. Bunter came out of the kitchen and padded softly into the scullery.

"Is that our dog, Bunter?"

"The owner brought him this morning, my lady, to inquire whether his lordship might desire to purchase an animal of that description. I understand he is an excellent watch-dog. I suggested that he should be left here to await his lordship's convenience."

Harriet looked at Bunter, who returned her gaze unmoved.

"Have you thought of aeroplanes, Bunter? We might put a swan on the roof."

"I have not been able to hear of a swan, my lady. But there is a person who owns a goat. . . ."

"Mr. Hardy was rather fortunate."

"The cattle-driver," said Bunter, with sudden wrath, "was late. His instructions were perfectly clear. The lost time will be deducted from his remuneration. We must not be paltered with. His lordship is not accustomed to it. Excuse me, my lady—the goat is just arriving, and I fear there may be a little difficulty with the dog on the door-step."

Harriet left him to it.

CHAPTER XIV

♦

Crowner's Quest

Love? Do I love? I walk
Within the brilliance of another's thought,
As in a glory. I was dark before,
As Venus' chapel in the black of night:
But there was something holy in the darkness,

Softer and not so thick as other where;
And as rich moonlight may be to the blind,
Unconsciously consoling. Then love came,
Like the out-bursting of a trodden star.
—Thomas Lovell Beddoes, *The Second Brother*

The coroner did not, after all, confine himself to taking evidence of identity; but he showed a laudable discretion in handling his witnesses. Miss Twitterton, in a brand-new black frock, a perky little close-fitting hat and a black coat of old-fashioned cut, clearly resurrected for the occasion, testified, with sniffs, that the body was that of her uncle, William Noakes, and that she had not seen him since the last Sunday week. She explained her uncle's habit of dividing his time between Broxford and Paggleham, and about the two sets of keys. Her endeavours to explain also about the sale of the house and the astonishing financial situation disclosed were kindly but firmly cut short, and Lord Peter Wimsey, in act more graceful, took her place and gave a brief and rather nonchalant *résumé* of his surprising wedding-night experiences. He handed the coroner various papers concerning the purchase of the house and sat down amid a murmur of sympathetic comment. Then came an accountant from Broxford, with a statement about the moribund condition of the wireless business, as revealed by a preliminary examination of the books. Mervyn Bunter, in well-chosen language, recounted the visit of the sweep and the subsequent discovery of the body. Dr. Craven spoke to the cause and probable time of death, described the injuries, and gave it as his opinion that they could not have been self-inflicted or produced by an accidental fall.

Next came Joe Sellon, very white in the face, but in official control of himself. He said he had been summoned to see the dead body, and described how it lay in the cellar.

"You are the village constable?"

"Yes, sir."

"When did you last see the deceased alive?"

"On the Wednesday night, sir, at five minutes past nine."

"Will you tell us about that?"

"Yes, sir. I had a certain matter of a private nature to discuss with the deceased. I proceeded to the house and spoke to him at the sitting-room window for about ten minutes."

"Did he then seem just as usual?"

"Yes, sir; except that words passed between us and he was a little excited. When we had finished our conversation he shut and bolted the window. I tried both doors and found them locked. I then went away."

"You did not enter the house?"

"No, sir."

"And you left him at 9.15 p.m., alive and well?"

"Yes, sir."

"Very well."

Joe Sellon turned to go; but the lugubrious man whom Bunter had met in the pub rose up from among the jury and said:

"We should like to ask the witness, Mr. Perkins, what he had words with the deceased about."

"You hear," said the coroner, slightly put out. "The jury wish to know the cause of your dispute with the deceased."

"Yes, sir. The deceased threatened to report me for a breach of duty."

"Ah!" said the coroner. "Well, we are not here to examine into your official conduct. It was he that threatened you, not you that threatened him?"

"That's right, sir; though I admit I was annoyed and spoke a bit sharp to him."

"I see. You did not return to the house that night?"

"No, sir."

"Very well; that will do. Superintendent Kirk."

The little stir of excitement aroused by Sellon's evidence died down before the enormous impassivity of Mr. Kirk, who described, very slowly and at considerable length, the arrangement of the rooms in the house, the nature of the fastenings on the doors and windows and the difficulty of ascertaining the facts due to the (quite fortuitous though very unfortunate) disturbance caused by the arrival of the new occupiers. The next witness was Martha Ruddle. She was in a great state of excitement, and almost excessively ready to assist the law. It was, indeed, her own readiness that undid her.

"... that taken aback," said Mrs. Ruddle, "you could a-knocked me down with a feather. Driving up to the door in the middle of the night as you might say, in sech a big motor-car as I never did see in all my born days, not without it was on the picturs— Lord what? I says, not believing him, which I'm sure, sir, it ain't surprising, more like film-stars I says, begging your pardon, and of course I were mistook, but that there car being so big and the lady in a fur coat and the gentleman with a glass in his eye jest like Ralph Lynn, which was all I could see in the—"

Peter turned the monocle on the witness with so outraged an astonishment that the giggles turned to loud laughter.

"Kindly keep to the question," said Mr. Perkins, vexed; "you were surprised to hear that the house was sold. Very well. We have heard how you got in. Will you please describe the condition of the house as you observed it."

From a tangle of irrelevancies, the coroner disengaged the facts that the bed had not been slept in, that the supper things were on the table, and that the cellar-door had been found open. With a weary sigh (for his cold was a severe one and he wanted to finish and get home), he took the witness back to the events of the preceding Wednesday.

"Yes," said Mrs. Ruddle, "I did see Joe Sellon, and a nice sorter pleeceman 'e is, usin' language not fit for a respectable woman to listen to, I don't wonder Mr. Noakes shet the window in 'is face. . . ."

"You saw him do that?"

"Plain as the nose on your face, I see 'im. Standin' there 'e was with the candlestick in 'is 'and, same as I couldn't miss seein' 'im, and laffin' fit to bust, and well 'e might, 'earin' Joe Sellon carryin' on that ridiculous. Well, I says to meself, a nice pleeceman you are, Joe Sellon, and I oughter know it, seein' you 'ad ter come ter me to find out 'oo took them 'ens of Miss Twitterton's. . . ."

"We are not inquiring into that," began the coroner, when the lugubrious man again rose up and said:

"The jury would like to know whether the witness heard what the quarrel was about."

"Yes, I did," said the witness, without waiting for the coroner. "They was quarrellin' about 'is wife, that's what they was quarrellin' about, and I say it's a—"

"Whose wife?" asked the coroner; while the whole room rustled with expectation.

"Joe's wife, o'course," said Mrs. Ruddle. "What 'ave you done wi' my wife, you old villain, 'e says, usin' names wot I wouldn't put me tongue to."

Joe Sellon sprang to his feet.

"That's a lie, sir!"

"Now, Joe," said Kirk.

"We'll hear you in a moment," said Mr. Perkins. "Now, Mrs. Ruddle. You're sure you heard those words?"

"The bad words, sir?"

"The words, 'What have you done with my wife'?"

"Oh, yes, sir—I heard that, sir."

"Did any threats pass?"

"N'no, sir," admitted Mrs. Ruddle, regretfully, "only sayin' as Mr. Noakes was bound for the bad place, sir."

"Quite so. No suggestions about how he was likely to get there?"

"Sir?"

"No mention of killing or murder?"

"Not as I 'eard, sir, but I wouldn't be surprised if 'e did offer to kill Mr. Noakes. Not a bit, I wouldn't."

"But actually you heard nothing of the sort?"

"Well, I couldn't rightly say I did, sir."

"And Mr. Noakes was alive and well when he shut the window?"

"Yes, sir."

Kirk leaned across the table and spoke to the coroner, who asked:

"Did you hear anything further?"

"I didn't *want* to 'ear nothing further, sir. All I 'eard was that Joe Sellon a-'ammerin' on the door."

"Did you hear Mr. Noakes let him in?"

"Let 'im in?" cried Mrs. Ruddle. "Wot 'ud Mr. Noakes want ter be lettin' 'im in for? Mr. Noakes wouldn't let nobody in wot used language to 'im like wot Joe used. 'E was a terrible timid man, was Mr. Noakes."

"I see. And the next morning you came to the house and got no answer?"

"That's right. And I says, lor', I says, Mr. Noakes must a-gone over to Broxford. . . ."

"Yes; you told us that before. And although you had heard all this terrible quarrel the night before, it never occurred to you that anything might have happened to Mr. Noakes?"

"Well, no, I didn't. I thought 'e'd gone off to Broxford, same as 'e often did. . . ."

"Quite. In fact, until Mr. Noakes was found dead, you thought nothing of this quarrel and attached no importance to it?"

"Well," said Mrs. Ruddle, "only w'en I knowed as 'e must a-died afore 'ar-pas'-nine."

"How did you know that?"

Mrs. Ruddle, with many circumlocutions, embarked upon the story of the wireless. Peter Wimsey wrote a few lines on a scrap of paper, which he folded and passed to Kirk. The Superintendent nodded, and passed it on to the coroner, who, at the conclusion of the story, asked:

"Wireless was Mr. Noakes's business?"

"Oh, yes, sir."

"If anything had gone wrong with the set, could he have put it right?"

"Oh, yes, sir. 'E was very clever with them things."

"But he only cared to listen to the news-bulletin?"

"That's right, sir."

"What time did he usually go to bed?"

"Eleven o'clock, sir. Reg'lar as clockwork 'e was, supper at 'ar-pas'-seven, Noos at 'ar-pas'-nine, bed at eleven, w'en 'e wos at 'ome, that is."

"Quite. How did you come to be near enough at half past nine to know whether the wireless was on?"

Mrs. Ruddle hesitated.

"I jest stepped over to the shed, sir."

"Yes?"

"Jest ter fetch something, sir."

"Yes?"

"Only a mite o' paraffin, sir," said Mrs. Ruddle, "which I'd a-put it back faithful in the morning, sir."

"Ah, yes. Well, that's none of our business. Thank you. Now, Joseph Sellon—you want to make a further statement?"

"Yes, sir. Only this, sir. Them words about Mrs. Sellon wasn't never mentioned at all. I might a-said, 'Now, don't you report me, sir, or I'll be in trouble, and what'll become of my wife?' That's all, sir."

"The deceased never interfered with your wife in any way?"

"No, sir. Certainly not, sir."

"I think I had better ask you whether the last witness bears you any grudge, to your knowledge."

"Well, sir, about them 'ens o' Miss Twitterton's. In the execution of my duty I 'ad to interrogate 'er son Albert, and I think she took it amiss, sir."

"I see. I think that's— Yes, Superintendent?"

Mr. Kirk had just received another message from his noble colleague. It appeared to perplex him; but he faithfully put the question.

"Well," said Mr. Perkins, "I should have thought you could have asked him yourself. However. The Superintendent wishes to know the length of the candle deceased had in his hand when he came to the window."

Joe Sellon stared.

"I don't know, sir," he said, finally. "I never noticed. I don't think it was special one way or the other."

The coroner turned interrogatively to Kirk, who, not knowing what was behind the question, shook his head.

Mr. Perkins, blowing his nose irritably, dismissed the witness and turned to the jury.

"Well, gentlemen, I don't see that we can finish this inquiry today. You see that it is impossible to fix the exact moment when deceased met his death, since he may have been prevented from hearing the news-bulletin by a temporary defect in the wireless apparatus, which he may have subsequently repaired. You have heard that the police are in a considerable difficulty as regards the collecting of evidence, since (by a most unfortunate accident for which nobody is at all to blame) various possible clues were destroyed. I understand that the police would like an adjournment—is that so?"

Kirk said that it was so; and the coroner adjourned the inquiry to that day fortnight, thus putting a tame end to a very promising affair.

As the audience scrambled from the little court, Kirk caught Peter.

"That old catamaran!" he said, angrily. "Mr. Perkins came down pretty sharp on her, but if he'd listened to me, he wouldn't have taken any evidence, only to identity."

"You think that would have been wise? To let her put her story all round the village, and everybody saying you didn't dare to let it come out at the inquest? He did at least give her the opportunity for an open display of spite. I think he's done better for you than you realise."

"Maybe you're right, my lord. I didn't see it that way. What was the point about that candle?"

"I wondered how much he really did remember. If he's not sure about the candle, he may only have imagined the clock."

"That's so," said Kirk, slowly. He was not sure about the implications of this. Nor, to tell the truth, was Wimsey.

"He might," Harriet suggested softly in her husband's ear, "have lied about the time."

"So he might. The queer thing is that he didn't. Mrs. Ruddle's clock said the same."

"Hawkshaw the Detective, in *Who Put Back the Clock?*"

"Here!" said Kirk, exasperated; "look at that!"

Peter looked. Mrs. Ruddle, on the doorstep, was holding a kind of court among the reporters.

"Goodness!" said Harriet. "Peter, can't you take them away? Who was the chap who leapt into the gulf?"

"Rome prizes most her citizens—"

"But every Englishman loves a lord. That's the idea."

"My wife," said Peter mournfully, "would cheerfully throw me to the lions, if required. *Moriturus*—very well, we'll try."

He advanced resolutely on the group. Mr. Puncheon, seeing this noble prey at his mercy, unprotected by fat bulls of Basan, flung himself upon him with a gleeful cry. The other hounds closed in about them.

"I say," said a grumbling voice close by, "I ought to 'ave given evidence. The law ought to know about them forty quid. Trying to 'ush it up, that's what they are."

"I don't suppose it seems so important to them, Frank."

"It's important to me. 'Sides, didn't 'e tell me as 'e was goin' to pay me on Wednesday? I reckon the coroner ought to a-been told about it."

Salcombe Hardy, having had his chance with Peter, had not abandoned his hold on Mrs. Ruddle. Mischievously, Harriet determined to pry him loose.

"Mr. Hardy—if you want an inside story, you'd better get hold of the gardener, Frank Crutchley. There he is, over there, talking to Miss Twitterton. He wasn't called at the inquest, so the others may not realise he's got anything to tell them."

Sally bubbled over with gratitude.

"If you make it worth his while," said Harriet, with serpent malice, "he *might* keep it exclusive."

"Thanks very much," said Sally, "for the tip."

"That's part of our bargain," said Harriet, beaming upon him. Mr. Hardy was rapidly coming to the conclusion that Peter had married a most fascinating woman. He made a rapid dart at Crutchley and in a few moments was seen to depart with him in the direction of the Four-Ale bar. Mrs. Ruddle, suddenly deserted, gazed indignantly about her.

"Oh, *there* you are, Mrs. Ruddle! Where's Bunter? We'd better let him drive us home and come back for his lordship, or we shall get no lunch. I'm simply starving. What an impertinent, tiresome lot these newspaper men are!"

"That's right, m'lady," said Mrs. Ruddle. "I wouldn't talk to the likes of them!"

She tossed her head, setting some curious jet ornaments on her bonnet jingling, and followed her mistress to the car.

Sitting up in all that grandeur she would feel just like a film-star herself. Reporters, indeed!

As they drove away, six cameras clicked.

"There now," said Harriet. "You'll be in all the papers."

"Well, to be sure!" said Mrs. Ruddle.

"Peter."

"Madam?"

"Funny, after what we said, that suggestion cropping up about Mrs. Sellon."

"Village matron instead of village maiden. Yes; very odd."

"There can't be anything in it?"

"You never know."

"You didn't think so when you said it?"

"I am always trying to say something too silly to be believed; but I never manage it. Have another cutlet?"

"Thanks, I will. Bunter cooks like an angel in the house. I thought Sellon got through his examination surprisingly well."

"Nothing like telling the exact official truth and no more. Kirk must have coached him pretty thoroughly. I wonder if Kirk— No, dash it! I won't wonder. I won't be bothered with all these people. We seem curiously unable to get any time to ourselves this honeymoon. And that reminds me—the vicar wants us to go round to his place this evening for a sherry-party."

"A sherry-party? Good heavens!"

"We provide the party and he provides the sherry. His wife will be so delighted to see us, and will we excuse her not calling first, as she has a Women's Institute this afternoon."

"Must we?"

"I think we must. Our example has encouraged him to start a sherry-fashion in these parts, and he has sent for a bottle on purpose."

Harried gazed at him in dismay.

"Where from?"

"From the best hotel in Pagford. . . . I accepted with pleasure for both of us. Was that wrong?"

"Peter, you're not *normal*. You have a social conscience

far in advance of your sex. Public-house sherry at the vicarage! Ordinary, decent men shuffle and lie till their wives drag them out by the ears. There must be *something* you'll jib at. Will you refuse to put on a boiled shirt?"

"Do you think a boiled shirt would please them? I suppose it would. Besides, you've got a new frock you want to show me."

"You're definitely too good to live. . . . Of course we'll go and drink their sherry, if we die of it. But couldn't we just be selfish and naughty this afternoon?"

"As how?"

"Go off somewhere by ourselves."

"By God, we will! . . . Is that really your notion of happiness?"

"To that depth have I fallen. I admit it. Don't dance on a woman when she's down. Have some of this—I don't know what it is—this thing Bunter's made. It looks absolutely marvellous."

"Just how naughty and selfish may I be? . . . May I drive fast? . . . I mean, really fast?"

Harriet repressed a shudder. She liked to drive, and even liked being driven, but anything over seventy miles an hour made her feel hollow inside. Still, married people cannot have everything their own way.

"Yes, really fast—if you feel like that."

"Definitely too good to live!"

"I should say, definitely too good to die. . . . But really fast means the main road."

"So it does. Well, we'll do the main road really fast and get rid of it."

The ordeal lasted only as far as Great Pagford. Happily they encountered none of Superintendent Kirk's black sheep parked on bends, though, just outside, they shot past Frank Crutchley driving a taxi and were rewarded by his astonished and admiring stare. Passing the police-station at a demure legal thirty, they turned out westward and took to the sideroads. Harriet, who could not distinctly recollect having breathed at all since they left Paggleham, filled her lungs and observed in resolutely steady tones that it was a lovely day for a run.

"Isn't it? Do you approve of this road?"

"It's beautiful," said Harriet, fervently. "*All* corners!" He laughed.

"*Prière de ne pas brutaliser la machine*. I ought to know better—God knows I'm frightened of enough things myself. I must have a streak of my father in me. He was one of the old school—you either faced a fence of your own accord or were walloped over and no nonsense. It worked—after a fashion. One learnt to pretend one wasn't a coward, and take out the change in bad dreams."

"You certainly don't show any signs of it."

"One of these days you'll find me out, I expect. I don't happen to be afraid of speed—that's why I like to show off. But I give you my word I won't do it again, this trip."

He let the needle drop back to twenty-five and they dawdled on through the lanes in silence, with no particular direction. About the mid-afternoon, they found themselves in a village some thirty miles from home—an old village with a new church and a pond flanking a trim central green, all clustered at the base of a little rise. On a side opposite the church, a narrow and rather ill-made lane appeared to rise towards the brow of the hill.

"Let's go up there," said Harriet, appealed to for instructions. "It looks as though we should get a good view."

The car swung into the lane and wound its way up with lazy ease between low hedges already touched with autumn. Below and to their left was spread the pleasant English country, green and russet with well-wooded fields sloping to a stream that twinkled placidly in the October sunshine. Here and there the pale glint of stubble showed amid the pasture; or the blue smoke drifted above the trees from the red chimneys of a farm. On their right, at a bend of the road, they came upon a ruined church, only the porch and a portion of the chancel arch left standing. The other stone-work had doubtless been carried away to build the new church in the centre of the village; but the abandoned graves with their ancient headstones had been trimly kept, and just within the open gate a space had been levelled and made into a kind of garden-plot with flower-beds and a sun-dial and a wooden seat on which visitors could rest to view the distant prospect. Peter gave an exclamation, and let the car slide to a standstill on the grass verge.

"May I lose my last dollar," he said, "if that isn't one of our chimney-pots!"

"I believe you're right," said Harriet, staring at the sun-dial, whose column did indeed bear a remarkable resemblance to a "Tooder pot." She followed Peter out of the car and through the gate. Seen close to, the sun-dial revealed itself as a miscellany; the dial and gnomon were ancient; the base was a millstone; the column, when sharply tapped, sounded hollow.

"I will have my pot back," said Peter in determined tones, "if I die for it. We will present the village with a handsome stone pillar in its place. Jack shall have Jill, Nought shall go ill, the man shall have his mare again and all go well. This suggests a new variation of the time-honoured sport of pot-hunting. We will track down our bartered chimneys from end to end of the county, as the Roman legions sought the lost eagles of Varus. I think the luck went out of the house with the chimney-pots, and it's our job to bring it back."

"That will be fun. I counted this morning: there are only four of them missing. This looks exactly like the three that are left."

"I'm positive it is ours. Something tells me so. Let us register our claim to it by a trifling act of vandalism which the first rain will blot out." He solemnly took out a pencil and inscribed upon the pot: "Talboys, *Suam quisque homo rem meminit*. Peter Wimsey." He handed the pencil to his wife, who added, "Harriet Wimsey," with the date below.

"First time of writing it?"

"Yes. It looks a little drunk, but that's because I had to squat down to it."

"No matter—it's an occasion. Let's occupy this handsome seat and contemplate the landscape. The car's well off the road if anybody wants to get up the lane."

The seat was solid and comfortable. Harriet pulled off her

hat and sat down, pleased to feel the soft wind stir her hair. Her gaze wandered idly over the sunlit valley. Peter hung his hat on the extended hand of a stout eighteenth-century cherub engaged in perusing a lichenous book on an adjacent tombstone, sat down on the other end of the seat and stared reflectively at his companion.

His spirits were in a state of confusion, into which the discovery of the murder and the problem of Joe Sellon and the clock had introduced only a subsidiary set of disturbing factors. These he dismissed from his mind, and set himself to reduce the chaos of his personal emotions to some sort of order.

He had got what he wanted. For nearly six years he directed his resolution stubbornly to a single end. Up to the very moment of achievement he had not paused to consider what might be the results of his victory. The last two days had given him little time for thought. He only knew that he was faced with an entirely strange situation, which was doing something quite extraordinary to his feelings.

He forced himself to examine his wife with detachment. Her face had character, but no one would ever think of calling it beautiful, and he had always—carelessly and condescendingly—demanded beauty as a pre-requisite. She was long-limbed and sturdily made, with a kind of loosely-knit freedom of movement that might, with a more controlled assurance, grow into grace; yet he could have named—and if he had chosen might have had—a score of women far lovelier in form and motion. Her speaking voice was deep and attractive; yet, after all, he had once owned the finest lyric soprano in Europe. Otherwise, what?—A skin like pale honey and a mind of a curious, tough quality that stimulated his own. Yet no woman had ever so stirred his blood; she had only to look or speak to make the very bones shake in his body.

He knew now that she could render back passion for passion with an eagerness beyond all expectation—and also with a kind of astonished gratitude that told him more than she knew. While a mannerly reticence forbade that the name of her dead lover should ever be mentioned between them, Peter, interpreting phenomena in the light of expert knowledge, found himself mentally applying to that unhappy young man quite a number of epithets, among which "clumsy lout" and "egotistical puppy" were the kindest. But the passionate exchange of felicity was no new experience: what was new was the enormous importance of the whole relationship. It was not merely that the present bond could not be sundered without scandal and expense and the troublesome interference of lawyers. It was that, for the first time in his experience, it really mattered to him what his relations with a lover were. He had somehow vaguely imagined that, the end of desire attained, soul and sense would lie down together like the lion and the lamb; but they did nothing of the sort. With orb and sceptre thrust into his hands, he was afraid to take hold on power and call his empire his own.

He remembered having said to his uncle (with a solemn dogmatism better befitting a much younger man): "Surely it is possible to love with the head as well as the heart." Mr. Delagardie had replied, somewhat drily: "No doubt; so long as you do not end by thinking with your entrails instead of your brain." This, he felt, was precisely what was happening to him. As soon as he tried to think, a soft, inexorable clutch seemed to fasten itself upon his bowels. He had become vulnerable in the very point where always, until now, he had been most triumphantly sure of himself. His wife's serene face told him that she had somehow gained all the confidence he had lost. Before their marriage, he had never seen her look like that.

"Harriet," he said, suddenly, "what do you think about life? I mean, do you find it good on the whole. Worth living?"

(He could, at any rate, trust her not to protest, archly: "That's a nice thing to ask on one's honeymoon!")

She turned to him with a quick readiness, as though here was the opportunity to say something she had been wanting to say for a long time:

"Yes! I've always felt absolutely certain it was good—if only one could get it straightened out. I've hated almost everything that ever happened to me, but I *knew* all the time it was just things that were wrong, not everything. Even when I felt most awful I never thought of killing myself or wanting to die—only of somehow getting out of the mess and starting again."

"That's rather admirable. With me it's always been the other way round. I can enjoy practically everything that comes along—while it's happening. Only I have to keep on doing things, because, if I once stop, it all seems a lot of rot and I don't care a damn if I go west tomorrow. At least, that's what I should have said. Now—I don't know. I'm beginning to think there may be something in it after all . . . Harriet—"

"It sounds like Jack Sprat and his wife."

"If there was any possible chance of straightening it out for *you*. . . . We've begun well, haven't we, with this awful bloody mess? When once we get clear of it, I'd give anything. But there you are, you see, it's the same thing over again."

"But that's what I'm trying to tell you. It ought to be, but it isn't. Things have come straight. I always knew they would if one hung on long enough, waiting for a miracle."

"Honestly, Harriet?"

"Well, it *seems* like a miracle to be able to look forward—to—to see all the minutes in front of one come hopping along with something marvellous in them, instead of just saying, Well, that one didn't actually hurt and the next may be quite bearable if only something beastly doesn't come pouncing out—"

"As bad as that?"

"No, not really, because one got used to it—to being everlastingly tightened up to face things, you see. But when one doesn't have to any more, it's different—I can't tell you what a difference it makes. You—you—you— Oh, damn and blast you, Peter, you *know* you're making me feel exactly like Heaven, so what's the sense of trying to spare your feelings?"

"I don't know it and I can't believe it, but come here and I'll try. That's better." His chin was pressed upon her head when the sword came back from the sea. "No, you are not too heavy—you needn't insult me. Listen, dear, if that's true or even half true, I shall begin to be afraid of death. At my age it's rather disturbing. All right—you needn't apologise. I like new sensations."

Women had found paradise in his arms before now—and told him so, with considerable emphasis and eloquence. He had accepted the assurance cheerfully, because he had not really cared whether they found paradise or only the Champs Elysées, so long as the place was a pleasant one. He was as much troubled and confused now as though somebody had credited him with the possession of a soul. In strict logic, of course, he would have had to admit that he had as much right to a soul as anybody else, but the mocking analogy of the camel and the needle's eye was enough to make that claim stick in his throat as a silly piece of presumption. Of such was not the kingdom of heaven. He had the kingdoms of the earth, and they should be enough for him: though nowadays it was in better taste to pretend neither to desire nor deserve them. But he was filled with a curious misgiving, as though he had meddled in matters too high for him; as though he were being forced, body and bones, through some enormous wringer that was squeezing out of him something undifferentiated till now, and even now excessively nebulous and inapprehensible. *Vagula, blandula*, he thought—pleasantly erratic and surely of no consequence—it couldn't possibly turn into something that had to be reckoned with. He made the mental gesture of waving away an intrusive moth, and tightened his bodily hold on his wife as though to remind himself of the palpable presence of the flesh. She responded with a small contented sound like a snort—an absurd sound that seemed to lift the sealing stone and release some well-spring of laughter deep down within him. It came bubbling and leaping up in the most tremendous hurry to reach the sunlight, so that all his blood danced with it and his lungs were stifled with the rush and surge of this extraordinary fountain of delight. He felt himself at once ridiculous and omnipotent. He was exultant. He wanted to shout.

Actually, he neither moved nor spoke. He sat still, letting the mysterious rapture have its way with him. Whatever it was, it was something that had been suddenly liberated and was intoxicated by its new freedom. It was behaving very foolishly and its folly enchanted him.

"Peter?"

"What is it, lady?"

"Have I got any money?"

The preposterous irrelevance of the question made the fountain shoot sky-high.

"My darling fool, yes, of course you have. We spent a whole morning signing papers."

"Yes, I know, but where is it? I mean, can I draw a cheque on it? I was thinking, I'd never paid my secretary her salary and at the moment I haven't got a penny in the world except what's yours."

"It isn't mine, it's your own. Settled on you. Murbles explained all that, though I don't suppose you were listening. But I know what you mean, and yes, it's there, and yes, you can draw a cheque on it straight away. Why this state of sudden destitution?"

"Because, Mr. Rochester, I wasn't going to be married in grey alpaca. And I spent every blessed thing I had to do you proud, and then some. I left poor Miss Bracey lamenting *and* borrowed ten bob of her at the last minute for enough petrol to get me to Oxford. That's right, laugh! I did kill my pride—but, oh, Peter! it had a lovely death."

"Full sacrificial rites. Harriet, I really believe you love me. You couldn't do anything so unutterably and divinely right by accident. *Quelle folie—mais quel geste!*"

"I thought it would amuse you. That's why I told you instead of borrowing a stamp from Bunter and writing a formal inquiry to the bank."

"Meaning that you don't grudge me my victory. Generous woman! While you're about it, tell me something else. How the blazes, with all the other things, did you manage to afford the Donne autograph?"

"That was a special effort. Three five-thousand-word shorts at forty guineas each for the *Thrill Magazine*."

"What? the story about the young man who murdered his aunt with a boomerang?"

"Yes; and the unpleasant stockbroker who was found in the curate's front parlour with his head bashed in, like old Noakes—Oh, dear! I was forgetting all about poor Mr. Noakes."

"Damn old Noakes! At least, perhaps I'd better not say that. It might be true. I remember the curate. What was the third? The cook who put prussic acid in the almond icing?"

"Yes. Where did you get hold of that exceedingly low-class rag? Does Bunter pore over it in his leisure moments?"

"No; he reads photographic journals. But there are such things as press-cutting agencies."

"Are there, indeed? How long have you been collecting cuttings?"

"Nearly six years, isn't it, by now? They lead a shamefaced existence in a locked drawer, and Bunter pretends to know nothing about them. When some impertinent beast of a bone-headed reviewer has turned me dyspeptic with fury, he politely attributes my ill-temper to the inclement season. Your turn to laugh. I had to be maudlin over something, curse it, and you didn't overwhelm me with material. I once lived three weeks on a belated notice in *Punch*. Brute, fiend, devil-woman—you might say you're sorry."

"I can't be sorry for anything. I've forgotten how."

He was silent. The fountain had become a stream that ran chuckling and glittering through his consciousness, spreading as it went into a wide river that swept him up and drowned him in itself. To speak of it was impossible; he could only have taken refuge in inanities. His wife looked at him, thoughtfully drew her feet up on to the seat so as to take her weight from his knees and settled herself into acquiescence with his mood.

Whether, left to themselves, they would have succeeded in emerging from this speechless trance, and might not, in the manner of Donne's ecstatic couple, have remained like sepulchral statues in the same posture and saying nothing until nightfall, is uncertain. Three quarters of an hour later an elderly bearded person came creaking up the lane with a horse and waggon. He looked at them with ruminative eyes, showing no particular curiosity; but the spell was broken. Harriet swung herself hurriedly off her husband's knees and stood up; Peter, who in London would rather have been seen dead than embracing anybody in public, astonishingly showed no embarrassment, but cried out a cordial greeting to the carter.

"Is my bus in your way?"

"No, sir, thank 'ee. Don't disturb yourself."

"Lovely day it's been." He strolled down to the gate, and the man checked his horse.

"That it has. A real lovely day."

"Pleasant little spot, this. Who put up the seat?"

"That's squire done that, sir; Mr. Trevor over at the big house. He done it along of the women as likes to come up Sunday arternoons with their flowers and such. The new church ain't only been built five year, and there's a sight of folks likes to 'tend to the graves in the old churchyard. It's closed for buryings now, of course, but squire says, why not make it pleasant and comfor'ble-like. It's a stiffish pull up the lane and weariful to the children and the old people. So that's what he done."

"We are very much beholden to him. Was the sun-dial here before that?"

The carter chuckled.

"Lord love you, no, sir. She's a regular job, is that there sun-dial. Vicar, he found the top of her put away in the rubbish-'ole when they was clearing away the old church, and Bill Muggins he says, 'There's the stone outer the old mill 'ud make a beautiful base for 'er, if so be we 'ad a bit of a drain-pipe or summat to put between 'em.' And Jim Hawtrey, *he* says, 'I know a man,' he says, 'over at Paggleham wot 'as 'arf-a-dozen of them ancient old chimbley-pots for sale. What's the matter with that?' So they tells vicar and he tells squire and they gets the bits together and Joe Dudden and 'Arry Gates, they puts 'em up with a lick o' mortar in their spare time, vicar puttin' the top on with 'is watch in 'is 'and and a little book so she'll tell the time correct. You'll find 'er middlin' right now, sir, if you look. 'Course, in summer she's an hour out, her keepin' to God's time and us 'aving to go by Gov'ment time. It's a cur'ous thing you askin' about that there sun-dial, because why? The very man wot sold vicar the chimbley-pot, 'e wos found dead in his own 'ouse only yesterday, and they do say it was murder."

"You don't say so. It's a queer world, isn't it? What's the name of this village? Lopsley? Thanks very much. Get yourself a drink. . . . By the way, you know you've got a loose shoe on your near hind?"

The carter said he had not noticed it and thanked the observant gentleman for his information. The horse lolloped on.

"Time we were getting back," said Peter, with a reluctant note in his voice, "if we're to change in time for the vicar's sherry. We'll call on the squire, though, before we're many days older. I'm determined to have that pot."

CHAPTER XV

♦

Sherry—and Bitters

Fool, hypocrite, villain—man! Thou canst not call me that.

—George Lillo, *Tragedy of George Barnwell*

Harriet was glad they had taken the trouble to dress. The vicar's wife (whom she vaguely remembered to have seen in the old days at bazaars and flower shows, perpetually stout, amiable and a little red in the face) had done honour to the occasion with a black lace dress and a daring little bridge coat in flowered chiffon velvet. She advanced with a beaming face to meet them.

"You poor things! What an upset for you! It is so nice of you to come and see us. I hope Simon apologised for my not calling, but what with my house and the parish work and the Women's Institute I was quite busy all day. Do come and sit down by the fire. *You*, of course, are an old friend, my dear, though I don't suppose you remember me. Let my husband help you off with your coat. *What* a pretty frock! Such a lovely colour. I hope you don't mind my saying so. I do so love to see bright colours and bright faces about me. Come and sit on the sofa, against this green cushion—you'll make quite a picture. . . . No, no, Lord Peter, don't sit on that! It's a rocking-chair; it always takes people by surprise. Most men like *this* one, it's nice and deep. Now, Simon, where did you put those cigarettes?"

"Here they are, here they are. I hope they're the kind you like. I'm a pipe-smoker myself and not very knowledgeable, I fear. Oh, thank you, thank you, no—not a pipe just before dinner. I will try a cigarette, just for a change. Now, my dear, will you join us in this little dissipation?"

"Well, I don't *usually*," said Mrs. Goodacre, "because of the parish, you know. It's very absurd, but one has to set an example."

"These particular parishioners," said Peter, striking a match persuasively, "are corrupted already beyond hope of repentance."

"Very well, then, I will," said the vicar's lady.

"Bravo!" said Mr. Goodacre. "That really makes it quite a gay party. Now! It is my prerogative to distribute the sherry. I believe I am right in saying that sherry is the only wine with which the goddess Nicotina does not quarrel."

"Quite right, padre."

"Ah! You confirm that opinion. I am very glad—very glad indeed to hear you say so. And here—ah, yes! Will you have some of these little biscuits? Dear me, what a remarkable variety! Quite an *embarras de richesses!*"

"They come assorted in boxes," said Mrs. Goodacre, simply. "Cocktail biscuits, they call them. We had them at the last whist drive."

"Of course, of course! Now which is the kind that has cheese inside it?"

"These, I think," said Harriet, from a plenitude of experience, "and those long ones."

"So they are! How clever of you to know. I shall look to

you to guide me through this delectable maze. I must say, I think a little social gathering like this before dinner is a most excellent idea."

"You are sure you would not like to stay and dine with us?" said Mrs. Goodacre, anxiously. "Or to spend the night? Our spare room is always ready. Are you *really* comfortable at Talboys, after all this terrible business? I told my husband to tell you that if there was anything at all we could do—"

"He faithfully delivered your kind message," said Harriet. "It's ever so good of you. But really and truly we're quite all right."

"Well," said the vicar's wife, "I expect you would rather be alone, so I won't be an officious old busybody. In our position one's always interfering with people for their good, you know. I'm sure it's a bad habit. By the way, Simon, poor little Mrs. Sellon's very much upset. She was taken quite ill this morning, and we had to send for the district nurse."

"Oh, dear, dear!" said the vicar. "Poor woman! That was a very extraordinary suggestion Martha Ruddle made at the inquest. There can't, surely, be anything in it."

"Certainly not. Nonsense. Martha likes to make herself important. She's a spiteful old thing. Though I can't help saying, even now he's dead, that William Noakes was a nasty old creature."

"Not in *that* way, surely, my dear?"

"You never know. But I meant, I couldn't blame Martha Ruddle for disliking him. It's all very well for you, Simon. You always think charitably of everyone. And besides, you never talked to him about anything except gardening. Though as a matter of fact, Frank Crutchley did all the work."

"Frank is a very clever gardener, indeed," said the vicar. "In fact he is clever all round. He found the defect in my motor-car engine immediately. I'm sure he will go far."

"He's going a little too far with that girl Polly, if you ask me," retorted his wife. "It's about time they asked you to put up the banns. Her mother came up to see me the other day. Well, Mrs. Mason, I said, you know what girls are, and I admit it's very difficult to control them these days. If I were you, I should speak to Frank and ask him what his intentions are. However, we mustn't begin talking about parish matters."

"I should be sorry," said the vicar, "to think ill of Frank Crutchley. Or of poor William Noakes, either. I expect there is nothing in it but talk. Dear me! To think that when I called at the house last Thursday morning, he was lying there dead! I particularly wanted to see him, I remember. I had a small offering of a *Teesdalia nudicaulis* for his rock-garden—he was fond of rock-plants. I felt very melancholy when I planted it here, myself, this morning."

"You are even fonder of plants than he was," said Harriet, glancing round the shabby room, which was filled with pot-plants on stands and tables.

"I am afraid I must admit the soft impeachment. Gardening is an indulgence of mine. My wife tells me it runs away with too much money, and I dare say she is right."

"I said he ought to get himself a new cassock," said Mrs. Goodacre, laughing. "But if he prefers rock-plants, that's his business."

"I wonder," said the vicar, wistfully, "what will become of William Noakes's plants. I suppose they will belong to Aggie Twitterton."

"I don't know," said Peter. "The whole thing may have to be sold, I suppose, for the benefit of the creditors."

"Dear, dear!" exclaimed the vicar. "Oh, I do hope they will be properly looked after. Especially the cacti. They are delicate creatures, and it is getting rather late in the year. I remember peeping in at the window last Thursday and thinking it was hardly safe for them to be left in that room without a fire. It's time they were put under glass for the winter. Particularly the big one in the hanging pot and that new variety he's got in the window. Of course, *you* will be keeping up good fires."

"We shall, indeed," said Harriet. "Now that we have got the chimneys clear, with your assistance. I hope your shoulder isn't still painful."

"I can feel it, I can feel it a little. But nothing to speak of. Just a slight bruise, that is all. . . . If there is to be a sale, I shall hope to make an offer for the cacti—if Aggie Twitterton doesn't want to buy them in for herself. And with your permission, my dear, of course."

"Frankly, Simon, I think them detestably hideous things. But I'm quite ready to offer a home to them. I know you've been coveting those cacti for years."

"Not coveting, I hope," said the vicar. "But I fear I must confess to a great weakness for cacti."

"It's a morbid passion," said his wife.

"Really, my dear, really—you shouldn't use such exaggerated language. Come, Lady Peter—another glass of sherry. Indeed, you mustn't refuse!"

"Shall I put them peas on, Mr. Bunter?"

Bunter paused in his occupation of tidying the sitting-room and strode with some haste to the door.

"*I* will see to the peas, Mrs. Ruddle, at the proper time." He looked up at the clock, which marked five minutes past six. "His lordship is very particular about peas."

"Is he now?" Mrs. Ruddle seemed to take this as a signal for conversation, for she appeared on the threshold. "That's jest like my Bert. 'Ma,' 'e allus says, 'I 'ates peas 'ard.' Funny, 'ow often they *is* 'ard. Or biled right away outer their shells. One or other."

Bunter offered no comment, and she tried again. "'Ere's them things you arst me to polish. Come up lovely, ain't they?"

She offered for inspection a brass toasting-fork and the fragment of a roasting-jack that had so unexpectedly made its appearance from the chimney.

"Thank you," said Bunter. He hung the toasting-fork on a nail by the fireplace and, after a little consideration, set the other specimen upright on the what-not.

"Funny" pursued Mrs. Ruddle, "the way the gentry is about them old bits o' things. Curios! Rubbish, if you ask me."

"This is a very old piece," replied Bunter, gravely, stepping back to admire the effect.

Mrs. Ruddle sniffed. "Reckon them as shoved it up the chimbley knew wot they wos doin'. Give me a nice gas-oven any day. Ah! I'd like that—same as my sister's wot lives in Biggleswade."

"People have been found dead in gas-ovens before now," said Bunter, grimly. He took up his master's blazer, shook it, appeared to estimate its contents by their weight, and removed a pipe, a tobacco-pouch and three boxes of matches from one pocket.

"Lor' now, Mr. Bunter, don't you talk like that! Ain't we 'ad enough corpusses about the 'ouse already? 'Ow they can go on livin' 'ere I *don't* know!"

"Speaking for his lordship and myself, we are accustomed to corpses." He extracted several more match-boxes and, at the bottom of the nest, discovered a sparking-plug and a cork-screw.

"Ah!" said Mrs. Ruddle, with a deep, sentimental sigh. "And we're *'e's* 'appy, *she's* 'appy. Ah! It's easy to see she worships the ground 'e treads on."

Bunter drew out two handkerchiefs, male and female, from another pocket and compared them indulgently. "That is a very proper sentiment in a young married woman."

"'Appy days! But it's early days yet, Mr. Bunter. A man's a man w'en all's said and done. Ruddle, now—'e useter knock me about something shocking w'en 'e'd 'ad a drop—though a good 'usband, and bringin' the money 'ome reg'lar."

"I beg," said Bunter, distributing match-boxes about the room, "you will not institute these comparisons, Mrs. Ruddle. I have served his lordship twenty years, and a sweeter-tempered gentleman you could not wish to find."

"You ain't married to 'im, Mr. Bunter. *You* can give 'im a munce warning any day."

"I hope I know when I am well situated, Mrs. Ruddle. Twenty years' service, and never a harsh word nor an unjust action in all my knowledge of him." A tinge of emotion crept into his tone. He laid a powder-compact aside on the what-not; then folded the blazer together with loving care and hung it over his arm.

"You're lucky," said Mrs. Ruddle. "I couldn't rightly say the same of pore Mr. Noakes, which though he's dead and gone I will say 'e wos a sour-tempered, close-fisted, suspicious brute, pore old gentleman."

"Gentleman, Mrs. Ruddle, is what I should designate as an elastic term. His lordship—"

"There now!" interrupted Mrs. Ruddle. "If there ain't love's young dream a-comin' up the path."

Bunter's brows beetled awfully. "To *whom* might you be referring, Mrs. Ruddle?" he demanded in a voice like Jupiter Tonans.

"W'y, that Frank Crutchley, to be sure."

"Oh!" Jupiter was appeased. "Crutchley? Is he your choice for a second?"

"Go along with you, Mr. Bunter! Me? No fear! No—Aggie Twitterton. Runs after 'im like an old cat with one kitten."

"Indeed?"

"At '*er* age! Mutton dressed as lamb. Makes me fair sick. If she knowed wot I knows—but there!"

This interesting revelation was cut short by the entrance of Crutchley himself.

"'Evenin'," said he, generally, to the company. "Any special orders tonight? I ran over, thinkin' there might be. Mr. 'Ancock don't want me for an hour or two."

"His lordship gave instructions that the car was to be cleaned; but now it's out again."

"Ah!" said Crutchley, apparently taking this as an intimation that gossip might proceed unchecked. "Well, they've got a nice day for it."

He made a tentative motion to seat himself, but caught Bunter's eye and compromised by leaning negligently against the end of the settle.

"'Ave you 'eard when they've fixed for the funeral?" inquired Mrs. Ruddle.

"'Leven-thirty termorrer."

"And 'igh time too—with 'im layin' there a week or more. There won't be many wet eyes, neither, if you ask me. There's one or two couldn't abide Mr. Noakes, not countin' 'im wot did away with 'im."

"They didn't get much forrader at the inquest, seems to me," observed Crutchley.

Bunter opened the what-not, and began to select wine-glasses from among its miscellaneous contents.

"'Ushin' it up," said Mrs. Ruddle, "that's wot they wos. Tryin' to make out there wasn't nothing atween Joe Sellon and 'im. That Kirk, 'is face was a treat w'en Ted Puddock got askin' all them questions."

"Seemed to me they went a bit quick over all that part of it."

"Didn't want nobody to think as a bobby might a-been mixed up in it. See 'ow the crowner shut me up w'en I started to tell 'im? Ah! But them noospaper men wos on to it sharp enough."

"Did you communicate your opinion to them, may I ask?"

"I might a-done, or I might not, Mr. Bunter, only jest at that instant minnit, out comes me lord, and they wos all on to 'im like wopses round a jam-pot. 'Im and 'is lady'll be in all the papers termorrer. They took a photer o' me too, with 'er ladyship. It's nice to see your friends in the papers, ain't it now?"

"The laceration of his lordship's most intimate feelings can afford no satisfaction to me," said Bunter, reprovingly.

"Ah! if I'd telled 'em all I thinks about Joe Sellon they'd 'ave me on the front page. I wonder they lets that young feller go about at large. We might all be murdered in our beds. The moment I see pore Mr. Noakes's body, I says to myself, 'Now, wot's Joe Sellon doin' in this 'ere—'im bein' the last to see the pore man alive?'"

"Then you were already aware that the crime had been committed on the Wednesday night?"

"Well, o'course I—No, I didn't, not then—See 'ere, Mr. Bunter, don't you go a-puttin' words in a woman's mouth—I—"

"I think," said Bunter, "you had better be careful."

"That's right, Ma," agreed Crutchley. "You go on imaginin' things, you'll land yourself in Queer Street one o' these days."

"Well," retorted Mrs. Ruddle, backing out of the door, "*I* didn't bear no pertickler grudge against Mr. Noakes. Not like some as I could name—with their forty poundses."

Crutchley stared at her retreating form.

"Gawdamighty, wot a tongue! I wonder 'er own spit didn't poison 'er. I wouldn't 'ang a dog on '*er* evidence. Mangy old poll-parrot!"

Bunter voiced no opinion, but picked up Peter's blazer and a few other scattered garments and walked upstairs. Crutchley, relieved of his vigilant eye and stern regard for the social proprieties, strolled quietly over to the hearth.

"Ho!" said Mrs. Ruddle. She brought in a lighted lamp, set it on a table on the far side of the room and turned on Crutchley with a witch-like smile. "Waitin' for kisses in the gloamin'?"

"Wotcher gettin' at?" demanded Crutchley, morosely.

"Aggie Twitterton's a-comin' down the 'ill on 'er bicycle."

"Gawd!" The young man shot a quick look through the window. "It's 'er all right." He rubbed the back of his head and swore softly.

"Wot it is to be the answer to the maiden's prayer!" said Mrs. Ruddle.

"Now, see 'ere, Ma. Polly's my girl. You know that. There ain't never been nothin' atween me and Aggie Twitterton."

"Not between you and 'er—but there might be atween 'er and you," replied Mrs. Ruddle, epigrammatically, and went out before he could reply. Bunter, coming downstairs, found Crutchley thoughtfully picking up the poker.

"May I ask why you are loitering about here? Your work is outside. If you want to wait for his lordship, you can do so in the garage."

"See 'ere, Mr. Bunter," said Crutchley, earnestly. "Let me bide in here for a bit. Aggie Twitterton's on the prowl, and if she was to catch sight o' me—you get me? She's a bit—"

He touched his forehead significantly.

"H'm!" said Bunter. He went across to the window and saw Miss Twitterton descend from her bicycle at the gate. She straightened her hat and began to fumble in the basket attached to the handle-bars. Bunter drew the curtains rather sharply. "Well, you can't stop here long. His lordship and her ladyship may be back any minute now. What is it now, Mrs. Ruddle?"

"I've put out the plates like you said, Mr. Bunter," announced that lady with meek self-righteousness. Bunter frowned. She had something rolled in the corner of her apron and was rubbing at it as she spoke. He felt that it would take a long time to teach Mrs. Ruddle a good servant's-hall manner.

"And I've found the other vegetable-dish—only it's broke."

"Very good. You can take these glasses out and wash them. There don't seem to be any decanters."

"Never you mind that, Mr. Bunter. I'll soon 'ave them bottles clean."

"Bottles?" said Bunter. "What bottles?" A frightful suspicion shot through his brain. "What have you got there?"

"Why," said Mrs. Ruddle, "one o' them dirty old bottles you brought along with you." She displayed her booty in triumph. "Sech a state as they're in. All over whitewash."

Bunter's world reeled about him and he clutched at the corner of the settle.

"My God!"

"You couldn't put a thing like that on the table, could you now?"

"Woman!" cried Bunter, and snatched the bottle from her, "that's the Cockburn '96!"

"Ow, is it?" said Mrs. Ruddle, mystified. "There now! I thought it was summink to drink."

Bunter controlled himself with difficulty. The cases had been left in the pantry for safety. The police were in and out of the cellar, but by all the laws of England, a man's pantry was his own. He said in a trembling voice:

"You have not, I trust, handled any of the other bottles?"

"Only to unpack 'em and set 'em right side up," Mrs. Ruddle assured him cheerfully. "Them cases'll come in 'andy for kindling."

"Gawdstrewth!" cried Bunter. The mask came off him all in one piece, and nature, red in tooth and claw, leapt like a tiger from ambush. "Gawdstrewth, would you believe it? All his lordship's vintage port!" He lifted shaking hands to heaven. "You lousy old nosey-parking bitch! You ignorant, interfering old bizzom! Who told you to go poking your long nose into my pantry?"

"Really, Mr. Bunter!" said Mrs. Ruddle.

"Go it," said Crutchley, with relish. "'Ere's someone at the front door."

"'Op it out of here!" stormed Bunter, unheeding, "before I take the skin off you!"

"Well, I'm sure! 'Ow was I to know?"

"Get out!"

Mrs. Ruddle retired, but with dignity.

"Sech manners!"

"Put yer flat foot right into it that time, Ma," observed Crutchley. He grinned. Mrs. Ruddle turned in the doorway.

"People can do their own dirty work after this," she remarked, witheringly, and departed.

Bunter took up the violated bottle of port and cradled it mournfully in his arm.

"All the port! all the port! Two and a half dozen, all shook up to blazes! And his lordship bringing it down in the back of the car, driving as tender and careful as if it was a baby in arms."

"Well," said Crutchley, "that's a miracle, judgin' by the way he went into Pagford this afternoon. Nearly blew me and the old taxi off the road."

"Not a drop fit to drink for a fortnight!—And him looking forward to his glass after dinner!"

"Well," said Crutchley again, with the philosophy we keep for other men's misfortunes, "he's unlucky, that's all."

Bunter uttered a Cassandra-like cry:

"There's a curse upon this house!"

As he turned, the door was flung violently open to admit Miss Twitterton, who shrank back with a small scream, on receiving this blast of eloquence full in the face.

"'Ere's Miss Twitterton," said Mrs. Ruddle, unnecessarily, and banged out.

"Oh, dear!" gasped the poor lady. "I beg your pardon. Er

. . . is Lady Peter at home? . . . I've just brought her a . . . Oh, I suppose they are out. . . . Mrs. Ruddle is so stupid. . . . Perhaps . . ." She looked appealingly from one man to the other. Bunter, pulling himself together, recaptured his mask, and this stony metamorphosis put the finishing touch to Miss Twitterton's discomfort.

"If it isn't troubling you too much, Mr. Bunter, would you be so kind as to tell Lady Peter that I've brought her a few eggs from my own hens?"

"Certainly, Miss Twitterton." The social solecism had been committed and could not now be redeemed. He received the basket with the condescending kindness due from my lord's butler to a humble dependant of the house.

"The Buff Orpingtons," explained Miss Twitterton. "They—they lay such pretty brown eggs, don't they? And I thought, perhaps—"

"Her ladyship will greatly appreciate the attention. Would you care to wait?"

"Oh, thank you. . . . I hardly know . . ."

"I am expecting them back very shortly. From the vicarage."

"Oh!" said Miss Twitterton. "Yes." She sat down rather helplessly on the proffered chair. "I meant just to hand the basket to Mrs. Ruddle, but she seems very much put about."

Crutchley gave a short laugh. He had made one or two attempts at escape; but Bunter and Miss Twitterton were between him and the door, and now he appeared to resign himself. Bunter seemed glad of the opportunity for an explanation.

"*I* have been very much put about, Miss Twitterton. Mrs. Ruddle has violently agitated all his lordship's vintage port, just as it was settling down nicely after the journey."

"Oh, how dreadful!" cried Miss Twitterton, her sympathetic mind grasping that the disaster, however incomprehensible, was of the first magnitude. "Is it all spoilt? I believe they have some very good port wine at the Pig and Whistle—only it's rather expensive—4*s*. 6*d*. a bottle and nothing on the empties."

"I fear," said Bunter, "that would scarcely meet the case."

"Or if they would like some of my parsnip wine I should be delighted to—"

"Huh!" said Crutchley. He jerked his thumb at the bottle in Bunter's arm. "What does that stand his nibs in for?"

Bunter could bear no more. He turned to go.

"Two hundred and four shillings the dozen!"

"Cripes!" said Crutchley. Miss Twitterton could not believe her ears.

"The dozen *what?*"

"Bottles!" said Bunter. He went out shattered, with drooping shoulders, and shut the door decisively. Miss Twitterton, reckoning rapidly on her fingers, turned in dismay to Crutchley, who stood with a derisive smile, making no further effort to avoid the interview.

"Two hundred and four—seventeen shillings a bottle! Oh, it's impossible! It's . . . it's wicked!"

"Yes. Cut above you and me, ain't it? Bah! there's a chap could give away forty pound out of his pocket and never miss it. But does he? No!"

He strolled over to the hearth and spat eloquently into the fire.

"Oh, Frank! You mustn't be so bitter. You couldn't expect Lord Peter—"

"'Lord Peter!'—who're you to be calling him by his pet name? Think you're somebody, don't you?"

"That is the correct way to speak of him," said Miss Twitterton, drawing herself up a little. "I know quite well how to address people of rank."

"Oh, yes!" replied the gardener, sarcastically, "I dessay. And you say 'Mister' to his blasted valet. Come off of it, my girl. It's 'me lord' for you, same as for the rest of us. . . . I know your mother was a school-teacher, all right. *And* your father was old ted Baker's cow-man. If she married beneath 'er, it ain't nothing to be stuck up about."

"I'm sure," Miss Twitterton's voice trembled—"*you're* the last person that ought to say such a thing to me."

Crutchley's face lowered.

"That's it, is it? Tryin' to make out you been lowerin'

yourself by associating with me, eh? All right! You go and hobnob with the gentry. *Lord* Peter!"

He thrust his hands deep down in his pockets and strode irritably towards the window. His determination to work up a quarrel was so evident that even Miss Twitterton could not mistake it. It could have only one explanation. With fatal archness, she wagged a reproving finger.

"Why, Frank, you silly old thing! I believe you're jealous!"

"Jealous!" He looked at her and began to laugh. It was not a pleasant laugh, though it showed all his teeth. "That's good! that's rich, that is! What's the idea? Startin' to make eyes at his lordship now?"

"Frank! He's a married man. How can you say such things?"

"Oh, he's married all right. Tied up good and proper. 'Ead well in the noose. 'Yes, darling!' 'No, darling!' 'Cuddle me quick, darling.' Pretty, ain't it?"

Miss Twitterton thought it *was* pretty, and said so.

"I'm sure it's beautiful to see two people so devoted to one another."

"Quite a ro-mance in 'igh life. Like to be in *'er* shoes, wouldn't you?"

"You don't really think I'd want to change places with anybody?" cried Miss Twitterton. "But, oh, Frank! If only you and I could get married at once—"

"Ah, yes!" said Crutchley, with a kind of satisfaction. "Your Uncle Noakes has put a bit of spoke in that wheel, ain't 'e?"

"Oh!—I've been trying all day to see you and talk over what we were to do."

"What *we're* going to do?"

"It isn't for myself, Frank. I'd work my fingers to the bone for you."

"And a fat lot o' good that 'ud do. 'Ow about my garridge? If it 'adn't a-been for your soft soap I'd a-got my forty quid out o' the old devil months ago."

Miss Twitterton quailed before his angry eyes.

"Oh, please don't be so angry with me. We couldn't either of us know. And oh!—there's another terrible thing—"

"What's up now?"

"I—I—I'd been saving up a little bit—just a little here and there, you know—and I'd got close on £50 put away in the savings bank—"

"Fifty pounds, eh?" said Crutchley, his tone softening a little. "Well, that's a tidy little bit. . . ."

"I meant it for the garage. It was to be a surprise for you—"

"Well, and what's gone wrong with it?" The sight of her imploring eyes and twitching, bony hands brought back his irritation. "Post-office gone bust?"

"I—I—I lent it to Uncle. He said he was short—people hadn't paid their bills—"

"Well," said Crutchley with impatience, "you got a receipt for it, I suppose." Excitement seized him. "That's *your* money. They can't get at that. You 'ave it out o' them—you got a receipt for it. You give me the receipt and I'll settle with that MacBride. That'll cover my forty quid, anyhow."

"But I never thought to ask Uncle for a *receipt*. Not between relations. How could I?"

"You never thought—? Nothing on paper—? Of all the blasted fools—!"

"Oh, Frank dear, I'm so sorry. Everything seems to have gone wrong. But you know, you never dreamt, any more than I did—"

"No; or I'd 'ave acted a bit different, I can tell you."

He ground his teeth savagely and struck a log on the hearth with his heel so that the sparks flew. Miss Twitterton watched him miserably. Then a new hope came to sustain her.

"Frank, listen! Perhaps Lord Peter might *lend* you the money to start the garage. He's ever so rich."

Crutchley considered this. Born rich and born soft were to him the same thing. It was possible, if he made a good impression—though it did mean truckling to a blasted title.

"That's a fact," he admitted. "He might."

In a rosy flush, Miss Twitterton saw the possibility as an accomplished fact. Her eager wishes flew ahead into a brilliant future.

"I'm sure he would. We could get married at once, and

have that little corner cottage—you know—on the main road, where you said—and there'd be ever so many cars stopping there. And I could help quite a lot with my Buff Orpingtons!"

"You and your Buff Orpingtons!"

"And I could give piano-lessons again. I know I could get pupils. There's the stationmaster's little Elsie—"

"Little Elsie's bottom! Now, see here, Aggie, it's time we got down to brass tacks. You and me getting spliced with the idea of coming into your uncle's money—that was one thing, see! That's business. But if there's no money from you, it's off. You get that?"

Miss Twitterton uttered a faint bleat. He went on, brutally:

"A man that's starting in life wants a wife, see? A nice little bit to come 'ome to. Some'un he can cuddle—not a skinny old hen with a brood o' Buff Orpingtons."

"How can you speak like that?"

He caught her roughly by the shoulder and twisted her round to face the mirror with the painted roses.

"Look at yourself in the glass, you old fool! Talk about a man marrying his grandmother—"

She shrank back and he pushed her from him.

"Coming the schoolmarm over me, with yer 'Mind yer manners, Frank,' and 'mind yer aitches,' and bum-sucking round to his lordship—'Frank's so clever'—t'sha! making me look a blasted fool."

"I only wanted to help you get on."

"Yes—showing me off, like as if I was your belongings. You'd like to take me up to bed like the silver tea-pot—and a silver tea-pot 'ud be about as much use to you, I reckon."

Miss Twitterton put her hands over her ears. "I won't listen to you—you're mad—you're—"

"Thought you'd bought me with yer uncle's money, didn't you? Well—where is it?"

"How can you be so cruel?—after all I've done for you?"

"You've done for me, all right. Made me a laughing-stock and got me into a blasted mess. I suppose you've been blabbing about all over the place as we was only waitin' for vicar to put up the banns—"

"I've never said a word—truly, truly I never have."

"Oh, ain't you? Well, you should a-heard old Ruddle talk."

"And if I had," cried Miss Twitterton with a last, desperate burst of spirit, "why shouldn't I? You've told me over and over again you were fond of me—you said you were—you said you were—"

"Oh, can that row!"

"But you did say so. Oh, you can't, you can't be so cruel! You don't know—you don't know—Frank, please! Dear Frank—I know it's been a dreadful disappointment—but you can't mean this—you can't! I—I—I—oh, do be kind to me, Frank—I love you so—"

In frantic appeal, she flung herself into his arms; and the contact with her damp cheeks and stringy body drove him to an ugly fury.

"Damn you, get off! Take your blasted claws out of my neck. Shut up! I'm sick and tired of the sight of you."

He wrenched her loose and flung her heavily upon the settle, bruising her, and knocking her hat grotesquely over one ear. As he looked at her with a sort of delight in her helpless absurdity and her snuffling humiliation, the deep roar of the Daimler's exhaust zoomed up to the gate and stopped. The latch clicked and steps came along the path. Miss Twitterton sobbed and gulped, hunting vaguely for her handkerchief.

"Hell's bells!" said Crutchley, "they're comin' in."

Above the creak of the gravel came the sound of two voices singing together softly.

"Et ma joli' colombe
Qui chante jour et nuit,
Et ma joli' colombe
Qui chante jour et nuit,
Qui chante pour les filles
Qui n'ont pas de mari—
Auprès de ma blonde
Qu'il fait bon, fait bon, fait bon,
Auprès de ma blonde
Qu'il fait bon dormi."

"Get up, you fool!" said Crutchley, hunting in a hurry for his cap.

> *"Qui chante pour les filles*
> *Qui n'ont pas de mari,*
> *Qui chante pour les filles*
> *Qui n'ont pas de mari—"*

He found the cap on the window-sill and pulled it on with a jerk. "You'd better clear out, sharp. I'm off."

The woman's voice rang out, alone and exultant:

> *"Pour moi ne chante guère*
> *Car j'en ai un joli—"*

The tune, if not the words, stabbed Miss Twitterton into a consciousness of that insolent triumph, and she stirred wretchedly on the hard settle as the duet was joined again:

> *"Auprès de ma blonde*
> *Qu'il fait bon, fait bon, fait bon,*
> *Auprès de ma blonde*
> *Qu'il fait bon dormi."*

She lifted a blotched and woe-begone face; but Crutchley was gone—and the words of the song came back to her. Her mother, the schoolmistress, had had it in that little book of French songs—though, of course, it was not a thing one could teach the school-children. There were voices in the passage outside.

"Oh, Crutchley!" casual and commanding. "You can put the car away."

And Crutchley's, colourless and respectful, as though it did not know how to use cruel words:

"Very good, my lord."

Which way out? Miss Twitterton dabbed the tears from her face. Not into that passage, among them all—with Frank there—and Bunter perhaps coming out of the kitchen—and what would Lord Peter think?

"Anything further tonight, my lord?"

"No, thanks. That's all. Good night."

The door-knob moved under his hand. Then her ladyship's voice—warm and friendly:

"Good night, Crutchley."

"Good night, my lord. Good night, my lady."

Seized with panic, Miss Twitterton fled blindly up the bedroom stair as the door opened.

CHAPTER XVI

♦

Crown Matrimonial

NORBERT: *Explain not: let this be!*
This is life's height.
CONSTANCE: *Yours, yours, yours!*
NORBERT: *You and I—*
Why care by what meanders we are here
I' the centre of the labyrinth! Men have died
Trying to find this place, which we have found.
—Robert Browning, *In a Balcony*

"Well, well, well!" said Peter. "Here we are again." He lifted his wife's cloak from her shoulders and gently saluted the nape of her neck.

"In the proud consciousness of duty done."

His eyes followed her as she crossed the room. "Wonderfully inspiring thing, doing one's duty. Gives one a sort of exalted sensation. I feel quite light-headed."

She dropped on to the couch, laying lazy arms along its back.

"I'm feeling slightly intoxicated, too. It couldn't possibly be the vicar's sherry?"

"No," he said firmly, "not possibly. Though I fancy I have drunk worse. Not much, and not more than once. No—it's just the stimulating effects of well-doing—or perhaps it's the country air—or something."

"Rather giddy-making, but nice."

"Oh, definitely." He unwound the scarf from his neck, hung it with the cloak over the settle and drifted irresolutely to a position behind the couch. "I mean to say—yes, definitely. Like champagne. Almost like being in love. But I don't think it could be that, do you?"

She tilted her face to smile at him, so that he saw it oddly and intriguingly inverted.

"Oh, surely not." She caught his roving hands, held them, dumbly protesting, away from her breast, brought them up under her chin and imprisoned them there.

"I thought not. Because, after all, we are married. Or aren't we? One can't be married *and* in love. Not with the same person, I mean. It isn't done."

"Absolutely not."

"Pity. Because I'm feeling rather youthful and foolish to-night. Tender and twining, like a very young pea. Positively romantic."

"That, my lord, is disgraceful in a gentleman of your condition."

"My mental condition is simply appalling. I want the violins to strike up in the orchestra and discourse soft music while the limelight merchant turns up the moon. . . ."

"And the crooners are crooning in tune!"

"Damn it, why not? I *will* have my soft music! Unhand me, girl! Let's see what the B.B.C. can do for us."

She released him; and her eyes, in their turn, followed him to the radio cabinet.

"Stand there a moment, Peter. No—don't turn round."

"Why?" he said, standing obediently. "Has my unfortunate face begun to get on your nerves?"

"No—I was just admiring your spine, that's all. It has a

kind of sort of springy line about it that pleases me. Completely enslaving."

"Really? I can't see it. But I must tell my tailor. He always gives me to understand that he invented my back for me."

"Does he also imagine he invented your ears and the back of your skull and the bridge of your nose?"

"No flattery can be too gross for my miserable sex. I am purring like a coffee-mill. But you might have picked a more responsive set of features. It's difficult to express devotion with the back of one's head."

"That's just it. I want the luxury of a hopeless passion. There, I can say to myself, there is the back of his adorable head, and nothing I can say will soften it."

"I'm not so sure of that. However, I'll try to live up to your requirements—my true love hath my heart, but my bones are my own. Just at the moment, though, the immortal bones obey control of dying flesh and dying soul. What the devil did I come over here for?"

"Soft music."

"So it was. Now my little minstrels of Portland Place! Strike, you myrtle-crownèd boys, ivied maidens, strike together!"

"Arrch!" said the loud speaker, ". . . and the beds should be carefully made up beforehand with good, well-rotted horse-manure or . . ."

"Help!"

"That," said Peter, switching off, "is quite enough of that."

"The man has a dirty mind."

"Disgusting. I shall write a stiff letter to Sir John Reith. Isn't it an extraordinary thing that just when a fellow's bubbling over with the purest and most sacred emotions—when he's feeling like Galahad and Alexander and Clark Gable all rolled into one—when he so to speak bestrides the clouds and sits upon the bosom of the air—"

"Dearest! are you sure it's not the sherry?"

"Sherry!" His rocketing mood burst in a shower of spangles. "Lady, by yonder blessèd moon I swear . . ." He halted, gesturing into the shadows. "Hullo! they've put the moon on the wrong side."

"Very careless of the limelight merchant."

"Drunk again, drunk again. . . . Perhaps you're right about the sherry. . . . Curse this moon, it leaks. O more than moon, Draw not up seas to drown me in thy sphere!" He wrapped his handkerchief about the stem of the lamp, brought it across from the table and set it beside her, so that the red-orange of her dress shone in the pool of light like an oriflamme. "That's better. Now we begin all over again. Lady, by yonder blessèd moon I swear, That tips with silver all these fruit-tree tops. . . . Observe the fruit-trees. *Malus aspidistriensis*. Specially imported by the management at colossal expense. . . ."

The voices came faintly to Aggie Twitterton, crouched shiveringly in the room overhead. She had meant to escape by the back stair; but at the bottom of it stood Mrs. Ruddle, engaged in a long expostulation with Bunter, whose replies from the kitchen were inaudible. Apparently on the point of departure, she kept on coming back to make some fresh remark. Any minute she might take herself off, and then—

Bunter came out so silently that Miss Twitterton did not hear him till his voice boomed suddenly from just below her:

"I have nothing more to say, Mrs. Ruddle. Good night to you."

The back door shut sharply and there was the noise of the drawing of bolts. One could not now escape unheard. In another moment, feet began to ascend the stair. Miss Twitterton withdrew hastily into Harriet's bedroom. The feet came on; they passed the branching of the stair; they were coming in. Miss Twitterton retired still further, shocked to find herself trapped in a gentleman's bedroom that smelt faintly of bay rum and Harris tweed. Next door she heard the crackle of a kindled fire, the rattle of curtain rings upon the rods, a subdued clink, the pouring of fresh water into the ewer. Then the door-latch lifted, and she fled breathless back into the darkness of the stairs.

* * *

"... Romeo was a green fool, and all his trees had green apples. Sit there, Aholibah, and play the queen, with a vineleaf crown and a sceptre of pampas-grass. Lend me your cloak, and I will be the kings and all their horsemen. Speak the speech, I pray you, trippingly on the tongue. Speak it! My snow-white horses foam and fret—sorry, I've got into the wrong poem, but I'm pawing the ground like anything. Say on, lady of the golden voice. 'I am the Queen Aholibah—'"

She laughed; and let the magnificent nonsense roll out organ-mouthed:

> "*My lips kissed dumb the word of* Ah
> *Sighed on strange lips grown sick thereby.*
> *God wrought to me my royal bed;*
> *The inner work thereof was red,*
> *The outer work was ivory.*
> *My mouth's heat was the heat of flame*
> *With lust towards the kings that came*
> *With horsemen riding royally—*

Peter, you'll break that chair. You *are* a lunatic!"

"My dearest, I've got to be." He flung the cloak aside and stood before her. "When I try to be serious, I make such a bloody fool of myself. It's idiotic." His voice wavered with uncertain over-tones. "Think of it—laugh at it—a well-fed, well-groomed, well-off Englishman of forty-five in a boiled shirt and an eyeglass going down on his knees to his wife—to his own wife, which makes it so much funnier—and saying to her—and saying—"

"Tell me, Peter."

"I can't. I daren't."

She lifted his head between her hands, and what she saw in his face stopped her heart.

"Oh, my dear, don't. . . . Not all that. . . . It's terrifying to be so happy."

"Ah, no, it's not," he said quickly, taking courage from her fear.

"All other things to their destruction draw,
Only our love hath no decay;
This no tomorrow hath, nor yesterday;
Running it never runs from us away
But truly keeps his first, last, everlasting day."

"Peter—"

He shook his head, vexed at his own impotence.

"How can *I* find words? Poets have taken them all, and left me with nothing to say or do—"

"Except to teach me for the first time what they meant."

He found it hard to believe.

"Have I done that?"

"Oh, Peter—" Somehow she must make him believe it, because it mattered so much that he should. "All my life I have been wandering in the dark—but now I have found your heart—and am satisfied."

"And what do all the great words come to in the end, but that?—I love you—I am at rest with you—I have come home."

There was such a stillness in the room that Miss Twitterton thought it must be empty. She crept down softly, stair by stair, afraid lest Bunter should hear her. The door was ajar and she pushed it open inch by inch. The lamp had been moved, so that she found herself in darkness—but the room was not empty, after all. On the far side, framed in the glowing circle of the lamplight, the two figures were bright and motionless as a picture—the dark woman in a dress like flame, with her arms locked about the man's bowed shoulders and his golden head in her lap. They were so quiet that even the great ruby on her left hand shone steadily without a twinkle.

Miss Twitterton, turned to stone, dared neither advance nor retreat.

"Dear." The word was no more than a whisper, spoken without a movement. "My heart's heart. My own dear lover and husband." The locked hands must have tightened their hold, for the red stone flashed sudden fire. "You are mine, you are mine, all mine."

The head came up at that and his voice caught the triumph and sent it back in a mounting wave:

"Yours. Such as I am, yours. With all my faults, all my follies, yours utterly and for ever. While this poor, passionate, mountebank body has hands to hold you and lips to say, I love you—"

"Oh!" cried Miss Twitterton, with a great strangling sob, "I can't bear it! I can't bear it!"

The little scene broke like a bubble. The chief actor leapt to his feet and said very distinctly:

"Damn and blast!"

Harriet got up. The sudden shattering of her ecstatic mood and a swift, defensive anger for Peter's sake made her tone sharper than she knew:

"Who is it? What are you doing there?" She stepped out of the pool of light and peered into the dusk. "*Miss Twitterton?*"

Miss Twitterton, incapable of speech and terrified beyond conception, went on choking hysterically. A voice from the direction of the fireplace said grimly:

"I knew I should make a bloody fool of myself."

"Something's happened," said Harriet, more gently, putting out a reassuring hand. Miss Twitterton found her voice:

"Oh, forgive me—I didn't know—I never meant—" The remembrance of her own misery got the upper hand of her alarm. "Oh, I'm so dreadfully unhappy."

"I think," said Peter, "I had better see about decanting the port."

He retreated quickly and quietly, without waiting to shut the door. But the ominous words had penetrated to Miss Twitterton's consciousness. A new terror checked her tears in midflow.

"Oh, dear, oh, dear! The port wine! Now he'll be angry again."

"Good heavens!" exclaimed Harriet, completely bewildered. "What has gone wrong? What is it all about?"

Miss Twitterton shuddered. A cry of "Bunter!" in the passage warned her that the crisis was imminent.

"Mrs. Ruddle has done something *dreadful* to the port wine."

"Oh, my poor Peter!" said Harriet. She listened anxiously. Bunter's voice now, subdued to a long, explanatory mumble. "Oh, dear, oh, dear, oh, dear!" moaned Miss Twitterton.

"But what *can* the woman have done?"

Miss Twitterton really was not sure.

"I *believe* she's shaken the bottle," she faltered. "Oh!"

A loud yelp of anguish rent the air within. Peter's voice lifted to a wail:

"What! *all* my pretty chickens and their dam?"

The last word sounded to Miss Twitterton painfully like an oath.

"O-o-oh! I do *hope* he won't be violent."

"Violent?" said Harriet, half amused and half angry. "Oh, I shouldn't think so."

But alarm is infectious . . . and much-tried men have been known to vent their exasperation upon their servants. The two women clung together, waiting for the explosion.

"Well," said the distant voice, "all I can say is, Bunter, don't let it happen again. . . . All right. . . . Good God, man, you needn't tell me that . . . of course you didn't. . . . We'd better go and view the bodies."

The sounds died away, and the women breathed more freely. The dreadful menace of male violence lifted its shadow from the house.

"Well!" said Harriet, "that wasn't so bad after all. . . . My dear Miss Twitterton, what *is* the matter? You're trembling all over. . . . Surely, *surely* you didn't really think Peter was going to—to throw things about or anything, did you? Come and sit down by the fire. Your hands are like ice."

Miss Twitterton allowed herself to be led to the settle.

"I'm sorry—it was silly of me. But . . . I'm always so terrified of . . . gentlemen being angry . . . and . . . and . . . after all, they're all men, aren't they? . . . and men are so horrible!"

The end of the sentence came out in a shuddering burst. Harriet realised that there was more here than poor Uncle

William or a couple of dozen of port.

"Dear Miss Twitterton, what is the trouble? Can I help? Has somebody been horrible to you?"

Sympathy was too much for Miss Twitterton. She clutched at the kindly hands.

"Oh, my lady, my lady—I'm ashamed to tell you. He said such dreadful things to me. Oh, please forgive me!"

"Who did?" asked Harriet, sitting down beside her.

"Frank. Terrible things. . . . And I know I'm a little older than he is—and I suppose I've been very foolish—but he *did* say he was fond of me."

"Frank Crutchley?"

"Yes—and it wasn't my fault about Uncle's money. We were going to be married—only we were waiting for the forty pounds and my own little savings that Uncle borrowed. And they're all gone now and no money to come from Uncle—and now he says he hates the sight of me, and—and I *do* love him so!"

"I *am* so sorry," said Harriet, helplessly. What else was there to be said? The thing was ludicrous and abominable.

"He—he—he called me an old hen!" That was the almost unspeakable thing; and when it was out Miss Twitterton went on more easily. "He was so angry about my savings—but I never thought of asking Uncle for a receipt."

"Oh, my dear!"

"I was so happy—thinking we were going to be married as soon as he could get the garage started—only we didn't tell anybody, because, you see, I *was* a little bit older than him, though of course I was in a better position. But he was working up and making himself quite superior—"

How fatal, thought Harriet, how fatal! Aloud she said:

"My dear, if he treats you like that he's not superior at all. He's not fit to clean your shoes."

Peter was singing:

> "*Que donneriez-vous, belle,*
> *Pour avoir votre ami?*

Que donneriez-vous, belle,
Pour avoir votre ami?"

(He seems to have got over it, thought Harriet.)

"And he's so *handsome*. . . . We used to meet in the churchyard—there's a nice seat there. . . . Nobody comes that way in the evenings. . . . I let him kiss me. . . ."

"Je donnerais Versailles,
Paris et saint Denis!"

". . . and now he hates me. . . . I don't know what to do. . . . I shall go and drown myself. . . . Nobody *knows* what I've done for Frank. . . ."

"Auprès de ma blonde
Qu'il fait bon, fait bon, fait bon,
Auprès de ma blonde
Qu'il fait bon dormi!"

"Oh, *Peter!*" said Harriet in an exasperated undertone. She rose and shut the door upon this heartless exhibition. Miss Twitterton, exhausted by her own emotions, sat weeping quietly in a corner of the settle. Harriet was conscious of a whole series of emotions, arranged in layers like a Neapolitan ice.

What on earth am I to do with her? . . .
He is singing songs in the French language. . . .
And it must be nearly dinner-time. . . .
Somebody called Polly. . . .
Mrs. Ruddle will drive those men distracted. . . .
Bonté d'âme. . . .
Old Noakes dead in our cellar. . . .
(Eructavit cor meum!). . .
Poor Bunter! . . .
Sellon? . . .
(Qu'il fait bon dormi). . . .

If you know How, you know Who. . . .
This house. . . .
My true love hath my heart and I have his. . . .

She came back and stood by the settle. "Listen! Don't cry so terribly. He isn't worth it. Honestly, he couldn't be. There isn't a man in ten million that's worth breaking your heart over." (No good to tell people that.) "Try to forget him. I know it sounds difficult. . . ."

Miss Twitterton looked up.

"*You* wouldn't find it so easy?"

"To forget Peter?" (No; nor other things.) "Well, of course, Peter. . . ."

"Yes," said Miss Twitterton, without rancour. "You're one of the lucky ones. I'm sure you deserve it."

"I'm quite sure I don't." (God's bodikins, man, much better. . . . Every man after his desert?)

"And *what* you must have thought of me!" cried Miss Twitterton, suddenly restored to a sense of the actual. "I hope he isn't too terribly angry. You see, I heard you coming in—just outside the door—and I simply couldn't face anybody—so I ran upstairs—and then I didn't hear anything so I thought you'd gone and came down—and seeing you so happy together. . . ."

"It doesn't matter the very least bit," said Harriet, hastily. "*Please* don't think any more about it. He knows it was quite an accident. Now—don't cry any more."

"I must be going." Miss Twitterton made vague efforts to straighten her disordered hair and the jaunty little hat. "I'm afraid I look a sight."

"No, not a bit. Just a touch of powder's all you want. Where's my—oh! I left it in Peter's pocket. No, here it is on the what-not. That's Bunter. He always clears up after us. Poor Bunter and the port—it must have been a blow to him."

Miss Twitterton stood patiently to be tidied up, like a small child in the hands of a brisk nurse. "There—you look *quite* all right. See! No one would notice anything."

The mirror! Miss Twitterton shrank at the thought of it, but curiosity spurred her on. This was her own face, then—how strange!

"I've never had powder on before. It—it makes me feel quite fast."

She stared, fascinated.

"Well," said Harriet, cheerfully, "it's helpful sometimes. Let me tuck up this little curl behind—"

Her own dark, glowing face came into the mirror behind Miss Twitterton's and she saw with a shock that the trail of vine-leaves was still in her hair. "Goodness! how absurd I look! We were playing silly games—"

"You look lovely," said Miss Twitterton. "Oh, dear—I hope nobody will think—"

"Nobody will think anything. Now, promise me you won't make yourself miserable any more."

"No," said Miss Twitterton, mournfully. "I'll try not." Two large, lingering tears rolled slowly into her eyes, but she remembered the powder and removed them carefully. "You *have* been so kind. Now I *must* run."

"Good night." The opening of the door revealed Bunter, hovering with a tray in the background.

"I *hope* I haven't kept you from your supper."

"Not a bit," said Harriet, "it isn't time for it yet. Now good-bye and don't worry. Bunter, please show Miss Twitterton out."

She stood absently, gazing at her own face in the mirror, the vine-wreath trailing from her hand.

"Poor little soul!"

CHAPTER XVII

◆

Crown Imperial

One cried, "God bless us!" and "Amen" the other,
As they had seen me with these hangman's hands.
—William Shakespeare, *Macbeth*

Peter came in cautiously, carrying a decanter.

"It's all right," said Harriet. "She's gone."

He put down the wine at a carefully calculated distance from the fire and observed, in a conversational tone:

"We found some decanters, after all."

"Yes—I see you did."

"My God, Harriet—what was I saying?"

"It's all right, darling. You were only quoting Donne."

"Is that all? I rather fancied I had put in one or two little bits of my own. . . . Oh, well, what's it matter? I love you and I don't care who knows it."

"Bless you."

"All the same," he went on, determined to put the embarrassing topic in its place for good and all, "this house is making me jumpy. Skeletons in the chimney, corpses in the cellar, elderly females hiding behind the doors—I shall look under the bed tonight—Ough!"

He started nervously, as Bunter came in carrying a standard lamp; and covered his confusion by stooping, unnecessarily, to feel the decanter again.

"Is that the port, after all?"

"No, claret. It's a youngish but pleasant Hermitage, with only a very light sediment. It seems to have travelled all right—it's quite clear."

Bunter, setting the lamp near the hearth, cast a look of mute anguish at the decanter and retired with hushed footsteps.

"I'm not the only sufferer," said his master, with a shake of the head. "Bunter's nerves are very much affected. He feels this Ruddle muddle acutely—coming on top of everything else. I enjoy a little bustle and movement myself, but Bunter has his standards."

"Yes—and though he's charming to me, our marriage must have been an awful blow to him."

"More in the nature of an emotional strain, I think. And he's a little worried about this case. He fancies I'm not giving my mind to it. This afternoon, for instance—"

"I'm afraid so, Peter, yes. The woman tempted you—"

"O *felix culpa!*"

"Frittering away your time among the tombstones, instead of following up the clues. But there aren't any clues."

"If there ever were any, Bunter probably cleared them away with his own hands—he and Ruddle, his partner in crime. Remorse is eating his soul like a caterpillar in a cabbage. . . . But he's quite right; because all I've done so far is to throw suspicion on that wretched boy, Sellon—when I might just as well have thrown it on someone else, as far as I can see."

"On Mr. Goodacre, for instance. He *has* got a morbid passion for cacti."

"Or on the infernal Ruddles. I *could* climb through that window, by the way. I tried after lunch."

"Did you? And did you find out whether Sellon might have altered Mrs. Ruddle's clock?"

"Ah! . . . you took that point. Trust a detective novelist to go hot-foot for a clock problem. You're looking like the cat that's swallowed the canary. Out with it—what have you discovered?"

"It couldn't have been altered more than about ten minutes either way."

"Indeed? And how does Mrs. Ruddle come to have a clock with quarter-chimes?"

"It was a wedding-present."

"It would be. Yes, I see. You could put it forward, but you couldn't put it right again. And you couldn't put it back at all. Not more than ten minutes or so. Ten minutes might be valuable. Sellon said it was five past nine. Then, by all the rules, he should need an alibi for—Harriet, no! that makes no sense. It's no use having an alibi for the moment of the murder unless you take pains to *fix* the moment of the murder. If a ten-minute alibi is to work, the time must be fixed within ten minutes. And it's only fixed within twenty-five—and even then, we can't be *sure* about the wireless. Can't *you* do something with the wireless? That's the mystery-monger's white-headed boy."

"No, I can't. A clock and a wireless ought to add up to something, but they don't. I've thought and thought—"

"Well, you know, we only started yesterday. It seems longer, but that's all it is. Hang it! We've not been married fifty-five hours."

"It feels like a lifetime—no, I don't mean that. I mean, it feels as if we'd always been married."

"So we have—from the foundation of the world—Confound you, Bunter, what do you want?"

"The menu, my lord."

"Oh! Thanks. Turtle soup . . . That's a little citified for Paggleham—a trifle out of key. Never mind. Roast duck and green peas are better. Local produce? Good. Mushrooms on toast—"

"From the field behind the cottage, my lord."

"From the—? Good God, I hope they *are* mushrooms—we don't want a poison-mystery as well."

"No poison, my lord, no. I consumed a quantity myself to make sure."

"Did you? Devoted Valet Risks Life for Master. Very well, Bunter. Oh! and, by the way, was it you playing hide-and-seek with Miss Twitterton on our stairs?"

"My lord?"

"All right, Bunter," said Harriet, quickly.

Bunter took the hint and vanished, murmuring, "Very good."

"She was hiding from us, Peter, because she'd been crying when we came in and she didn't want to be caught."

"Oh, I see," said Peter. The explanation satisfied him, and he turned his attention to the wine.

"Crutchley's been behaving like a perfect beast to her."

"Has he, by jove?" He gave the decanter a half-turn.

"He's been making love to the poor little wretch."

As though to prove himself a man and no angel, his lordship gave utterance to a faintly derisive hoot.

"Peter—it isn't funny."

"I beg your pardon, my dear. You're quite right. It's not." He straightened himself suddenly and said, with some emphasis: "It's anything but funny. Is she fond of the blighter?"

"My dear, pathetically. And they were going to be married and start the new garage—with the forty pounds and her little savings—only they're gone, too. And now he finds she won't come into any money from her uncle. . . . What are you looking at me like that for?"

"Harriet, I don't like this at all." He was gazing at her with an expression of growing consternation.

"Of course, he's chucked her over now—the brute!"

"Yes, yes—but don't you see what you're telling me? She'd have given him the money, of course? Done anything in the world for him?"

"She said nobody knew what she *had* done for him—Oh, Peter! You can't mean *that!* It *couldn't* be the little Twitterton!"

"Why not?"

He flung the words out like a challenge; and she faced it squarely, standing up to him with her hands on his shoulders, so that their eyes met level.

"It's a motive—I see it's a motive. But you didn't want to hear about motive."

"But you're cracking my ear-drums with it," he cried, almost angrily. "Motive won't make a case. But once you've got the How, the Why drives it home."

"All right, then." He should fight on his own ground.

"*How?* You made no case against her."

"There was no need. Her How is child's play. She had the key of the house, and no alibi after 7.30. Killing hens is no alibi for killing a man."

"But to smash in a man's head with a blow like that—she's tiny, and he was a big man. I couldn't break your head open like that, though I'm nearly as tall as you are."

"You're about the one person who could. You're my wife. You could take me unawares—as a loving niece might her uncle. I can't see Noakes sitting down and letting Crutchley or Sellon go pussy-footing about behind him. But a woman one knows and trusts—that's different."

He sat down at the table, with his back towards her, and picked up a fork.

"Look! Here I am, writing a letter or doing my accounts. . . . You're fidgeting round somewhere in the background. . . . I take no notice; I'm used to it. . . . You take up the poker quietly . . . don't be afraid, you know I'm slightly deaf. . . . Come up on the left, remember; my head leans over a little to the side of the pen. . . . Now . . . two quick steps and a brisk rap on the skull—you needn't hit too hard—and you're an exceedingly wealthy widow."

Harriet put the poker down rather hastily.

"Niece—Widow's a hateful word; so weedy—let's stick to niece."

"I slump down, and the chair slips away, so that I bruise my right side against the table in falling. You remove any finger-prints from the weapon—"

"Yes—and then just let myself out with my own key and lock the door behind me. Quite simple. And you, I suppose, when you come to, obligingly tidy away whatever you were writing—"

"And tidy myself into the cellar. That's the idea."

"I suppose you've seen this all along."

"I have. But I was irrational enough to tell myself that the motive was insufficient. I couldn't see the Twitterton doing murder for money to extend her hen-runs. Serve me right for being weak-minded. The moral is, Stick to How, and somebody will hand you the Why on a silver salver."

He read remonstrance in her eyes, and added earnestly:

"It's a whacking great motive, Harriet. A middle-aged woman's last bid for love—and the money to make the bid."

"It was Crutchley's motive, too. Couldn't she have let him in? Or lent him the key, not knowing what he wanted it for?"

"Crutchley's times are all wrong. Though he may have been an accomplice. If so, he's got damned good reason for giving her the chuck now. In fact, it's the best move he can possibly make, even if he only *suspects* she did it."

His voice was like flint. It jarred on Harriet.

"It's all very well, Peter, but where's your proof?"

"Nowhere."

"What did you say yourself? It's no good showing how it *might* have been done. Anybody *might* have done it—Sellon, Crutchley, Miss Twitterton, you, I, the vicar or Superintendent Kirk. But you haven't proved how it *was* done."

"Good God, don't I know that? We want proofs. We want facts. How? how? how?" He sprang up and struck at the air passionately with his hands. "This house would tell us, if roof and walls could but speak. All men are liars! Send me a dumb witness that cannot lie!"

"The house? . . . we've silenced the house ourselves, Peter. Gagged and bound it. If we'd asked it on Tuesday night—but it's hopeless now."

"That's what's biting me. I hate fooling about with maybe and might-have-been. And Kirk isn't likely to examine the thing too closely. He'll be so damned thankful to get a likelier suspect than Sellon that he'll hare off after the Crutchley-Twitterton motive—"

"But, Peter—"

"And then, as like as not," he went on, absorbed in the technical aspect of the thing, "he'll fall down on it in court for lack of direct proof. If only—"

"But, Peter—you're not going to tell Kirk about Crutchley and Miss Twitterton!"

"He'll have to know, of course. It's a fact, as far as it goes. The point is, will he see—"

"Peter—no! You can't do that! That poor little woman and her pathetic love-affair. You can't be so cruel as to tell the police—the police, good heavens!"

For the first time he seemed to realise what she was saying. "Oh!" he said, softly, and turned away towards the fire. "I was afraid it might come to this." Then, over his shoulder:

"One can't suppress evidence, Harriet. You said to me, 'Carry on.'"

"We didn't *know* these people then. She told me in confidence. She—she was grateful to me. She trusted me. You can't take people's trust and make it into a rope for their necks. Peter—"

He stood staring down into the flames. "It's abominable!" cried Harriet, in a sort of consternation. Her excitement broke against his rigidity like water against a stone. "It's—it's brutal."

"Murder is brutal."

"I know—but—"

"You have seen what murdered men look like. Well, I saw this old man's body." He swung round and faced her. "It's a pity the dead are so quiet; it makes us ready to forget them."

"The dead—are dead. We've got to be decent to the living."

"I'm thinking of the living. Till we get at the truth, every soul in this village is suspect. Do you want Sellon broken and hanged, because we wouldn't speak? Must Crutchley be left under suspicion because the crime was never brought home to anybody else? Are they all to go about in fear, knowing there's an undiscovered murderer among them?"

"But there's no proof—no proof!"

"It's evidence. We can't pick and choose. Whoever suffers, we *must* have the truth. Nothing else matters a damn."

She could not deny it. In desperation, she broke through to the real issue:

"But must it be *your* hands—?"

"Ah!" he said, in a changed voice. "Yes. I have given you the right to ask me that. You married into trouble when you married my work and me."

He spread out his hands as though challenging her to look at them. It seemed strange that they should be the same hands that only last night . . . Their smooth strength fascinated her. License my roving hands and let them go before, behind, between—His hands, so curiously gentle and experienced. . . . With what sort of experience?

"These hangman's hands," he said, watching her. "You knew that, though, didn't you?"

Of course she had known it, but—She burst out with the truth:

"I wasn't married to you then!"

"No. . . . That makes the difference, doesn't it? . . . Well, Harriet, we are married now. We are bound. I'm afraid the moment has come when something will have to give away—you, or I—or the bond."

(So soon? . . . Yours, utterly and for ever—He was hers, or else all faith was mockery.)

"No—no! . . . Oh, my dear, what is happening to us? What has become of our peace?"

"Broken," he said. "That's what violence does. Once it starts, there's no stopping it. It catches us all, sooner or later."

"But . . . it mustn't. Can't we escape?"

"Only by running away." He dropped his hands in a hopeless gesture. "Perhaps it would be better for us to run. I have no right to drag any woman into this mess—least of all, my wife. Forgive me. I have been my own master so long—I think I have forgotten the meaning of an obligation." The stricken whiteness of her face startled him. "Oh, my dear—don't upset yourself like this. Say the word, and we'll go right away. We'll leave this miserable business and never meddle again."

"Do you really mean that?" she said, incredulously.

"Of course I mean it. I have said it."

His voice was the voice of a beaten man. She was appalled, seeing what she had done.

"Peter, you're mad. Never dare to suggest such a thing. Whatever marriage is, it isn't that."

"Isn't what, Harriet?"

"Letting your affection corrupt your judgment. What kind of life could we have if I knew that you had become less than yourself by marrying me?"

He turned away again, and when he spoke, it was in a queerly shaken tone:

"My dear girl, most women would consider it a triumph."

"I know, I've heard them." Her own scorn lashed herself—the self she had only just seen. "They boast of it—'My husband would do *anything* for me. . . .' It's degrading. No human being ought to have such power over another."

"It's a very real power, Harriet."

"Then," she flung back passionately, "we won't use it. If we disagree, we'll fight it out like gentlemen. We won't stand for matrimonial blackmail."

He was silent for a moment, leaning back against the chimney-breast. Then he said, with a lightness that betrayed him:

"Harriet, you have no sense of dramatic values. Do you mean to say we are to play out our domestic comedy without the great bedroom scene?"

"Certainly. We'll have nothing so vulgar."

"Well—thank God for that!"

His strained face broke suddenly into the familiar mischievous smile. But she had been too much frightened to be able to smile back—yet.

"Bunter isn't the only person with standards. You *must* do what you think right. Promise me that. What I think doesn't matter. I swear it shall never make a difference."

He took her hand and kissed it gravely.

"Thank you, Harriet. That is love with honour."

They stood so for a moment, both conscious that something had been achieved that was of enormous—of overmastering importance. Then Harriet said, practically:

"In any case, you were right, and I was wrong. The thing has got to be done. By any means, so long as we get to the bottom of it. That's your job, and it's worth doing."

"Always provided I can do it. I don't feel very brilliant at the moment."

"You'll get there in the end. It's all *right*, Peter."

He laughed—and Bunter came in with the soup.

"I regret that dinner is a little late, my lady."

Harriet looked at the clock. It seemed to her that she had lived through interminable ages of emotion. But the hands stood at a quarter past eight. Only an hour and a half had gone by since they had entered the house.

CHAPTER XVIII

♦

Straws in the Hair

Follow the knave; and take this drab away.
—William Shakespeare, *II Henry VI. II. I*

"The really essential thing," said Peter, executing a sketch on the table-cloth with the handle of his soup-spoon, "is to put in a workable hot-water system and build out a bathroom over the scullery. We can make the furnace-house *here*, so as to get a straight fall from the cistern *there*. And that will give us a direct outfall for the bath to the sewer—if I may dignify it by that name. I think there'd be room to make another little bedroom near the bathroom; and when we want more space, we can convert the attics. The electric plant can live in the stable."

Harriet agreed and offered her own contribution:

"Bunter speaks none too kindly of the kitchen range. He says he would designate it as a period piece, my lady, but, if I will permit him to say so, of an inferior period. I think it's mid-Victorian."

"We will take it a few periods back and have it Tudor. I propose to instal an open fire and roasting-spit and live in the baronial manner."

"With a scullion to turn the spit? Or one of those bandy-legged period dogs?"

"Well—no; I was going to compromise about that, and have the spit turned by electricity. And an electric cooker for the days when we didn't feel so period. I like the best of both worlds—I'm quite ready to be picturesque but I draw the line at inconvenience and hard work. I'm sure it would be hard work training a modern dog to turn a spit."

"Talking of dogs—are we keeping that terrific bull-mastiff?"

"We've only hired him till after the funeral. Unless you feel a fancy for him. He is almost embarrassingly affectionate and demonstrative; but he'd do to play with the children. The goat, on the other hand, I have sent home. It got loose while we were out and ate a row of cabbages and Mrs. Ruddle's apron."

"Are you sure you don't want to keep it to provide milk for the nursery tea?"

"Quite sure. It's a billy-goat."

"Oh! well, that's very smelly and useless. I'm glad he's gone. Are we going to keep things?"

"What should you like to keep? Peacocks?"

"Peacocks need a terrace. I was thinking of pigs. They're comfortable; and when you feel dreamy and indolent you can go and scratch their backs like Mr. Baldwin. And ducks make a pleasant noise. But I don't care much for hens."

"Hens have peevish faces. By the way, I'm not sure you weren't right before dinner. On principle, it's the proper thing to give Kirk information, but I wish one knew how he was going to use it. If once he gets a fixed idea—"

"There's someone at the door. If that's Kirk, we'll have to make up our minds."

Bunter entered, bringing with him the fragrance—but only the fragrance—of sage and onion.

"My lord, there is an individual—"

"Oh, send him away. I can't stand any more individuals."

"My lord—"

"We're at dinner. Send him away. Tell him to call again later."

There was the noise of swift footsteps on the gravel outside; and at the same moment a stout, elderly Hebrew burst into the room.

"Very thorry to intrude," said this gentleman, in a breathless and hasty manner. "No wish to cause inconvenience. I," he added helpfully, "am Moss & Isaacs—"

"You were wrong, Bunter. It's not an individual—it's a company."

"—and here in my hand I have—"

"Bunter, take the company's hat."

"Very thorry," said the company, whose failure to uncover seemed due rather to oblivion than to want of natural courtesy. "No intention to offend. But I have here a bill of thale on the furniture in this house, and I have run—"

A thunderous knocking on the door caused him to fling up despairing hands. Bunter hurried out.

"A bill of sale?" cried Harriet.

The intruder turned eagerly to her:

"For a debt of theventy-three, thickthteen, thickth," he said, emotion choking his speech—"and I have run all the way from the buth-thtop—all the way—and there ith a man—"

He was right; there was a man. He pushed his way past Bunter, crying out in reproachful tones:

"Mr. Solomons, Mr. Solomons! that's not fair. Everything in this house is the property of my clients, and the executrix has agreed—"

"Good evening, Mr. MacBride," said the master of the house, politely.

"I can't help that," said Mr. Solomons, his voice drowning Mr. MacBride's reply. He mopped his forehead with his handkerchief. "We hold a bill of sale on the furniture—look at the date on this document—"

Mr. MacBride said firmly:

"Ours has been running five years."

"I don't care," retorted Mr. Solomons, "if it's been running as long as Charley's Aunt!"

"Gentlemen, gentlemen!" said Peter, in conciliatory accents, "cannot this matter be amicably arranged?"

"Our van," said Mr. Solomons, "will call for the goods tomorrow."

"Our clients' van," replied Mr. MacBride, "is on the way now."

Mr. Solomons uttered a loud expostulatory howl, and Peter tried again:

"I implore you, gentlemen, have some consideration for my wife, if not for me. We are in the middle of dinner, and you propose to remove the table and chairs. We have to sleep—will you not leave us so much as a bed to lie on? We also, if it comes to that, have some claim upon the furniture, since we hired it. Pray do not be so precipitate. . . . Mr. MacBride, you have known us long and (I hope) loved us well—you will, I am sure, have compassion on our nerves and feelings, and not turn us out dinnerless to sleep under the nearest haystack."

"My lord," said Mr. MacBride, somewhat moved by this appeal, but conscious of his duty, "in the interests of our clients—"

"In the interests of our firm," said Mr. Solomons.

"In all our interests," said Peter, "will you not sit down and share our roast duck with apple sauce and sage and onion stuffing? You, Mr. Solomons, have run fast and far—your strength needs sustaining. You, Mr. MacBride, spoke feelingly yesterday morning about our English family life—will you not for once consent to see it at its best? Do not break up the happy home! Over a slice of the breast and a glass of the best any little differences may be adjusted."

"Yes, indeed," said Harriet. "Do join us. Bunter will break his heart if the bird gets dried up in the oven."

Mr. MacBride hesitated.

"It's very good of you," began Mr. Solomons, wistfully. "If your ladyship—"

"No, no, Solly," said Mr. MacBride; "it ain't fair."

"My dear," said Peter, with a polite inclination, "you know very well that it is a husband's incurable habit to invite his business friends to dine under any circumstances and on the shortest possible notice. Without that habit, home life would not be what it is. Therefore I make no apology."

"Of course not," said Harriet. "Bunter, these gentlemen will dine with us."

"Very good, my lady." He laid dexterous hands on Mr. Solomons and relieved him of his overcoat. "Allow me." Mr. MacBride, without further argument, valeted himself and then helped Peter to bring two more chairs to the table, observing as he did so: "I don't know what you advanced on these, Solly, but they weren't worth it."

"So far as we are concerned," said Peter, "you may have the whole lot tomorrow and welcome. Now—are we all quite comfortable? Mr. Solomons on the right—Mr. MacBride on the left. Bunter—the claret!"

Mr. Solomons and Mr. MacBride, mellow with Hermitage and cigars, departed fraternally at a quarter to ten, having previously made a brief tour of the house, so as to check their inventories together. Peter, who had accompanied them in order to establish his right to his own belongings, returned, bearing in his hand one of the little straw wig-wams in which wine-bottles are housed while travelling.

"What's that for, Peter?"

"Me," said his lordship. He detached the straws methodically, one by one, and began to thread them through his hair. He had succeeded in making a very passable bird's-nest of himself when Superintendent Kirk was announced.

"Good evening, Mr. Kirk," said Harriet, with as much warmth of welcome as she could put into words.

"Good evening," said the Superintendent. 'I'm afraid I'm intruding." He looked at Peter, who made a horrible face at him. "It's a bit late for a call."

"This," said Peter, wildly, "is the foul fiend Flibbertigibbet: he begins at Curfew and walks till the first cock. Have a straw, Superintendent. You'll need one before you've finished."

"Have nothing of the sort," said Harriet. "You look tired. Have a glass of beer or some whisky or something and don't mind my husband. He sometimes gets taken that way."

The Superintendent thanked her absent-mindedly; he seemed to be in travail with an idea. He slowly opened his mouth, and looked at Peter again.

"Sit down, sit down," said the latter, hospitably. "I'll talk a word with this same learned Theban."

"Got it!" cried Mr. Kirk. "King Lear! Though their injunction be to bar my doors And let this tyrannous night take hold upon you, Yet have I ventur'd to come seek you out."

"You're very nearly right about that," said Harriet. "We really thought we were going to be turned out into the tyrannous night. Hence the distraction and the straws."

Mr. Kirk inquired how this might be.

"Well," said Harriet, installing him on one of the settles, "there's a Mr. Solomons of Moss & Isaacs, who holds a bill of sale on the furniture, and your old friend Mr. MacBride, who wants to distrain on the furniture for his writ, and they both came in together to take the furniture away. But we gave them dinner and they went peaceably."

"You may ask," added Peter, "why they rather choose to have a weight of carrion flesh than to receive three thousand ducats—I cannot tell you, but so it was."

Mr. Kirk paused so long this time that both Peter and Harriet thought he must have become stricken with aphasia; but at last, and with a wide smile of triumph, he gave tongue:

"He is well paid that is well satisfied! Merchant of Venice!"

"A Daniel come to judgment! Harriet, the Superintendent has caught the hang of our half-witted manner of conversation. He is a man, take him for all in all, we shall not look upon his like again. Give him his drink—he has deserved it. Say when. Shall I make spirits fetch me what I please, Resolve me of all ambiguities?"

"Thank you," said the Superintendent, "not too stiff, my lord, if you don't mind. We'll have it gentle and the elements so mixed—"

"That a spoon might stand up in it," suggested Peter.

"No," said Mr. Kirk. "That bit doesn't seem to finish up quite right. But thanks all the same. Here's health."

"And what have you been doing all afternoon?" inquired

Peter, bringing a stool to the fire and seating himself on it between his wife and Kirk.

"Well, my lord," said Kirk. "I've been up to London."

"To London?" said Harriet. "That's right, Peter. Come a little further this way and let me take the straws out. *Il m'aime—un peu—beaucoup—*"

"But not to see the Queen," pursued the Superintendent. "I went to see Frank Crutchley's young woman. In Clerkenwell."

"Has he got one there?"

"*Passionément—à la folie—*"

"He *had,*" said Kirk.

"*Pas du tout. Il m'aime—*"

"I got the address from that chap Williams over at Hancock's. Seems she's a good-looking young woman—"

"*Un peu—beaucoup—*"

"With a bit of money—"

"*Passionément—*"

"Lived with 'er dad and seemed dead struck on Frank Crutchley. But there—"

"A *la folie—*"

"You know what girls are. Some other fellow turned up—"

Harriet paused, with the twelfth straw in her fingers.

"And the long and the short of it is, she married the other bloke three months back."

"*Pas du tout!*" said Harriet; and flung the straws into the fire.

"The devil she did!" said Peter. He caught Harriet's eye.

"But what got me all worked up," said Kirk, "was finding out what 'er father was."

"It was a robber's daughter, and her name was Alice Brown. Her father was the terror of a small Italian town."

"Not a bit of it. He's a—There!" said Mr. Kirk, arresting his glass half way to his mouth, "of all the trades and professions open to a man, what should you say he was?"

"From your air," replied Peter, "of having, so to speak, found the key that cuts the Gordian knot—"

"I can't imagine," said Harriet, hastily. "We give it up."

"Well," announced Kirk, eyeing Peter a little dubiously, "if you give it up, then I'll tell you. 'Er father is an ironmonger and locksmith as cuts keys when wanted."

"Good God, you don't say so!"

Kirk, putting down a mouthful, nodded emphatically.

"And what's more," he went on, setting the glass down on the table with a smack, "what's more, none so long ago—six months more or less—young Crutchley comes along, bright as you please, and asks him to cut a key for him."

"Six months ago! Well, well!"

"Six months. But," resumed the Superintendent, "now this I'm going to tell you *will* surprise you. I don't mind saying it surprised me. . . . Thank you, I don't mind if I do. . . . Well—the old boy didn't make no secret of the key. Seems there'd a-been a bit of a tiff between the young people before they parted brass-rags. Anyhow, he didn't seem to feel no special call to speak up for Frank Crutchley. So when I asked the question, he answered straight off, and what's more, he took me round to his workshop. He's a methodical old bird, and when he makes a new key, he keeps a cast of it. Says people often lose their keys, and it comes in 'andy to have a record. I dunno. Shouldn't wonder if he'd had official inquiries round there before. But that's neether here nor there. He took me round and he showed me the cast what he'd made of the key. And what do you think that key was like?"

Peter, having been once rebuked, did not this time venture on so much as a veiled guess. But Harriet felt that some sort of reply was called for. Mustering up all the astonishment the human voice is capable of expressing, she said:

"You *can't* mean it was the key to one of the doors in this house?"

Mr. Kirk smote his thigh with a large hand.

"Aha!" he cried. "What did I say? I knew I should catch you there! No—it was not, and nothing like, neether. Now! What do you think of that?"

Peter picked up the remains of the bottle-straw and began

to weave himself a fresh head-dress. Harriet felt that her effort had gone even better than she had intended.

"How astonishing!"

"Nothing like it," repeated the Superintendent. "A huge great thing it was, more like a church key."

"Was it," asked Peter, his fingers working rapidly among the straws, "made from a key or from a wax mould?"

"From a key. He brought it along with him. Said it was the key to a barn he'd hired to keep some stuff in. Said the key belonged to the owner and he wanted another for himself."

"I should have thought it was the owner's business to supply a key for the tenant," said Harriet.

"So should I. Crutchley explained he'd had one once and lost it. And mind you, that might be true. Anyhow, that's the only key the old man had cut for him—or so he said, and I don't think he was lying, neether. So away I come, by the evening train, no wiser. But after I'd had me bit o' supper, I says to myself, Well, I says, it's a line—never leave a line, I says, till you've followed it up. So out I goes to Pagford to look for our young friend. Well, he wasn't in the garage, but Williams said he'd seen him go out on his bike along the road to Ambledon Overbrook—you may know it—about a mile and a half out o' Pagford on the Lopsley road."

"We came through it this afternoon. Pretty little church with a brooch spire."

"Yes, it's got a spire. Well, I thought I'd have a look for my gentleman, so I pushed along and—do you remember seeing a big old barn with a tiled roof about three quarters to a mile out of Pagford?"

"I noticed it," said Harriet. "It stands all by itself in a field."

"That's right. Well, going past there, I see a light, as it might be a bicycle-lamp, going across that field, and it came to me all of a sudden that about six months ago, Crutchley did a bit of work on a tractor for Mr. Moffatt as owns that barn. See? I just put them things together in my mind. So I gets out of the car, and I follows the bicycle light across the field. He wasn't going fast—just walking with it—and I went pretty quick, and when he was about half way across, he must a-heard me coming, because he stopped. So I come up and then I see who it was."

The Superintendent paused again.

"Go on," said Peter. "We'll buy it this time. It wasn't Crutchley. It was Mr. Goodacre or the landlord of the Crown."

"Caught you again," said Kirk, jovially. "Crutchley it was, all right. I asked him what he was doing there, and he said that was his business and we argued a bit, and I said I'd like to know what he was doing with a key to Mr. Moffatt's barn, and he wanted to know what I meant by that and—anyhow, the long and the short was, I said I was going to see what there was in the barn and he was damn well going to come with me. So we went along, and he sounded pretty sulky, but he says: 'You're barking up the wrong tree,' and I says, 'We'll see about that.' So we got to the door and I says, 'Give me that key,' and he says, 'I tell you I ain't got no key,' and I says, 'Then what do you want in this field, because it don't lead nowhere, and anyhow,' I says, 'I'm going to see.' So I puts me 'and on the door and it come open as easy as winking. And what do you think was inside that barn?"

Peter contemplated his plait of straw and twisted the ends together to form a crown.

"At a guess," he replied, "I should say—Polly Mason."

"Well, there!" exclaimed the Superintendent. "Just as I was all set to catch you again! Polly Mason it was, and she wasn't half scared to see me, neether. 'Now, my girl,' I said to her, 'I don't like to see you here,' I says. 'What's all this?' And Crutchley says, 'No business of yours, you stupid cop. She's over the age of consent.' 'Maybe,' I said, 'but she's got a mother,' I said, ''as brought her up decent; and what's more,' I said, 'it's breaking and entering, and that's a civil trespass, and Mr. Moffatt'll have something to say about it.' So there was more words passed, and I said to the girl, 'You 'and over that key, which you ain't got no right to, and if you've got any sense or feeling,' I said, 'you'll come along home with me.' And the end of it was, I brought her back—and a lot of sauce she gave me, the young piece. As for me lord, I left him to twiddle his thumbs—I beg your pardon, my lord—no offence intended."

Peter finished his crown and put it on.

"It's an odd thing," he observed, "that men like Crutchley, with quantities of large white teeth, are practically always gay Lotharios."

"Not frivolously gay, either," said Harriet. "Two strings to the bow for use and one for pleasure."

"Frank Crutchley," said Kirk, "has got too much o' what the cat cleans 'er paws with. Stupid cop, indeed—I'll cop 'im, the cheeky 'ound, one o' these days."

"There is a certain lack of the finer feelings," said Peter. "Euphelia serves to grace my measure but Chloe is my real flame, no doubt. But to get Euphelia's father to cut the key for Chloe is—tactless."

"'Tain't my business to run a Sunday school," said the Superintendent, "but that Polly Mason's asking for trouble. 'The banns is going up next Sunday,' says she, bold as brass. 'Are they?' says I. 'Well, if I was you, my girl, I'd run round to parson with 'em myself, straight away, before your young man changes his mind. If you and him's walking out in a proper way, there's no need to have keys to other folks' barns.' I didn't say anything about the young lady in London, because that's over and done with, but where there's one there might be two."

"There were two," said Harriet resolutely; "and the other one was here, in Pagford."

"What's that?" said Kirk.

Harriet told her story for the second time that evening.

"Well, I'm bothered!" exclaimed Mr. Kirk, laughing heartily. "Poor old Aggie Twitterton! Kissing Frank Crutchley in the churchyard. That's a good 'un!"

Neither of the other two made any comment. Presently, Kirk's mirth subsided and he showed signs of being once more in a state of mental gestation. His eyes became fixed and his lips moved silently. "'Alf a moment, 'alf a moment," said Kirk while they watched him breathlessly; "Aggie Twitterton, eh? And young Crutchley? Now, that's made me think of something, that has. . . . Now, don't you tell me. . . . There! I knew I'd get it!"

"I thought you would," said Peter, only half aloud.

"Twelfth Night!" cried Mr. Kirk, exultantly. "Orsino, that's it! 'Too old, by heaven, Let still the woman take An elder than herself'—I knew there was something in Shakespeare." He fell silent again. "Hullo!" he said, in a changed tone, "that's all right, but see here! If Aggie Twitterton wanted the money for Frank Crutchley and had the keys to the house, what was to prevent her—eh?"

"Nothing whatever," said Peter. "Only you've got to prove it, you know."

"I've had my eye on Aggie Twitterton all along," said the Superintendent. "After all, you can't get over them things she said. And her knowing about the will and all. And, come to look at it, whoever did it had to get into the house, now, hadn't they?"

"Why?" demanded Peter. "How do you know Noakes didn't come out and get killed in the garden?"

"No," said Kirk, "that's the one thing he couldn't, and you know that as well as I do; and for why? There wasn't no earth nor gravel on his shoes nor yet on his coat where he fell on it. And this time of the year, and with the rain we had last week there would a-been. No, my lord, springes to catch woodcocks! You don't catch me that way."

"Hamlet," said Peter, meekly. "Very well. Now we'd better tell you all the ways we've thought of for getting into the house."

After nearly an hour, the Superintendent was shaken, but not convinced.

"See here, my lord," he said at last. "I see your point, and you're quite right. It's no good saying, He might or She might, because there'd always be a clever counsel to say, might ain't necess*ar*ily right. And I see I been a bit hasty, overlooking that window and the trap-door and about something having been thrown at deceased. Better late than never. I'll be round again in the morning, and we'll go into all them points. And here's another thing. I'll bring Joe Sellon with me, and you can try for yourself about him gettin' through them—mullions, d'you call them? Because, not to put too fine a point upon it, he'd make two of you, my lord—and what's more, it's my belief *you* could get through pretty well almost anything, including a judge and jury, if you'll pardon me saying so. . . . No, don't you mistake me. I ain't out to put nothing on Aggie Twitterton—I'm out to find who killed deceased, and prove it. And I *will* prove it, if I have to go through the place with a tooth-comb."

"Then," said Peter, "you have to be up pretty early in the morning, to stop our London friends from carrying away the furniture, lock, stock and barrel."

"I'll see they don't take the trap-door," retorted the Superintendent. "Nor yet the door and windows. And now I'll be getting off home, and I'm very sorry for keeping you and her ladyship up like this."

"Not at all," said Peter. "Parting is such sweet sorrow—We've had quite a Shakespearean evening, haven't we?"

"Well," said Harriet, as her lord returned from seeing the Superintendent to the door, "he wasn't unreasonable, after all. But oh! I do hope there won't be any more people tonight."

"*Nous menons une vie assez mouvementée*. I've never known such a day. Bunter looks quite haggard—I have sent him to bed. As for me, I don't feel like the same person I was before breakfast."

"I don't even feel the same person I was before dinner. Peter—about that. It's frightened me rather. I've always so loathed and dreaded any sort of possessiveness. You know how I've always run away from it."

"I've reason to know it." He made a wry face. "You ran like the Red Queen."

"I know I did. And now—I start it, of all people! I simply can't think what came over me. It's frightful. Is that sort of thing always going to happen to me?"

"I don't know," he said, lightly. "I can't imagine. In an experience of women extending, like the good Dr. Watson's, over many nations, and three separate continents—"

"Why separate? Do ordinary continents come blended, like teas?"

"I don't know. That's what it says in the book. Three separate continents. In all my experience, you are completely unprecedented. I never met anybody like you."

"Why? Possessiveness isn't unprecedented."

"On the contrary—it's as common as mud. But to recognise it in one's self and chuck it overboard is—unusual. If you want to be a normal person, my girl, you should let it rip and give yourself and everybody else hell with it. And you should call it something else—devotion or self-sacrifice and that sort of thing. If you go on behaving with all this reason and generosity, everybody will think we don't give a damn for one another."

"Well—if ever I do anything like that again, for heaven's sake don't give in . . . you wouldn't have, really?"

"If it had come to the point—yes, I should. I couldn't live in a wrangle. Not with you, anyway."

"I wouldn't have believed you could be so weak. As if a possessive person is *ever* going to be satisfied. If you gave in once, you'd have to do it again and again. Like Danegeld."

"Don't be harsh with me, Domina. If it happens again, I'll take a stick to you. I promise. But I wasn't sure what I was up against—*la femme jalouse de l'oeuvre*, or a perfectly reasonable objection, or just marriage as such. I can't expect being married to be just like not being married, can I? I thought I might be heading the wrong way. I thought if I show you where the hitch was—I don't know what I thought. It doesn't matter. I only know what you said, and that it took my breath away."

"I only know that I started to behave like a pig and thought better of it. Peter—it hasn't upset the—the things you said before? It hasn't spoilt anything?"

"To know that I can trust you better than myself? What do you think? . . . But listen, dear—for God's sake let's take that word 'possess' and put a brick round its neck and drown it. I will not use it or hear it used—not even in the crudest physical sense. It's meaningless. We can't possess one another. We can only give and hazard all we have—Shakespeare, as Kirk would say. . . . I don't know what's the matter with me tonight. Something seems to have got off the chain. I've said things I didn't think I could say if I lived to be a hundred—by which time most of them wouldn't be worth saying."

"It seems to be that kind of day. I've said things too. I think I've said everything, except—"

"That's true. You never have said it. You've always found some other phrase for it. *Un peu d'audace, que diable!* . . . Well?"

"I love you."

"Bravely said—though I had to screw it out of you like a cork out of a bottle. Why should that phrase be so difficult? I—personal pronoun, subjective case; L-O-V-E, love, verb active, meaning—Well, on Mr. Squeers's principle, go to bed and work it out."

The window was still open; for October, the air was strangely mild and still. From somewhere close at hand a cat—probably the ginger tom—lifted its voice in a long-drawn wail of unappeasable yearning. Peter's right hand searched the sill, and closed upon the granite paperweight. But even in the act, he changed his mind, released his grip and with the other hand drew the casement to and fastened it.

"Who am I," said he aloud, "to cast stones at my fellow-mortal?"

He lit his candle, extinguished the lamps and made his way upstairs.

Two minutes later, Bunter, prompted by God knows what savage libido, flung a boot from the back bedroom; and on the mere the wailing died away.

CHAPTER XIX

◆

Prickly Pear

This is the dead land
This is cactus land
Here the stone images
Are raised, here they receive
The supplication of a dead man's hand
Under the twinkle of a fading star. . . .

Between the idea
And the reality
Between the motion
And the act
Falls the Shadow.
—T. S. Eliot, *The Hollow Men*

"Peter, what were you dreaming about early this morning? It sounded pretty awful."

He looked vexed.

"Oh, my God, have I started that again? I thought I'd learnt to keep my dreams to myself. Did I say things? Tell me the worst."

"I couldn't make out what you said. But it sounded as though—to put it mildly—you had something on your mind."

"What an agreeable companion I must be," he said, bitterly. "I know. I've been told about it before. The perfect bedfellow—so long as I keep awake. I'd no business to risk it; but one always hopes one's going to come right again sometime. In future I'll remove myself."

"Don't be an idiot, Peter. You stopped dreaming as soon as I got hold of you."

"So I did. It comes back to me now. . . . Fifteen of us marching across a prickly desert, and we were all chained together. There was something I had forgotten—to do or tell somebody—but I couldn't stop, because of the chain. . . . Our mouths were full of sand, and there were flies and things. . . . We were in dark blue uniforms, and we had to go on. . . ."

He broke off. "I don't know why blue uniforms—it's usually something to do with the War. And telling one's dreams is the last word in egotism."

"I want to hear it; it sounds perfectly foul."

"Well, it was, in a way. . . . Our boots were broken with the march. . . . When I looked down, I saw the bones of my own feet, and they were black, because we'd been hanged in chains a long time ago and were beginning to come to pieces."

"Mais priez dieu que tous nous veuille absoudre."

"Yes, that's it. Very like the Ballade des Pendus. Only it was hot, with a sky like brass—and we knew that the end of the journey would be worse than the beginning. And it was all my fault, because I'd forgotten—whatever it was."

"What was the end of it?"

"It didn't end. It changed when you touched me—something about rain and a bunch of chrysanthemums. . . . Oh, it was only the old responsibility-dream, and a mild one at that. The funny thing is that I know there *is* something I've forgotten. I woke up with it on the tip of my tongue—but it's gone."

"It'll come back if you don't worry it."

"I wish it would; and then I shouldn't feel so guilty about it. . . . Hullo, Bunter, what's that? The post? Heaven above, man, what have you got there?"

"Our silk hat, my lord."

"Silk hat? Don't be ridiculous, Bunter. We don't want that in the country."

"The funeral is this morning, my lord. I thought it possible your lordship might desire to attend it. The prayer-books are in the other parcel with the black suit."

"But surely to goodness I can go to a village funeral without a mourning suit and a top-hat!"

"The conventional marks of esteem are highly appreciated in rural communities, my lord. But it is as your lordship wishes. Two vans have arrived to take the furniture, my lord, and Superintendent Kirk is below with Mr. MacBride and Mr. Solomons. With your lordship's permission, I will suggest that I should take the car over to Broxford and order a few temporary necessities—such as a couple of camp-beds and a kettle."

"Peter," said Harriet, looking up from her correspondence, "there's a letter from your mother. She says she is going down to the Dower House this morning. The shooting-party at the Hall has broken up, and Gerald and Helen are going for the week-end to Lord Attenbury's. She wonders whether we should like to join her for a day or two. She thinks we may need rest and change—not from one another, she is careful to explain, but from what she calls housekeeping."

"My mother is a very remarkable woman. Her faculty for hitting the right nail on the head is almost miraculous—especially as all her blows have the air of being delivered at random. Housekeeping! The house is about all we're likely to keep, by the looks of it."

"What do you think of her idea?"

"It's rather for you to say. We've got to go somewhere or other, unless you really prefer the kettle and the camp-bedstead to which Bunter so feelingly alludes. But it is said to be unwise to introduce the mother-in-law complication too early on."

"There are mothers-in-law and mothers-in-law."

"True; and you wouldn't be bothered with the others-in-law, which makes a difference. We once talked about seeing the old place when we could do it on our own."

"I'd like to go, Peter."

"Very well, then, you shall. Bunter, send Her Grace a wire to say we're coming down tonight."

"Very good, my lord."

"Heartfelt satisfaction," said Peter, as Bunter left them. "He will be sorry to abandon the investigation, but the camp-beds and the kettle would break even Bunter's spirit. In a way I feel rather thankful to Mr. Solomons for precipitating matters. We haven't run away; we've received the order to retreat and can march out with all the honours of war."

"You really feel that?"

"I think so. Yes, I do."

Harriet looked at him and felt depressed, as one frequently does when one gets what one fancied one wanted.

"You'll never want to come back to this house again."

He shifted uneasily. "Oh, I don't know. I could be bounded in a nutshell . . . were it not that I have bad dreams."

But he would always have bad dreams in that house while the shadow of failure lay on it. . . . He pushed the subject aside by asking:

"Any other news from the Mater?"

"Not news, exactly. Of course, she's awfully sorry we've been tr-r-roubled by all this. She thinks she has found us a very suitable pair of housemaids, to come in November. The chandelier is up, and every drop has been separately silenced so as not to jingle; she had the piano-tuner playing the piano at it for an hour on end, and it didn't let out a single ting-a-ling. Ahasuerus caught a mouse on Tuesday night and put it in Franklin's bedroom slipper. Your nephew Jerry had a little difference of opinion with a policeman, but explained that he had been marrying off his uncle and escaped with a fine and a caution. That's all. The rest is—well, it more or less amounts to saying she's glad I can give you a good chit and it may not be a bad thing to begin with a little adversity."

"Perhaps she's right. I'm thankful it was a good chit, anyhow. Meanwhile, here's a note for you from Uncle Pandarus—I mean, Uncle Paul—enclosed in a letter to me in which he has the impertinence to hope that my addiction of late years to what he calls 'intemperate orgies of virtue' have not left me too much out of practice for my *métier d'époux*. He recommends *une vie réglée* and begs I will not allow myself to become *trop émotionné*, since emotion tends to impair *les forces vitales*. I do not know anybody who can cram more cynical indelicacy into a letter of good advice than my Uncle Pandarus."

"Mine's good advice, too; but it isn't exactly cynical."

(Mr. Delagardie had, in fact, written:

> MY DEAR NIECE—I hope that my absurd, but on the whole agreeable nephew is contriving to fill your cup with the wine of life. May an old man who knows him well remind you that what is wine to you is bread to him. You are too sensible to be offended by *cette franchise*. My nephew is not sensible at all—il n'est que sensible et passablement sensuel. Il a plus besoin de vous que vous de lui; soyez généreuse—c'est une nature qu'on ne saurait gâter. Il sent le besoin de se donner—de s'épancher; vous ne lui refuserez certes pas ce modeste plaisir. La froideur, la coquetterie même, le tuent; il ne sait pas s'imposer; la lutte lui répugne. Tout cela, vous le savez déjà—Pardon! je vous trouve extrèmement sympathique, et je crois que son bien-être nous est cher à tous deux. Avec cela, il est marchand du bonheur à qui en veut; j'espère que vous trouverez en lui ce qui pourra vous plaire. Pour le rendre heureux, vous n'avez qu'à être heureuse; il supporte mal les souffrances d'autrui. Recevez, ma chère nièce, mes voeux les plus sincères.)

Peter grinned.

"I won't ask what it is. The least said about Uncle Paul's good advice, the soonest mended. He is a most regrettable old man, and his judgment is disgustingly sound. According to him I suffer from a romantic heart, which plays the cat-and-banjo with my realistic mind."

(Mr. Delagardie had, in fact, written:

> . . . Cette femme te sera un point d'appui. Elle n'a connu jusqu'ici que les chagrins de l'amour; tu lui en apprendra les délices. Elle trouvera en toi des délicatesses imprévues, et qu'elle saura apprécier. Mais

surtout, mon ami, pas de faiblesse! Ce n'est pas une jeune fille niaise et étourdie; c'est une intelligence forte, qui aime à résoudre les problèmes par la tête. Il ne faut pas être trop soumis; elle ne t'en saura pas gré. Il faut encore moins l'enjôler; elle pourra se raviser. Il faut convaincre; je suis persuadé qu'elle se montrera magnanime. Tâche de comprimer les élans d'un coeur chaleureux—ou plutôt réserve-les pour ces moments d'intimité conjugale où ils ne seront pas déplacés et pourront te servir à quelque chose. Dans toutes les autres circonstances, fais valoir cet esprit raissoneur dont tu n'es pas entièrement dépourvu. A vos âges, il est nécessaire de préciser; on ne vient plus à bout d'une situation en se livrant à des étreintes effrénées et en poussant des cris déchirants. Raidis-toi, afin d'inspirer le respect à ta femme; en lui tenant tête tu lui fourniras le meilleur moyen de ne pas s'ennuyer. . . .)

Peter folded this epistle away with a grimace, and inquired: "Do you mean to go to the funeral?"

"I don't think so. I've got no black frock to do your top-hat credit, and I'd better stay here to keep an eye on the Solomons-MacBride outfit."

"Bunter can do that."

"Oh, no—he's panting to attend the obsequies. I've just seen him brushing his best bowler. Are you coming down?"

"Not for a moment. There's a letter from my agent I've simply got to attend to. I thought I'd cleared everything up nicely, but one of the tenants has chosen this moment to create a tiresomeness. And Jerry has got himself into a jam with a woman and is really frightfully sorry to bother me, but the husband has turned up with the light of blackmail in his eye and what on earth is he to do?"

"Great heavens! That boy again?"

"What I shall *not* do is to send him a cheque. As it happens, I know all about the lady and gentleman in question, and all that is required is a firm letter and the address of my solicitor, who knows all about them too. But I can't write downstairs, with Kirk oiling in and out of the windows and brokers' men wrangling over the what-not."

"Of course you can't. I'll go and see to things. Be busy and good. . . . And I used to think you were God's own idler, without a responsibility in the world!"

"Property won't run itself, worse luck! Nor yet nephews. Aha! Uncle Pandarus likes giving avuncular advice, does he? Trust *me* to distribute a little avuncular advice in the quarter where it will do most good. Every dog has his day. . . . *C'est bien, embrasse-moi. . . . Ah, non! voyons, tu me dépeignes. . . . Allons, hop! il faut être sérieux.*"

Peter, having dealt with his correspondence and been persuaded, fretfully protesting, into a black suit and a stiff collar, came downstairs and found Superintendent Kirk about to take his leave, and Mr. MacBride just issuing victor from a heated three-cornered argument between himself, Mr. Solomons and a dusty-looking professional person who explained that he represented the executrix. What precise business arrangement had been come to, Peter did not ask and never discovered. The upshot seemed to be that the furniture was to go, Harriet (on Peter's behalf) having waived all claim to it on the grounds (a) that they had so far paid nothing for the use of it, (b) that they would not have it if it were given away with a pound of tea and (c) that they were going away for the week-end and (d) would be glad to have it out of the house as soon as possible to make room for their own goods.

This point having been settled, Mr. MacBride appealed to the Superintendent for leave to carry on. Kirk nodded gloomily.

"No luck?" asked Peter.

"Not a ha'porth," said Kirk. "It's as you said. Puffett and Bert Ruddle have left their marks all over the place upstairs, but there's no telling if some of them wasn't made last week. There's no dint on this floor, as there might be if a stone had been thrown down—but *on* the other 'and, this old oak is that 'ard, you couldn't make any impression on it if you heaved rocks at it for a week. I dunno, I'm sure. I never see such a case. There don't seem to be nothing you can lay your fingers on, like."

"Have you tried squeezing Sellon through the window?"

"Joe Sellon?" Kirk snorted. "If you was to go down to the village, you'd see Joe Sellon. Coo! Talk of a traffic jam! I never see nothing like it in all my born days. There's 'alf Pagford here and pretty well the 'ole of Broxford, and all them newspaper men from London, and the *Broxford and Pagford Gazette* and the *North-Herts Advertiser* and a chap with one of them moving-picture cameras, and cars that thick in front of the Crown nobody can't get in, and such a mob around the bar, they can't get served when they are in. Joe's got more'n he can do. I've left my sergeant down there to lend 'im a hand. And," said the Superintendent, indignantly, "jest as we'd got about twenty cars parked neat and tidy in the lane by Mr. Giddy's field, up comes a kid and squeaks, 'Oh, please, mister—can't you let me by? I've brought the cow to bull'—and we 'ad to move 'em all out again. Aggravating ain't the word. But there! It can't last for ever, that's a comfort; and I'll bring Joe up here when the funeral's over and out of the way."

Mr. MacBride's men worked expertly. Harriet, watching the swift disintegration of her honeymoon house into a dusty desert of straw and packing-cases, rolled-up curtains and spidery pictures spreading their loose wires like springes, wondered whether the whole of her married life would have the same kaleidoscopic quality. Character is destiny: probably there was something in her and Peter that doomed them never to carry any adventure to its close without preposterous interruptions and abrupt changes of fortune. She laughed, as she assisted matters by tying a bunch of fire-irons together, and remembered what a married friend had once confided to her about her own honeymoon.

"Jim wanted a peaceful place, so we went to a tiny fishing village in Brittany. It was lovely, of course, but it rained a good deal, and I think it was rather a mistake we had so little to do.

We were very much in love, I don't mean we weren't—but there were a great many hours to get through, and it didn't seem somehow quite the right thing just to sit down quietly and read a book. There's something to be said, after all, for the sightseeing kind of honeymoon—it does give one a programme."

Well; things did not always go according to programme. Harriet looked up from the fire-irons and with some surprise observed Frank Crutchley.

"Were you wanting any help, my lady?"

"Well, Crutchley, I don't know. Are you free this morning?"

Crutchley explained that he had brought a party over from Great Pagford for the funeral; but they were going to lunch at the Crown and would not be wanting him again till later on.

"But don't you want to go to the funeral? You're in the Paggleham choir, aren't you? And the vicar said something about a choral service."

Crutchley shook his head.

"I've had words with Mrs. Goodacre—leastways, she 'ad words with me. That Kirk . . . interfering. It ain't no business of Vicar's wife about me and Polly Mason. I went up about 'aving the banns published, and Mrs. Goodacre set on me."

"Oh!" said Harriet. She was not very well pleased with Crutchley herself; but since he obviously had no idea that Miss Twitterton had made her troubles public, it seemed better not to refer to the subject. By this time, Miss Twitterton was probably regretting that she had spoken. And to take the matter up with Crutchley would only emphasise the poor little woman's humiliation by giving it importance. Besides, one of the removal-men was kneeling in the window, laying the bronze horsemen and other objects of art tenderly away in a packing-case, while another, on the step-ladder, had relieved the walls of the painted mirror and was contemplating an attack on the clock.

"Very well, Crutchley. You can give the men a hand if they need it."

"Yes, my lady. Shall I get some of this stuff out?"

"Well—no, not for the moment." She turned to the man

in the window, who had just placed the last atrocity in the case and was putting the lid on.

"Do you mind leaving the rest of this room to the last? My husband will be coming back here after the funeral and may have one or two people with him. We shall need some chairs to sit on."

"Right you are, lady. Could we do a bit upstairs?"

"Yes; certainly. And we shan't want this room very long."

"O.K., lady. Come along, Bill, this way."

Bill, a thin man with an apologetic moustache, came obediently down from the steps.

"Right-ho, George. It'll take us a bit o' time to take down them four-posters."

"Can this man give you any help? He's the gardener here."

George eyed Crutchley, who had taken the steps and brought them back to the centre of the room. "There's them plants in the green'us," said George. "We ain't got no special instructions about them, but we was told to take everything."

"Yes; the plants will have to go, and the ones in here as well. But these will do later. Go and see to the greenhouse, Crutchley."

"And there's a sight o' things in the outhouse," said George. "Jack's out there; he'd be glad of a hand with them."

Crutchley put the steps back against the wall and went out. George and Bill departed upstairs. Harriet remembered that Peter's tobacco and cigars were in the what-not and collected them. Then, smitten by a sudden pang, she hastened out into the pantry. It was already stripped. With the Furies at her heels, she bounded down the cellar steps, not even pausing to remember what had once lain at the foot of them. The place was dark as Egypt, but she struck a match, and breathed again. All was well. The two-and-a-half dozen of port lay carefully ranged upon the racks; and in front of them was tacked a notice in large letters: HIS LORDSHIP'S PROPERTY. DO NOT TOUCH. Coming up again into the light, she encountered Crutchley entering by the back door. He started at seeing her.

"I went to see if the wine was all right. I see Bunter has put up a notice. But please tell the men specially that they mustn't on any account lay a finger on those bottles."

Crutchley broke into a wide smile that showed Harriet how attractive his face could be and threw light on the indiscretions of Miss Twitterton and Polly Mason.

"They ain't likely to forget, my lady. Mr. Bunter, he spoke to them himself—very solemn. He sets great store by that wine, seemin'ly. If you could a-heard him yesterday ticking off Martha Ruddle—"

Harriet wished she had heard it, and was greatly tempted to ask for an eye-witness account of the scene; but considered that Crutchley's forwardness of manner scarcely called for encouragement; besides, whether he knew it or not, he was in her bad books. She said, repressively:

"Well, take care they don't forget it."

"Very good. They can't take the barrel, I suppose."

"Oh, yes—that doesn't belong to us. Only the bottled beer."

"Very good, my lady."

Crutchley went out again, without taking whatever it was he had come for, and Harriet returned to the sitting-room. With a kind of tolerant pity, she lifted the aspidistras from their containing pots and gathered them into a melancholy little group on the floor, together with a repellent little cactus like an over-stuffed pincushion and a young rubber-plant. She had seldom seen plants she could care less for, but they were faintly hallowed by sentimental association: Peter had laughed at them. She reflected she must be completely besotted about Peter, if his laughter could hallow an aspidistra.

"Very well," said Harriet aloud to herself, "I will *be* besotted." She selected the largest aspidistra and kissed one of its impassive shining surfaces. "But," she added cheerfully to the cactus, "I won't kiss *you* till you've shaved." A head came suddenly through the window and startled her.

"Excuse me, lady," said the head. "Is that there perambulator in the outhouse yourn?"

"What? Oh, dear, no," said Harriet, with a vivid and sympathetic appreciation of Peter's feelings the evening before. *(I knew I should make a bloody fool of myself*—they both seemed to be fated that way.) "It must be something the late owner picked up in a sale."

"Right you are, lady," said the head—Jack's, presumably—and disappeared whistling.

Her own clothes were packed. Bunter had come up shortly after breakfast—while Peter was writing letters—and had discovered her struggling with the orange frock. After watching her thoughtfully for a few moments he had offered his assistance, and it had been accepted with relief. The more intimate parts of the business had, after all, been effected previously—though, when Harriet saw her underwear unpacked later on, she could not remember having used so much tissue paper and was surprised to know herself such a neat packer.

Anyhow; it was all done.

Crutchley came into the sitting-room, with a number of glasses on a tray.

"Thought you might be needing these, my lady."

"Oh, thank you, Crutchley. How very sensible of you. Yes, we probably shall. Just put them down over there, would you?"

"Yes, my lady." He seemed disposed to linger.

"That fellow Jack," he said suddenly, after a pause, "wants to know what he's to do with some of that tinned and bottled stuff."

"Tell him to leave it in the pantry."

"He don't know which is yours, my lady."

"Everything with a Fortnum-&-Mason label. If there's anything else, it probably belongs to the house."

"Very good, my lady. . . . Shall you and his lordship be coming back here again, later on, if I might ask?"

"Oh, yes, Crutchley—I'm sure we shall. Were you thinking about your job here? Of course. We may be going away for a time while alterations are done, but we should like you to keep the garden in order."

"Thank you, my lady. Very good." There was a slightly embarrassed silence. Then:

"Excuse me, my lady. I was wonderin'—" He had his cap in his hands, twisting it rather awkwardly . . . "—seein' as me and Polly Mason is goin' to get married, whether his lordship . . . We was meanin' to start that garridge, only me 'avin' lost that forty pound . . . If it might be a loan, my lady, we'd pay it back faithful—"

"Oh, I see. Well, Crutchley, I can't say anything about that. You must speak to his lordship yourself."

"Yes, my lady . . . If you was to put in a word for me, maybe . . ."

"I'll think about it."

For the life of her, she could not infuse any genuine warmth into her tone; she wanted so much to say, "Are we to advance you the amount of Miss Twitterton's savings, too?" On the other hand, there was nothing unreasonable about the request, since Crutchley could not know how much she knew. The interview was ended, but the young man lingered, so that she was relieved to hear the car at the gate.

"They're coming back. They haven't been very long."

"No, my lady; it don't take long."

Crutchley hesitated for a second, and went out.

It was quite a large party that entered—if they had all come in the Daimler they must have looked like an undertakers' bean feast; but no! the vicar was there, and he might have brought some of them in his own little car. He came in, wearing his cassock, with his surplice and Oxford hood over one arm while with the other he gave fatherly support to Miss Twitterton. She, Harriet saw at a glance, was in a much more resilient mood than she had been the evening before. Though her eyes were red with funerary tears, and she clutched a handkerchief with a sable border in her black-kid-gloved hand, the excitement of being chief mourner behind so important a hearse had evidently restored all her lost self-importance. Mrs. Ruddle followed. Her mantle, of strange and ancient cut, glittered with black beads, and the jet ornaments on her bonnet danced even more gaily than they had done at the inquest. Her face was beaming. Bunter, following upon her heels, and burdened with a pile of prayer-books and a severe-looking bowler, might, by contrast, have been the deceased's nearest and dearest relative, so determined was his countenance in an appropriate gloom.

After Bunter came, rather unexpectedly, Mr. Puffett, in a curious greenish-black cutaway coat of incredible age, buttoned perilously across his sweaters over his working trousers. Harriet felt sure he must have been married in that coat. His bowler was not the bowler of Wednesday morning, but of the mashing curly-brimmed pattern affected by young bloods of the 'nineties.

"Well!" said Harriet, "here you all are!"

She hastened forward to greet Miss Twitterton, but was arrested mid-way by the entrance of her husband, who had stopped to put a rug over the radiator. He came in now with a touch of bravura, probably induced by self-consciousness. The effect of his sombre suit and scarf, rigidly tailored black overcoat, and tightly furled silk umbrella was slightly marred by the irresponsible tilt of his top-hat.

"Hullo-ullo-ullo," said his lordship, genially. He grounded the umbrella, smiled diffidently, and removed the topper with a flourish.

"Do come and sit down," said Harriet, recovering herself, and leading Miss Twitterton to a chair. She took the black-kid hand and squeezed it comfortingly.

"Jerusalem, my happy home!" His lordship surveyed his domain and apostrophised it with some emotion. "Is this the city that men call the perfection of beauty? Woe to the spoiler—the chariots of Israel and the horsemen thereof!"

He appeared to be in that rather unreliable mood which is apt to follow upon attendance at funerals and other solemn functions. Harriet said severely, "Peter, behave yourself," and turned quickly to ask Mr. Goodacre:

"Were there many people at the funeral?"

"A very large attendance," replied the vicar. "Really a remarkable attendance."

"It's *most* gratifying," cried Miss Twitterton, "—all this respect for Uncle." A pink flush spread over her cheeks—she looked almost pretty. "Such a *mass* of flowers! Sixteen wreaths—including your *beautiful* tribute, dear Lady Peter."

"Sixteen!" said Harriet. "Just fancy!" She felt as though she had received a sharp jolt over the solar plexus.

"And fully choral!" continued Miss Twitterton. "Such *touching* hymns. And *dear* Mr. Goodacre—"

"The Reverend's words," pronounced Mr. Puffett, "if I may say so, sir, went right to the 'eart."

He pulled out a large red cotton handkerchief with white spots and trumpeted into it briskly.

"Ow," agreed Mrs. Ruddle, "it was all just beautiful. I never seen a funeral to touch it, and I been to every buryin' in Paggleham these forty year and more."

She appealed to Mr. Puffett for confirmation, and Harriet seized the opportunity to question Peter:

"Peter—*did* we send a wreath?"

"God knows. Bunter—*did* we send a wreath?"

"Yes, my lord. Hothouse lilies and white hyacinths."

"How very chaste and appropriate!"

Bunter said he was much obliged.

"*Everybody* was there," said Miss Twitterton, "Dr. Craven came over, and old Mr. and Mrs. Sowerton, and the Jenkinses from Broxford and that rather odd young man who came to tell us about Uncle William's misfortunes, and Miss Grant had all the school-children carrying flowers—"

"And Fleet Street in full force," said Peter. "Bunter, I see glasses on the radio cabinet. We could do with some drinks."

"Very good, my lord."

"I'm afraid they've commandeered the beer-barrel," said Harriet, with a glance at Mr. Puffett.

"That's awkward," said Peter. He stripped off his overcoat, and with it his last vestige of sobriety. "Well, Puffett, I dare say you can make do for once with the bottled variety. First discovered, so they say, by Izaak Walton, who while fishing one day—"

Into the middle of this harangue there descended unexpectedly from the stairs Bill and George, carrying, the one a dressing-mirror and a wash-basin, and the other, a ewer and a small bouquet of bedroom utensils. They seemed pleased to see the room so full of company, and George advanced gleefully upon Peter.

"Excuse me, guv'nor," said George, flourishing the utensils vaguely in the direction of Miss Twitterton, who was sitting near the staircase. "All them razors and silver-mounted brushes up there—"

"Tush!" said his lordship, gravely, "nothing is gained by coarseness." He draped his coat modestly over the offending crockery, added his scarf, crowned the ewer with his top-hat, and completed the effect by hanging his umbrella over George's extended arm. "Trip it featly here and there through the other door and ask my man to come up presently and tell you which things are what."

"Right-oh, guv'nor," said George, ambling away a trifle awkwardly—for the topper showed a tendency to over-balance. The vicar, surprisingly, relieved the general embarrassment by observing with a reminiscent smile:

"Now, you might not believe it, but when I was up at Oxford I once put one on the Martyr's Memorial."

"Did you?" said Peter. "I was one of the party that tied an open umbrella over each of the Caesars. They were the Fellows' umbrellas. Ah! here come the drinks."

"Thank you," said Miss Twitterton. She shook her head sadly at the glass. "And to think that last time we partook of Lord Peter's sherry—"

"Dear me, dear me!" said Mr. Goodacre. "Thank you. Ah! yes, indeed."

He turned the wine musingly upon his tongue and appeared to compare its flavour favourably with that of the best sherry in Pagford.

"Bunter—you've got some beer in the kitchen for Puffett."

"Yes, my lord."

Mr. Puffett, reminded that he was, in a manner of speaking, in the wrong place, picked up his curly bowler and said heartily:

"That's very kind of your lordship. Come along, Martha. Get off your bonnet and shawl and we'll give these lads a 'and outside."

"Yes," said Harriet. "Bunter will be wanting you, Mrs. Ruddle, to see about getting some lunch of some sort. Will you stay and have something with us, Miss Twitterton?"

"Oh, no, really. I must be getting home. It's so good of you—"

"But you mustn't hurry," said Harriet, as Puffett and Mrs. Ruddle vanished. "I only said that because Mrs. Ruddle—though an excellent servant in her way—sometimes needs a reminder. Mr. Goodacre, won't you have a drop more sherry?"

"No, really—I must be moving homewards."

"Not without your plants," said Peter. "Mr. Goodacre has prevailed on Mr. MacBride, Harriet, to let the cacti go to a good home."

"For a consideration, no doubt?"

"Of course, of course," said the vicar. "I paid him for them. That was only right. He has to consider his clients. The other person—Solomons, I think his name is—made a slight difficulty, but we managed to get over that."

"How did you manage?"

"Well," admitted the vicar, "I paid him too. But it was a small sum. Quite a small sum, really. Less than the plants are worth. I did not like to think of their going to a warehouse with no one to care for them. Crutchley has always looked after them so well. He is very knowledgeable with cacti."

"Indeed?" said Miss Twitterton, so sharply that the vicar stared at her in mild astonishment. "I am *glad* to hear that Frank Crutchley fulfilled *some* of his obligations."

"Well, padre," said Peter, "rather you than me. I don't like the things."

"They are not to everybody's taste, perhaps. But this one, for instance—you must acknowledge that it is a superb specimen of its kind."

He shuffled his shortsighted way towards the hanging cactus and peered at it with an anticipatory pride of possession.

"Uncle William," said Miss Twitterton in a quavering voice, "always took great pride in that cactus."

Her eyes filled with tears, and the vicar turned quickly towards her.

"I know. Indeed, Miss Twitterton, it will be quite happy and safe with me."

Miss Twitterton nodded, speechlessly; but any further

demonstration was cut short by the entrance of Bunter, who said, coming up to her:

"Excuse me. The furniture removers are about to clear the attics and have desired me to inquire what is to be done with the various trunks and articles labelled 'Twitterton.'"

"Oh! dear me! Yes, of course. Oh, dear—yes, please tell them I think I had better come and see to that myself. . . . You see—dear me!—however did I come to forget?—there are quite a lot of my things here." She fluttered towards Harriet. "I *hope* you won't mind—I *won't* trespass on your time—but I'd *better* just see what's mine and what isn't. You see, my cottage is so very *small*, and Uncle very kindly let me store my little belongings—some of dear Mother's things—"

"But of course," said Harriet. "Do go anywhere you like, and if you want any help—"

"Oh, thank you so much. Oh, Mr. Goodacre, thank you."

The vicar, politely holding open the staircase door, extended his hand.

"As I shall be going in a very few minutes, I'll say goodbye now. Just for the moment. I shall of course come and see you. And now, you mustn't allow yourself to brood, you know. In fact, I'm going to ask you to be very brave and sensible and come and play the organ for us on Sunday as usual. Now, will you? We've all come to rely on you so much."

"Oh, yes—on Sunday. Of course, dear Mr. Goodacre, if you wish it, I'll do my best—"

"Oh, thank you. I—you—everybody's so good to me."

Miss Twitterton vanished upstairs in a little whirl of gratitude and confusion.

"Poor little woman! poor little soul!" said the vicar. "It's most distressing. This unsolved mystery hanging over us—"

"Yes," said Peter, absently; "not too good."

It gave Harriet a shock to see his eyes, coldly reflective, still turned towards the door by which Miss Twitterton had gone out. She thought of the trap-door in the attic—and the boxes. Had Kirk searched those boxes, she wondered. If not—well, then, what? Could there be anything in a box? A blunt instrument, with perhaps a little skin and hair on it? It seemed to her that they had all been standing silent a very long time, when Mr. Goodacre, who had resumed his doting contemplation of the cactus, suddenly said:

"Now, this is very strange—very strange indeed!"

She saw Peter start as it were out of a trance and cross the room to see the strange thing. The vicar was staring up into the nightmare vegetable above his head with a deeply puzzled expression. Peter stared too; but since the bottom of the pot was three or four inches over his head, he could see very little.

"Look at that!" said Mr. Goodacre, in a voice that positively shook. "Do you see what that is?"

He fumbled in his pocket for a pencil, with which he pointed excitedly to something in the centre of the cactus.

"From here," said Peter, stepping back, "it looks like a spot of mildew, though I can't see very well from this distance. But perhaps in a cactus that's merely the bloom of a healthy complexion."

"It *is* mildew," said the vicar, grimly. Harriet, feeling that intelligent sympathy was called for, climbed on the settle, so that she could look at the plant on a level.

"There's some more of it on the upper side of the leaves—if they are leaves, and not stalks."

"Somebody," said Mr. Goodacre, "has been giving it too much water." He looked accusingly from husband to wife.

"We haven't any of us touched it," said Harriet. She stopped, remembering that Kirk and Bunter had handled it. But they were scarcely likely to have watered it.

"I'm a humane man," began Peter, "and though I don't *like* the prickly brute—"

Then he, too, broke off; and Harriet saw his face change. It frightened her. It became the kind of face that might have belonged to that agonised dreamer of the morning hours.

"What is it, Peter?"

He said in a half whisper:

"Here we go round the prickly pear, the prickly pear, the prickly pear—"

"Once the summer is over," pursued the vicar, "you must administer water very sparingly, very sparingly indeed."

"Surely," said Harriet, "it couldn't have been the knowledgeable Crutchley."

"I think it was," said Peter, as though returning to them from a long journey. "Harriet—you heard Crutchley tell Kirk how he watered it last Wednesday week and wound the clock before collecting his wages from old Noakes."

"Yes."

"And the day before yesterday you saw him water it again."

"Of course; we all saw him."

Mr. Goodacre was aghast.

"But, my dear Lady Peter, he couldn't have done that. The cactus is a desert plant. It only requires watering about once a month in the cooler weather."

Peter, having emerged to clear up this minor mystery, seemed to be back on his nightmare trail. He muttered: "I can't remember—" But the vicar took no notice.

"*Somebody* has touched it lately," he said. "I see you've put it on a longer chain."

Peter's gasp was like a sob.

"That's it. The chain. We were all chained together."

The struggle passed from his face, leaving it empty as a mask. "What's that about a chain, padre?"

CHAPTER XX

◆

When You Know How, You Know Who

And here an engine fit for my proceeding!
—William Shakespeare, *Two Gentlemen of Verona*

To be interrupted at a crisis had become so much a feature of daily life at Talboys that Harriet felt no surprise to see Bunter enter upon these words, as upon a cue. Behind him hovered the forms of Puffett and Crutchley.

"If it will not inconvenience your lordship, the men are anxious to get these pieces of furniture out."

"You see," added Mr. Puffett, stepping forward, "they works on contract. Now, if we could jest slip some of these 'ere things out to them—" He waved a fat hand persuasively towards the sideboard, which was a massive dresser, made all in one piece and extremely heavy.

"All right," said Peter; "but be quick. Take them and go."

Bunter and Puffett seized upon the near end of the dresser, which came staggering away from the wall, its back festooned with cobwebs. Crutchley seized the far end and backed with it to the door.

"Yes," continued Mr. Goodacre, whose mind, once it fastened on anything, clung to it with the soft tenacity of a sea-anemone. "Yes, I suppose the old chain had become unsafe. This is an improvement. You get a much better idea of the cactus now."

The sideboard was moving slowly across the threshold; but the amateurs were not making too good a job of it, and it stuck. Peter, with sudden impatience, pulled off his coat.

"How he hates," thought Harriet, "to see anything bungled."

"Easy does it," said Mr. Puffett.

Whether by good luck or superior management, no sooner had Peter set his hand to it than the topheavy monstrosity abandoned the position and went sweetly through.

"That's done it!" said Peter. He shut the door and stood before it, his face slightly flushed with exertion. "Yes, padre—you were saying about the chain. It used to be shorter?"

"Why, yes. I'm positive it was. Quite positive. Let me see—the bottom of the pot used to come about here."

He raised his hand slightly above the level of his own tall head.

Peter came down to him.

"About four inches higher. You're sure?"

"Oh, yes, quite. Yes—and the—"

Through the unguarded door came Bunter once more, armed with a clothes-brush. He made for Peter, seized him from behind and began to brush the dust from his trousers. Mr. Goodacre, much interested, watched the process.

"Ah!" he said, dodging out of the way as Puffett and Crutchley came in to remove the settle nearest the window—"that's the worst of those heavy old sideboards. It's so difficult to clean behind them. My wife always complains about ours."

"That'll do, Bunter. Can't I be dusty if I like?"

Bunter smiled gently and began on the other leg.

"I am afraid," went on the vicar, "I should give your excellent man many hours of distress if I were his employer. I am always being scolded for my untidiness." Out of the tail of his eye he saw the door shut behind the other two men, and his mind, lagging behind his vision, made a sudden bound to catch up with it. "Wasn't that Crutchley? We ought to have asked him—"

"Bunter," said Peter, "you heard what I said. If Mr. Goodacre likes, you can brush him. I will *not* be brushed. I refuse."

He spoke with more sharpness, under his light tone, than Harriet had ever heard him use. She thought: "For the first time since we were married he has forgotten my existence." She went over to the coat he had thrown off and began to search it for cigarettes; but she did not miss Bunter's quick upward glance or the almost imperceptible jerk of Peter's head.

Bunter, without a word, went to brush the vicar, and Peter, released, walked straight up to the fireplace. Here he stopped, and his eye searched the room.

"Well, really," said Mr. Goodacre, with a refreshing delight in novelty. "Being valeted is quite a new experience for me."

"The chain," said Peter. "Now, where—?"

"Oh, yes." Mr. Goodacre took up his thread again. "I was about to say, that is certainly a new chain. The old one was of brass to match the pot, whereas this—"

"Peter!" said Harriet, involuntarily.

"Yes," he said, "I know now." He seized upon the ornamental drain-pipe, tossed the pampas-grasses out of it and tilted it up, just as Crutchley came in—this time with the man Bill—and advanced upon the other settle.

"If you don't mind, guv'nor."

Peter jerked the pipe swiftly back and sat on it.

"No," he said. "We haven't finished here. Take yourselves off. We must have something to sit on. I'll make it right with your employer."

"Oh!" said Bill. "Well—right y'are, guv'nor. But mind you, this job's got to be done today."

"It will be," said Peter.

George might have stood out; but Bill evidently possessed a more sensitively balanced temperament or a livelier eye to the main chance. He said submissively, "Right-ho, guv'nor," and went out, taking Crutchley with him.

As the door shut, Peter lifted the drain-pipe. At the bottom of it lay a brass chain, curled together like a sleeping serpent.

Harriet said: "The chain that came down the chimney."

Peter's glance swept over her as though she had been a stranger.

"A new chain was fixed up and the other one hidden up the chimney. Why?" He lifted the chain and looked at the cactus as it hung centred over the radio cabinet. Mr. Goodacre was deeply intrigued.

"Now, that," he said, taking the end of the chain in his hand, "looks remarkably like the original chain. See. It is darkened with soot, but it's quite bright when you rub it."

Peter dropped his end of the chain, leaving it dangling in the vicar's hand. He picked out Harriet from the rest and said to her, as though propounding a problem to the brightest-looking of a not-too-hopeful class:

"When Crutchley had watered the cactus, which he had watered the week before and which should only be watered once a month—"

"—*in* the colder weather," said Mr. Goodacre.

"—he was on the steps here. He wiped the pot. He got down. He put back the steps over here by the clock. He came back here to the cabinet. Can you remember what he did next?"

Harriet shut her eyes, once more seeing the room as it had been on that strange morning.

"I believe—"

She opened them again. Peter laid his hands gently, one on each side of the cabinet.

"Yes—he did. I know he did. He pulled the cabinet forward to bring it centrally under the pot. I was sitting quite close to him at the end of the settle—that's why I noticed."

"I noticed it too. That's the thing I couldn't remember."

He pushed the cabinet gently back, moving forward with it so that the pot now hung directly over his head and about three inches above it.

"Dear me," said Mr. Goodacre, surprised to discover that something of importance was apparently going on, "this is all very mysterious."

Peter made no reply, but stood gently lifting and letting fall the lid of the radio cabinet. "Like this," he said, softly. "Like this . . . This is London calling."

"I'm afraid I'm being very stupid," ventured the vicar again.

This time Peter looked up and smiled at him.

"Look!" he said. He put up his hand and lightly touched the pot, setting it gently swinging at the end of its eight-foot chain. "It's possible," he said. "My God! it's possible. Mr. Noakes was about your height, wasn't he, padre?"

"Just about. Just about. I may have had the advantage of him by an inch, but not more."

"If I'd had more inches," said Peter, regretfully (for his height was a sensitive point with him), "I might have had more brains. Better late than never." His eye roamed the room, passed over Harriet and the vicar and rested on Bunter. "You see," he said, "we've got the first and last terms of the progression—if we could fill in the middle terms."

"Yes, my lord," agreed Bunter, in a colourless voice. His heart had leapt within him. Not the new wife this time, but the old familiar companion of a hundred cases—the appeal had been to him. He coughed. "If I might make a suggestion, it would be as well to verify the difference in the chains before we proceed."

"Quite right, Bunter. Clear as you go. Get the steps."

Harriet watched Bunter as he mounted and took the brass chain that the vicar mechanically handed to him. But it was Peter who heard the step on the stair. Before Miss Twitterton was in the room he was half-way across it, and when she turned from shutting the door after her, he stood at her elbow.

"So *that's* all seen to," said Miss Twitterton, brightly. "Oh, Mr. Goodacre—I didn't think I should see you again. It *is* nice to think you're having Uncle William's cactus."

"Bunter's just coping with it," said Peter. He stood between her and the steps and his five-foot nine was an effectual screen to her four-foot eight. "Miss Twitterton, if you've really finished, I wonder if you would do something for me?"

"But of *course*—if I *can!*"

"I think I must have dropped my fountain-pen somewhere in the bedroom, and I'm rather afraid one of those fellows up there may put his foot on it. If I might trouble you—"

"Why, with pleasure!" cried Miss Twitterton, delighted that the task was not beyond her powers. "I'll run up and look for it at once. I always say I'm *remarkably* good at finding things."

"It's extraordinarily kind of you," said Peter. He manoeuvred her gently to the door, opened it for her, and shut it after her. Harriet said nothing. She knew where Peter's pen was, for she had seen it in the inner breast pocket of his coat when she was looking for cigarettes, and she felt a cold weight at the pit of her stomach. Bunter, who had slipped quickly down from the steps, stood, chain in hand, as though ready to put the gyves on a felon when he heard the word. Peter came back with urgency in his step.

"Four inches difference, my lord."

His master nodded.

"Bunter—no, I shall want you." He saw Harriet and spoke to her as though she had been his footman. "Here, you, go and fasten the door at the top of the back stair. Don't let her hear you if you can help it. Here are the house-keys. Lock the doors, front and back. Make sure that Ruddle and Puffett and Crutchley are all inside. If anyone says anything, those are my orders. Then bring the keys back—do you understand?... Bunter, take the steps and see if you can find anything in the way of a hook or a nail in the wall or ceiling on that side of the chimney-place."

Harriet was out of the room, and tip-toeing along the passage. Voices in the kitchen and a subdued clinking told her that lunch was being got ready—and probably eaten. Through the open door she glimpsed the back of Crutchley's head—he was tilting a mug to his lips. Beyond him stood Mr. Puffett, his wide jaws moving slowly on a large mouthful. She could not see Mrs. Ruddle, but in a moment her voice came through from the scullery. "... See it was that there Joe, plain as the nose on 'is face, and goodness knows that's big enough, but there! 'e's too much taken up with 'is good lady..." Somebody laughed. Harriet thought it was George. She scurried past the kitchen, ran up the privy as she went and found herself panting, more with excitement than haste, at the door of her own room. The key was on the inside. She turned the handle softly and crept in. Nothing was there but her own boxes, packed and waiting, and the component parts of what had been the bed, stacked ready for removal. In the next room she could hear little scuffling sounds, and then Miss Twitterton chirping agitatedly to herself (like the White Rabbit, thought Harriet): "Oh, dear, oh, dear! what has become of it?" (or was it, "What will become of me?") For a flash of time Harriet stood, her hand already on the key. If she were to go in and say, "Miss Twitterton, *he knows* who killed your uncle, and..." Like the White Rabbit—a white rabbit in a cage....

Then she was out and locking the door behind her.

Back in the passage now... and quietly past that open door. Nobody seemed to take any notice. She locked the front door, and the house was fast, as it had been on the night of the murder.

She returned to the sitting-room, and found she had been so quick that Bunter was still on the steps by the fireplace, searching the dark beams with a pocket-torch.

"A cup-hook, my lord, painted black and screwed into the beam."

"Ah!" Peter measured the distance with his eye, from the hook to the cabinet and back again. Harriet held out the keys to him and he pocketed them absentmindedly without so much as a nod.

"Proof," he said. "Proof of something at last. But where is the—?"

The vicar, who seemed to have been putting two and two carefully together in his mind, cleared his throat:

"Do I understand," he said, "that you have discovered a—what they call a *clue* to the mystery?"

"No," said Peter. "We're looking for that. The clue. Ariadne's clue of thread—the little ball of twine to thread the labyrinth—th—Yes, twine. Who said twine? Puffett, by Jove! He's our man!"

"Tom Puffett!" exclaimed the vicar. "Oh, I should not like to think that Puffett—"

"Fetch him here," said Peter.

Bunter was off the steps before he spoke. "Yes, my lord," he said, and was gone like lightning. Harriet's eye fell on the chain, which lay, where Bunter had left it, on top of the cabinet. She picked it up and the clink of the links caught Peter's ear.

"Best get rid of that," he said. "Give it me." He scanned the room for a hiding-place—then, with a sort of chuckle, made for the chimney.

"We'll put it back where it came from," he said, as he dived under the cowl. "Safe bind, safe find, as Puffett is fond of observing." He emerged again, dusting his hands.

"There's a ledge, I suppose," said Harriet.

"Yes. The gun dislodged the chain. If Noakes had kept his chimneys swept, his murderer might have been safe. What's that, padre, about doing evil that good may come?"

Mr. Goodacre was spared discussion of this doctrinal point by the arrival of Mr. Puffett with Bunter at his elbow.

"Did you want me, my lord?"

"Yes, Puffett. When you were clearing up this room on Wednesday morning after we'd loosened the soot, do you remember picking up a bit of string from the floor?"

"String?" said Mr. Puffett. "If it's string you're looking

for, I reckon you've come to the right place for it. When I sees a bit o' string, my lord, I picks it up and puts it away, 'andy when wanted." He pulled up his sweaters with a grunt and began to produce rolls of string from his pockets as a conjuror produces coloured paper. "There's all sorts 'ere, you can take your choice. As I says to Frank Crutchley, safe bind, safe find, I says. . . ."

"That was about a piece of string, wasn't it?"

"That's right," said Mr. Puffett, extracting with some difficulty a thick piece of small-cord. "I picks up a piece of string off this very floor, and I says to him—alloodin' to that there forty pound of his—I says to him—"

"I thought I saw you pick some up. I suppose you can't tell by this time *which* piece it was?"

"Oh!" said Mr. Puffett, enlightened. "I get you now, me lord. You was wantin' that pertickler bit o' string. Well, now, I dunno as I could rightly say which was that identical piece of string. Not the *string*, I couldn't. Not but what it was a good bit of string, too—a good thick piece, reckon it might be a yard long without knots. But whether it was *this* piece now, or *that* piece I wouldn't pretend to say."

"A yard long?" said Peter. "It must have been more than that."

"No," said Mr. Puffett. "Not the string—well, it might a-been four foot, not more. There was a rare good bit o' black fishin'-line, mebbe twenty feet or so—But it's string you're lookin' for."

"I made a mistake," said Peter. "I ought, of course, to have said fishing-line. Naturally, it would be fishing-line. And black. It had to be. Have you got that on you?"

"Oh!" said Mr. Puffett, "if it's fishin'-line you're after, w'y didn't you say so? Safe bind—"

"Thank you," said Peter. He whipped the roll of black line deftly from the sweep's slow fingers. "Yes. That's it. That would hold a twenty-pound salmon. And I'll bet you there's a sinker at each end. I thought so—yes."

He threaded one end of the line through one of the rings at the lip of the pot, brought the two ends with their sinkers together and handed them to Bunter, who took them without a word, mounted the steps and passed the double line over the hook in the ceiling.

"Oh!" said Harriet. "I see now. Peter, how horrible!"

"Haul up," said Peter, unheeding. "Take care you don't foul the line."

Bunter hauled on the line, grunting a little as it cut into his fingers. The pot, steadied from below by Peter's outstretched hand, stirred, lifted, moved up and away out of his reach, rising in a great semicircle at the end of the iron chain.

"It's all right," said Peter. "The plant won't fall out. It's a dead tight fit—as *you* know. Haul steady."

He went to take the slack of the line as it came down over the hook. The pot now lay level, strung out flat below the rafters, the cactus emerging sideways, so that it looked in the dimness like a monstrous hermit crab clawing out greedily from its shell.

The vicar, peering up at it, ventured a remonstrance.

"Pray, be careful, my man. If that thing was to slip and come down it might easily kill somebody."

"Very easily," said Peter. "That's what I was thinking." He walked backwards towards the radio cabinet, keeping the double string taut in his hand.

"It must weigh getting on for fourteen pound," said Bunter.

"I can feel it," said Peter, grimly. "How did you come not to notice its weight when you and Kirk were examining it? It's been loaded with something—lead shot from the feel of it. This must have been planned some time ago."

"So that," said Harriet, "is how a woman could have broken a tall man's head. A woman with strong hands."

"Or anybody," said Peter, "who didn't happen to be there at the time. Anyone with a cast-iron alibi. God makes power, padre, and man makes engines."

He brought the two ends of the line to the edge of the cabinet, to which they reached exactly. He lifted the lid and slipped them under; then brought the lid down upon them. The spring catch stood up to the strain, and the sinkers held firm against the flange, though Harriet noticed that the pull of the heavy pot had raised the near side of the cabinet slightly from the ground. But it could not lift far; since its feet were jammed close against the end of the settle, over which the thin black line stretched taut and nearly invisible to the hook in the beam.

A sharp knock on the window made them all start. Kirk and Sellon stood outside, beckoning excitedly. Peter walked quickly across and opened the lattice, while Bunter came down from the steps, folded them and set them quietly back against the wall.

"Yes?" said Peter.

"My lord!" Sellon's voice was quick and eager. "My lord, I never told you no lie. You *can* see the clock from the window. Mr. Kirk, he's just told me—"

"That's right," said Kirk. "Half-past twelve, plain as a pike-staff. . . . Hullo!" he added, able to see better now that the window was open—"they've took the cactus down."

"No, they haven't," said Peter. "The cactus is still there. You'd better come along in. The front door's locked. Take the keys and lock it again behind you. . . . It's all right," he added, speaking into Kirk's ear. "But come in quietly—you may have to make an arrest."

The two policemen vanished with surprising speed.

Mr. Puffett, who had been scratching his head in a contemplative manner, accosted Peter.

"That's an orkerd-looking arrangement of yours, me lord. Are you dead sure it won't come down?"

As some safeguard against this possibility, he clapped on his bowler.

"Not unless somebody opens the cabinet for the 12.30 gramophone orgy. . . . For God's sake, padre, stand away from that lid!"

The vicar, who had advanced towards the cabinet, started away guiltily at the peremptory tone.

"I was only looking more closely at the string," he explained. "You can't see it at all against the panelling, you know. Most remarkable. It's being so black and so fine, I suppose."

"That," said Peter, "is the idea of fishing-line. I'm sorry I shouted, but do keep back in case of accident. Do you realise you're the one person in this room who isn't safe?"

The vicar retired into a corner to work this out. The door was flung open, and Mrs. Ruddle, uncalled and unwanted, announced in loud tones:

"'Ere's the p'leece!"

"There!" said Mr. Puffett. He tried to urge her out, but Mrs. Ruddle was determined to know what all this long conference was about. She planted herself firmly beside the door with arms akimbo.

Kirk's ox-like eyes went to Peter and then followed his glance up to the ceiling, where they encountered the astonishing phenomenon of the cactus, floating Houdini-fashion, without visible means of support.

"Yes," said Peter. "That's where it is. But don't touch that cabinet, or I won't answer for the consequences. I fancy that's where that cactus was at 9.5 P.M. last Wednesday week, and that's why Sellon was able to see the clock. This is what's called reconstructing the crime."

"The crime, eh?" said Kirk.

"You wanted a blunt instrument that could strike a tall man from behind and above. There it is. That would break the skull of an ox—with the power we've put behind it."

Kirk looked at the pot again.

"H'm," he said slowly. "Pretty—but I'd like a bit o' proof. There weren't no blood nor 'air on that there pot we'en I last see it."

"Of course not!" cried Harriet. "It was wiped."

"When and how?" said Peter, slewing round on her sharply.

"Why, not till last Wednesday morning. The day before yesterday. You reminded us only just now. On Wednesday morning, under our very eyes, while we all sat round and watched. That's How, Peter, that's How!"

"Yes," he said, smiling at her excitement. "That's How. And now we know How, we know Who."

"Thank God, we know something at last," said Harriet. At the moment she cared little for How or Who. Her jubilee was for the alert cock of Peter's head, as he stood and smiled at her, balancing himself lightly and swaying a little on his toes. A job finished—and after all, no failure—no more frustrated dreams about chained and defeated men seeking a lost memory among hot deserts horrid with prickly cactus.

But the vicar, not being Peter's wife, took the thing otherwise.

"You mean," he said, in a shocked voice, "that when Frank Crutchley watered the cactus and wiped the pot—oh! but that is a dreadful conclusion to come to! Frank Crutchley—one of my own choirmen!"

Kirk was better satisfied.

"Crutchley?" said he. "Ah! *now* we're getting at it. He had his grudge about the forty pound—and 'e thought he'd get even with the old man and marry the heiress—two birds with one blunt instrument, eh?"

"The heiress?" exclaimed the vicar, in fresh bewilderment. "But he's marrying Polly Mason—he came round about the banns this morning."

"That's rather a sad story, Mr. Goodacre," said Harriet. "He was secretly engaged to Miss Twitterton and he—hush!"

"D'you think they were in it together?" began Kirk—and then suddenly woke up to the fact that Miss Twitterton was in the room with them.

"I couldn't find your fountain-pen *anywhere*," said Miss Twitterton, earnest and apologetic. "I do hope—" She became aware of something odd and strained in the atmosphere, and of Joe Sellon, who was stupidly gaping in the one direction that everybody else was avoiding.

"Good gracious!" said Miss Twitterton. "*What* an extraordinary thing! How ever did Uncle's cactus get up there?"

She made a bee-line for the cabinet. Peter caught her and pulled her back.

"I don't think so," he said, cryptically to Kirk over his shoulder; and led Miss Twitterton away to where the vicar still stood petrified with astonishment.

"Now," said Kirk, "let's get this clear. How exactly do you make out he worked it?"

"If that trap was set like that on the night of the murder

when Crutchley left at 6.20"—Miss Twitterton uttered a faint squeak—"then, when Noakes came in, as he always did at half-past nine, to turn on the wireless for the news-bulletin—"

"Which he did," said Mrs. Ruddle, "reg'lar as clock-work—"

"Why, then—"

But Harriet had thought of an objection, and whatever Peter thought of her she must put it.

"But, Peter—could anybody—even by candlelight, walk right up to that cabinet without noticing that the cactus wasn't there?"

"I think—" said Peter.

The door opened so quickly that it caught Mrs. Ruddle sharply on the elbow—and Crutchley walked in. In one hand he carried the standard lamp, and had apparently come in to fetch something on his way to the van outside, for he called back to some invisible person behind him:

"All right—I'll get it and lock it up for you."

He was abreast of the cabinet before Peter could say:

"What do you want, Crutchley?"

His tone made Crutchley turn his head.

"Key o' the radio, my lord," he said briefly and, still looking at Peter, lifted the lid.

For the millionth part of a second, the world stood still. Then the heavy pot threshed down like a flail. It flashed as it came. It skimmed within an inch over Crutchley's head, striking white terror into his face with its passing, and shattered the globe of the lamp into a thousand tinkling fragments.

Then, and only then, Harriet realised that they had all cried out, and she among them. And after that, there was silence for several seconds, while the great pendulum swung over them in a gleaming arc.

Peter spoke, warningly:

"Stand back, padre."

His voice broke the tension. Crutchley turned on him with a face like the face of a beast.

"You devil! you damned cunning devil! How did you

Curse you—how did you know I done it? I'll have the throat out of you!"

He leapt, and Harriet saw Peter brace himself; but Kirk and Sellon caught him as he sprang from under the death-swing of the pot. He wrestled with them, panting and snarling.

"Let me go, blast you! Let me get at him! So you set a trap for me, did you? Well, I killed him. The old brute cheated me. So did you, Aggie Twitterton, blast you! I been done out o' my rights. I killed him, I tell you, and all for nothing."

Bunter went quietly up, caught the pot as it swung and brought it to a standstill.

Kirk was saying:

"Frank Crutchley, I arrest you. . . ."

The rest of the words were lost in the prisoner's frenzied shouting. Harriet went over and stood by the window. Peter had not moved. He left Bunter and Puffett to help the police. Even with this assistance, they had their work cut out to drag Crutchley from the room.

"Dear me!" said Mr. Goodacre. "This is a most shocking thing." He picked up his surplice and stole.

"Keep him off!" shrieked Miss Twitterton, as the struggling group surged past her. "How horrible! Keep him off! To think that I ever let him come near me!" Her small face was distorted with fury. She ran after them, shaking her clenched fists and crying out grotesquely: "Beast! beast! how dare you kill poor Uncle!"

The vicar turned to Harriet.

"Forgive me, Lady Peter. My duty is with that unhappy young man."

She nodded, and he followed the rest out of the room. Mrs. Ruddle, arrested on her way to the door by the sight of the fishing-line dangling from the pot, was illuminated with sudden understanding.

"Why, there!" she cried, triumphantly. "That's a funny thing, that is. That's the way it was when I come in 'ere Wednesday morning to clear for the sweep. I took it off meself and throwed it down on the floor."

She looked about her for approbation, but Harriet was past

all power of comment and Peter still stood unmoving. Gradually, Mrs. Ruddle realised that the moment for applause had gone by, and shuffled out. Then from the group in the doorway Sellon detached himself and came back, his helmet askew and his tunic torn open at the throat.

"My lord—I don't rightly know how to thank you. This clears me."

"All right, Sellon. That'll do. Buzz off now like a good chap."

Sellon went out; and there was a pause.

"Peter," said Harriet.

He looked round, in time to see Crutchley hauled past the window, still struggling in the four men's hands.

"Come and hold my hand," he said. "This part of the business always gets me down."

EPITHALAMION

◆

CHAPTER I

◆

London: Amende Honorable

> VERGES: *You have always been called a merciful man, partner.*
>
> DOGBERRY: *Truly, I would not hang a dog by my will, much more a man.*
>
> —William Shakespeare, *Much Ado About Nothing*

Miss Harriet Vane, in those admirable detective novels with which she was accustomed to delight the hearts of murder-fans (see blurb), usually made a point of finishing off on a top-note. Mr. Robert Templeton, that famous though eccentric sleuth, would unmask his murderer with a flourish of *panache* in the last chapter and retire promptly from the stage amid a thunder of applause, leaving somebody else to cope with the trivial details of putting the case together.

What happened in real life, she discovered, was that the famous sleuth, after cramming down a hasty lunch of bread and cheese, which he was almost too preoccupied to eat, spent the rest of the afternoon at the police-station, making an interminable statement. The sleuth's wife and servant also made statements, and all three were then bundled unceremoniously out while statements were taken from the sweep, the charwoman and the vicar; after which, the police were prepared, if the going looked good, to sit up all night taking a statement from the prisoner. A further agreeable feature was a warning that neither the sleuth nor any of his belongings was to leave the country, or indeed go anywhere, without previously informing the police, since the next part of the procedure might take the form of a batch of summonses to appear before the magistrates. Returning home from the police-station, the sleuth family found the house occupied by a couple of constables taking photographs and measurements, preparatory to removing the wireless cabinet, the brass chain, the hook and the cactus to figure as Exhibits A to D. These were by now the only portable objects left in the house, other than the owner's personal property; since George and Bill had finished the job and left with their van. There had been difficulty and delay in persuading them to leave without the wireless set; but here the arm of the law at length prevailed. At last the police went away and left them alone.

Harriet looked round the empty sitting-room with a curiously blank sensation. There was nothing to sit on except the window-sill, so she sat on that. Bunter was upstairs, locking trunks and suit-cases. Peter walked aimlessly up and down the room.

"I'm going up to Town," he said abruptly. He looked vaguely at Harriet. "I don't know what you'd care to do."

This was disconcerting, because she could not tell from his tone whether he wanted her in London or not. She asked:

"Shall you be staying the night in Town?"

"I don't think so, but I must see Impey Biggs."

So that was the difficulty. Sir Impey Biggs had been her own counsel when she had stood her trial, and Peter was wondering how she would take the mention of his name.

"Do they want him for the prosecution?"

"No; I want him for the defence."

Naturally—what a stupid question.

"Crutchley must be defended, of course," pursued Peter, "though at the moment he's in no state to discuss anything. But they've persuaded him to let a solicitor act for him. I've seen the man and offered to get Biggy for them. Crutchley needn't know we've had anything to do with it. He probably won't ask."

"Must you see Sir Impey today?"

"I'd rather. I rang him up from Broxford. He's in the House tonight, but he can see me if I go round after the debate on some Bill or other he's concerned in. That will make it rather late for you, I'm afraid."

"Well," said Harriet, resolved to be reasonable whatever happened, "I think you had better run me up to Town. Then we can sleep at an hotel, if you like, or in your mother's house, if the servants are there; or if you'd rather stay at your club, there's a friend I can always ring up; or I can get out my own car and run down to Denver ahead of you."

"Resourceful woman! We'll go to Town, then, and wait upon the event."

He seemed relieved by her readiness to accommodate herself, and presently went out to do something or other to the car. Bunter came down, looking worried.

"My lady, what would you wish to have done with the heavy luggage?"

"I don't know, Bunter. We can't very well take it to the Dower House, and if we take it to Town, there's nowhere much to put it, except the new house—and I don't suppose we shall be going there, yet awhile. And I don't care to leave it here, with no one to see to it, since we can't possibly come back for some time. Even if his lordship—That is to say, we should have to get some furniture in."

"Precisely, my lady."

"I suppose you have no idea what his lordship is likely to decide?"

"No, my lady, I regret to say I have not."

For nearly twenty years, Bunter had known no plans which did not include the Piccadilly flat; and he was for once at a loss.

"I'll tell you what," said Harriet. "Go up to the vicarage and ask Mrs. Goodacre for me whether we may leave it with her for a few days till we have made our plans. She can then send it on, carriage forward. Make some excuse for my not going myself. Or find me a piece of paper and I will write a note. I would rather his lordship could find me here when he wants me."

"I understand perfectly, my lady. If I may say so, I think that will be an excellent arrangement."

One felt rather shabby, perhaps, for not going to say *au revoir* to the Goodacres. But, quite apart from what Peter might or might not want, the thought of Mrs. Goodacre's questions and Mr. Goodacre's lamentations was a daunting one. When Bunter returned, bringing a cordial note of assent from the vicar's wife, he reported that Miss Twitterton was also at the parsonage, and Harriet was more than ever thankful to have escaped.

Mrs. Ruddle seemed to have disappeared. (She and Bert were, indeed, having a sumptuous six o'clock tea with Mrs. Hodges and a few neighbours, eager to have their news served up piping hot.) The only person who lingered to bid them farewell was Mr. Puffett. He did not intrude; only, as the car moved out into the lane, he popped into ken from the top of a neighbouring gate, where he seemed to have been enjoying a peaceful smoke.

"Jest," said Mr. Puffett, "to wish you luck, me lord and me lady, and 'ope as we shall be seein' you 'ere again afore long. You ain't 'ad things so comfortable as you might 'ave 'oped, but there's more than one 'ud be sorry if you wos to take a misliking to Paggleham on that account. And if you'd like them chimneys given a thorough over'aul, or any other little job in the sweepin' or buildin' line, you've only to mention it and I'd be 'appy to oblige."

Harriet thanked him very much.

"There's one thing," said Peter. "Over at Lopsley there's a sun-dial in the old churchyard, made from one of our chimney-pots. I'm writing to the squire to offer him a new sun-dial in exchange. May I tell him that you will call for the old one and see to getting it put back?"

"I'll do that and welcome," said Mr. Puffett.

"And if you know where any of the others have gone, you might let me know."

Mr. Puffett promised readily that he would. They shook

hands with him, and left him standing in the middle of the lane, cheerfully waving his bowler till the car had turned the corner.

They drove for five miles or so in silence. Then Peter said:

"There's a little architect who would make a good job of that bathroom extension. His name's Thipps. He's a common little blighter, but he has very real feeling for period stuff. He did the church at Duke's Denver, and he and I got really friendly about thirteen years ago, when he was troubled with a corpse in his bathroom. I think I'll send him a line."

"He sounds just right. . . . You haven't taken what Puffett calls a misliking to Talboys, then? I was afraid you might want to get rid of it."

"While I live," he said, "no owner but ourselves shall ever set foot in it."

She was satisfied and said no more. They ran into London in time for dinner.

Sir Impey Biggs extricated himself from his debate about midnight. He greeted Harriet with a cheerful friendliness, Peter as the lifelong friend and connection that he was, and both with all proper congratulations on their marriage. Although there had been no further discussion of the subject, it had somehow been taken for granted that there was now no more question of Harriet's going to sleep with a friend or driving to Denver alone. After dinner, Peter had merely said, "It's no good going down to the House yet," and they had turned into a news-cinema and seen a Mickey Mouse and an educational film about the iron and steel industry.

"Well, well," said Sir Impey. "So you want me to tackle a defence for you. This business down in Hertfordshire, I suppose."

"Yes. I warn you beforehand you haven't a very good case."

"Never mind. We've tackled some pretty hopeless jobs before now. With you on our side I know we can put up a good fight."

"I'm not, Biggy. I'm a witness for the prosecution."

The K.C. whistled.

"The devil you are. Then why are you briefing counsel for the prisoner? Conscience-money?"

"More or less. It's rather a rotten show altogether, and we'd like to do our best for the man. I mean to say, don't you know—there we were, just married and everything pleasant about us. And then this happens, and the local bobbies can make nothing of it. And we horn in, looking all silklined, and fasten the crime on a poor devil who hasn't got a bean in the world and hasn't done *us* any harm except dig the garden—Well, anyway, we'd like you to defend him."

"You'd better begin at the beginning."

Peter began at the beginning, and went on, interrupted only by the older man's shrewd questions, to the end. It took a long time.

"Well, Peter, you're handing me a nice pup. Including the criminal's own confession."

"He didn't give that on oath. Shock—nerves—frightened into it by my unfair trick with the pot."

"Suppose he's made it again to the police?"

"Badgered into it by questions. Surely you're not going to be worried by a little thing like that."

"There's the chain and the hook and the lead in the pot."

"Who's to say Crutchley put them there? They may have been part of one of old Noakes's little games."

"And the watering of the cactus and wiping of the pot?"

"*Bagatelles!* We've only the vicar's opinion about the metabolism of cacti."

"Can you dispose of the motive, too?"

"Motive doesn't make a case."

"It does, for nine juries out of ten."

"Very well—several other people had motives."

"Your Twitterton woman, for instance. Had I better try to hint that she might have done it?"

"If you fancy she'd have the wits to realise that a pendulum must always pass directly beneath its point of suspension."

"H'm!—by the way, supposing you people hadn't turned up, what would have been the murderer's next step? What did he think would happen?"

"If Crutchley was the murderer?"

"Well, yes. He must have expected that the body would be found lying on the sitting-room floor by the next person who entered the house."

"I've thought this out. The next person to enter would, in the ordinary way, have been Miss Twitterton, who had the key. She was completely under his thumb. Remember, they used to meet in the evenings in Great Pagford churchyard. He'd have no difficulty in finding out whether she intended to go over at any time during the week to see her uncle. If she'd announced any such intention, he'd have taken steps—asked for an hour off from the garage on private business and contrived to run across Miss Twitterton on her way to the house. If Mrs. Ruddle had thought to tell Miss Twitterton that old Noakes had disappeared, it would have been easier still. The first person to be consulted would have been dear Frank, who knew all about everything. Best of all would have been what nearly happened—that Mrs. Ruddle should have taken the situation for granted and said nothing to anyone. Then Crutchley would have arrived at Talboys as usual on the Wednesday morning, found (to his surprise) he couldn't get in, gone to fetch the key from Miss Twitterton and discovered the body for himself. In any case, he'd have been first on the scene, with or without Miss Twitterton. If he was alone, very good. If not, he'd have dispatched her on her bicycle to fetch the police and taken the opportunity while her back was turned to rescue the string, polish the pot, remove the other chain from the chimney and generally see that the whole place presented an innocent appearance. I don't know why the chain was put up the chimney in the first instance; but I imagine old Noakes came in on him unexpectedly, just as he'd made the exchange, and he had to get rid of it quickly. Probably he thought it would be safe enough there, and didn't bother too much."

"And suppose Noakes had come into the sitting-room between 6.20 and 9 o'clock?"

"That was the risk. But old Noakes was 'reg'lar as clockwork.' He had his supper at 7.30. The sun set at 6.38 and the room is low-windowed and darkish. At any time after 7 the chances were that he would notice nothing. But make what play you like with that."

"He must have had a disagreeable morning the day you arrived," said Sir Impey. "Always supposing, of course, that this prosecution is justified. I wonder he made no efforts, after the crime was discovered, to get the chain removed."

"He did," said Harriet. "He came in three times while the furniture-movers were there; and made a quite determined effort to get me out of the room to investigate some tinned goods. I did go out once, and met him in the passage, making for the sitting-room."

"Ah!" said Sir Impey. "And you'd be prepared to go into the box and swear to that. You don't leave me much chance between you. If you'd had any consideration for me, Peter, you'd have married a less intelligent woman."

"I'm afraid I've been selfish about that. But you'll take the case, Biggy, and do your best?"

"To please you, I will. I shall enjoy cross-examining you. If you think of any awkward questions to put to yourself, let me know. Now be off with you. I'm getting old, and bed's the place for me."

"So that's that," said Peter. They stood on the pavement, shivering a little. It was nearly three in the morning and the air was sharp. "What now? Do we seek a hotel?"

(What was the right answer to that? He looked at once tired and restless—a state of body in which almost any answer is the wrong one. She decided to risk a bold shot.)

"How far is it to Duke's Denver?"

"Just over ninety miles—say ninety-five. Would you like to drive straight down? We could pick up the car and be out of Town by half-past three. I'd promise not to drive fast—and you might be able to get a bit of sleep on the way."

Miraculously, the answer had been the right one. She said, "Yes; let's do that." They found a taxi. Peter gave it the address of the garage where they had left the car and they trundled away through the silent streets.

"Where's Bunter?"

"He's gone on down by train, with a message to say we might be a little late."

"Will your mother mind?"

"No. She's known me forty-five years."

CHAPTER II

♦

Denver Ducis: The Power and the Glory

"And the moral of that is," said the Duchess. . . .
—Lewis Carroll, *Alice in Wonderland*

The Great North Road again, mile upon mile, through Hatfield, Stevenage, Baldock, Biggleswade, north and east to the Hertfordshire border—the same road they had travelled four days earlier, with Bunter sitting behind and two-and-a-half dozen of port stowed under his feet in an eiderdown. Harriet found herself dozing. Once, Peter's touch on her arm roused her to hear him say, "That's the turn for Pagford. . . ." Huntingdon, Chatteris, March—still north and east, with the wind blowing keener over the wide flats from the bitter northern sea, and the greyness that heralds the dawn lifting coldly into the sky ahead.

"Where are we now?"

"Coming into Downham Market. We've just passed through Denver—the original Denver. Duke's Denver is about fifteen miles further on."

The car swung through the little town and turned due east.

"What time is it?"

"Just upon six. I've only averaged thirty-five."

The fen lay behind them now, and the country was growing more wooded. As the sun rose, they slipped into a tiny village with a church from whose tower a clock struck the quarter.

"Denver Ducis," said Peter. He let the car dawdle down the narrow street. In the cottages, lighted windows showed where men and women were rising to go early to work. A man came out from a gate, stared at the car and touched his hat. Peter acknowledged the salute. Now they were out of the village, and running along beside a low wall, with high forest trees hanging over it.

"The Dower House is on the other side," said Peter. "It'll save time to go through the park." They swung into a tall gateway, with a lodge beside it. The growing light showed the stone beasts crouched upon the posts, holding each a shield of arms. At the noise of the horn, a man hurried out of the lodge in his shirt-sleeves and the gates swung back.

"'Morning, Jenkins," said Peter, and let the car stop. "Sorry to bring you out so early."

"No call to be sorry, my lord." The lodge-keeper turned to call over his shoulder. "Mother! here's his lordship!" He was an elderly man, and spoke with the familiarity of long service. "We were expecting you any time, and the sooner the better for us. Will this be her new ladyship?"

"Got it in one, Jenkins."

A woman appeared wrapping a shawl about her and curtsying. Harriet shook hands with the pair of them.

"This is no way to bring your bride home, my lord," said Jenkins, reprovingly. "We had the bells rung for you o'Tuesday, and we were meaning to give you a good welcome when you came."

"I know, I know," said Peter, "but I never could do anything right from a boy, could I? Talking of that, are the boys all well?"

"Doing first-rate, my lord, thank you. Bill's got his sergeant's stripes last week."

"Good luck to it," said Peter heartily. He let the clutch in, and they moved on up a wide avenue of beeches.

"I suppose it's a mile from your gate to the front door?"

"Just about."

"And do you keep deer in the park?"

"We do."

"And peacocks on the terrace?"

"I'm afraid so. All the story-book things."

At the far end of the avenue, the great house loomed grey against the sunlight—a long Palladian front, its windows still asleep, and behind it the chimneys and turrets of rambling wings and odd, fantastic sprouts of architectural fancy.

"It's not very old," said Peter, apologetically, as they turned away, leaving the house on their left. "Nothing before Queen Elizabeth. No donjon keep. No moat. The castle fell down a good many years ago, I'm thankful to say. But we've got specimens of all the bad periods since then and one or two of the good ones. And the Dower House is impeccable Inigo Jones."

Harriet, stumbling sleepily up the impeccable Inigo Jones staircase in the wake of a tall footman, was aware of a scurry of high heels on the landing and a cry of delight. The footman flattened himself swiftly against the wall as the Dowager Duchess shot past him in a rose pink dressing-gown, her white plaits flying and Ahasuerus clinging for dear life to her shoulder.

"My darlings, how lovely to see you!—Morton, go and get Franklin out of bed and send her to her ladyship immediately—You must be tired and famished—How dreadful about that poor young man!—Your hands are frozen, my dear—I do hope Peter hasn't been driving at a hundred miles an hour this horrid cold morning—Morton, you silly man, can't you see Ahasuerus is scratching me? Take him off at once—I've put you in the Tapestry Room, it's warmer—Dear me! I feel as though I hadn't seen either of you for a month—Morton, tell them to bring breakfast up here instantly—and what *you* want, Peter, is a hot bath."

"Baths," said Peter, "real baths are definitely a good idea." They walked along a wide landing, with aquatints along the wall, and two or three tables in Queen Anne Chinoiserie, with Famille Rose jars upon them. At the door of the Tapestry Room was Bunter—who must either have got up very early or never gone to bed, for he was dressed with an impeccability worthy of Inigo Jones. Franklin, also impeccable, but slightly flurried in her manner, arrived almost at the same moment. The grateful sound of running water broke refreshingly upon the ear. The Duchess kissed them both, announcing that they were to do exactly as they liked and that she wasn't going to bother them; and before the door shut they heard her energetically scolding Morton for not having gone to see the dentist and threatening him with gumboils, pyorrhea, septic poisoning, indigestion and a complete set of false teeth if he persisted in behaving like a baby.

"This," said Peter, "is one of the presentable Wimseys—Lord Roger; he was a friend of Sidney's and wrote poetry and died young of a wasting fever, and all that kind of thing. That, as you see, is Queen Elizabeth; she slept here in the usual way and nearly bust the family bank. The portrait is said to be by Zucchero, but it's not. The contemporary duke, on the other hand, really is by Antonio Moro, and that's the best thing about it. He was one of the tedious Wimseys, and greed was his leading characteristic. This old harridan was his sister, Lady Stavesacre, who slapped Francis Bacon's face. She's no business to be here, but the Stavesacres are hard up, so we bought her in. . . ."

The afternoon sun slanted in through the long windows of the gallery, picking out here a blue Garter ribbon, there a scarlet uniform, lighting up a pair of slender hands by Van Dyck, playing among the powdered curls of a Gainsborough, or throwing into sudden startling brilliance some harsh white face set in a sombre black periwig.

"That awful ill-tempered-looking brute is the—I forget which duke, but his name was Thomas and he died about 1775—his son made a sad, imprudent marriage with a hosier's widow—here she is, looking rather fed-up about it. And there's the prodigal son—rather a look of Jerry about him, don't you think?"

"Yes, it's very like him. Who's this one? He's got a queer, visionary sort of face, rather nice."

"That's their younger son, Mortimer; he was as mad as a

hatter and founded a new religion with himself as its only follower. That's Dr. Gervase Wimsey, Dean of St. Paul's; he was a martyr under Queen Mary. This is his brother, Henry—he raised the standard for Queen Mary in Norfolk at her accession. Our family's always been very good at having a foot in both camps. That's my father, like Gerald, but much better looking. . . . That's a Sargent, which is about its only excuse for existence."

"How old were you then, Peter?"

"Twenty-one; full of illusions and trying hard to look sophisticated. Sargent saw through that, damn the fellow! Here is Gerald, with a horse, by Furse; and downstairs in the horrible room he calls his study, you will find a picture of a horse, with Gerald, by Munnings. Here's my mother, by Laszlo—a first-class portrait of her, a good many years ago, of course. Not that anything but a very rapidly moving picture could really convey her quality."

"She fills me with delight. When I came down just before lunch I found her in the hall, putting iodine on Bunter's nose, where Ahasuerus had scratched him."

"That cat scratches everybody. I saw Bunter—he was very self-conscious about it. 'I am thankful to say, my lord, that the colour of the application is exceedingly transient.' My mother is rather wasted upon a small household. She was at her best with the staff at the Hall, who all went in mortal terror of her. There is a legend that she personally ironed our old butler's back for lumbago; but she says it wasn't a flatiron but a mustard-plaster. Have you seen enough of this Chamber of Horrors?"

"I like looking at them, though they make me feel sympathetic to the hosier's widow. And I'd like to hear some more about their histories."

"You'll have to get hold of Mrs. Sweetapple. She's the housekeeper and knows them all by heart. I'd better show you the library, though it isn't what it ought to be. It's full of the most appalling rubbish and the good stuff isn't properly catalogued. Neither my father nor my grandfather did anything about it, and Gerald's hopeless. We've got an old bird muddling round there now—he's my third cousin, not the one who's potty and lives at Nice, his younger brother. He hasn't got a bean, so it quite suits him to toddle about down here; and he does his best, and really knows quite a bit of antiquarian stuff, only he has very short sight and no method, and never can keep to one subject at a time. This is the great ballroom—it's rather fine, really, if you don't object to pomp on principle. You get a good view from here over the terraces down to the water-garden, which would look much more impressive if the fountains were turned on. That silly-looking thing among the trees there is one of Sir William Chambers's pagodas, and you can just see the roof of the orangery. . . . Oh, look! there you are—you insisted on peacocks; don't say we didn't provide them for you."

"You're right, Peter—it *is* a story-book place."

They went down the great staircase and across a hall chilly with statuary and thence by way of a long cloister to another hall. A footman came up with them as they paused before a door ornamented with classical pilasters and a carved cornice.

"Here's the library," said Peter. "Yes, Bates, what is it?"

"Mr. Leggatt, my lord. He wanted to see His Grace urgently. I told him he was away, but that your lordship was here, and he asked, could you spare him a moment?"

"It's about that mortgage, I expect—but *I* can't do anything about it. He must see my brother."

"He seems very anxious to speak to your lordship."

"Oh—very well, I'll see him. Do you mind, Harriet?—I won't be long. Have a look round the library—you may find Cousin Matthew there, but he's quite harmless, only very shy and slightly deaf."

The library, with its tall bays and overhanging gallery, looked east and was already rather dark. Harriet found it restful. She wandered along, pulling out here and there a calf-bound volume at random, sniffing the sweet, musty odour of ancient books, smiling at a carved panel over one of the fireplaces, on which the Wimsey mice had escaped from the coat of arms and played in and out of a heavily undercut swag of flowers and wheat-ears. A large table, littered deep in books and papers, she judged to belong to Cousin Matthew—a half-written sheet in an elderly man's rather tremulous writing appeared to be part of a family chronicle; propped open on a stand beside it was a fat manuscript book, containing a list of household expenses for the year 1587. She pored over it for a few moments, making out such items as "to i paire quysshons of redd sarsnet for my lady Joans chambere" and "to ii li tenterhooks, and iii li nayles for the same," and then continued to explore, till rounding the corner of the bookshelves into the end bay, she was quite startled to come upon an elderly gentleman, in a dressing-gown. He was standing by the window, with a book in his hand, and the family features were so clearly marked on him—especially the nose—that she could have no doubt of his identity.

"Oh!" said Harriet, "I didn't know anyone was here. Are you—" Cousin Matthew must have a surname, of course; the potty cousin at Nice was the next heir, she remembered, after Gerald's and Peter's lines, so they must be Wimseys—"are you Mr. Wimsey?" (Though, of course, he might quite well be Colonel Wimsey, or Sir Matthew Wimsey, or even Lord Somebody.) "I'm Peter's wife," she added, by way of explaining her presence.

The elderly gentleman smiled very pleasantly and bowed, with a slight wave of the hand as though to say, "Make yourself at home." He was slightly bald, and his grey hair was cropped very closely above his ears and over the temples. She judged him to be sixty-five or so. Having thus made her free of the place, he returned to his book, and Harriet, seeing that he seemed disinclined for conversation, and remembering that he was deaf and shy, decided not to worry him. Five minutes later, she glanced up from examining a number of miniatures displayed in a glass case, and saw that he had made his escape and was, in fact, gazing down at her from a little stair that ran up to the gallery. He bowed again and the flowered skirts of the dressing-gown went whisking up out of sight, just as somebody clicked on the lights at the inner end of the room.

"All in the dark, lady? I'm sorry to have been so long. Come and have tea. That bloke kept me talking. I can't stop Gerald if he wants to foreclose—as a matter of fact, I advised him to. The Mater's come over, by the way; and there's tea going in the Blue Room. She wants you to look at some china there. She's rather keen on china."

With the Duchess in the Blue Room was a slight, oldish man, rather stooping, dressed neatly in an old-fashioned knickerbocker suit, and wearing spectacles and a thin grey beard like a goat's. As Harriet entered, he rose from his chair and came forward with extended hand, uttering a faint nervous bleat.

"Oh, hullo, Cousin Matthew!" cried Peter, heartily, clapping the old gentleman smartly on the shoulder. "Come and be introduced to my wife. This is my cousin, Mr. Matthew Wimsey, who keeps Gerald's books from falling to pieces with age and neglect. He's writing the history of the family from Charlemagne downwards, and has just about got to the Battle of Roncevaux."

"How do you do?" said Cousin Matthew. "I—I hope you had a pleasant journey. The wind's rather chilly today. Peter, my dear boy, how are you?"

"All the better for seeing you. Have you got a new chapter to show me?"

"Not a *chapter*," said Cousin Matthew. "No. A few more pages. I'm afraid I got rather led away upon a sideline of research. I *think* I have got upon the track of the elusive Simon—the twin, you know, who disappeared and was supposed to have turned pirate."

"Have you, by Jove? Sound work. Are these muffins? Harriet, I hope you share my passion for muffins. I meant to find out before I married you, but the opportunity never arose."

Harriet accepted the muffin, and said, turning to Cousin Matthew:

"I made a silly mistake just now. I met somebody in the library and thought it must be you, and addressed him as Mr. Wimsey."

"Eh?" said Cousin Matthew. "What's that? Somebody in the library?"

"I thought everybody was away," said Peter.

"Perhaps Mr. Liddell came in to look up the *County His-*

tories," suggested the Duchess. "Why didn't he ask them to give him tea?"

"I think it was someone living in the house," said Harriet, "because he was in his dressing-gown. He's sixty-ish and a little bald on top, with the rest of his hair very short, and he's rather like you, Peter—side-face, anyhow."

"Oh, dear me," said the Duchess; "it must have been Old Gregory."

"Good lord! so it must," agreed Peter, with his mouth full of muffin. "Well, really now, I take that very kind of Old Gregory. He doesn't usually venture out so early in the day—not for a visitor, at any rate. It's a compliment to you, Harriet. Very decent of the old boy."

"Who is Old Gregory?"

"Let me see—he was some sort of cousin of the eighth—ninth—which duke was it, Cousin Matthew?—the William-and-Mary one, anyway. He didn't speak, I suppose? . . . No, he never does, but we always hope that one day he'll make up his mind to."

"I quite thought he was going to, last Monday evening," said Mr. Wimsey. "He was standing up against the shelves in the fourth bay, and I was positively obliged to disturb him to get at the Bredon Letters. I said, 'Pray excuse me, just for one moment,' and he smiled and nodded and seemed about to say something. But he thought better of it, and vanished. I was afraid I might have offended him, but he reappeared in a minute or two in the politest way, just in front of the fireplace, to show there was no ill feeling."

"You must waste quite a lot of time bowing and apologising to the family spooks," said Peter. "You should just walk slap through them as Gerald does. It's much simpler, and doesn't seem to do either party any harm."

"*You* needn't talk, Peter," said the Duchess. "I distinctly saw you raise your hat to Lady Susan one day on the terrace."

"Oh, come, Mother! That's pure invention. Why on earth should I be wearing a hat on the terrace?"

Had it been possible to imagine either Peter or his mother

capable of discourtesy, Harriet would have suspected an elaborate leg-pull. She said tentatively:

"This sounds almost too story-book."

"Not really," said Peter, "because it's all so pointless. They never foretell deaths or find hidden treasures or reveal anything or alarm anybody. Why, even the servants don't mind them. Some people can't see them at all—Helen, for example."

"There!" said the Duchess, "I knew there was something I meant to tell you. Would you believe it?—Helen's insisted on making a new guests' bedroom in the west wing, right in the middle of where Uncle Roger always walks. So stupid and thoughtless. Because, however well one knows they're not solid, it *is* disconcerting for anyone like Mrs. Ambrose to see a captain of the guard step out of the towel-cupboard when she's in no state either to receive him or retreat into the passage. Besides, I can't think that all that damp heat is good for his vibrations, or whatever they call them—last time I saw him he looked quite foggy, poor thing!"

"Helen is sometimes a trifle tactless," said Mr. Wimsey. "The bathroom was certainly needed, but she could quite well have put it further along and given Uncle Roger the housemaid's pantry."

"That's what I told her," said the Duchess; and the conversation took another turn.

Well, no! thought Harriet, sipping her second cup of tea; the idea of being haunted by old Noakes was not likely to worry Peter much.

". . . because, if I'm interfering, you know," said the Duchess, "I had much better be put in a lethal chamber at once, like poor Agag—not in the Bible, of course, but the one before Ahasuerus, he was a blue Persian—and why everybody shouldn't be if they feel like it, I don't know, when they get old and sick and a nuisance to themselves—but I was afraid you might find it a little worrying the first time it happened, so I mentioned it . . . though being married may make a difference and it may not happen at all. . . . Yes, that's Rockingham—one of the good designs—most of it is too two-pence-coloured, but this is one of Brameld's landscapes. . . . You wouldn't think anyone who talked so much could be so inaccessible, really, but I always tell myself it's that absurd pretence that one hasn't got any weaknesses—so silly, because we all have, only my husband never would hear of it. . . . Now isn't this bowl amusing?. . . . You can see it's Derby by the glaze, but the painting was done by Lady Sarah Wimsey, who married into the Severn-and-Thameses—it's a group of her and her brother and their little dog, and you can recognise the funny little temple, it's the one down by the lake. . . . They used to sell the white china, you know, to amateur artists, and then it went back to be fired in the factory. It's sensitive work, isn't it? Wimseys are either very sensitive, or not sensitive at all, to things like painting and music."

She put her head on one side and looked up at Harriet over the rim of the bowl with bright brown eyes like a bird's.

"I thought it might be rather like that," said Harriet, going back to what the Duchess had really said. "I remember one time, when he'd just finished up a case, he came out to dinner and really seemed quite ill."

"He doesn't like responsibility, you know," said the Duchess, "and the War and one thing and another was bad for people that way. . . . There were eighteen months . . . not that I suppose he'll ever tell you about that, at least, if he does, then you'll know he's cured. . . . I don't mean he went out of his mind or anything, and he was always perfectly sweet about it, only he was so dreadfully afraid to go to sleep . . . and he couldn't give an order, not even to the servants, which made it really very miserable for him, poor lamb! . . . I suppose if you've been giving orders for nearly four years to people to go and get blown to pieces it gives you a—what does one call it nowadays?—an inhibition or an exhibition, or something, of nerves. . . . You needn't sit holding that tea pot, my dear, I'm so sorry—give it to me, I'll put it back. . . . Though really I'm chattering away quite in the dark, because I don't *know* how he takes these things now, and I shouldn't think anybody did, except Bunter—

and considering how much we owe Bunter, Ahasuerus should have known better than to scratch him like that. I do hope Bunter isn't being difficult or anything."

"He's a marvel—and quite amazingly tactful."

"Well, that's nice of the man," said the Duchess, frankly, "because sometimes these attached people *are* rather difficult . . . and seeing that if anybody can be said to have pulled Peter round again it was Bunter, one might have to make allowances."

Harriet asked to be told about Bunter.

"Well," said the Duchess, "he was a footman at Sir John Sanderton's before the War and he was in Peter's unit . . . sergeant or something eventually . . . but they were in some—what's that American word for a tight place?—jam, isn't it?—yes, some jam or other together, and took a fancy to one another . . . so Peter promised Bunter that, if they both came out of the War alive, Bunter should come to him. . . . Well, in January 1919, I think it was—yes, it was, because I remember it was a dreadfully cold day—Bunter turned up here, saying he'd wrangled himself out. . . ."

"Bunter never said that, Duchess!"

"No, dear, that's my vulgar way of putting it. He said he had succeeded in obtaining his demobilisation, and had come immediately to take up the situation Peter had promised him. Well, my dear, it happened to be one of Peter's very worst days, when he couldn't do anything but just sit and shiver. . . . I liked the look of the man, so I said, 'Well, you can try—but I don't suppose he'll be able to make up his mind one way or the other.' So I took Bunter in, and it was quite dark, because I suppose Peter hadn't had the strength of mind to switch the lights on . . . so he had to ask who it was. Bunter said, 'Sergeant Bunter, my lord, come to enter your lordship's service as arranged'—and he turned on the lights and drew the curtains and took charge from that moment. I believe he managed so that for months Peter never had to give an order about so much as a soda-siphon. . . . He found that flat and took Peter up to Town and did everything. . . . I remember . . . I hope I'm not boring you with Bunter, my dear, but it really was rather touching. . . . I'd come up to Town one morning early and looked in at the flat. Bunter was just taking in Peter's breakfast . . . he used to get up very late in those days, sleeping so badly . . . and Bunter came out with a plate in his hand and said, 'Oh, your Grace! His lordship has told me to take away these damned eggs and bring him a sausage.' . . . He was so much overcome that he put down the hot plate on the sitting-room table and took all the polish off. . . . From those sausages," concluded the Duchess, triumphantly, "I don't think Peter ever looked back!"

Harriet thanked her mother-in-law for these particulars. "If there is a crisis," she said, "when the Assizes come on, I'll take Bunter's advice. Anyway, I'm very grateful to you for warning me. I'll promise not to be wifely and solicitous—that would probably put the lid on."

"By the way," said Peter, the following morning, "I'm terribly sorry and all that, but could you possibly bear being hauled off to church? . . . I mean, it'll be kind of well-thought-of if we turn up in the family pew . . . gives people something to talk about and all that sort of thing. Not, of course, if it makes you feel *absolutely* like Saint Thingummy on the grid-iron—all hot and beginning to curl at the corners—only if it's a comparatively mild martyrdom, like the little-ease or the stocks."

"Of course I'll come to church."

It felt a little odd, all the same, to stand virtuously in the hall with Peter, waiting for a parent to come and shepherd one away to Morning Service. It took, for one thing, so many years off one's age. The Duchess came down, putting on her gloves, just as one's mother had always done, and saying, "Don't forget, dear, there's a collection today," as she handed her prayer-book to her son to carry.

"And oh!" said the Duchess, "the vicar sent up a message that his asthma's rather bad and the curate away; so as Gerald isn't here he'd be very grateful if you'd read the Lessons."

Peter said amiably that he would, but hoped it wouldn't be anything about Jacob, whose personality irritated him.

"No, dear. It's a nice gloomy piece out of Jeremiah. You'll

do it so much better than Mr. Jones, because I was always very careful about adenoids, making you breathe through the nose. We'll pick up Cousin Matthew on the way. . . ."

The small church was packed. "Good house," said Peter, surveying the congregation from the porch. "The peppermint season has begun, I notice." He removed his hat and followed his female belongings up the aisle with preternatural decorum.

". . . world without end, amen."

The congregation sat down with a creak and a shuffle, and disposed itself to listen with approval to his lordship's rendering of Jewish prophecy. Peter, handling the heavy red-silk markers, glanced round the building, collected the attention of the back pews, clasped the brass eagle firmly by either wing, opened his mouth, and then paused, to direct his eyeglass awfully upon a small boy sitting just beneath the lectern.

"Is that Willy Blodgett?"

Willy Blodgett became petrified.

"Now, don't you pinch your sister again. It's not cricket."

"There," said Willy Blodgett's mother in an audible whisper, "sit still! I declare I'm ashamed of you."

"Here beginneth the Fifth Chapter of the Book of the Prophet Jeremiah.

"Run ye to and fro through the streets of Jerusalem, and see now, and know, and seek in the broad places thereof, if ye can find a man, if there be any that executeth judgment. . . ."

(Yes, indeed. Frank Crutchley in the local gaol—was he listening to execution and judgment? Or didn't you have to attend Divine Service until after you were tried and sentenced?)

"Wherefore a lion out of the forest shall slay them, and a wolf of the evenings shall spoil them, a leopard shall watch over their cities. . . ."

(Peter seemed to be rather enjoying the zoo. Harriet noticed that the family pew had crouching cats in place of the ordinary poppy-heads, in compliment no doubt to the Wimsey crest. There was a chantry at the east end of the south aisle, with canopied tombs. Wimseys again, she supposed.)

"Hear now this, O foolish people, and without understanding; which have eyes and see not . . ."

(To think how they had looked on while that pot was wiped clean. . . . The reader, untroubled by this association of ideas, had passed happily on into the next verse—the exciting one, about waves tossing and roaring.)

"For among my people are found wicked men: they lay wait, as he that setteth snares; they set a trap, they catch men."

(Harriet looked up. Had she fancied that slight check in the voice? Peter's eyes were steadily fixed on the page.)

". . . and my people love to have it so: and what will ye do in the end thereof?

"Here endeth the First Lesson."

"Very well read," said Mr. Wimsey, leaning across Harriet, "excellent; I can always hear everything you say."

Peter said in Harriet's ear:

"You ought to hear old Gerald, when he gets in among the Hivites and the Perizzites and the Girgashites."

As the Te Deum started, Harriet again thought of Paggleham, and wondered whether Miss Twitterton had found courage to preside at the organ.

CHAPTER III

Talboys: Crown Celestial

So here I'll watch the night and wait
To see the morning shine
When he will hear the stroke of eight
And not the stroke of nine.

—A. E. Housman,
A *Shropshire Lad*

After the magistrates' court they were free until the Assizes. So they finished their honeymoon in Spain, after all.

* * *

The Dowager Duchess wrote that the furniture had been sent up to Talboys from the Hall and that the painting and plastering were done. It would be better to leave work on the new bathroom until the frosts were over. But the house was habitable.

And Harriet wrote back that they were coming home in time for the trial, and that no marriage had ever been so happy as theirs—only, Peter was dreaming again.

Sir Impey Biggs, cross-examining:

"And you expect the jury to believe that this remarkable piece of mechanism went unnoticed by the deceased from 6.20 to 9 o'clock?"

"I expect nothing. I have described the mechanism as we constructed it."

Then the judge:

"The witness can only speak to his knowledge of the facts, Sir Impey."

"Quite so, m'lud."

The point made. The suggestion implanted that the witness was a little unreasonable. . . .

"Now, this booby-trap you set for the prisoner. . . ."

"I understood the witness to say that the trap was set by way of experiment, and that the prisoner arrived unexpectedly and sprang it before he could be warned."

"That is so, my lord."

"I am obliged to your lordship. . . . What effect did the accidental springing of this booby-trap have upon the prisoner?"

"He seemed very much frightened."

"We may easily believe that. And astonished?"

"Yes."

"When suffering under this very natural surprise and alarm, was he able to speak coolly and collectedly?"

"He was anything but cool and collected."

"Did you think he was aware of what he was saying?"

"I can scarcely be a judge of that. He was agitated."

"Would you go as far as to call his manner frenzied?"

"Yes; that word describes it very well."

"He was out of his mind with terror?"

"I am not qualified to say so."

"Now, Lord Peter. You have explained very clearly that this engine of destruction at the lowest point of its swing was not less than six feet from the ground?"

"That is so."

"Anybody less than six feet in height would be perfectly safe from it?"

"Exactly."

"We have heard that the prisoner's height is five feet and ten inches. He was, therefore, not at any time in danger from it?"

"Not in the slightest."

"If the prisoner himself had arranged the pot and chain as the prosecution suggest, he would know better than anybody else that it could not even touch him?"

"In that case, certainly he must have known it."

"Yet he was very much alarmed?"

"Very much alarmed indeed."

An exact and non-committal witness.

Agnes Twitterton, an excited and spiteful witness, whose very obvious resentment against the prisoner did him if anything more good than harm. Dr. James Craven, a highly technical witness. Martha Ruddle, a talkative and circumlocutory witness. Thomas Puffett, a deliberate and sententious witness. The Rev. Simon Goodacre, a reluctant witness. Lady Peter Wimsey, a very quiet witness. Mervyn Bunter, a deferential witness. P.C. Joseph Sellon, a witness of few words. Superintendent Kirk, an officially impartial witness. A strange ironmonger from Clerkenwell, who had sold the prisoner a quantity of lead shot and an iron chain, a damaging witness.

Then, the prisoner himself, witness in his own defence: a very bad witness indeed, sullen and impudent by turns.

Sir Impey Biggs, eloquent on behalf of the prisoner—"this industrious and ambitious young man"; hinting at prejudice—

"a lady who may have some cause to fancy herself ill-used"; indulgently sceptical about "the instrument of destruction so picturesquely constructed by a gentleman whose ingenuity is notorious"; virtuously indignant at the construction placed upon "words uttered at random by a terrorised man"; astonished to discover in the case for the Prosecution "not a scintilla of direct proof"; passionately moving in his appeal to the jury not to sacrifice a young and valuable life on evidence so flimsily put together.

Counsel for the Prosecution, gathering up the threads of proof that Sir Impey had tossed into disorder, weaving them into a rope as thick as a cable.

The Judge, undoing the twist again to show the jury exactly what was the strength of each separate strand, and handing the materials back to them, neatly assorted.

The Jury, absent for an hour.

Sir Impey Biggs came over. "If they hesitate all this time, they may acquit him in spite of himself."

"You ought to have kept him out of the box."

"We advised him to stay out. I think he got swollen head."

"Here they come."

"Members of the jury, are you agreed upon your verdict?"

"We are."

"Do you find the prisoner guilty or not guilty of the murder of William Noakes?"

"Guilty."

"You say he is guilty and that is the verdict of you all?"

"Yes."

"Prisoner at the bar, you have been arraigned upon a charge of murder, and have placed yourself upon your country. That country has now found you guilty. Have you anything to say why judgment of death should not be pronounced upon you according to law?"

"I say I don't care a damn for the lot of you. You've proved nothing against me. His lordship's a rich man and he had a down on me—him and Aggie Twitterton."

"Prisoner at the bar, the jury, after a careful and patient hearing, have found you guilty of murder. In that verdict I entirely concur. The sentence of the court upon you is that you be taken from hence to the place from which you came, and thence to a place of execution, and you be there hanged by the neck until you be dead and your body buried in the precincts of the prison in which you shall last have been confined, and may the Lord have mercy upon your soul."

"Amen."

One of the most admirable features of the English criminal law is said to be its dispatch. You are tried as soon as possible after your arrest, the trial takes three or four days at most, and after your conviction (unless, of course, you appeal), you are executed within three weeks.

Crutchley refused to appeal, preferring to announce that he done it, that he'd do it again, and let them get on with it, it made no odds to him.

Harriet, in consequence, was left to form the opinion that three weeks was quite the worst period of waiting in the world. A prisoner should be executed the morning after his conviction, as after a court-martial, so that one could get all the misery over in a lump and have done with it. Or the business should be left to drag on for months and years, as in America, till one was so weary of it as to have exhausted all emotion.

The worst feature, she thought, about those three weeks, was Peter's determined courtesy and cheerfulness. Whenever he was not over at the county gaol, patiently inquiring whether there was anything he could do for the prisoner, he was at Talboys, being considerate, admiring the arrangement of the house and furniture, or putting himself at his wife's disposal to tour the country in search of missing chimney-pots or other objects of interest. This heart-breaking courtesy was punctuated by fits of exigent and exhausting passion, which alarmed her not only by their reckless abandonment, but by being apparently automatic and almost impersonal. She welcomed them, because he would sleep afterwards as though stunned. But every day found him more firmly entrenched behind some kind of protective fortification, and herself becoming less and less a person to him. In his present mood, she felt unhappily, almost any woman would have done.

She was unspeakably grateful to the Duchess, who had forewarned and so, to some extent, fore-armed her. She wondered whether her own decision "not to be wifely and solicitous" had been a wise one. She wrote, asking for counsel. The Duchess's reply, ranging over a variety of subjects, amounted to saying, "Let him find his own way out." A postscript added: "One thing, my dear—*he is still there*, and that's encouraging. It's so easy for a man to be somewhere else."

About a week before the execution, Mrs. Goodacre turned up in a state of considerable agitation. "That wretched man Crutchley!" she said. "I *knew* he would get Polly Mason into trouble, and he *has!* And now what's to be done? Even supposing he could get leave to marry her and wanted to do it—and I don't suppose he cares a rap for the girl—is it better for the child to have no father or one who's been hanged for murder? I'm sure *I* don't know! Even Simon doesn't know—though naturally he says he ought to marry her. I don't see why he shouldn't—it won't make the least difference to him. But now the girl doesn't want him to, either—says she doesn't want to be married to a murderer, and I'm sure I can't blame her. Her mother's in a great way, of course. She should have kept Polly at home or sent her into good service—I told her she was much too young to go into that drapery shop at Pagford, and *not* really steady, but it's too late to say that now."

Peter asked whether Crutchley knew anything about this development.

"The girl says not. . . . And goodness me!" said Mrs. Goodacre, suddenly waking up to a whole series of possibilities, "suppose old Mr. Noakes hadn't lost his money and Crutchley hadn't been found out, what would have happened to Polly? He meant to have that money by hook or by crook . . . if you ask me, my dear Lady Peter, Polly's had a narrower escape than she thought for."

"Oh, it mightn't have come to that," said Harriet.

"Perhaps not; but one undiscovered murder makes many. However, that isn't the point. The point is what we're to do about this baby that's on the way."

Peter said he thought Crutchley ought at least to be told about it. He thought it was only fair that the man should be given the chance to do what he could. He offered to take Mrs. Mason over to see the governor of the prison. Mrs. Goodacre said it was very good of him.

Harriet, escorting Mrs. Goodacre down the path to the gate, said it would do her husband good to have something definite to do about Crutchley; he worried a good deal.

"Very likely he does," said Mrs. Goodacre. "You can see he's that sort. Simon's just the same if he has had to be severe with anybody. But that's men all over. They want the thing done and then, of course, they don't like the consequences. Poor dears, they can't help it. They haven't got logical minds."

Peter reported in the evening that Crutchley had been very angry and refused categorically to have anything further to do with Polly or any more blasted women. He had, in fact, refused to see either Mrs. Mason or Peter or anybody else, and had told the governor to damn well leave him alone. Peter then began to worry about what ought to be done for the girl. Harriet let him wrestle with this problem (which had at least the merit of being a practical one) and then said:

"Couldn't you put Miss Climpson on to it? With all her High-Church connections she ought to be able to hear of some job that would do. I've been to see the girl, and she doesn't seem to be a bad sort, really. And you could help with money and that sort of thing."

He looked at her as though seeing her for the first time for a fortnight.

"Why, of course. I think my brain must have gone mushy. Miss Climpson is the obvious person. I'll write to her at once."

He got pen and paper, wrote the address and "Dear Miss Climpson," and sat blankly, pen in hand.

"Look here—I think you could write this better than I

could. You've been to see the girl. You can explain. . . . Oh, God! I'm so tired."

It was the first crack in the defences.

He made his last effort to see Crutchley on the night before the execution. He was armed with a letter from Miss Climpson containing the outline of some very excellent and sensible arrangements for Polly Mason.

"I don't know when I shall be back," he said. "Don't wait up for me."

"Oh, Peter—"

"I say, for God's sake don't wait up for me."

"Very well, Peter."

Harriet went to look for Bunter, and found him running over the Daimler from bonnet to back axle.

"Is his lordship taking you with him?"

"I couldn't say, my lady. I have had no instructions."

"Try and go with him."

"I will do my best, my lady."

"Bunter . . . what usually happens?"

"It depends, my lady. If the condemned man is able to display a friendly spirit, the reaction is less painful for all concerned. On the other hand, I have known us take the next boat or aeroplane to a foreign country at a considerable distance. But the circumstances have, of course, been different."

"Yes, Bunter, his lordship has particularly said he does not wish me to sit up for him. But if he should return tonight, and he doesn't . . . if he should be very restless . . ." That sentence did not seem to be ending properly. Harriet began again. "I shall go upstairs, but I don't see how one could possibly sleep. I shall sit by the fire in my room."

"Very good, my lady."

Their eyes met with perfect understanding.

The car was brought round to the door.

"All right, Bunter. That will do."

"Your lordship does not require my services?"

"Obviously not. You can't leave her ladyship alone in the house."

"Her ladyship has been good enough to give me permission to go."

"Oh!"

A pause during which Harriet, standing in the porch, had time to think: Suppose he asks me whether I imagine he needs a keeper!

Then Bunter's voice, with exactly the right note of dignified injury:

"I had anticipated that your lordship would wish me to accompany you as usual."

"I see. Very well. Hop in."

The old house was Harriet's companion in her vigil. It waited with her, its evil spirit cast out, itself swept and garnished, ready for the visit of devil or angel.

It was past two o'clock when she heard the car return. There were steps on the gravel, the opening and shutting of the door, a brief murmur of voices—then silence. Then, unheralded by so much as a shuffle on the stair, came Bunter's soft tap at the little door.

"Well, Bunter?"

"Everything has been done that could be done, my lady." They spoke in hushed tones, as though the doomed man lay already dead. "It was some considerable time before he would consent to see his lordship. At length the governor persuaded him, and his lordship was able to deliver the message and acquaint him with the arrangements made for the young woman's future. I understand that he seemed to take very little interest in the matter; they told me there that he continued to be a sullen and intractable prisoner. His lordship came away very much distressed. It is his custom under such circumstances to ask the condemned man's forgiveness. From his demeanour, I do not think he had it."

"Did you come straight back?"

"No, my lady. On leaving the prison at midnight, his

lordship drove away in a westerly direction, very fast, for about fifty miles. That is not unusual; I have frequently known him drive all night. Then he stopped the car suddenly at a cross-roads, waiting for a few minutes as though he were endeavouring to make up his mind, turned round and came straight back here, driving even faster. He was shivering very much when we came in, but refused to eat or drink anything. He said he could not sleep, so I made up a good fire in the sitting-room. I left him seated on the settle. I came up by the back way, my lady, because I think he might not wish to feel that you were in any anxiety about him."

"Quite right, Bunter—I'm glad you did that. Where are you going to be?"

"I shall remain in the kitchen, my lady, within call. His lordship is not likely to require me, but if he should do so, he will find me at hand, making myself a little supper."

"That's an excellent plan. I expect his lordship will prefer to be left to himself, but if he should ask for me—not on any account unless or until he does—will you tell him—"

"Yes, my lady?"

"Tell him there is still a light in my room, and that you think I am very much concerned about Crutchley."

"Very good, my lady. Would your ladyship like me to bring you a cup of tea?"

"Oh, Bunter, thank you. Yes, I should."

When the tea came, she drank it thirstily, and then sat listening. Everything was silent, except the church clock chiming out the quarters; but when she went into the next room she could hear faintly the beat of restless feet on the floor below.

She went back and waited. She could think only one thing, and that over and over again. I must not go to him; he must come to me. If he does not want me, I have failed altogether, and that failure will be with us all our lives. But the decision must be his and not mine. I have got to accept it. I have got to be patient. Whatever happens, I must not go to him.

It was four by the church clock when she heard the sound she had been waiting for: the door at the bottom of the stair creaked. For a few minutes nothing followed, and she thought he had changed his mind. She held her breath till she heard his footsteps mount slowly and reluctantly and enter the next room. She feared they might stop there, but this time he came straight on and pushed open the door which she had left ajar.

"Harriet. . . ."

"Come in, dear."

He came over and stood close beside her, mute and shivering. She put her hand out to him and he took it eagerly, laying his other hand in a fumbling gesture on her shoulder.

"You're cold, Peter. Come nearer the fire."

"It's not cold," he said, half-angrily, "it's my rotten nerves. I can't help it. I suppose I've never been really right since the War. I hate behaving like this. I tried to stick it out by myself."

"But why should you?"

"It's this damned waiting about till they've finished. . . ."

"I know. I couldn't sleep either."

He stood holding out his hands mechanically to the fire till he could control the chattering of his teeth.

"It's damnable for you too. I'm sorry. I'd forgotten. That sounds idiotic. But I've always been alone."

"Yes, of course. I'm like that, too. I like to crawl away and hide in a corner."

"Well," he said, with a transitory gleam of himself, "you're my corner and I've come to hide."

"Yes, my dearest."

(And the trumpets sounded for her on the other side.)

"It's not as bad as it might be. The worst times are when they haven't admitted it, and one goes over the evidence and wonders if one wasn't wrong, after all. . . . And sometimes they're so damned decent . . ."

"What was Crutchley like?"

"He doesn't seem to care for anybody or regret anything except that he didn't pull it off. He hates old Noakes just as much as the day he killed him. He wasn't interested in Polly—only said she was a fool and a bitch, and I was a bigger fool to waste time and money on her. And Aggie Twitterton could go and rot with the whole pack of us, and the sooner the better."

"Peter, how horrible!"

"If there *is* a God or a judgment—what next? What have we done?"

"I don't know. But I don't suppose anything we could do would prejudice the defence."

"I suppose not. I wish we knew more about it."

Five o'clock. He got up and looked out into the darkness, which as yet showed no sign of day's coming.

"Three hours more. . . . They give them something to make them sleep. . . . It's a merciful death compared with most natural ones. . . . It's only the waiting and knowing beforehand. . . . And the ugliness. . . . Old Johnson was right; the procession to Tyburn was kinder. . . . 'The hangman with his gardener's gloves comes through the padded door.' . . . I got permission to see a hanging once. . . . I thought I'd better know . . . but it hasn't cured me of meddling."

"If you hadn't meddled, it might have been Joe Sellon or Aggie Twitterton."

"I know that. I keep telling myself that."

"If you hadn't meddled six years ago, it would almost certainly have been me."

That stopped him in his caged pacing to and fro.

"If you had had to live through that night, Harriet, knowing what was coming to you, I would have lived it through in the same knowledge. Death would have been nothing, though you were little to me then compared with what you are now. . . . What the devil am I doing, to remind you of that horror?"

"If it hadn't been for that, we shouldn't be here—we should never have seen one another. If Philip hadn't been murdered, we shouldn't be here. If I'd never lived with Philip, I shouldn't be married to you. Everything wrong and wretched—and out of it all I've somehow got *you*. What can one make of that?"

"Nothing. There seems to be no sense in it at all."

He flung the problem away from him and began his restless walk again.

Presently he said:

"My gracious silence—who called his wife that?"

"Coriolanus."

"Another tormented devil. . . . I'm grateful, Harriet—No, that's not right; you're not being kind, you're being yourself. Aren't you horribly tired?"

"Not the least bit."

She found it difficult to think of Crutchley, baring his teeth at death like a trapped rat. She could see his agony only at second-hand through the mind that it dominated. And through the mind's distress and her own there broke uncontrollably the assurance that was like the distant note of a trumpet.

"They hate executions, you know. It upsets the other prisoners. They bang on the doors and make nuisances of themselves. Everybody's nervous. . . . Caged like beasts, separately. . . . That's the hell of it . . . we're all in separate cells. . . . I can't get out, said the starling. . . . If one could only get out for one moment, or go to sleep, or stop thinking. . . . Oh, damn that cursed clock! . . . Harriet, for God's sake, hold on to me . . . get me out of this . . . break down the door. . . ."

"Hush, dearest. I'm here. We'll see it out together."

Through the eastern side of the casement, the sky grew pale with the forerunners of the dawn.

"Don't let me go."

The light grew stronger as they waited.

Quite suddenly, he said, "Oh, damn!" and began to cry—in an awkward, unpractised way at first, and then more easily. So she held him, crouched at her knees, against her breast, huddling his head in her arms that he might not hear eight o'clock strike.

Now, as in Tullia's tomb one lamp burnt clear
Unchanged for fifteen hundred year,
May these love-lamps we here enshrine,
In warmth, light, lasting, equal the divine.
Fire ever doth aspire,

And makes all like itself, turns all to fire,
But ends in ashes; which these cannot do,
For none of these is fuel, but fire too.
This is joy's bonfire, then, where love's strong arts
Make of so noble individual parts
One fire of four inflaming eyes, and of two loving hearts.

—John Donne, *Eclogue for the Marriage of the Earl of Somerset*